英語 Make Me High 系列

From Cloze Test to Translation Practice

從克漏字到翻譯練習

附解析本

王郁惠、鄭翔嬬 編著

獨家首創
反覆練習
模式

三民書局

國家圖書館出版品預行編目資料

From Cloze Test to Translation Practice 從克漏字到翻譯練習／王郁惠,鄭翔嬬編著.－－初版九刷.－－臺北市: 三民,2022
面; 公分.－－（英語Make Me High系列）

ISBN 978-957-14-5663-8 （平裝）
1. 英語 2. 讀本

805.18   101005443

英語 *Make Me High* 系列

From Cloze Test to Translation Practice 從克漏字到翻譯練習

編 著 者	王郁惠　鄭翔嬬
發 行 人	劉振強
出 版 者	三民書局股份有限公司
地　　址	臺北市復興北路 386 號 (復北門市) 臺北市重慶南路一段 61 號 (重南門市)
電　　話	(02)25006600
網　　址	三民網路書店 https://www.sanmin.com.tw
出版日期	初版一刷 2012 年 5 月 初版九刷 2022 年 9 月
書籍編號	S809460
I S B N	978-957-14-5663-8

三民書局

序

英語 Make Me High 系列的理想在於超越，在於創新。

這是時代的精神，也是我們出版的動力；

這是教育的目的，也是我們進步的執著。

針對英語的全球化與未來的升學趨勢，

我們設計了一系列適合普高、技高學生的英語學習書籍。

面對英語，不會徬徨不再迷惘，學習的心徹底沸騰，

心情好 High！

實戰模擬，掌握先機知己知彼，百戰不殆決勝未來，

分數更 High！

選擇優質的英語學習書籍，才能激發學習的強烈動機；

興趣盎然便不會畏懼艱難，自信心要自己大聲說出來。

本書如良師指引循循善誘，如益友相互鼓勵攜手成長。

展書輕閱，你將發現⋯⋯

學習英語原來也可以這麼 High！

給讀者的話

　　克漏字測驗不管是在小考、定期考或大考中，一直是許多學生最難克服的題型，這是因為克漏字測驗是一種綜合測驗，不但檢測學生對單字的意思與用法是否確實了解，也測驗學生是否會運用各種文法規則，甚至考驗學生對整篇文章的承轉與理解是否準確，學生不但要掌握文章細節也需抓住大方向。

　　本書編寫的目的就是希望幫助學生學習能同時兼顧字句的用法與段落的主旨，期望透過確實的練習，不僅能熟習解題技巧和應答策略，更能厚植自己的英語實力。在編排上以各類主題為主軸，內容包羅萬象，有自然生物、歷史文明、人物介紹、醫療保健、科技新知、生活型態、人文藝術等主題共三十個單元。每個單元皆有兩短篇與一長篇的克漏字練習，接著每個單元還有兩個常用句型的講解與三組針對該篇句型所提供的連貫式翻譯練習，期望學生透過充份及反覆的練習，強化各種技巧，提昇測驗的速度與能力。

　　本書在使用上，每個單元的分量大約為一堂（五十分鐘）課的時間，老師可彈性視上課時間於一學期（大約每周兩個單元）或一學年（大約每周一個單元）中完成所有範圍。若課堂時間有限，亦可當回家作業練習，因此，本書最後附上每篇文章的全文翻譯，同時克漏字與翻譯練習的每道題目都附上詳解，一一說明解題的邏輯分析過程，方便學生自修使用。

　　本書編寫力求完善，但難免有疏漏之處，希望讀者與各界賢達隨時賜教。

Contents

Part I : Cloze Test

Ⓐ Most bats are only active at night when they come out to feed. To get around in the dark, they rely on a special adaptation called echolocation. A bat makes high-pitched sounds and sends them out in pulses. The sound pulses come back as echoes, which lets the bat know ___1___ away from objects. Since this system relies on sound, most bats have large ears that are super ___2___.

Besides, many species have strange-looking growths of skin around their mouths and noses. These growths are like flaps that can be used ___3___ the sound pulses.

To snatch bugs in total darkness, bats also need to be skillful fliers. Their wings are ___4___ leathery skin that is stretched between the fingers of each hand. That's right—bat wings are actually their hands!

These ___5___ are truly amazing adaptations that allow bats to fly, hunt, and get around in the dark.

_____ 1. (A) how far is it   (B) it is how far   (C) how far it is   (D) how it is far

_____ 2. (A) sensible   (B) sensitive   (C) sensational   (D) sentimental

_____ 3. (A) to control   (B) to controlling   (C) control   (D) controlling

_____ 4. (A) made up   (B) made of   (C) made out   (D) made from

_____ 5. (A) attitudes   (B) breakthroughs   (C) demonstrations   (D) features

---

rely on 依賴   *adaptation* n. 適應   *echolocation* n. 回聲定位   *flap* n. 皮瓣
sound pulse n. 聲脈衝   *snatch* v. 抓取   *leathery* adj. 似皮革的

關於 adaptation 的搭配用法

special/successful adaptation 特殊的 / 成功的適應
make adaptation to... 對於…的適應 (能力)
adaptation for/to... 對於…的適應
a process of adaption 適應過程

B Before babies can master speech, it is important that they can learn to match vocal sounds with the expressions on their parents' face. Interestingly, an animal research reveals that rhesus monkeys have a(n) __1__ ability similar to humans.

In the experiment, monkeys were placed in front of two TVs, each __2__ a silent film. On one monitor, it showed the monkey making the typical expression for a friendly "coo" sound. On __3__, the monkey made a different facial expression when making an angry "threatening" sound. Next, the scientists used loudspeakers to play either the "coo" or "threatening" sounds. __4__ hearing the auditory cue, the monkeys went over to the correct screen and looked at the right face for the right sound. The researchers also noticed that the monkeys looked longer when the matching face made the friendly "coo" sound.

For humans as well as monkeys, their ability to link speech with meaning enables them to __5__ with their own kind.

_____ 1. (A) acting	(B) matching	(C) reading	(D) speaking
_____ 2. (A) play	(B) to play	(C) playing	(D) played
_____ 3. (A) other	(B) another	(C) others	(D) the other
_____ 4. (A) After	(B) Before	(C) Though	(D) Until
_____ 5. (A) combine	(B) command	(C) communicate	(D) compete

---

master v. 掌控　*rhesus monkey* n. 獼猴　*silent film* n. 無聲影片
loudspeaker n. 擴音器　*auditory cue* 聲音提示

動物聲響相關動詞

鳥類：chirp 吱喳叫，twitter 啁啾，tweet 吱喳，sing 啼，whistle 囀鳴
雄雞：crow 啼叫　布穀鳥 (cuckoo)、鴿子 (dove)：coo 咕咕地叫
鴨鵝：quack 呱呱叫 嘎嘎叫　蛙：croak 呱呱叫　鼠：squeak 吱吱叫
貓：hiss 嘶嘶聲，meow 喵，purr 呼嚕，yowl 號哭　狗：bark 吠叫，woof 吠叫
豬：grunt 呼嚕，oink 豬叫，squeal 尖叫　羊：bleat 咩咩叫
驢：bray 驢叫　馬：neigh 馬嘶，snort 鼻息聲，whinny 馬嘶

Ⓒ　Many animals have an ability called camouflage that serves to prevent them from being seen by attackers. Camouflage is the animal's color or shape that appears to ___1___ its surroundings.

Animals such as deer, squirrels, and mice have the colors of the trees and soil on the forest floor. Many sea creatures like sharks and dolphins have a grayish-blue coloring, which makes ___2___ easier to blend in with the soft light underwater. Many animals have developed special adaptations that let them ___3___ their coloration as their surroundings change. One of the biggest shifts in an animal's surroundings occurs during the change of the seasons. The forest may be green and brown in summer, but it is covered with snow in winter, making colorful animals an easy ___4___ . Many birds and animals like foxes and rabbits ___5___ this by producing different colors of fur or feathers ___6___ the time of year. Some skillful hiders, such as chameleons and octopuses, have learned how to change their colors instantly ___7___ the changes in their surroundings. And some animals such as some species of butterflies do not hide at all, but confuse predators by ___8___ themselves as something dangerous.

In different parts of the world, you'll find all kinds of animal camouflage. Often this adaptation is a more effective survival tool than ___9___ weapons of defense like teeth or claws. ___10___ , it is much better to be entirely overlooked by an attacker than to have to put up a fight.

_____ 1. (A) bring about　(B) live on　(C) mix with　(D) turn to

_____ 2. (A) such　(B) much　(C) them　(D) it

_____ 3. (A) alter　(B) to alter　(C) be altered　(D) altering

_____ 4. (A) desire　(B) instrument　(C) promise　(D) target

_____ 5. (A) deal with　(B) head for　(C) see to　(D) look into

_____ 6. (A) depend on　(B) to depend on　(C) depended on　(D) depending on

_____ 7. (A) on behalf of　(B) not to mention　(C) in relation to　(D) in accordance with

_____ 8. (A) designing　(B) disguising　(C) dividing　(D) dominating

_____ 9. (A) aggressive　(B) constructive　(C) experimental　(D) influential

_____ 10. (A) What's worse　(B) By contrast　(C) After all　(D) In addition

---

camouflage n. 偽裝　　*squirrel* n. 松鼠　　*chameleon* n. 變色龍　　*octopus* n. 章魚
predator n. 掠奪者　　*defense* n. 防衛

 **Part II : Translation Practice**

Sentence Patterns

1. allow + O + to V

動詞 allow（准許）之後接受詞，再接不定詞 to V，意思為「准許…做…」或有「讓…做…」之意。此類的動詞還包括 cause, challenge, enable, encourage, expect, force, forbid, invite, order, permit, persuade, remind, tell, warn。此外，allow 之後也可直接接動名詞 V-ing。

例：These features are truly amazing adaptations that **allow** bats **to fly** in the dark.

例：We do not **allow smoking** in this area.

2. let + O + V

意為「讓…做…」。使役動詞 let 之後接受詞，再接原形動詞作受詞補語，此時受詞與其後動詞為主動關係。若為被動關係則須用 be + V-en。

例：Many animals have developed special adaptations that **let** them **alter** their coloration as their surroundings change.

例：**Let** the work **be done** at once.

Ⓐ

 Keywords •

1. 海豚：*dolphin* (n.)　肌肉：*muscle* (n.)　蛋白質：*protein* (n.)　潛水：*dive* (v.)

　氧氣：*oxygen* (n.)

2. 流線形的：*streamlined* (adj.)　快速地：*with great speed*

 Sample •

1. 海豚肌肉中的一種特殊蛋白質能讓牠們在潛入水中時儲存氧氣。

A special protein in dolphins' muscles **allows** them **to** save oxygen while they dive underwater.

2. 此外，海豚流線形的身形讓牠們快速地游泳。

Besides, dolphins' streamlined shape **lets** them **swim** with great speed.

Ⓑ

Keywords

1. 纖細的、修長的：*slender* (adj.)　喙：*beak* (n.)　（用探針等）探索、細察：*probe* (v.)
2. 堅硬的：*stiff* (adj.)　羽毛：*feather* (n.)　拍打：*beat* (v.)

Practice

1. 蜂鳥 (hummingbird) 細長的喙讓牠們能探入花朵中尋找食物。

　　　　　　　　　　　　　　　　　　　　　　　　　　　　　　

2. 此外，牠們硬直的羽毛，使得翅膀能一次快速拍打好幾個小時。

　　　　　　　　　　　　　　　　　　　　　　　　　　　　　　

　　　　　　　　　　　　　　　　　　　　　　　　　　　　　　

Ⓒ

Keywords

1. 北極熊：*polar bear* (n.)　融入：*blend* (*in*) *with*　北極：*the Arctic* (n.)
2. 脂肪：*fat* (n.)　嚴寒的：*freezing/biting/bitter cold*

Practice

1. 北極熊的白毛讓牠們容易地融入北極的冰與雪。

　　　　　　　　　　　　　　　　　　　　　　　　　　　　　　

2. 此外，牠們厚厚的毛和脂肪讓牠們能在嚴寒的氣候下保持溫暖。

Unit 2 Animals (II)

Part I : Cloze Test

(A)   Some kinds of whales are among the rarest creatures in the world. The biggest __1__ to their survival is hunting by humans—whaling.

In 1868 the first whaling ship with harpoon guns—guns designed to shoot spears into whales—sailed from Norway. These new whaling ships were fast and could chase the biggest whales. For over 100 years, commercial whaling __2__ a huge industry. Hundreds of these whaling ships took thousands of whales, and very soon Blue whales, Sperm whales, Humpback whales, and many more were nearly __3__. In the 1980s, the International Whaling Commission decided to stop all whaling. Only Norway and Japan still hunt whales __4__ protests from many other countries.

Even today, 20 years after most whaling stopped, there are only about 600 Northern Right whales __5__. The population is not growing because whales do not have children fast enough to replace the whales which die.

_____ 1. (A) attempt   (B) effort   (C) support   (D) threat

_____ 2. (A) reminded   (B) remained   (C) retained   (D) retreated

_____ 3. (A) broken out   (B) put out   (C) stood out   (D) wiped out

_____ 4. (A) despite   (B) though   (C) regardless   (D) even

_____ 5. (A) leave   (B) to leave   (C) left   (D) leaving

---

survival n. 生存　　*whaling* n. 捕鯨　　*harpoon gun* n. 捕鯨槍、魚叉　　*spear* n. 矛
commercial adj. 商業的　　*Sperm whale* n. 抹香鯨　　*Humpaback whale* n. 座頭鯨
International Whaling Commission 國際捕鯨委員會　　*Norway* n. 挪威
Northern Right whale n. 北露脊鯨　　*population* n. (動物) 數量

Ⓑ　First discovered around 1598, the dodo, a large flightless bird, was found only on the island of Mauritius in the Indian Ocean. Many believe that early seafarers saw the dodo as a source of fresh meat and hunted them into extinction. ___1___, this has been disproved as dodo meat was said to be very unappetizing.

　　The dodo's extinction was caused by man's intrusion into their unique environment. Early settlers ___2___ the dodo's habitat and introduced new animals that either ___3___ them or destroyed their nests. The last confirmed sighting of a dodo was in 1681. The disappearance of the dodo was the first official extinction of a species in recorded history. Because of this, the dodo has become a ___4___ of extinction. Expressions like "dead as a dodo" or "gone the way of the dodo" are used today to describe things that are or will soon ___5___ forever.

_____ 1. (A) Additionally　　(B) However　　(C) Moreover　　(D) Therefore

_____ 2. (A) conserved　　(B) disturbed　　(C) provided　　(D) sustained

_____ 3. (A) carried on　　(B) depended on　　(C) preyed on　　(D) switched on

_____ 4. (A) consequence　　(B) delegation　　(C) privilege　　(D) symbol

_____ 5. (A) lose　　(B) lost　　(C) be lost　　(D) losing

Mauritius 模里西斯島　*Indian Ocean* 印度洋　*seafarer* n. 水手　*extinction* n. 絕種
disprove v. 證明…不正確　*unappetizing* adj. 難吃的　*intrusion* n. 入侵
settler n. 拾荒者、移民　*habitat* n. 棲息地　*species* n. 物種

Ⓒ More and more animals are in danger of becoming extinct. Even America's beloved national symbol, the bald eagle, 1 this terrible fate. Once, bald eagles could be found in all of the fifty states except Hawaii, but by 1967 only several hundred remained.

Two things were causing the bald eagle's decline. Starting in the 1940's, American cities had been growing quickly to 2 the growing population. As the cities pushed further into the countryside, many trees were cut down, destroying the forests 3 were the bald eagle's habitat.

It was also around this time 4 farmers began spraying a poison called DDT on their crops to control pests. Mice ate the crops and the poison with it. DDT was also making its way into lakes and rivers, 5 the fish. When the eagles ate the poisoned mice and fish, DDT made its way up the food chain. The poison caused female eagles 6 eggs with unusually thin shells, meaning many eggs never hatched. Scientists warned that 7 something was done immediately to save the bald eagle, it would soon disappear forever.

In 1972, the United States government responded by 8 the use of DDT. As the poison was removed from the food chain, the bald eagle population began to bounce back. In 1974, there were only around 791 nesting pairs of bald eagles in the United States. By 1998, this number 9 to around 5,948 pairs. It shows that if people make a serious, determined effort, even the most desperate situation can be 10 .

_____ 1. (A) was faced with (B) confronting (C) was met (D) encountering

_____ 2. (A) keep up with (B) make up with (C) put up with (D) take up with

_____ 3. (A) where (B) that (C) what (D) ✕

_____ 4. (A) which (B) that (C) how (D) ✕

_____ 5. (A) poison (B) poisoned (C) poisoning (D) to poison

_____ 6. (A) lay (B) laid (C) to lie (D) to lay

_____ 7. (A) now that (B) once (C) while (D) unless

_____ 8. (A) allowing (B) banning (C) noticing (D) promoting

_____ 9. (A) went up to (B) was gone up (C) has gone up (D) had gone up

_____ 10. (A) analyzed (B) complicated (C) reversed (D) tolerated

---

DDT (*dichlorodiphenyltrichloroethane*) 殺蟲劑 (雙對氯苯基三氯乙烷)

Part II : Translation Practice

Sentence Patterns

1. There is/are + N + $\begin{cases} \text{V-ing} \\ \text{V-en} \end{cases}$

若 N 可以主動做某個動作，則用現在分詞 (V-ing) 為「有…在 (做)…」之意；若 N 為某個動作的接受者，也就是被動，則用過去分詞 (V-en)，為「有…被…」之意。

例：__There are__ only about 600 Northern Right whales __left__.

2. $\begin{cases} \text{By + 未來時間，S + will + have + V-en} \\ \text{By + 過去時間，S + had + V-en} \end{cases}$

若 by 之後接尚未發生的未來某個時間，則主要子句用未來完成式 (will have + V-en)，表示「在未來某時間前，某事將完成」；若 by 之後接過去某個時間，則主要子句用過去完成式 (had + V-en)，表示「在過去某時間前，某事已完成」。

例：By 1998, this number __had gone__ up to around 5,948 pairs.

Ⓐ

 Keywords ••

1. 商業的：*commercial* (adj.)
2. 世界野生動物基金會：*World Wildlife Fund*　努力：*effort* (n.)　減少：*reduce* (v.)

 Sample ••

1. 每年約有超過一千隻鯨魚因為商業市場而被殺害。

There are over 1,000 whales **killed** for the commercial market every year.

2. 透過世界野生動物基金會的努力，他們希望到 2016 年時，殺害將會大大減少。

Through World Wildlife Fund's effort, they hope that **by 2016** killings will **have been** greatly **reduced**.

Ⓑ

✈ Keywords •─────────────────────────────────•

1. 目前：*at present*　　在野外：*in the wild*

2. 全球暖化：*global warming*　　破壞：*damage* (v.)　　棲息地：*habitat* (n.)

　　生態：*ecology* (n.)　　改變：*change/alter* (v.)

✈ Practice •─────────────────────────────────•

1. 目前約有兩萬頭北極熊存活在野外。

　_____

　_____

2. 等到科學家了解到全球暖化破壞牠們的棲息地時，北極的生態早已變了。

　_____

　_____

Ⓒ

✈ Keywords •─────────────────────────────────•

1. 維持：*sustain* (v.)　　大貓熊：*giant panda* (n.)

2. 竹林：*bamboo forest* (n.)　　復原、恢復：*restore* (v.)　　餓死：*starve to death*

✈ Practice •─────────────────────────────────•

1. 世界上沒有存留足夠的自然棲息地能維持大貓熊。

　_____

　_____

2. 等到足夠的竹林被復原時，貓熊將早已經餓死了。

　_____

　_____

Part I : Cloze Test

Ⓐ   When you play sports, it is important that you do your best to win. But top athletes also understand that it's not whether you win or lose ___1___ how you play the game that really counts.

    Bad sportsmanship can destroy a game in many ways. By ___2___ a rival or complaining about something that happened during the game, an athlete will cause negative feelings for everyone and ___3___ others who are watching. Most of the best athletes show class on the field whatever happens.

    Being a good sport also has other ___4___ . By controlling your emotions, you will play better as well. The best coaches and parents teach their children to play hard and to respect the game they play. These tips work well not only in the game, but also at school and work. ___5___ , no one likes to play against a bad sport.

_____ 1. (A) and   (B) but   (C) for   (D) rather

_____ 2. (A) competing   (B) defeating   (C) insulting   (D) launching

_____ 3. (A) look forward to   (B) put an end to

             (C) set a bad example for   (D) take advantage of

_____ 4. (A) benefits   (B) drawbacks   (C) facilities   (D) honors

_____ 5. (A) For one thing   (B) In contrast   (C) Before long   (D) After all

---

athlete n. 運動員   *count* v. 有重要性、影響   *sportsmanship* n. 運動精神
rival n. 對手   *class* n. 氣質、天份   *be a good/bad sport* 做個有／沒有風度的運動員
coach n. 教練

Ⓑ   Sports are a fun and healthy activity that many people enjoy but athletic activities carry with them the risk of injury.

Sports injuries can be described as __1__ acute __1__ chronic. An acute injury is one that happens suddenly such as a bruise, a pulled muscle, or a broken bone. A chronic injury, __2__, develops over time. For example, stress fractures are tiny cracks that develop in a bone due to repeated __3__.

Of course, no matter how careful people are, sometimes injuries happen. If you get hurt, do not try to play through pain. You can help yourself by following "RICE." The letters in this __4__ remind you to **R**est, **I**ce, **C**ompress, and **E**levate your injury. These actions will help prevent swelling and allow healing to begin.

The risk of injury should not make you fear athletic activities. __5__, proper awareness of the danger can make sports both fun and safe.

_____ 1. (A) both...and　　　　　　　　　(B) either...or
　　　　　(C) neither...nor　　　　　　　 (D) not only...but also

_____ 2. (A) consequently　(B) however　　(C) moreover　　(D) similarly

_____ 3. (A) overdose　　　(B) overthrow　 (C) overuse　　　(D) overweight

_____ 4. (A) definition　　 (B) implication　(C) acronym　　　(D) wisdom

_____ 5. (A) Besides　　　 (B) Therefore　　(C) Otherwise　　(D) Rather

---

acute adj. 急性的　　*chronic* adj. 慢性的　　*bruise* n. 瘀傷　　*pulled muscle* 肌肉拉傷
broken bone 骨折　　*develop* v. 罹患 (病)；出現 (症狀)　　*over time* 逐漸地
crack n. 裂痕　　*swelling* n. 腫脹　　*fracture* n. 骨折

---

sports injuries 運動傷害

因為短暫時間中的過度運動、姿勢不良、暖身運動不足所造成的急性傷害 (acute injuries)，或是運動員因長期運動而造成身體局部的重複性壓力傷害 (repetitive stress injury) 稱為累積傷害 (overuse injury)。一般人會因為慢跑、打籃球、網球、重量訓練，造成傷害。除了 RICE 治療法外，還有 Danger, Response, Airway, Breathing, Circulation(DR ABC) 及 Talk, Observe, Touch, Active movement, Passive movement, Skills test (TOTAPS) 等。

Ⓒ　Held every four years, the Paralympic Games are similar to the Olympics. They are __1__ only for the people who have physical or mental injuries. The first Paralympics were held in 1948. Its first games were wheelchair competitions for the disabled soldiers of World War II, many of __2__ had suffered spinal cord injuries. It was not until 1960 __3__ the first official Paralympic Games were held. Since 2001, both the summer and winter Paralympic Games have been held __4__ the regular Olympics. Starting in 2012, any city __5__ to host the Olympics must also host the Paralympics.

　　Some people may question why sports for the disabled should be __6__. In fact, sports can help them in many ways. It can increase their physical strength as well as __7__ them mentally stronger. Sports can also help the disabled to build up their belief in themselves. This is very important because only when they have belief in themselves __8__ and make their life a success. Getting involved in sports gives them a chance to prove that they too can work like others and this helps inspire millions of other disabled people. For instance, Ms. Annemie Schneider of Germany is a gold medal skier who consistently won her competitions, despite having had one leg __9__ above the knee. When she is not training, she teaches and inspires young disabled athletes and their parents, and visits recovery centers to encourage young patients. Like many other Paralympians, she __10__ a role model for all.

_____ 1. (A) furthermore　(B) however　(C) indeed　(D) probably
_____ 2. (A) them　(B) those　(C) whom　(D) which
_____ 3. (A) when　(B) which　(C) that　(D) so that
_____ 4. (A) in view of　　　　　　　(B) in spite of
　　　　(C) in case of　　　　　　(D) in conjunction with
_____ 5. (A) chooses　(B) choosing　(C) chosen　(D) to choose
_____ 6. (A) discriminated　(B) eliminated　(C) interrupted　(D) promoted
_____ 7. (A) make　(B) makes　(C) making　(D) to make
_____ 8. (A) they can try　(B) can they try　(C) that they can try　(D) that can they try
_____ 9. (A) remove　(B) removed　(C) removing　(D) to be removed
_____ 10. (A) appeals to　(B) brings about　(C) runs into　(D) serves as

Paralympic Games 殘障奧運　*spinal cord* 脊髓　*consistently* adv. 一致地

 **Part II : Translation Practice**

Sentence Patterns

1. A as well as B
   → not only B but (also) A
   → not only B but A as well

意為「不僅 B 而且 A」。as well as 為連接詞，需連接對等的詞性，亦即 A 和 B 在文法結構上需相同。使用 as well as 時，將要強調的部份置於前面，若改為 not only...but (also)... 則將要強調的部份置於後面。此外，若連接的部分為主詞，動詞與 A 一致。

例：It can increase their physical strength **as well as** make them mentally stronger.

2. not A but B

此句型為「不是 A，而是 B」之意。A 和 B 在文法結構上需相同，此外，若連接的部分為主詞，動詞與 B 一致。

Ⓐ

 Keywords

1. 運動家精神：*sportsmanship* (n.)　樹立榜樣：*set an example*　運動員：*athlete* (n.)
   觀眾：*spectator* (n.)
2. 有重要意義、有價值：*count* (v.)　過程：*process* (n.)

 Sample

1. 有運動家精神的人不僅為觀眾也為運動員立下好的榜樣。

   People who have good sportsmanship set a good example for athletes **as well as** spectators/**not only** for spectators **but also** for athletes.

2. 他們知道重要的並非比賽結果而是學習過程。

   They know what counts is **not** the result of the game **but** the process of learning.

Ⓑ

Keywords

1. 運動員：*sportsman/player/athlete*（n.）　教練：*coach*（n.）　運動傷害：*sports injury*（n.）
   避免：*avoid*（v.）
2. 伸展：*stretch*（v.）　放鬆：*relax*（v.）　保護：*protect*（v.）

Practice

1. 不僅是運動員，教練也都瞭解運動傷害很難避免。

   _____

   _____

2. 因此，他們做伸展練習不是要放鬆肌肉，而是要保護自己。

   _____

   _____

Ⓒ

Keywords

1. 傑出的：*outstanding*（adj.）　表揚：*honor*（v.）　表現：*performance*（n.）
2. 紀錄：*record*（n.）　毅力：*perseverance*（n.）

Practice

1. 透過奧運還有殘障奧運，傑出運動員因為出色的表現得以得到表揚。

   _____

   _____

2. 他們的名字將被記住，不是因為他們的紀錄而是因為他們的毅力。

   _____

   _____

Part I : Cloze Test

Ⓐ One of the worst moments in baseball history is the 1919 World Series. The Cincinnati Reds won that year, but __1__ everyone remembers is their rival team: the Chicago White Sox.

A group of gamblers wanted to make a fortune from the series. The White Sox were expected to win, so betting against them would mean getting good odds if the team lost. To make sure that the White Sox __2__, the gamblers paid eight of the players to make mistakes __3__. The plan worked and the gamblers got very rich from the games.

After the series, many people felt suspicious of the White Sox's performance; thus, a grand jury was created to investigate the game. In the end, all eight players __4__ in the case were banned from playing Major League Baseball.

The Chicago White Sox were shamed and even cursed. They didn't win a World Series again until 2005, 86 years after the __5__.

_____ 1.(A) which   (B) that   (C) what   (D) where

_____ 2.(A) loses   (B) lost   (C) will lose   (D) would lose

_____ 3.(A) at least   (B) on purpose   (C) in touch   (D) within reach

_____ 4.(A) involve   (B) involved   (C) involving   (D) to involve

_____ 5.(A) scandal   (B) profit   (C) campaign   (D) budget

World Series 世界大賽   *Cincinnati Reds* 辛辛那提紅人隊
Chicago White Sox 芝加哥白襪隊   *odds* n. 機會、機率   *suspicious* adj. 可疑的
grand jury 陪審團   *Major League Baseball* 大聯盟   *curse* v. 詛咒

B All sports are "spectator sports"—this means that spectators or fans watch the athletes competing at a safe distance. But this "invisible" __1__ has holes. Fans have crossed through, often with __2__ results. For example, in 1993, tennis's number-one player, Monica Seles, was stabbed by a German fan. In 2002, Tom Gamboa, a baseball first-base coach, was attacked by a father and his son.

What causes fan violence? Some say the alcohol __3__ in most sporting arenas fuels fan enthusiasm and turns it into something abusive. History and culture also plays a part. If two countries are playing each other and they are also political rivals, violence is not __4__ .

Sports authorities have considered banning alcohol during events; some have increased security. They have also showed no hesitation to charge fans and players __5__ crimes. Fans, after all, should be stopped from fanning the flames of violence.

_____ 1. (A) barrier   (B) distance   (C) geography   (D) measurement

_____ 2. (A) concrete   (B) disastrous   (C) encouraging   (D) positive

_____ 3. (A) sells   (B) sold   (C) selling   (D) to sell

_____ 4. (A) at any cost   (B) out of control   (C) beyond doubt   (D) far away

_____ 5. (A) of   (B) for   (C) with   (D) at

---

spectator n. 觀眾　　*safe distance* 安全距離　　*Monica Seles* 莫妮卡・莎莉絲
stab v. 刺、捅　　*Tom Gamboa* 湯姆・甘博　　*first-base* n. 一壘　　*fan violence* 球迷暴力
alcohol n. 酒精　　*arena* n. 運動場館　　*fuel* v. 刺激、加劇　　*enthusiasm* n. 熱情
abusive adj. 辱罵的、施虐的　　*authority* n. 管理當局　　*ban* v. 禁止　　*hesitation* n. 猶豫
fan v. 煽動

Ⓒ   The crowd leaped to their feet and their screams filled the air as Ben Johnson of Canada crossed the 100m line at the Seoul Olympics in the record time of 9.79 seconds, __1__ him the fastest human ever.

Only 3 days later, Johnson was found __2__ of using steroids. He was stripped off his medal and banned from competing. However, he's not the only person __3__ for the use of drugs. Since winning is the only thing that matters in today's cruel world of sports, no one bothers to think about __4__, about code of conduct. Time and again the world has been shocked by such derogatory events.

The development and use of such performance-enhancing drugs is one of the __5__ effects of developing technology. Doctors are paid to acquire the doses, and often ask for large sums to keep their lips __6__. Scientists are paid to develop new drugs that will give the athletes a competitive __7__ over the others.

To clean such spiteful occurrence off, World Anti-Doping Agency has been __8__ to test the athletes for the use of steroids before any major international sports meet. __9__, its success is hard to determine.

A gold medal at the Olympics is the ultimate goal of many athletes. In their hungry desire to win a medal, the athletes forget the whole purpose of the Olympics—the celebration of humanity. By __10__ foul play, the athletes spoil the reputation of their countries, their fans, and even humanity.

_____ 1. (A) makes	(B) made	(C) making	(D) to make
_____ 2. (A) conscious	(B) guilty	(C) suspicious	(D) typical
_____ 3. (A) punish	(B) punished	(C) punishing	(D) to punish
_____ 4. (A) ethics	(B) mortals	(C) objectives	(D) possessions
_____ 5. (A) beneficial	(B) remarkable	(C) temporary	(D) undesirable
_____ 6. (A) seal	(B) sealed	(C) sealing	(D) to seal
_____ 7. (A) edge	(B) rival	(C) triumph	(D) calling
_____ 8. (A) come across	(B) laid off	(C) set up	(D) turned into
_____ 9. (A) However	(B) Moreover	(C) Otherwise	(D) Therefore
_____ 10. (A) falling for	(B) looking after	(C) putting off	(D) resorting to

---

steroid n. 類固醇   _code of conduct_ 規範   _large sums_ 大額款項
spiteful adj. 惡質的   _World Anti-Doping Agency_ 世界反禁藥組織
sports meet 運動競賽

Part II : Translation Practice

Sentence Patterns

1. What (S +) V...is/was + $\begin{cases} \text{that S + V} \\ \text{N/Adj.} \end{cases}$
what 所引導的名詞子句作主詞用。what 為複合關係代名詞，通常視為第三人稱單數，所引導的子句當「名詞」用，其後接單數動詞。 例：**What** everyone remembers **is** their rival team.
2. be + V-en
「be 動詞 + 過去分詞」為被動語態的基本動詞型態。英文中有主動與被動兩種語態，主詞（或動作執行者）不重要或不清楚時，多用被動語態。 例：Doctors **are paid** to acquire the doses, and often ask for large sums to keep their lips sealed.

Ⓐ

Keywords ●

1. 表現：*perform*（v.）　膝蓋：*knee*（n.）　傷害：*injury*（n.）
2. 強迫…做：*force sb. + to V*　離場：*quit the game*

Sample ●

1. 讓這位籃球選手昨晚表現不佳的是他膝蓋的傷。

   What made the basketball player perform poorly last night **was** his knee injury.

2. 他被迫提早離場，並且在賽後就被送去醫院。

   He **was forced** to quit the game early and **taken** to the hospital right after the game.

Ⓑ

Keywords

1. 增進：*enhance* (v.)　表現：*performance* (n.)　可恥的、不名譽的：*disgraceful* (adj.)
2. 除去、剝奪：*strip sb. of sth.*　禁止：*ban sb. from V-ing*

Practice

1. 這位運動員在比賽中為了增進表現所做的事，令人不恥。

_____

_____

2. 他被摘除金牌，並且遭終生禁賽。

_____

_____

Ⓒ

Keywords

1. 發狂：*lose one's mind*　酒精飲料：*alcohol* (n.)
2. 逮捕：*arrest* (v.)　當場：*on the spot*　指控、控訴：*charge sb. with sth.*　當地的：*local* (adj.)

Practice

1. 讓足球球迷發狂的是他們喝了太多酒精飲料。

_____

_____

2. 他們當場被捕，且之後遭當地警方起訴。

_____

_____

Unit 5 Sports (III)

Part I : Cloze Test

Ⓐ If you feel tired, have backaches, or are simply out of shape, then yoga is the answer for you. Yoga is a 5,000-year-old form of exercise and meditation that __1__ all over the world.

Yoga is wonderful because it helps you treat all the __2__ in a safe, effective, and convenient way. Stretching eases aches and pains and helps strengthen muscles. Meditation releases the mind __3__ its worries. Deep breathing unlocks the inner energies of the body. By uniting mind and body, yoga may treat stress simultaneously, __4__ better results than other exercises.

Many people join gyms, buy exercise equipment, or play team sports. This can be expensive and time-consuming. Yoga, by contrast, can be practiced anywhere, requires no special equipment, and can be done __5__ or in a group. Most importantly, yoga provides permanent strength, helping to release future stress!

_____ 1. (A) practices   (B) practicing   (C) is practiced   (D) has practiced

_____ 2. (A) accidents   (B) failures   (C) hunger   (D) stress

_____ 3. (A) for   (B) from   (C) of   (D) with

_____ 4. (A) provide   (B) providing   (C) provided   (D) to provide

_____ 5. (A) alone   (B) beforehand   (C) daily   (D) free

---

out of shape 身材走樣　*meditation* n. 冥想　*release* v. 釋放、抒解　*unlock* v. 開啟
simultaneously adv. 同時地　*gym* n. 健身房　*equipment* n. 器材
team sport 團體運動　*time-consuming* adj. 耗費時間的　*permanent* adj. 持久的
stress n. 壓力

Ⓑ Sometimes we may be envious of fish swimming freely in a colorful underwater garden. To visit the underwater world, we need to learn SCUBA diving. SCUBA diving gets its name from the words it ___1___ —Self Contained Underwater Breathing Apparatus. It means divers carry everything they need to stay alive under the water, ___2___ relying on hoses feeding them air from the surface of the water.

Scuba divers carry a tank of compressed air. They also wear a wetsuit to keep warm, fins or flippers to help kick through the water, and a weight belt to ___3___ them ___3___ coming to the surface. They also wear a special vest. Air from the tank is pumped in and out of the vest to help them stay at the right depth. Too much air will send them up, ___4___ too little will have them dropping to the seafloor. Once you have been ___5___ with the skills, you're free to explore the exciting sea world.

_____ 1. (A) breaks out (B) gets over (C) puts out (D) stands for

_____ 2. (A) instead of (B) regardless of (C) in spite of (D) as a result of

_____ 3. (A) deprive...of (B) inform...of (C) stop...from (D) dissuade...from

_____ 4. (A) although (B) since (C) when (D) while

_____ 5. (A) accessed (B) equipped (C) commented (D) involved

---

SCUBA (Self Contained Underwater Breathing Apparatus) 水肺潛水
tank n. （氣）罐　　*compressed* adj. 壓縮的　　*wetsuit* n. 潛水保暖衣　　*fin* n. 鰭
flipper n. 蛙鞋　　*weight belt* n. 配重帶　　*pump* v. （用幫浦）抽取、注入
seafloor n. 海底

---

scuba diving 水肺潛水

指著是自行攜帶水下呼吸系統進行潛水，除了一般觀光休閒用途 (leisure/recreation) 外、另外還有作為海洋研究 (marine sciences) 用途、漁業用途 (fishing) 或是水底機械修復、海底探勘考古 (archeology)、爆破 (demolition)、搜索救難 (search and rescue) 等專業潛水。

Ⓒ   Also called adventure sports, extreme sports involve more risk, adrenaline, and personal achievement than traditional sports. They also come along with a whole new breed of   1   !

Playing extreme sports is risky. For the athletes, this usually means   2   a dangerous version of a sport that already exists. For example, take springboard diving   3   and you have a dangerous sport like cliff diving. If you miss your landing during a cliff dive, you could break your back on a bed of rocks   4   just land with a clumsy splash!

Scientists believe that extreme athletes are naturally designed for these risks. Adrenaline, which causes extreme levels of excitement, drives these individuals to do stunts that most of us can barely   5   to watch. They become addicted to their sports because of chemicals   6   in the brain after they perform their dangerous tricks. That's   7   they do them again and again, no matter how hard they fall.

Extreme sports attract athletes who are obsessed with personal achievement. There are few rules or referees in these sports, and athletes   8   creativity, skills and fearlessness to achieve their personal bests.

Though not all of us dare try these sports, curiosity can't keep us away from watching these daredevils. If you're bored of watching traditional sports, you can   9   to an extreme alternative. Though you won't win any medals from your comfortable couch, you can get a sense of the adrenaline rush   10   taking the dangerous risks!

_____ 1. (A) attacks   (B) athletes   (C) audiences   (D) awards
_____ 2. (A) attempt   (B) attempting   (C) attempted   (D) to attempt
_____ 3. (A) by surprise   (B) for granted   (C) into account   (D) to the extreme
_____ 4. (A) rather than   (B) more than   (C) in time to   (D) with regard to
_____ 5. (A) fear   (B) keep   (C) stand   (D) wait
_____ 6. (A) release   (B) releasing   (C) released   (D) to release
_____ 7. (A) how   (B) why   (C) when   (D) where
_____ 8. (A) apply to   (B) indulge in   (C) make up   (D) rely on
_____ 9. (A) take off   (B) talk back   (C) tune in   (D) turn out
_____ 10. (A) but   (B) even   (C) except   (D) without

adrenaline n. 腎上腺素   *springboard* n. 跳板   *clumsy* adj. 笨拙的   *stunt* n. 特技
referee n. 裁判   *daredevil* n. 膽大的人   *alternative* n. 另類的選擇

Part II : Translation Practice

Sentence Patterns

1. keep/prevent/stop + O + from + V-ing

keep, prevent, stop 都作「使無法做某事」解,與 from 搭配使用,其後需接動名詞。

例:Curiosity can't **keep** us away from **watching** these daredevils.

2. Instead of + N/V$_1$-ing, S + V$_2$....
  → S + not + V$_1$.... (否定句). Instead, S + V$_2$

此句型為「沒有做 V$_1$…而做 V$_2$…」之意。instead of 後面接「沒有做的事」。此句型也可用副詞 instead 改寫,作「取而代之的是」、「相反地」解,instead 可置於句首或句末。

例:It means divers carry everything they need to stay alive under the water, **instead of** relying on hoses feeding them air from the surface of the water.

Ⓐ

 Keywords ••

1. 工作量:*workload* (n.)

2. 上健身房:*go to the gym*　做瑜珈:*do/practice yoga*　午休時間:*lunch break*

 Sample ••

1. **Mary** 繁重的工作量沒有阻止她每天運動。

Mary's heavy workload doesn't **keep/prevent/stop** her **from** doing some exercise every day.

2. 她沒有去上健身房,而是利用午餐休息時間做瑜珈。

Instead of going to the gym, she practices yoga during her lunch break.

= She doesn't go to the gym. **Instead**, she practices yoga during her lunch break.

Ⓑ

✈ Keywords •────────────────────────•

1. 極限運動：*extreme sport*　潛在的：*potential*（adj.）　追求刺激者：*thrill seeker*
   瘋狂的：*crazy*（adj.）
2. 放棄：*give up/quit*（v.）　願意：*be willing to + V*　冒險：*take the risk*　技巧：*trick*（n.）

✈ Practice •────────────────────────•

1. 極限運動的潛在危險無法阻止追求刺激者做這些瘋狂的運動。

   _____

   _____

2. 他們不會放棄，反而願意冒險、嘗試困難的技巧。

   _____

   _____

Ⓒ

✈ Keywords •────────────────────────•

1. 密集的：*intensive*（adj.）　訓練課程：*training course*　額外的：*additional*（adj.）
   花費：*expense*（n.）　熱衷：*take to sth.*
2. 渴望：*be eager to + V*

✈ Practice •────────────────────────•

1. 密集的訓練課程和額外的花費無法阻止海洋愛好者熱衷水肺潛水。

   _____

   _____

2. 他們不願嘗試較容易的活動，反而渴望享受一種全新的經驗。

   _____

   _____

Unit 6 History: Human Rights Movement

Part I : Cloze Test

Ⓐ Nelson Mandela (1918−) plays an important role in ending discrimination in his country. He was born in a time __1__ South Africa was a considerably unjust country. __2__ from the white population through the "apartheid" system, the non-whites were refused the right to vote and were treated unfairly. To fight this injustice, Mandela became a lawyer and in 1944 joined the African National Congress. In 1962, he went to Ethiopia to promote African freedom, but when he returned, he was __3__ for illegal exit and sentenced to life imprisonment. When he was in prison, he continued to fight for his cause. In 1990, President F. W. de Klerk (1936−) __4__ the racist laws and freed many political prisoners, including Mandela. Three years later, De Klerk and Mandela shared the Nobel Peace Prize "for their work for the peaceful termination of the apartheid regime." In 1994, Mandela became the first non-white President of South Africa. Though he retired from public life in 1999, he remains an __5__ for freedom fighters everywhere.

_____ 1. (A) which   (B) of which   (C) where   (D) when

_____ 2. (A) They separate   (B) Separated   (C) Separating   (D) To separate

_____ 3. (A) accused   (B) afforded   (C) annoyed   (D) arrested

_____ 4. (A) abolished   (B) enforced   (C) observed   (D) violated

_____ 5. (A) achievement   (B) explanation   (C) inspiration   (D) occupation

---

discrimination n. 歧視　*South Africa* 南非　*considerably* adv. 非常、很
apartheid n. 種族隔離政策　*non-white* adj. 非白種人的　*injustice* n. 不公不義
African National Congress 非洲民族議會　*Ethiopia* 衣索比亞　*sentence* v. 判刑
life imprisonment 終生監禁　*cause* n. 理念　*termination* n. 終結　*regime* n. 政權

Ⓑ　Born into a rich family, Mahatma Gandhi (1869−1948) went to England as a young man to study law. When he returned to India, he worked hard for causes he believed in. These included fair taxes, improving the situation of women, assisting the poor, ___1___ brotherhood and equal treatment between Indians of different social levels. Like many of his countrymen, Gandhi believed that India should be a free country, not ruled by Britain. He began doing everything he could to make this ___2___ happen.

　　Because of his beliefs, Gandhi ___3___ a rebel, but he was a rebel with an important difference. He believed in ___4___ resistance. He encouraged his followers to resist, but never to fight back. He taught that fighting only led to more fighting, and that nonviolence was the best way to ___5___ change. In this way, Gandhi was finally successful in leading India to independence in 1947.

_____ 1. (A) encourage　　(B) encouraged　　(C) encouraging　　(D) to encourage

_____ 2. (A) change　　(B) fact　　(C) mission　　(D) practice

_____ 3. (A) considered to be　(B) was considered　(C) regarded as　　(D) was regarded

_____ 4. (A) military　　(B) organized　　(C) peaceful　　(D) religious

_____ 5. (A) come up with　　(B) make up for　　(C) take over　　(D) bring about

---

fair taxes 公平稅賦　　*brotherhood* n. 手足情誼　　*rebel* n. 叛亂份子
difference n. 差異　　*resist* v. 抗爭　　*resistance* n. 抗爭

Mahatma Gandhi (1869−1948) 甘地

全名為 Mohandas Karamchand Gandhi，印度獨立運動領袖，被譽為印度獨立建國的國父，另有「聖雄」之稱號。曾在印度駐南非的公司工作期間，參與南非的公民運動，因而遭到逮捕監禁。以「非暴力」的不合作、絕食運動，多次遭遇逮捕，但最終仍帶領印度人民脫離英國殖民。1948 年在前往祈禱會途中遭受印度教狂熱分子槍擊身亡。

Ⓒ The African-American minister Martin Luther King, Jr. (1929–1968) was one of the most important black leaders of his time. He is famous for planting the __1__ of nonviolence within the activist civil rights movement.

King first learned about nonviolence in college, and later he was __2__ by the teachings of Henry David Thoreau and Mahatma Gandhi on nonviolent resistance. King foresaw that organized, non-violent protest against the racist system __3__ a wave of pro-civil rights movement. To King, nonviolence was more __4__ than violence, which simply continued the cruelty of one group against the other. He recognized that violence could never bring real justice. Instead of diminishing evil, violence would __5__ it.

King's first victory was the Montgomery Bus Boycott he led, __6__ the black citizens of Montgomery, Alabama refused to use the city buses for eleven months, __7__ an end to the policy of segregated bus seats for blacks and whites. The city governors finally gave up, and from then on, black citizens could sit __8__ they pleased. The Southern Christian Leadership Conference (SCLC), an organization of black churches and ministers, was created after this success. Under King's leadership, the SCLC applied the principles of nonviolent protest __9__ astonishing success.

King became the youngest recipient of the Nobel Peace Prize, which was awarded to him for leading non-violent resistance to end racial prejudice in the US. He is now recognized around the world as a __10__ of freedom, peace, and nonviolent civil disobedience.

_____ 1. (A) challenge   (B) result   (C) strategy   (D) tendency

_____ 2. (A) followed   (B) impressed   (C) possessed   (D) rejected

_____ 3. (A) create   (B) to create   (C) creating   (D) would create

_____ 4. (A) economical   (B) political   (C) radical   (D) technical

_____ 5. (A) divide   (B) multiply   (C) reduce   (D) prohibit

_____ 6. (A) that   (B) when   (C) which   (D) in which

_____ 7. (A) demand   (B) demanded   (C) demanding   (D) to be demanded

_____ 8. (A) wherever   (B) whenever   (C) whatever   (D) however

_____ 9. (A) with   (B) in   (C) out of   (D) from

_____ 10. (A) breakthrough   (B) milestone   (C) signal   (D) symbol

African-American n. 非裔美籍的　　*minister* n. 牧師　　*diminish* v. 削弱
Montgomery Bus Boycott 蒙哥馬利市拒乘公車運動
SCLC (*The Southern Christian Leadership Conference*) 南方基督教領袖會議
recipient n. 受獎者　　*prejudice* n. 偏見　　*disobedience* n. 不服從

 ## Part II : Translation Practice

Sentence Patterns

1. N(P), which/who/when/where

此句型為關係子句的非限定用法。先行詞為專有名詞或獨一無二的人或事物時，關係代名詞之前需加上逗點，表示「非限定用法」，此時關係子句是用於補充說明先行詞。

例：Nonviolence was more radical than violence, **which** simply continued the cruelty of one group against the other.

2.時間 + when

(表示時間的) 關係副詞 when 前面的先行詞可以省略，若先行詞為 the time 則關係副詞 when 可以省略。

例：I can't remember the time **when** we first met.
　　→ I can't remember the time we first met.
　　→ I can't remember **when** we first met.

Ⓐ

 ### Keywords

1. 獨立宣言：*Declaration of Independence*　　起草、草擬：*draft* (v.)
　聲明、陳述：*state/claim* (v.)　　平等的：*equal* (adj.)

2. 採用：*adopt* (v.)　　殖民地：*colony* (n.)　　和…打仗：*be at war with*

 ### Sample

1. 由湯瑪士・傑佛遜 (Thomas Jefferson) 起草的獨立宣言清楚地聲明人人生而平等。

   The Declaration of Independence, **which** was drafted by Thomas Jefferson, clearly states that all men are created equal.

2. 此宣言於 1776 年 7 月 4 日被採用，當時美國殖民地正和英國交戰中。

   The Declaration was adopted on July 4, 1776, **when** American colonies were at war with Great Britain.

Ⓑ

✈ Keywords

1. 被認為：*be regarded/thought of as*　重申：*restate* (v.)　原則：*principle* (n.)
   平等：*equality* (n.)
2. 發表：*deliver* (v.)　內戰：*civil war* (n.)　使分裂、拆散：*tear apart*　奴隸制度：*slavery* (n.)
   議題：*issue* (n.)

✈ Practice

1. 在被認為是最偉大演講之一的蓋茲堡演說 (Gettysburg Address) 中，亞柏拉罕‧林肯 (Abraham Lincoln) 重申人人平等的原則。

   _____

2. 此演說在美國內戰期間發表，當時美國正為奴隸議題所分裂。

   _____

   _____

Ⓒ

✈ Keywords

1. 當選演說：*acceptance speech*　發表演說：*address* (v.)　支持者：*supporter* (n.)
   恢復、重建：*restore* (v.)　信念：*faith/belief* (n.) *(+ in)*
2. 降臨、發生：*come to*

✈ Practice

1. 巴拉克‧歐巴馬 (Barack Obama) 對超過 20 萬名的支持者發表的當選演說，重建了人們的信念。

   _____

   _____

2. 他們相信任何事都可能做得到的時代已降臨美國。

   _____

   _____

Part I : Cloze Test

Ⓐ Possessing an on-going civilization for over 4,000 years, Egypt is an ancient land that has not yet given up all of its secrets. One mystery, which has fascinated historians, involves a lost Egyptian city—Heracleion. About 1,300 years ago, it simply ___1___. No one is sure what caused the destruction of this city.

Recently, divers ___2___ the lost city of Heracleion in the Mediterranean Sea, a few miles off the coast of Egypt. The well-preserved ruins were found under thirty feet of water in Aboukir Bay. Divers have ___3___ items that have been hidden for centuries from below the ocean sands. Initial studies reveal that Heracleion may have resembled modern Venice, with canals, lovely villas, and temples. Historians point out that the city was quite ___4___, and renowned for its many pleasures. Hopefully, these artifacts will help ___5___ the last years of Egypt's great civilization.

_____ 1. (A) emerged   (B) prospered   (C) removed   (D) vanished

_____ 2. (A) discover   (B) have discovered (C) are discovered (D) had discovered

_____ 3. (A) retrieved   (B) retreated   (C) relieved   (D) received

_____ 4. (A) coastal   (B) primitive   (C) native   (D) wealthy

_____ 5. (A) keep up with   (B) look forward to (C) shed light on   (D) take pride in

---

possess v. 擁有   *civilization* n. 文明   *fascinate* v. 迷住、吸引   *historian* n. 歷史學家
Heracleion 希拉克里昂   *destruction* n. 滅亡   *Mediterranean* adj. 地中海的
Aboukir Bay 阿布奇爾海灣   *item* n. 物件、項目   *resemble* v. 看起來像
renowned adj. 聞名的   *artifact* n. 工藝品

B Founded around 600 B.C., Pompeii became a Roman colony in 80 B.C. It was very close to the volcano Vesuvius, but people were ___1___ afraid ___1___ worried. Despite clear warning signs before the eruption, the inhabitants were caught ___2___. In 79 A.D., Vesuvius erupted, projecting wet ashes and toxic gas. The eruption lasted one day, changing the course of the local rivers and ___3___ the sea beach. After the tragedy, Pompeii was no longer a charming and peaceful city, but a tomb for thousands of people.

Pompeii was not rediscovered until 1748. Many buildings, temples and wall paintings, ___4___ by the ashes, have been found, offering us a rare opportunity to understand Roman everyday life in a provincial city. Pompeii is not only a rare chance for historians to understand Roman society and culture, but also an exceptional spot, attracting millions of tourists who are ___5___ by this extraordinary city.

_____ 1. (A) not only...but also   (B) either...or

     (C) neither...nor   (D) both...and

_____ 2. (A) by heart   (B) by surprise   (C) in touch   (D) in vain

_____ 3. (A) raise   (B) raised   (C) raising   (D) to raise

_____ 4. (A) preserve   (B) preserved   (C) preserving   (D) to preserve

_____ 5. (A) fascinated   (B) dominated   (C) conveyed   (D) abandoned

---

Pompeii 龐貝城   *colony* n. 殖民地   *volcano* n. 火山   *Vesuvius* 維蘇威火山
eruption n. 噴發   *inhabitant* n. 居民   *erupt* v. 爆發、噴發   *project* v. 拋射
toxic adj. 有毒的   *course* n. 航道   *provincial* adj. 省級的，地方的
exceptional adj. 罕見的、特殊的

Ⓒ   In the 1800s, in the dense jungles of Mexico and Guatemala, huge ancient cities were discovered among the trees and vines. Perfectly straight roads   1   these cities, and they were filled with beautiful stone temples and palaces. These were Mayan cities, but who were the Maya?

The Maya were   2   various tribes of American Indians who lived in Central America from about 1000 B.C. to 1572 A.D., a period of over 2,500 years. Their culture was based on   3 , mainly the growing of maize, or corn. Because they depended so much   4   the cycles of the seasons, they became very accomplished   5   and developed extremely accurate calendars—more accurate even than the Roman calendar that is widely used today. They built large domed structures to view the heavens,   6   windows positioned to frame specific planets and stars on religious celebration days.

Women were well-respected in Mayan communities, and had   7   standing with men. In many cases, they held positions of power, and some women were considered goddesses. The Maya were a very   8   people, and worshipped rain, fertility, and the earth.

The Mayan culture was at its greatest from about the third to the sixteenth centuries. But despite all of its accomplishments during that time, it has all but disappeared. Was it   9   the failure of crops, fighting within the tribes, or being overtaken by another culture? No one is sure. Today only the language, a few traditions, and the great accomplishments of the ancients   10 .

_____	1. (A) communicated	(B) competed	(C) connected	(D) constructed
_____	2. (A) consisted of	(B) made up of	(C) contained of	(D) constituted of
_____	3. (A) agriculture	(B) commerce	(C) handicrafts	(D) industry
_____	4. (A) in	(B) on	(C) at	(D) of
_____	5. (A) astronomers	(B) consultants	(C) mechanics	(D) philosophers
_____	6. (A) and	(B) for	(C) by	(D) with
_____	7. (A) higher	(B) lower	(C) equal	(D) social
_____	8. (A) industrious	(B) violent	(C) professional	(D) religious
_____	9. (A) because	(B) because of	(C) in spite of	(D) in regard to
_____	10. (A) maintain	(B) disappear	(C) survive	(D) preserve

---

vines n. 藤蔓   *maize* n. 玉米   *accomplished* adj. 有成就的   *domed* adj. 圓頂的
frame v. 加框   *fertility* n. 沃土

 **Part II : Translation Practice**

Sentence Patterns

1. 整體 +
{
consist of
be made up of
be composed/comprised of
comprise
}
+ N (部分／成分)

此句型為「由…所組成」之意。請注意各種動詞片語主動或被動的用法，以及整體與部分／成分所放置的位置。

例：The Maya **were made up of** various tribes of American Indians who lived in central America from about 1000 B.C. to 1572 A.D.

2. wh-疑問詞 + (S) + V

wh- 疑問詞所引導的子句為名詞子句，為間接問句，請注意疑問詞後面的主詞與動詞不需倒裝，此句型常接在 know, wonder, ask, doubt, tell 等動詞之後。

Ⓐ

 Keywords •

1. 人（類）的：*human* (adj.)　圖形：*figure* (n.)
2. 研究人員：*researcher* (n.)　複雜的：*complex* (adj.)
   樣式、花樣：*pattern* (n.)　表面：*surface* (n.)

 Sample •

1. 納茲卡線 (the Nazca lines) 是由不同的人形和動物圖形所組成的。

   The Nazca lines **are composed of/are comprised of/are made up of/consist of/comprise** different human and animal figures.

2. 研究人員想找出為什麼這些複雜的花樣會刻在沙漠的表面。

   Researchers want to find out **why** these complex patterns were cut into the desert's surface.

Ⓑ

✈ **Keywords** •··•

1. 主要地：*mainly*（adv.）

2. 考古學家：*archeologist*（n.）   解釋：*explain*（v.）   搬運：*transport*（v.）

✈ **Practice** •··•

1. 巨石陣 (Stonehenge) 主要是由許多高大的石頭所組成。

_____

_____

2. 考古學家試著解釋這些巨石是如何搬運到這裡。

_____

_____

Ⓒ

✈ **Keywords** •··•

1. 數十個：*dozens of*   石廟：*stone temple*

2. 建造：*construct*（v.）

✈ **Practice** •··•

1. 吳哥窟 (Angkor Wat) 是由數十個石寺廟所組成。

_____

_____

2. 遊客都想知道誰創造了它，還有它如何建造的。

_____

_____

Unit 8 History: Business

Ⓐ All over the world a Rolex watch represents wealth, good taste and high quality. Its __1__ and survival has been built on its inventions and its decision to stay with the mechanical wristwatch technology it perfected long ago.

The company's founder, Hans Wilsdorf, dreamed of replacing the standard pocket watches __2__ a perfectly functioning wristwatch. Wristwatches were fashion items, but no one had yet produced a wristwatch as accurate and reliable as the larger, but less convenient, pocket watch. __3__, in 1910, Wilsdorf made a wristwatch which was acclaimed by the School of Horology in Switzerland, the world's premier watch-making school. In 1926 Wilsdorf caused __4__ sensation with the first waterproof wristwatch, and then again in 1931 with the first automatic wristwatch.

Nowadays, as it was in the 1920s, Rolex is the foremost brand name in the watch industry. It has successfully lived through the __5__ from mechanical to new digital technology.

_____ 1. (A) fame   (B) idol   (C) slogan   (D) urge

_____ 2. (A) for   (B) of   (C) with   (D) to

_____ 3. (A) Therefore   (B) However   (C) Similarly   (D) Otherwise

_____ 4. (A) other   (B) the other   (C) others   (D) another

_____ 5. (A) translation   (B) transition   (C) transportation   (D) transmission

---

taste n. 品味　*mechanical* adj. 機械的　*wristwatch* n. 腕錶　*perfect* v. 使完美完善
accurate adj. 準確的　*reliable* adj. 可靠的　*acclaim* v. 讚揚
School of Horology in Switzerland 瑞士鐘錶學院　*premier* adj. 頂級的
sensation n. 轟動的事件　*waterproof* adj. 防水的　*foremost* adj. 一流的

B　The success of McDonald's Corporation is brought about by three men. The first two were the McDonald brothers, who created a new kind of restaurant in the 1940s. They had a simple menu and designed a factory-like kitchen __1__ trained staff could produce the menu items, like workers on __2__. People were attracted by the efficient service and soon the brothers opened more restaurants. They also started franchising, which means __3__ other businessmen to open restaurants with the McDonald's name and standard operating procedures. In exchange the brothers were paid a small percentage of the sales.

　　The third man was Ray Kroc. Surprised at the long but fast-moving line of customers, he persuaded the brothers __4__ nationwide by putting him in control of franchising. By the time he died in 1984, McDonald's was opening a restaurant somewhere in the world every seventeen hours! Thanks to them, McDonald can enjoy such a phenomenal __5__.

_____ 1. (A) which 　　　(B) what 　　　　(C) where 　　　　(D) that
_____ 2. (A) an hourly pay　(B) an assembly line (C) a daily routine　(D) a dress code
_____ 3. (A) allow 　　　　(B) to allow 　　　(C) allowing 　　　(D) allows
_____ 4. (A) expand 　　　(B) to expand 　　(C) expanding 　　(D) expanded
_____ 5. (A) depth 　　　　(B) breadth 　　　(C) warmth 　　　(D) growth

---

corporation n. 公司、集團　　*efficient* adj. 有效率的　　*franchising* v. 連鎖加盟
standard operating procedure 標準化作業流程　　*phenomenal* adj. 驚人的

McDonald's 麥當勞

世界最大漢堡速食連鎖餐飲，總部設於美國伊利諾州，在全球 119 個國家中設有約 3 萬 3 千多家分店。主要販售大麥克漢堡 (Big Mac)、吉事漢堡 (cheeseburger)、薯條 (French fries)、麥克雞塊 (Chicken McNuggets)、奶昔 (milkshakes) 及專為兒童提供的快樂兒童餐 (The Happy Meal) 等。因為麥當勞速食在全球的熱賣，讓其商標品牌成為一個流行文化的象徵，代表著「速食文化」、「美國式生活」、「美國文化入侵」及「垃圾食物」等正反兩極的反應。

Ⓒ Serving the world's most popular soft drink, the Coca-Cola Company can be characterized by its genius in promoting its products __1__ with its drive to continually expand its markets.

Coca-Cola was already being promoted by an advertisement in a local American newspaper in 1886, just a few months after its original formula __2__ by Dr. John Pemberton. He marketed Coca-Cola as a tonic drink to cure headaches but the __3__ was effective and simple, "Drink Coca-Cola."

Nationwide expansion followed the formation of The Coca-Cola Company in 1892. __4__ the leadership of Asa G. Chandler, the company established bottling factories outside Atlanta, enabling Coca-Cola consumption __5__ to every U.S. state. This expansion was __6__ by Coca-Cola advertisements on barn doors and the sides of buildings throughout America and by hiring famous singers, actors and sports stars to promote Coca-Cola.

In the twentieth century Coca-Cola expanded __7__, setting up bottling plants in Europe, South America, Africa and Asia. From the 1920s, the image of the Coca-Cola trademark has bombarded people with electric signs in cities around the world. Coca-Cola exploited the new __8__, advertising on radio and then on TV, creating catchy slogans such as "Coke is it!"

Robert Woodruff, the 1923 Coca-Cola Company Chairman, said that he wanted Coca-Cola to be "within an arm's __9__ of desire" for everyone. The company has maintained his drive and vision and continues its relentless pursuit of new __10__ to ensure that, as the 1927 advertisement stated, Coca-Cola is "around the corner from everywhere."

_____ 1. (A) couple   (B) to couple   (C) coupling   (D) coupled

_____ 2. (A) had been invented   (B) would be invented

      (C) invented   (D) was being invented

_____ 3. (A) identity   (B) slogan   (C) offense   (D) permit

_____ 4. (A) By   (B) For   (C) Under   (D) With

_____ 5. (A) spread   (B) to spread   (C) spreading   (D) to spreading

_____ 6. (A) accompanied   (B) delayed   (C) published   (D) restricted

_____ 7. (A) domestically   (B) internationally   (C) secretly   (D) visibly

_____ 8. (A) solar energy   (B) steam engines   (C) mass media   (D) public transport

_____ 9. (A) arrival   (B) length   (C) touch   (D) reach

_____ 10. (A) techniques   (B) inventions   (C) markets   (D) products

genius n. 才能   *tonic drink* 提神的飲料   *bottle* v. 裝瓶   *consumption* n. 消費

 Part II : Translation Practice

Sentence Patterns

1. not as/so + Adj./Adv. + as

as...as 中間可加入形容詞或副詞，表示「和⋯一樣」，若加入否定詞 not 則第一個 as 亦可用 so 取代，表示「不如⋯一樣」。
例：This dictionary is **not so** good **as** that old one.

2. However/Nevertheless, S + V

however 和 nevertheless 皆為副詞，作「然而」解，用於表示語意轉折。

 A

 **Keywords** •

1. 沖水馬桶：*flush toilet* (n.)　發明：*invent* (v.)　便宜：*inexpensive* (adj.)
2. 改良：*improvement* (n.)　負擔得起的：*affordable* (adj.)
   家家戶戶：*household* (n.)

Sample •

1. 沖水馬桶剛發明時，並不像今天一樣便宜。
   When flush toilets were just invented, they were **not as/so** inexpensive **as** they are today.

2. 然而，在一些改良後，家家戶戶都買得起沖水馬桶。
   However/Nevertheless, after some improvements, flush toilets become affordable to every household.

B

Keywords •

1. 餡料：*topping* (n.)
2. 傳遍：*spread* (v.)　各式各樣的：*various* (adj.)　食材：*ingredient* (n.)
   添加、加入：*add* (v.)

Practice •

1. 人們以前並沒有像現在一樣放這麼多餡料在披薩。

_____

2. 然而，在這食物傳遍到世界各地後，加入各式各樣食材。

_____

_____

C

Keywords •

1. 牛仔褲：*blue jeans*　時髦的：*stylish* (adj.)
2. 時尚、流行的式樣：*fashion* (n.)　吸引：*attract* (v.)
   所有年齡層的人：*people of all ages*

Practice •

1. 牛仔褲做出來時，並沒有像現在一樣時髦。

_____

2. 然而，之後它變成一種時尚，並且吸引了所有年齡層的人。

_____

_____

Unit 9 History: Architecture

Part I : Cloze Test

Ⓐ Tourists who travel to Rome must visit one of its oldest and most famous places: the Colosseum.

In 72 A.D., the Roman Emperor Vespasian asked his people to build the Colosseum __1__ various sporting activities. It took thousands of workers eight years to build. About 157 feet high and almost 1,788 feet long around the outside wall, the Colosseum had a seating __2__ of 50,000.

In the past, activities held there were mainly divided into two groups. One is to show human's strength and the other, to __3__. In the former kind, trained fighters struggled against each other or with dangerous animals. In the __4__ kind, trained monkeys and lions performed tricks to make the crowd laugh.

By the 6th century, the Romans had stopped holding these activities. After that, through years of lack of care and two earthquakes, the Colosseum was seriously __5__. To date, its appearance is still not repaired completely.

_____ 1. (A) hold   (B) holding   (C) held   (D) to hold

_____ 2. (A) capability   (B) capacity   (C) possibility   (D) probability

_____ 3. (A) discipline   (B) entertain   (C) inform   (D) persuade

_____ 4. (A) late   (B) later   (C) latter   (D) last

_____ 5. (A) ruined   (B) haunted   (C) deserted   (D) isolated

---

Rome 羅馬   *Colosseum* n. 圓形競技場   *Roman Emperor* 羅馬皇帝
Vespasian 維斯帕先   *seating* n. 座位（數量）   *lack of* 缺乏   *to date* 至今

Ⓑ Towering over Taipei, Taipei 101 is one building that certainly stands out. But other than its amazing __1__, there are many things that make Taipei 101 special.

Taipei 101 is an architectural achievement. Frequent earthquakes and wind and rain brought by strong typhoons are its main challenges. __2__, the building has to be strong enough to withstand the intense weather in Taiwan. Its extreme __3__ can prevent large sideways movement and ensure structural integrity. In addition, the curtain walls enhance critical structural elements such as bracing.

Taipei 101 is divided into eight floors as a unit. In Chinese, "eight" sounds like "fa," which means being __4__ and blooming. The shape of Taipei 101 looks like a growing bamboo tree, symbolizing the positive spirit of Taiwan.

__5__, Taipei 101 is a solid example of people's ability to change the landscape. It is a building that we should be proud of.

_____ 1. (A) length   (B) width   (C) height   (D) weight

_____ 2. (A) Therefore   (B) Nevertheless   (C) Moreover   (D) Conversely

_____ 3. (A) characteristic (B) flexibility   (C) progress   (D) technique

_____ 4. (A) conservative   (B) intelligent   (C) optimistic   (D) prosperous

_____ 5. (A) Simply put   (B) Strange to say

          (C) To begin with   (D) Comparatively speaking

---

tower v. 高聳   *stand out* 顯眼   *architectural* adj. 建築的   *withstand* v. 抵擋
intense adj. 極端的   *sideways* adj. 向旁邊的   *integrity* n. 完整   *enhance* v. 強化
brace v. 支撐   *bloom* v. 盛開   *bamboo* n. 竹   *landscape* n. 地景、景色

Ⓒ From a distance the majestic Taj Mahal appears like a shimmering jewel floating in a vast stretch of blue. But do you know that behind the white stone walls of this magnificent palace ___1___ a sad tale of love?

Shah Jahan, a Mughal Emperor, ruled India ___2___ 1628 to 1658. In 1612, the emperor married Arjumand Banu, who was later known as Mumtaz Mahal. Ever since their marriage, the two lovers did everything together. The king even ___3___ his wife ___3___ when he went to battle. Mumtaz was a constant support to Shah Jahan through his victories and ___4___ —she was a wife, lover, and friend to the king.

Unfortunately, their time together soon ___5___. Mumtaz died while giving birth to their fourteenth child in 1631. The death of his beloved wife so deeply ___6___ Shah Jahan that it is said, all his hair grew as white as snow in only a few months. In his sadness and desire to create a memory of his love, Shah Jahan ordered that the Taj Mahal ___7___ as the last resting place for his lovely wife. Thus, in 1632, the ___8___ of the Taj Mahal began in Agra.

It ___9___ twenty thousand workers twenty-two years to translate Shah Jahan's passionate love into the most touching symphony in white marble. About three hundred years later, it still instills a tender feeling of love ___10___ the hearts of the onlookers.

_____ 1. (A) exist   (B) exists   (C) existed   (D) existing
_____ 2. (A) in   (B) at   (C) from   (D) since
_____ 3. (A) took...off   (B) took...over   (C) took...along   (D) took...away
_____ 4. (A) defeats   (B) destinies   (C) discoveries   (D) disputes
_____ 5. (A) came to their aid   (B) came to an end
        (C) came into existence   (D) came into effect
_____ 6. (A) flashed   (B) flushed   (C) crashed   (D) crushed
_____ 7. (A) build   (B) built   (C) to build   (D) be built
_____ 8. (A) hometown   (B) architecture   (C) construction   (D) decoration
_____ 9. (A) took   (B) cost   (C) spent   (D) used
_____ 10. (A) for   (B) into   (C) with   (D) from

---

shimmering adj. 閃閃發亮   *magnificent* adj. 宏偉的   *translate* v. 轉變
symphony n. 交響曲

Part II : Translation Practice

Sentence Patterns

1. S₁ + order + that S₂ + (should) + 原形 V...

order 之後所接的 that 子句中 should 可以省略，直接用原形動詞，除了 order 之外，其他表示命令（如：command）、堅持（如：insist）、建議（如：suggest, propose, recommend, advise）、要求（如：demand, request, require）等動詞，也有相同的用法。

例：Shah Jahan **ordered** that the Taj Mahal (should) **be built** as the last resting place for his lovely wife.

2.地方副詞 (片語) + V/be + S

將地方副詞置於句首時要用倒裝的句型。若主詞為普通名詞時，先放動詞再接主詞。

如：Here comes **the bus**.。

但若主詞為代名詞時，則主詞動詞順序不變，不需倒裝。

如：Here **it** comes.。

Ⓐ

 Keywords •

1. 埃及（的）：*Egypt*（n.）*Egyptian*（adj.）　金字塔：*pyramid*（n.）　安息地：*resting place*（n.）
2. 寶藏：*treasure*（n.）　收藏：*collection*（n.）　物品：*object*（n.）　來生、來世：*afterlife*（n.）

 Sample •

1. 大約西元前 2540 年，埃及法老 (pharaoh) 古夫 (Khufu) 下令興建吉薩大金字塔 (the Great Pyramid of Giza) 做為他的安息地。

   Around 2540 B.C., Egyptian pharaoh Khufu **ordered that** the Great Pyramid of Giza **be built** as his resting place.

2. 在金字塔裡收藏有寶藏和他來生所需的物品。

   Inside the pyramid is a collection of treasures and objects for his afterlife.

Ⓑ

✈ Keywords •——————————————————————————————————•

1. 皇帝：*emperor* (n.)　防禦：*defend* (v.)　帝國：*empire* (n.)
2. 謠傳、謠言：*rumor has it that*　數不盡的：*countless* (adj.)　奴隸：*slave* (n.)

✈ Practice •——————————————————————————————————•

1. 大約西元前 220 年，中國的秦始皇 (Qin Shi Huang) 命令興建萬里長城 (the Great Wall) 以保護帝國。

———————————————————————————————————————

———————————————————————————————————————

2. 謠傳說在長城裡面有數不盡的奴隸屍體。

———————————————————————————————————————

———————————————————————————————————————

Ⓒ

✈ Keywords •——————————————————————————————————•

1. 主教：*bishop* (n.)　紀念：*in honor of*
2. 大教堂：*cathedral* (n.)　舉世聞名的：*world-renowned* (adj.)　雕像、雕刻品：*sculpture* (n.)

✈ Practice •——————————————————————————————————•

1. 在 1163 年，巴黎主教莫里斯・德・書里 (Maurice de Sully) 下令建造巴黎聖母院 (Notre Dame de Paris) 以紀念聖母瑪利亞 (Virgin Mary)。

———————————————————————————————————————

———————————————————————————————————————

2. 在這座大教堂裡面有舉世聞名的彩繪玻璃 (stained glass) 和雕像。

———————————————————————————————————————

———————————————————————————————————————

Part I : Cloze Test

Ⓐ   Dressed in his black cap and gown, Henry felt very proud that he was finally graduating. The   1   speeches and benediction were over. When the dean called his name, he nervously walked onto the stage   2   his diploma. When the last student received his diploma, all of the students yelled and threw their mortarboard caps into the air.

   The college graduation ceremony has not changed much in almost a thousand years. In the twelfth century Europe, the Catholic Church set up the first colleges to train men for the priesthood. Upon graduation, the students were then priests and   3   wear a black gown. These colleges originally taught only theology, but as civilization progressed, the colleges   4   their curriculums.

   Although most colleges are now secular, the modern graduation traditions derive   5   the medieval, religious college ceremonies. The benediction and wearing caps and gowns are examples of the centuries-old tradition.

_____ 1. (A) acceptance   (B) commencement (C) campaign   (D) inaugural

_____ 2. (A) accept   (B) accepted   (C) accepting   (D) to accept

_____ 3. (A) entitled to   (B) devoted to   (C) refused to   (D) opposed to

_____ 4. (A) designed   (B) expanded   (C) followed   (D) introduced

_____ 5. (A) to   (B) for   (C) from   (D) with

---

benediction n. 祝福   *dean* n. 院長   *diploma* n. 畢業證書   *mortarboard cap* 學士帽
Catholic Church 羅馬天主教會   *priesthood* n. 神職人員   *gown* n. 袍子
theology n. 神學   *curriculum* n. 課程   *secular* adj. 世俗的   *medieval* adj. 中世紀

Ⓑ　Ancient civilizations had several famous centers for advanced study. Plato's Academy, __1__, might be considered the world's oldest university, and India's first "university," Nalanda University, was well-known for Buddhist study. But if "oldest" means "longest continuously operating," then neither Plato's Academy nor Nalanda University could hold the title because __2__ closed many centuries ago.

According to *The Guinness Book of World Records*, the world's oldest university is the University of Al Karaouine in Fez, Morocco. Founded in 859 A.D., it is still __3__.

This university began as part of a mosque, and although it now includes classes in politics, science, and language, it __4__ an important school of religious study. In the Middle Ages, this university was a major center for the sharing of knowledge and understanding between Muslims and Europeans. Today, its mission is much the same: to demonstrate the positive role that Islamic society can __5__ in the world.

_____ 1. (A) instead of　　(B) for example　　(C) on the contrary　(D) as a result

_____ 2. (A) both　　　　(B) either　　　　(C) neither　　　　(D) none

_____ 3. (A) under construction　　　　　(B) beyond description

　　　　　(C) in operation　　　　　　　　(D) without permission

_____ 4. (A) remains　　(B) reminds　　(C) reserves　　(D) resigns

_____ 5. (A) do　　　　(B) make　　　(C) take　　　(D) play

---

advanced study 高等教育　*Plato* 柏拉圖　*academy* n. 學院
Nalanda University 那難陀大學　*Buddhist* adj. 佛學、佛教的
continuously adv. 持續不斷地　*The Guinness Book of World Records* 金氏世界紀錄
University of Al Karouine 卡魯母大學　*Fez* 菲茲　*Moroco* 摩洛哥
mosque n. 清真寺　*Middle Ages* 中世紀　*Muslim* n. 穆斯林　*mission* n. 使命、任務
Islamic adj. 伊斯蘭的

Ⓒ During Medieval times, education was very different from it is today. It was not a requirement for children to be educated. The kind of education children received __1__ the social class of their family and their gender.

The first schools were __2__ by churches for rich boys. Priests who had only a basic education themselves taught these schools. The school day lasted from the time the sun rose to the time the sun set, so it could be __3__ 12 hours. Students did not have books __4__ printing was too expensive. They studied the Bible and learned to read and write. They studied logic, Latin, astronomy, philosophy and mathematics. They were also taught proper behavior. The first universities in Medieval Europe were established in the 12th century by the church. Boys were allowed __5__ at the age of 14 or 15.

Children who lived in towns and villages were sometimes taught in small schools by a local priest. Children of peasants were usually taught __6__ skills and household tasks by their parents or older brothers and sisters. However, they did not learn to read or write. Boys sometimes became __7__ in order to learn a trade. After studying and working under a master for several years, they could start their own business __8__ a bakery.

We now have a more __9__ approach to education. We realize that everyone, __10__ social class or gender, has a right to be educated. Moreover, in most countries churches and schools are separate.

_____ 1. (A) depended upon (B) indulged in (C) exposed to (D) recovered from
_____ 2. (A) attended (B) noticed (C) operated (D) regarded
_____ 3. (A) as far as (B) as long as (C) as soon as (D) as well as
_____ 4. (A) because (B) so (C) until (D) though
_____ 5. (A) start (B) starting (C) to start (D) started
_____ 6. (A) reading (B) study (C) language (D) farm
_____ 7. (A) accountants (B) apprentices (C) ambassadors (D) applicants
_____ 8. (A) according to (B) next to (C) because of (D) such as
_____ 9. (A) conventional (B) indirect (C) scientific (D) universal
_____ 10. (A) on behalf of (B) as a result of (C) regardless of (D) instead of

---

Medieval adj. 中世紀的   *requirement* n. 必需、規定   *gender* n. 性別   *logic* n. 邏輯
trade n. 技藝

Part II : Translation Practice

Sentence Patterns

$$
1. \left\{
\begin{array}{l}
\text{On/Upon + N/V}_1\text{-ing,} \\
\text{As soon as S}_1 + \text{V}_1, \\
\text{The moment/instant/minute (that) S}_1 + \text{V}_1,
\end{array}
\right\} \text{S}_2 + \text{V}_2\ldots
$$

upon 之後要接名詞或動名詞，而 as soon as/the moment/the instant/the minute (that) 之後要接子句，作「一…就…」解，前後兩句的動詞時態要一致。子句可以出現在句首或是句尾，位於句首時以逗號與主要子句分隔。

2. regardless of + N/V-ing

此句型作「不顧、無視於…」解，意思相當於 in spite of。

例：We realize that everyone, **regardless of** social class or gender, has a right to be educated.

Ⓐ

 Keywords •────────────────────────────────•

1. 畢業：*graduate* (v.)*; graduation* (n.)　履歷表：*resume* (n.)
2. 真誠的：*sincere* (adj.)　主動的：*active* (adj.)　機會：*opportunity/chance* (n.)
　沒經驗：*inexperience* (n.)

 Sample •────────────────────────────────•

1. Peter一從大學畢業後，就立刻寄履歷表到許多公司。

　On/**Upon** graduation/graduating from college, Peter sent his resume to several companies.

　→ **As soon as**/**The moment**/**The instant**/**The minute** Peter graduated from college, he sent his resume to several companies.

2. 因為他非常真誠與主動，儘管他沒經驗，有位經理給了他一個機會。

　Because he was very sincere and active, a manager gave him an opportunity **regardless of** his inexperience.

Ⓑ

✈ Keywords •

1. 碩士學位：*master degree* (n.)　出國：*go abroad*　深造：*further studies*
2. 進取的：*aggressive* (adj.)　理解力強的、聰明的：*intelligent* (adj.)　委員會：*committee* (n.)
   獎學金：*scholarship* (n.)　背景：*background* (n.)

✈ Practice •

1. Mary 一拿到碩士學位，就立刻出國深造。

   _____

2. 因為她很積極進取、理解力又強，委員會不管她的背景給了她獎學金。

   _____

   _____

Ⓒ

✈ Keywords •

1. 取得：*acquire/obtain* (v.)　教師證：*teaching certificate*　申請：*apply* (+ *for*)
   偏遠地區：*remote area*
2. 有熱忱的、積極的：*enthusiastic* (adj.)　熱情的：*passionate* (adj.)　校長：*principal* (n.)
   職位：*position* (n.)

✈ Practice •

1. Rick 一取得到教師證，就立刻申請偏遠地區的工作。

   _____

2. 因為他既積極又熱情，有位校長不顧他的年紀給了他這個職位。

   _____

   _____

Unit 11 History: Invention

(A) According to archeologists, chewing gum was known to prehistoric people, who actually chewed on lumps of tree resin for pure enjoyment.

In the United States, the very first gum __1__ 1848, when resin was used to make Spruce Gum. In the mid 1800s, a photographer named Thomas Adams mixed chicle (a sticky tasteless substance) __2__ rubber in order to make a better tire. Though Adams failed to do so, he created a pure chicle gum and sold it. After its success, Adams tried to add flavor to the gum. The new product was quite popular with the public, but had one __3__ : it could not hold flavor. The flavor issue was not fixed __4__ 1880. William White experimented with flavors and solved the problem by adding sugar and corn syrup __5__ the mix. The first flavor he used was peppermint and it stayed in the gum while being chewed.

_____ 1.(A) dates back to   (B) is gone back to   (C) traces back to   (D) is dating back to

_____ 2.(A) for   (B) to   (C) with   (D) up

_____ 3.(A) advantage   (B) benefit   (C) drawback   (D) failure

_____ 4.(A) unless   (B) until   (C) since   (D) when

_____ 5.(A) in   (B) up   (C) with   (D) to

---

archeologist n. 考古學家   *chewing gum* 口香糖   *prehistoric* adj. 史前的
lump n. 塊狀   *resin* n. 樹脂   *Spruce Gum* 雲杉口香糖   *photographer* n. 攝影師
Thomas Adams 湯瑪斯‧亞當斯   *chicle* n. 糖膠樹膠   *substance* n. 物質
hold flavor 維持味道   *corn syrup* 玉米糖漿   *peppermint* n. 薄荷

Ⓑ　Most people think the "Hula Hoop" was invented in America in 1950s, but this is untrue. As far back as 1000 B.C., Egyptian children used large rings of dried grape vines as toys. These hoops were __1__ around the waist or rolled along the ground. Then, in England in the late Middle Ages, an activity called "hooping" came to be popular. About 500 years later, British sailors visiting the Hawaiian Islands noticed that the "hula" dance there looked much like "hooping." It was at this time __2__ the name "Hula Hoop" first appeared.

　　In 1957, two American businessmen became aware __3__ wooden rings being sold as toys in Australia. Their toy company, Wham-O, began producing and selling its own "Hula Hoops" in 1958. After much __4__, their new, brightly colored plastic hoops became so popular with children __5__ Wham-O sold 25 millions of them in just four months.

_____ 1. (A) driven　　　(B) drawn　　　(C) shot　　　(D) swung
_____ 2. (A) that　　　　(B) which　　　(C) where　　　(D) ×
_____ 3. (A) of　　　　　(B) for　　　　(C) with　　　(D) that
_____ 4. (A) criticism　　(B) encounter　(C) promotion　(D) resistance
_____ 5. (A) and　　　　(B) that　　　　(C) for　　　　(D) when

---

hula hoop 呼拉圈

一種約 1 公尺長 (兒童用約為 71 公分) 的塑膠圈玩具。在被正式稱為呼拉圈之前，歷史有記載的也有以各式材質 (葡萄藤、竹編) 圈狀玩具出現。但在 1950 年代美國商人以塑膠材質的大量生產之後，呼拉圈的用途就不局限於娛樂。60 年代被用來當作馬戲雜耍團的道具，還有用於競賽或是健身減肥的最佳運動器材。

Ⓒ Although kites are found all over the world these days, many people may not know that they originally came from China. The first Chinese kites appeared in the fifth century B.C. The earliest kites were not toys. 1 , they were used in war, often to fly messages over enemy lines. A few may have even been large enough to take people up in the air and let them 2 the movement of their enemies. Kites in China had other uses, too. Some were equipped 3 hooks and bait, and used for fishing. Others had whistles and special strings 4 to them so that they would make musical sounds while they flew.

Kite flying soon spread across Asia, but it was not until the late 1500s 5 . In the 1700s, kites began to be used for scientific research. 6 more about the wind and the weather, scientists attached special instruments and cameras to kites and then flew them high into the sky. The creators of early flying machines, such as the airplane, used a kite as a 7 , as well.

Today, airplanes have replaced kites for most scientific and 8 purposes, and kites are mostly used for fun. Though many may regard them as toys, kites have been 9 with a special tribute in the National Aeronautics and Space Museum. There, in a section devoted to airplanes and spaceships, a sign states simply, "the earliest 10 are the kites of China."

_____ 1. (A) However   (B) Therefore   (C) Rather   (D) Otherwise

_____ 2. (A) produce   (B) observe   (C) suspect   (D) transport

_____ 3. (A) with   (B) for   (C) by   (D) along

_____ 4. (A) attach   (B) attached   (C) attaching   (D) to attach

_____ 5. (A) that the kite appeared in Europe   (B) did the kite appear in Europe
              (C) when the kite appeared in Europe (D) the kite appearing in Europe

_____ 6. (A) Learn   (B) Learned   (C) Learning   (D) To learn

_____ 7. (A) mode   (B) model   (C) mold   (D) mood

_____ 8. (A) educational (B) medical   (C) military   (D) social

_____ 9. (A) honored   (B) coincided   (C) impressed   (D) furnished

_____ 10. (A) popular amusements   (B) effective weapons
               (C) musical instruments   (D) air vehicles

> *National Aeronautics and Space Museum* 美國國家航太博物館

Part II : Translation Practice

Sentence Patterns

1. <u>S + Aux + not + V/be</u> + not...until....
   → Not until... + <u>Aux + S + V be + S</u>....　(倒裝句)
   → It is not until... + that S + V　(分裂句)

until 為表「時間」關係的連接詞，意思為「直到⋯為止」。若將 not until... 置於句首，主要子句則要改為倒裝句，用於加強語氣。此句型還可搭配分裂句 it is...that 來加強語氣，此時把 not until... 這部分置於 it is 和 that 之間，剩餘的主要子句部分則置於 that 之後，此強調用法要注意主要子句的部份<u>不用</u>倒裝。

例：The flavor issue **was not** fixed **until** 1880.

2. ...so + adj./adv. + that S + V

此句型為「如此⋯以至於」之意。so 之後可以接形容詞或副詞，that 子句表示「結果」。

例：Plastic hoops became **so** <u>popular</u> with children **that** Wham-O sold 25 millions of them in just four months.

Keywords

1. 雕像：*statue* (n.)　發現：*discover* (v.)
2. 精緻：*delicate* (adj.)　數量眾多：*numerous* (adj.)　使驚訝：*amaze* (v.)
   古代的：*ancient* (adj.)

Sample

1. 直到 1722 年才發現復活節島 (Easter Island) 上的巨大雕像。

   The giant statues on Easter Island **were not** discovered **until** 1722.

   → **Not until** 1722 **were** the giant statues on Easter Island **discovered**.

   → **It was not until** 1722 **that** the giant statues on Easter Island **were discovered**.

2. 它們是如此的精緻與數量眾多，以至於研究人員對於古代人的技術感到驚訝。

   They are **so** delicate and numerous **that** researchers are amazed by the skills of the ancient people.

Ⓑ

✈ Keywords ••

1. 條碼：*bar code*（n.）　食品雜貨店：*grocery store*　廣泛地：*widely*（adv.）
2. 掃瞄器：*scanner*（n.）　顧客：*customer*（n.）　結帳：*check out*

✈ Practice ••

1. 直到 1970 年代早期，條碼才在食品雜貨店中廣為使用。

_____

_____

2. 它們是如此容易地能用掃瞄器讀取到，所以顧客可以更快速地結帳。

_____

_____

Ⓒ

✈ Keywords ••

1. 微波爐：*microwave oven*　發明：*invent*（v.）
2. 操作：*operate*（v.）　現在：*nowadays/now*（adv.）　準備（食物）：*fix*（v.）
　費（很多／很少）力氣：*with much/little effort*

✈ Practice ••

1. 直到 1940 年代末期，微波爐才由一名美國科學家所發明。

_____

_____

2. 它們現在是如此容易操作，所以每個人都不用費太多力氣就能做好一頓飯。

_____

_____

Unit 12 History: Mysteries

Ⓐ Though most people have heard of the Loch Ness monster, few may know the history of this mysterious creature.

The monster was first written about 1,500 years ago. In this story, a priest saw a large creature getting ready to attack a man when walking by Loch Ness. With God's help, the priest was able to save the poor man by ordering the monster __1__.

The modern legend of the Loch Ness monster, __2__, began in 1933. A couple __3__ on a new road near the Loch said they had seen a large animal swimming in the water there. News of this strange creature quickly spread.

In 1957, a collection of the __4__ and drawings of the monster was published. Because of it, people began to take the search for the monster more seriously. Though no creatures were found, the researchers did discover __5__ of large underwater objects.

_____ 1. (A) go away   (B) going away   (C) to go away   (D) went away

_____ 2. (A) otherwise   (B) however   (C) accordingly   (D) consequently

_____ 3. (A) drive   (B) driving   (C) to drive   (D) drove

_____ 4. (A) accounts   (B) coins   (C) medals   (D) stamps

_____ 5. (A) mystery   (B) shadow   (C) organism   (D) evidence

Loch Ness 尼斯湖
loch 為克爾特語中「湖泊」之意，也稱作 lough。位於蘇格蘭高地的大格蘭斷層 (Great Glen Fault) 上，經由冰河侵蝕而成，蘇格蘭境內第二大的淡水湖泊。此湖長約 37 公里，寬約 1.5 公里，深約 230 公尺。因為水中大量的浮藻、泥炭 (peat)，使水中能見度很低，也因此讓尼斯湖充滿著神秘色彩。自古以來也因為傳說中的神秘生物 (cryptid) 尼斯湖水怪 (Loch Ness Monster) 著名。

Ⓑ   The Devil's Sea, also known as the Formosa Triangle, covers the sea area within a triangle drawn between Japan, Taiwan and Yap Island. Like the Bermuda Triangle off the eastern United States, the Devil's Sea has become known ___1___ the large number of ships and fishing boats lost there.

Reasons given to explain this differ. Some say that the losses are caused by UFOs. Others believe that as with the Bermuda Triangle, compass readings here differ from other sea areas, but this has been found to be ___2___. Still others think the violent volcanic nature of the sea floor beneath the triangle causes the ___3___ of the ships.

Whatever the reason for these strange events, so many vessels were lost during the 1940s and 1950s ___4___ the Japanese government sent a research vessel to investigate and it, too, went missing with 100 men on board. Japan then declared the area a ___5___.

_____ 1. (A) as   (B) for   (C) to   (D) of
_____ 2. (A) practical   (B) guilty   (C) innocent   (D) untrue
_____ 3. (A) disappearance (B) departure   (C) abandonment   (D) arrival
_____ 4. (A) and   (B) so   (C) that   (D) therefore
_____ 5. (A) comfort zone (B) danger zone   (C) war zone   (D) quake zone

---

The Devil's Sea/The Formosa Triangle 福爾摩沙三角 (魔鬼海)   *Yap Island* 雅蒲島
Bermuda Triangle 百慕達三角   *compass reading* 羅盤的指針讀數
volcanic adj. 火山的   *vessel* n. 船隻

Bermuda Triangle 百慕達三角

位於北大西洋，由英屬百慕達群島 (the Bermudas/Somers Islands)、美屬波多黎各 (Puerto Rico) 及美國佛羅里達州邁阿密 (Miami) 所形成的三角海域，又稱作魔鬼三角 (Devil's Triangle)，常被誤稱為百慕達三角洲，因此地方並非三角洲地形。以發生超自然現象 (supernatural phenomena)、科學無法解釋的「神秘失蹤」或外星人 (extraterrestrial beings) 活動著稱，但經許多航海資料證實，這些傳聞、失蹤事件多有誇大、誤傳及誤解。

Ⓒ   In November 2007, a series of footprints were found around Mount Everest, Nepal. The footprints __1__ approximately 12 inches in length and resembled those of drawings of a mysterious creature known as the Abominable Snowman, __2__ Yeti. The Yeti is an ancient creature that has been reported by native Himalayans for hundreds of years. They are described as having ape/monkey __3__, such as thumbs, hairless ears, and the ability to stand on their hind legs. The name of "Yeti" comes from the Tibetan word, yeh-teh, which __4__ "little, man-like animal".

Much research done on the Yeti has been accomplished by scientists that study __5__, legendary, or mythological animals. Findings collected have shown that most sightings were __6__ a misidentified forest creature, such as a bear, but there have been hair samples collected that __7__ unidentified. Some experts claim that most sightings are probably an endangered brown bear, capable of walking on its hind legs. Yet, new sightings are constantly surfacing, __8__ feeds new hope and attention to the Yeti.

Since the 1950's, the Yeti has been featured in many television shows and movies, bringing with it a large audience of both believers and nonbelievers. The Yeti has been featured in Warner Brothers cartoons, the television series *Doctor Who,* and the 1987 movie *Harry and the Henderson's.* __9__ the Yeti exists or not, it shall be an unsolved mystery __10__ further proof is found, and this makes him/her all the more exciting for people to watch!

_____ 1. (A) measure   (B) measured

         (C) were measured   (D) have been measured

_____ 2. (A) and   (B) or   (C) but   (D) so

_____ 3. (A) characteristics   (B) evolution   (C) intelligence   (D) representation

_____ 4. (A) stands up   (B) stands out   (C) stands for   (D) stands by

_____ 5. (A) extinct   (B) domestic   (C) marine   (D) stray

_____ 6. (A) anything but   (B) anything like

         (C) nothing to do with   (D) nothing more than

_____ 7. (A) maintain   (B) retain   (C) sustain   (D) remain

_____ 8. (A) that   (B) what   (C) which   (D) where

_____ 9. (A) Whatever   (B) Whether   (C) No matter   (D) If

_____ 10. (A) although   (B) since   (C) until   (D) while

> *approximately* adv. 接近、約　　*resemble* v. 像、類似
> *the Abominable Snowman* 喜馬拉雅山雪人　　*Tibetan* n. 西藏文

 **Part II : Translation Practice**

Sentence Patterns

1. be known for + N
be known for 之後接原因，作「以…原因而聞名」解，除了 known 之外，還可以使用 famous, well-known, noted, renowned 表示有名之意；此外若要表示「以…身分而聞名」，則可用 be known as + 身分。 例：James Joyce **is well-known as** one of the greatest novelists in the twentieth century.
2. Whether + S + V$_1$ + or not, S + V$_2$...
whether 為連接詞，所引導的子句為副詞子句，作「無論…與否」解。 例：**Whether** the Yeti exists **or not**, it shall be an unsolved mystery until further proof is found.

Ⓐ

 Keywords

1. 外星人 (的)：*alien* (adj.)　太空船：*spaceship* (n.)　墜機：*crash* (v.)
2. 事件：*incident* (n.)　成為：*find its way*　大眾的、流行的：*popular* (adj.)
   文化：*culture* (n.)

 Sample

1. 羅斯威爾 (Roswell) 因 1947 年某夜裡一架在該處墜機的外星人太空船而聲名大噪。
   Roswell **is well-known for** the alien spaceship which crashed there on one night of 1947.
2. 無論羅斯威爾事件是否屬實，它都成了美國大眾文化的一環。
   Whether the Roswell Incident is real **or not**, it finds its way into American popular culture.

Ⓑ

✈ **Keywords** •————————————————————————————•

1. 巨大的：*huge/enormous* (adj.)　雕像：*statue* (n.)　和…相似：*resemble* (v.)
   人類（的）：*human* (n.) (adj.)
2. 雕刻：*carve* (v.)　宗教的：*religious* (adj.)　理由、目的：*purpose* (n.)　依然：*remain* (v.)
   創造力：*creativity* (n.)

✈ **Practice** •————————————————————————————•

1. 復活節島 (Easter Island) 以狀似人頭的巨大石頭雕像群聞名。

   _____

   _____

2. 無論是否為了宗教的理由而雕刻，它們依然是人類創造力的實例。

   _____

   _____

Ⓒ

✈ **Keywords** •————————————————————————————•

1. 建築：*architecture* (n.)　完美地：*perfectly* (adv.)　結合：*combine* (+ with)
   自然環境：*natural surroundings*
2. 地點、遺址：*site* (n.)　皇室的：*royal* (adj.)　修養所：*retreat* (n.)
   觀光勝地：*tourist attraction*

✈ **Practice** •————————————————————————————•

1. 馬丘比丘 (Machu Picchu) 以它和自然環境完美結合的建築而聞名。

   _____

   _____

2. 無論此地是否為皇室修養所，它都是祕魯 (Peru) 最為人造訪的旅遊觀光勝地之一。

   _____

   _____

Unit 13 Inspirational Biography

 **Part I : Cloze Test**

Ⓐ   Terry Fox, a brave young Canadian, proved that his dream can make a difference. At the age of 18, he was diagnosed ___1___ bone cancer and his right leg was amputated. ___2___ the suffering of a cancer patient firsthand, Terry realized that more funds were needed for cancer research. Thus, he planned a charity run across Canada.

  The "Marathon of Hope" began in April 1980, and Terry ran over twenty miles every day. Besides the severe pain, he also faced tremendous ___3___. People driving past would honk to force him off the road. ___4___, Terry's heartfelt daily updates to Canada's CBC Radio slowly began to capture the public's attention. Soon, many citizens began to donate money to his cause.

  Unfortunately Terry passed away on June 28, 1981, unable to finish his run. Yet, his dream lives on—his efforts have ___5___ other people to raise money for cancer research.

_____ 1. (A) of   (B) on   (C) for   (D) with

_____ 2. (A) Experience   (B) Experienced   (C) Experiencing   (D) To experience

_____ 3. (A) compassion   (B) indifference   (C) pessimism   (D) revolution

_____ 4. (A) Consequently   (B) Similarly   (C) Moreover   (D) However

_____ 5. (A) inspired   (B) insulted   (C) intended   (D) interfered

---

diagnose v. 診斷　*bone cancer* 骨癌　*amputate* v. 截（肢）　*firsthand* adv. 第一手
charity n. 慈善事業　*marathon* n. 馬拉松　*tremendous* adj. 強烈的
heartfelt adj. 衷心的　*CBC Radio* 加拿大廣播電台
pass away 過世　*live on* 繼續活著、存在　*raise money for...* 為…募籌款

Ⓑ   May 27, 1995 was the day when everything changed for Christopher Reeve. The actor, who played Superman in the movies, was thrown from his horse in a riding competition. In seconds, he went from being a man who loved sports to one who was __1__ to a wheelchair. He could not move or even breathe by himself. However, Reeve __2__ the character he played on screen. Even while recovering, he started using his superstar status for the benefit of others. He established the Christopher Reeve Foundation, __3__ helped raise funds for research on spinal cord injury and improve the quality of life for the disabled.

He once said, "A hero is an ordinary individual who finds strength to persevere...in spite of overwhelming __4__." Measuring up to his own __5__ of a hero, Reeve refused to give up on himself. He is truly a hero.

_____ 1. (A) adapted   (B) confined   (C) devoted   (D) opposed

_____ 2. (A) lived up to   (B) looked up to   (C) did away with   (D) got away with

_____ 3. (A) that   (B) which   (C) what   (D) in which

_____ 4. (A) demands   (B) emotions   (C) responses   (D) obstacles

_____ 5. (A) acceptance   (B) creativity   (C) definition   (D) exception

---

be thrown from... 從⋯墜落   *wheelchair* n. 輪椅   *spinal cord* 脊椎神經
persevere v. 堅持   *measure up* 符合

Christopher Reeve 克里斯多福・李維 (1952–2004)

已故美國知名電影演員，以飾演電影《超人》系列 (*Superman*)(1978,1980, 1983, 1987)、《似曾相識》(Somewhere in Time) (1980) 聞名。1995 年在參與馬術比賽時發生意外，導致脊椎受傷因而全身癱瘓 (paralysis)。但因為此次的事件，讓他投入幹細胞 (stem cell) 研究的推動，並成立克里斯多福・戴娜・李維基金會，致力於脊椎受傷造成癱瘓的治療研究。

Ⓒ Imagine that you were blind and deaf. Do you think you could still have a career and contribute __1__ society? Before you answer, consider the story of Helen Keller.

Helen Keller was born a healthy baby in 1880. However, when at eighteen months a mysterious brain fever __2__ her blind and deaf, life became difficult. Helen was constantly smashing things, screaming, and throwing tantrums out of __3__. Unable to cope with this situation, her family found her a teacher, Anne Sullivan.

Anne started teaching Helen __4__ spelling things out on her hand. She also taught her table manners and tasks like combing her hair. Helen often behaved __5__, but Anne would punish her. Slowly, Helen learned to do small tasks. This was one of the hardest times of her life, but Helen did not give up.

__6__ Helen's disabilities, she insisted on leading a productive life. She wanted to go to college, so with the help of Miss Sullivan, who translated books and lectures into sign language for her, Helen became the first deaf-blind person __7__ a bachelor's degree. While still in college, Helen wrote her autobiography __8__ *The Story of My Life*. Realizing that she could inspire many people by writing, she wrote about disabilities, social issues, and women's rights. She was so influential and accomplished __9__ she received many honorary doctorate degrees from universities around the world.

Helen Keller's story shows the importance of never giving up. It was Helen's positive attitude __10__ helped her overcome difficulties and has now brought help to millions.

_____ 1. (A) to   (B) for   (C) of   (D) with

_____ 2. (A) caused   (B) left   (C) kept   (D) remained

_____ 3. (A) amusement   (B) curiosity   (C) frustration (D) relief

_____ 4. (A) with   (B) by   (C) to   (D) throughout

_____ 5. (A) gracefully (B) perfectly   (C) responsibly (D) violently

_____ 6. (A) Despite   (B) In spite   (C) Although   (D) However

_____ 7. (A) earn   (B) earning   (C) to earn   (D) earned

_____ 8. (A) entitle   (B) entitling   (C) to entitle (D) entitled

_____ 9. (A) and   (B) that   (C) as   (D) so

_____ 10. (A) which   (B) what   (C) that   (D) of which

---

brain fever 腦膜炎   *tantrum* n. 發怒   *cope with* 處理、調適
productive adj. 有收穫的   *honorary doctorate degree* n. 榮譽博士學位

Part II : Translation Practice

Sentence Patterns

1. $\left\{\begin{array}{l}\text{In spite of + N,}\\ \text{Despite + N,}\\ \text{Although } S_1 + V_1,\end{array}\right\} S_2 + V_2$

介系詞片語 in spite of 和 despite 以及連接詞 although，有「儘管；雖然⋯」之意。而介系詞片語 in spite of 和 despite 之後接名詞；although 之後接子句。另外 in spite of the fact that 與 despite the fact that S + V 也與此句型有相同的意思及用法。

2. It is/was...that...

此為分裂句的句型，用於加強語氣；it is/was 和 that 之間放入要強調的部份，句子剩餘的部份置於 that 之後；強調的部份可以是名詞、介系詞片語、時間副詞、或副詞子句。

例：**It was** Helen's positive attitude **that** helped her overcome difficulties.

Keywords

1. 遭遇：*encounter* (v.)　巨大的、龐大的：*enormous* (adj.)　阻礙：*obstacle* (n.)
   用⋯面對⋯：*face...with...*　樂觀：*optimism* (n.)
2. 積極的、正面的：*positive* (adj.)　態度：*attitude* (n.)　鼓勵：*encourage* (v.)
   灰心：*lose heart*　失敗：*defeat* (n.)

Sample

1. 儘管他遇到巨大的阻礙，他總是樂觀面對。

   In spite of/**Despite** the enormous obstacles he encountered, he always faced them with optimism.

   → **Although** he encountered enormous obstacles, he always faced them with optimism.

2. 正是他積極的態度鼓勵其他人在失敗時不要灰心。

   It was his positive attitude **that** encouraged others never to lose heart in defeat.

Ⓑ

Keywords ••

1. 身體殘障：*physical disability*　　放棄：*give up*　　夢想：*dream*（n.）（v.）　　運動員：*athlete*（n.）

2. 決心：*determination*（n.）　　鼓舞：*inspire*（v.）　　充分地、完全地：*to the full*

Practice ••

1. 儘管他身體殘障，他從不放棄想要成為運動員的夢想。

_____

_____

2. 正是他堅強的決心鼓舞其他人充分發揮生命。

_____

_____

Ⓒ

Keywords ••

1. 英年早逝：*die young*　　自由鬥士：*a fighter for freedom/liberty*

2. 驚人的、極大的：*tremendous*（adj.）　　勇氣：*courage/bravery*（n.）　　限制：*limitation*（n.）

Practice ••

1. 儘管他英年早逝，人們將永遠記得他是一位真正的自由鬥士。

_____

_____

2. 正是他極大的勇氣教導我們絕不接受任何限制。

_____

_____

Unit 14 Inspirational Stories

Ⓐ　　Many studies show that people are attracted to those with high confidence. In contrast, ___1___ confidence can drag you down. But fear not, there are easy tips to make you confident!

　　One tip is to learn to think positively. When you have unconfident thoughts, try to make an effort ___2___ them to positive thoughts. Then, try to find out if there is any other way to deal with the problems ___3___ being sad and doing nothing. ___4___ tip is to try to stop judging yourself by what happens to you and be sure to know that your frustration doesn't mean you are a failure. Confident people can take the rough with the smooth.

　　Being confident all the time is not easy. If you learn to follow these steps, not only ___5___ become more confident, but also you will start to really enjoy life!

_____ 1. (A) a lack of　　(B) a glimpse of　　(C) a number of　　(D) a sum of

_____ 2. (A) change　　(B) to change　　(C) to changing　　(D) changing

_____ 3. (A) for the sake of　　(B) in terms of　　(C) instead of　　(D) in case of

_____ 4. (A) Other　　(B) The other　　(C) Another　　(D) Others

_____ 5. (A) are you　　(B) you are　　(C) you will　　(D) will you

與 confident 相關字詞
assertive 堅定自信的　　bold 大膽的　　conceited 自負的　　extrovert 活潑自信的 forceful 強勢有說服力的　　proud 自豪的、驕傲的　　self-assured 胸有成竹的 self-confident 自信的　　self-possessed 沉著的

Ⓑ Our lives can be similar to a river in many ways.

A river is formed by water from many different __1__. Rainfall dribbling from hillsides and water trickling in from streams contribute to making a river and so do sewerage pipes and wastewater from factories. __2__ a river ends up being clean or polluted depends on what is put into it. The same applies to us. The sort of person we become is mainly __3__ by what we choose to put into ourselves.

The water in a river is constantly moving, bubbling against rocks, and flowing towards its __4__ goal, the ocean. This is perhaps the most positive lesson we can learn from watching a river—only when we are actively moving towards our goals __5__ reach them. If we are too afraid to pursue our goals, our lives will become stagnant.

_____ 1. (A) backgrounds   (B) instructions   (C) sources   (D) tastes

_____ 2. (A) That   (B) Whether   (C) Either   (D) What

_____ 3. (A) delivered   (B) determined   (C) described   (D) designed

_____ 4. (A) ultimate   (B) specific   (C) decisive   (D) ambitious

_____ 5. (A) we are   (B) are we   (C) we can   (D) can we

---

rainfall n. 下雨   *dribble* v. 滴下；細流   *trickle* v. 細流   *stream* n. 溪流
sewerage pipe 污水下水道   *wastewater* n. 廢水   *bubble* v. 起泡、冒泡
stagnant n. 停滯的

與 **river** 相關的字詞

① riverbank 河岸   riverbed 河床   riverfront 河濱   river mouth 河口   riverside 河畔
   sell sb down the river 出賣／背叛別人
② brook 溪   canal 運河   creek 小河   seaway (通往內陸) 航道   stream 小河、溪澗
   tributary 支流   watercourse 河道   waterway 水道

Ⓒ *The Road* is a terrifying story written by Cormac McCarthy about a boy and his loving father who wander together across a landscape of destruction after a terrible event has destroyed the world. ___1___ is dead, and only a cold, colorless shell of a planet, with a few survivors, remains. Forests and cities have been burned, ___2___ rivers of black water and a layer of gray ashes covering everything. Amidst this nuclear winter, the boy and his father move down "the road" among burned dead bodies, battling terrible weather, violence, and numerous other ___3___ of severe destruction. Occasionally, they pass by an object that reminds them ___4___ how the world used to be.

The novel takes on the concept of death itself, though the reader never learns what caused the wide destruction. McCarthy presents a lonely character who has difficulty ___5___ food, shelter, safety, companionship, or hope. The story is full of despair but there is also ___6___, and McCarthy has been complimented for his description of both the ___7___ lives and thoughts of the characters as well as their exterior circumstances.

The story is mainly about survival, the father's dedication to ___8___ his young son. The father has a strong will to live, and is determined to succeed despite the hopeless circumstances and an unknown future.

This is not a light story, but ___9___ questions of hope and faith in the face of a terrible situation. ___10___ how terrible the world is after the destruction, it reminds us, by the severe contrast, to celebrate life.

_____ 1. (A) Application   (B) Civilization   (C) Distribution   (D) Expansion

_____ 2. (A) leave   (B) to leave   (C) left   (D) leaving

_____ 3. (A) causes   (B) disadvantages   (C) examples   (D) systems

_____ 4. (A) to   (B) with   (C) of   (D) through

_____ 5. (A) find   (B) to find   (C) found   (D) finding

_____ 6. (A) depression   (B) harshness   (C) impression   (D) tenderness

_____ 7. (A) inner   (B) social   (C) family   (D) academic

_____ 8. (A) protect   (B) protecting   (C) be protected   (D) being protected

_____ 9. (A) addresses   (B) arises   (C) responds   (D) restores

_____ 10. (A) No wonder   (B) No matter   (C) However   (D) Whether

 **Part II : Translation Practice**

Sentence Patterns

1. No matter wh- + Adj./Adv...., S + V...
   → Whoever/Whatever/Wherever/Whenever/However..., S + V...

此為「無論」之意。no matter 之後接 wh-疑問詞（如：who, what, where, when, how 等），
可代換為 whoever, whatever, wherever, whenever, however；其中 no matter how、
however 之後接形容詞或副詞。

例：**No matter** how terrible the world is after the destruction, it reminds us, by the
severe contrast, to celebrate life.

2. Only + 副詞子句／副詞片語 + $\begin{cases} \text{be V} + \text{S} \\ \text{助動詞} + \text{S} + \text{V} \end{cases}$

此為「Only 的倒裝句型」。only 所引導的子句或片語置於句首時，主要子句的部份要倒裝；only
之後可以接副詞片語或副詞子句。

例：**Only** when we are actively moving towards our goals **can we** reach them.

Ⓐ

 Keywords ••

1. 經驗：*experience*（n.）　令人感到挫折的：*frustrating*（adj.）
   朝光明面看：*look on the bright side*
2. 保持：*remain*（v.）　樂觀：*optimistic*（adj.）　接受、承擔：*take on*　挑戰：*challenge*（n.）

 Sample ••

1. 無論這經驗多麼令人感到挫折，你應該試著朝光明面看。

   No matter how frustrating the experience is, you should try to look on the bright
   side.

   → **However** frustrating the experience is, you should try to look on the bright side.

2. 唯有當你保持樂觀，你才能欣然接受挑戰。

   Only when you remain optimistic can you take on the challenges willingly.

Ⓑ

Keywords ●

1.失敗：*failure* (n.)　慘烈的、悲慘的：*disastrous* (adj.)　坦然面對：*take...well*
2.知悉、了解：*be aware of*　缺點：*shortcoming/drawback/weakness* (n.)
　成功：*succeed* (v.)

Practice ●

1.無論這失敗有多麼慘烈，你應該學會坦然面對。

_____

_____

2.唯有當你知道自己的缺點，你在未來才能成功。

_____

_____

Ⓒ

Keywords ●

1.擋路：*in the way*　保持鎮定：*stay/keep/remain calm*　堅守：*stick to*　原則：*principle* (n.)
2.對…有信心：*have confidence/faith in*　設法做到：*manage to*　戰勝：*defeat/overcome* (v.)

Practice ●

1.無論什麼擋在你的路上，你應該保持鎮定、堅守你的原則。

_____

_____

2.唯有當你對自己有信心，你才能設法戰勝你的恐懼。

_____

_____

Part I : Cloze Test

Ⓐ   In 1854, cholera broke out in the SOHO neighborhood of London. Within the 250 yards around Broad Street, 500 people were dead in about a week. Some people blamed it on bad air;   1   thought it was God's punishment. But a physician named John Snow found that almost all of the victims lived around the water pump at Broad Street.   2 , 10 of them died even though they did not live near the pump. In the growing panic, he visited the victims' family. He found that, of the 10 victims, five   3   brought back water from the Broad Street pump because of its taste and three were children who attended a school nearby. Convinced, he appeared before the officials and asked the water pump handle   4 . Immediately the spreading stopped.   5   Snow did not discover Vibrio Cholerae—the bacteria that cause cholera, his detective-like methods helped create modern Epidemiology.

_____ 1.(A) other   (B) others   (C) the other   (D) the others

_____ 2.(A) Therefore   (B) However   (C) In addition   (D) In fact

_____ 3.(A) almost   (B) hardly   (C) regularly   (D) seldom

_____ 4.(A) removing   (B) to remove   (C) being removing   (D) to be removed

_____ 5.(A) Although   (B) Even   (C) Since   (D) Unless

---

cholera 霍亂   *break out* 爆發（疾病）   *SOHO* 蘇活區   *physician* n. 內科醫生
water pump 抽水幫浦   *convince* v. 確信   *Vibrio Cholerae* 霍亂弧菌
bacteria n. 細菌   *detective* n. 偵探   *Epidemiology* n. 流行病學

Ⓑ Aspirin, the wonder drug of the past 100 years, seems to offer more health benefits every year. Besides just easing pain or curing a headache, some studies show that aspirin may be effective in __1__ the risk of heart attacks and strokes. Since it is an over-the-counter drug, it is widely __2__ . For most people, when they take aspirin, their blood thins and a chemical called thromboxane is blocked. This chemical is responsible for creating blood clots, __3__ at times could lead to strokes. When thromboxane is blocked, these clots don't form. That may lower the danger of heart attacks or strokes. But for some, its benefits are unattainable. Those __4__ health conditions, such as clotting disorder or stomach ulcers are not allowed to take the wonder drugs regularly. Aspirin use may result in serious side effects on these patients who have a __5__ to aspirin. Every medicine has benefits as well as risks. Remember no medicine is absolutely safe, even the wonder drug.

_____ 1. (A) increasing   (B) measuring   (C) reducing   (D) taking

_____ 2. (A) accessible   (B) conventional   (C) prescribed   (D) regular

_____ 3. (A) that   (B) which   (C) what   (D) in which

_____ 4. (A) who have   (B) who having   (C) have   (D) to have

_____ 5. (A) prevention   (B) resistance   (C) symptom   (D) treatment

---

aspirin 阿斯匹靈   *wonder drug* 萬靈藥   *heart attack* 心臟病   *stroke* n. 中風
over-the-counter drug 非處方藥   *resistance* n. 抗藥性   *thromboxane* n. 血栓素
blood clot 凝結血液   *unattainable* adj. 達不到的   *stomach ulcer* 胃潰瘍
absolutely adv. 絕對地

Ⓒ   Have you ever thought that what you smell can affect the way you feel? A new therapy called "aromatherapy" __1__ that smells can influence our moods and even our health. The word "aromatherapy" was first used by a French scientist in the 1920s. It __2__ the word "aroma," or smell, with "therapy," or treatment.

Basically, aromatherapy is a kind of alternative medicine that uses essential oils and compounds __3__ from plants. In aromatherapy, the scents of essential oils and plants are inhaled. __4__, a person breathes deeply while holding a bottle of essential oil close to his or her nose. Essential oils can also be massaged directly into the skin or put into a hot bath.

Aromatherapy has become very popular __5__ people who want relief from stress. What's more, a few doctors are now using aromatherapy in hospitals to __6__ patients' pain, especially mothers with severe labor pain. But some people have __7__ aromatherapy. They say there is no scientific proof to show that it is really effective. __8__, some "aromatherapy" products that are sold smell good, but actually are fake.

__9__ these criticisms, the popularity of aromatherapy continues to grow. But the debate over its usefulness continues as well. Many people wonder __10__ aromatherapy is an effective therapy or just a way to make money. Only time will tell.

_____ 1. (A) claim   (B) claims   (C) claiming   (D) claimed

_____ 2. (A) combines   (B) communicates   (C) confines   (D) connects

_____ 3. (A) extract   (B) extracts   (C) extracting   (D) extracted

_____ 4. (A) As a consequence   (B) In other words
        (C) To some extent   (D) On the other hand

_____ 5. (A) with   (B) as   (C) for   (D) to

_____ 6. (A) endure   (B) increase   (C) relieve   (D) suffer

_____ 7. (A) argued   (B) confirmed   (C) criticized   (D) praised

_____ 8. (A) On the contrary   (B) On the whole   (C) In short   (D) In addition

_____ 9. (A) Although   (B) Even if   (C) In spite   (D) Despite

_____ 10. (A) whether   (B) what   (C) which   (D) that

---

aromatherapy n. 芳香療法   *compound* n. 混合物   *labor pain* 產痛

Part II : Translation Practice

Sentence Patterns

1.
$$\begin{cases} \text{With + N,} \\ \text{As + S}_1 \text{ + V}_1, \end{cases} \text{S}_2 \text{ + V}_2....$$

介系詞 with 和連接詞 as 有「隨著…」之意。with 之後接名詞或名詞片語；as 之後接子句。

2. To + V$_1$..., S + V$_2$....

此為表示正面「目的」的用法。不定詞 to 有「為了…」之意，之後接原形動詞，相當於 in order to + V 或 so as to + V。

例：To save money, Jenny walks to school every day.

In order to save money, Jenny walks to school every day.

Ⓐ

 Keywords •────────────────────────•

1. 禽流感：*avian/bird flu*　　爆發：*break out* (v.); *outbreak* (n.)　　恐慌：*panic* (n.)

   民眾、大眾：*the public*

2. 避免：*prevent...from...*　　擴散：*spread* (v.)　　呼籲：*urge* (v.)　　口罩：*mask* (n.)

   公共場所：*public place*

 Sample •────────────────────────•

1. 隨著禽流感的爆發，民眾的恐慌不斷上升。

   With the outbreak of avian flu/**As** avian flu broke out, the panic among the public was growing/rising.

2. 為了避免這疾病的擴散，政府呼籲人民在公共場所要戴口罩。

   To prevent the disease from spreading, the government urged people to wear masks in public places.

Ⓑ

Keywords

1. 快速的：*rapid* (adj.)　發展：*develop* (v.); *development* (n.)
2. 高齡化的社會：*an aging society*　注意：*pay attention to*　老年人：*senior citizen*
   福利：*welfare* (n.)

Practice

1. 隨著醫藥的快速發展，現代人能活得更久。

2. 為了迎接高齡化的社會，政府應注意老年人的福利。

Ⓒ

Keywords

1. 平均壽命：*lifespan/life expectancy*　有健康意識的：*health-conscious* (adj.)
2. 生活品質：*the quality of life*　願意：*be willing to*　休閒活動：*leisure activity*

Practice

1. 隨著平均壽命的延長，人們變得比以前更有健康意識。

2. 為了提升生活品質，越來越多人願意花更多時間在休閒活動上。

Part I : Cloze Test

Ⓐ Ebonics is often thought of as "Black English," or the style of speech used by African Americans. The word "ebonics" is a __1__ of the words "ebony" (black) and "phonics" (the study of sound). Ebonics is usually used by African Americans __2__ informal occasions. Users of this language in a casual environment may use Standard English in more formal circumstances such as at work. Usually, Ebonics can be recognized in several ways. For instance, "ain't" is used to __3__ "don't," "isn't" etc. Therefore, phrases like "Why you ain't tell me?" means "Why didn't you tell me?" In addition, "Ima tell you..." is often heard too. It means "I am going to tell you..." Some think Ebonics is an __4__ language because it is often used by those with low levels of education. However, it __5__ follow a system. It isn't just a lazy form of Standard English. Instead, it shows a different culture.

_____ 1. (A) mixture   (B) recipe   (C) pronunciation   (D) origin

_____ 2. (A) with   (B) in   (C) near   (D) on

_____ 3. (A) substitute   (B) exchange   (C) replace   (D) in place of

_____ 4. (A) average   (B) imaginary   (C) inferior   (D) offensive

_____ 5. (A) must   (B) does   (C) can't   (D) is to

> *Standard English* 標準英語   *Ebonics* 黑人英語   *phonics* n. 語音學
> *occasion* n. 場合   *casual* adj. 隨興的   *circumstance* n. 情況

Ⓑ　Chinese American novelists have popped up at literary conferences, award ceremonies and in glowing reviews. You ___1___ about some of them—Amy Tan, Gish Jen, and Ha Jin. These second and third generation American Chinese are growing up ___2___ of their ability and right to express themselves. Two important feelings have supported their work—first, the sense of belonging and secondly, an interest in history. Amy Tan's novels (*Joy Luck Club*, *The Bonesetter's Daughter*) often mix Chinese childhood memories with contemporary American life. Gish Jen explores identity and she has received praise from mainstream American ___3___ the Chinese communities. Ha Jin is a relatively newcomer whose grasp of English is ___4___ he has won the PEN/Faulkner awards twice. These writers have proved that the ___5___ expression in English is no flash in the pan indeed.

_____ 1. (A) should have read (B) must have read (C) do read (D) can't have read

_____ 2. (A) confidently (B) with confidence (C) confidence (D) confident

_____ 3. (A) as well as (B) instead of (C) in place of (D) except for

_____ 4. (A) too masterly to (B) so that
　　　　　 (C) so masterly that (D) such masterly that

_____ 5. (A) oriental (B) native (C) informal (D) innovative

Chinese American 華裔美籍（的）　*pop up* 突然出現　*conference* n. 研討會
glowing adj. 熱烈讚揚的　*Amy Tan* 譚恩美　*Gish Jen* 任璧蓮　*Ha Jin* 哈金
generation n. 代　*sense of belonging* 歸屬感　*Joy Luck Club* 喜福會
The Bonesetter's Daughter 接骨師的女兒　*contemporary* adj. 當代的
identity n. 身份認同　*mainstream* n. 主流　*relatively* adv. 相對地
newcomer n. 新進、新來的人　*grasp* n. 掌握（能力）　*Faulkner* 福克納
No flash in the pan. 並非曇花一現

Ⓒ Today, technology and advertising are changing English in new and unusual ways. __1__ has probably played the biggest role in the development of new English. Over the last ten years, e-mail, Internet chat rooms, instant and text messaging have become popular ways to communicate, and people who use them have created a new style of language. Abbreviations, for example, are often used. "LOL," for "laugh out loud," is written to show that something is very funny. Numbers are also sometimes used __2__ letters, as in "Gr8," for "great" or "L8r," for "later." Using this new type of English is convenient for people. This is important for faster communication in text messages, __3__ the space for messages is limited. __4__, some people believe that e-mail and instant messaging are less formal means of communication. Therefore, they do not have to follow the rules of punctuation and grammar that they would __5__ use on more formal occasions. Advertising has also made some contributions __6__ the new English. In order to be different—and to get attention—some advertisements use new types of English, especially new __7__. Today, ads for "x-treme" (extreme) or "x-tra valu" (extra value) products are often seen.

Of course, it is probably not appropriate to use many of these new abbreviations or terms when writing an essay or taking a test. In addition, though this new type of English is popular in messages and in e-mail, it has __8__ to become popular in spoken English. Very few people say "BTW" or "IMHO" when speaking with others; __9__, they say "by the way" or "in my (humble) opinion." However, __10__, the new English remains a growing part of the language.

_____ 1. (A) Either   (B) None   (C) The former   (D) The latter

_____ 2. (A) in place of   (B) in terms of   (C) in the name of   (D) in honor of

_____ 3. (A) where   (B) which   (C) when   (D) that

_____ 4. (A) On the contrary   (B) Nevertheless   (C) As a result   (D) In addition

_____ 5. (A) otherwise   (B) never   (C) rarely   (D) even

_____ 6. (A) in   (B) for   (C) to   (D) at

_____ 7. (A) pronunciations   (B) grammar   (C) vocabulary   (D) spellings

_____ 8. (A) almost   (B) yet   (C) ever   (D) not

_____ 9. (A) instead   (B) accordingly   (C) while   (D) furthermore

_____ 10. (A) sooner or later   (B) time after time   (C) for the time being   (D) now and then

abbreviation n. 縮寫   *punctuation* n. 標點符號

 **Part II : Translation Practice**

Sentence Patterns

1. replace/take the place of/be in place of/substitute for
A 取代 B 的句型如下： A **replace** B = A **take the place of** B = A **be in place of** B = A **substitute for** B 用 A 取代 B 句型如下： **replace** B **with** A = **substitute** A **for** B
2. the former..., the latter...
表示「前者…，後者…」之意。類似用法還有 "that..., this..." 例：She usually has coffee and chocolate cake for breakfast. **The former** (coffee) can boost her energy and **the latter** (chocolate cake) can keep her in a good mood. 　　→ She usually has coffee and chocolate cake for breakfast. **That** can boost her energy and **this** can keep her in a good mood.

Ⓐ

 Keywords •─────────────────────────────────────•

1. 母語：*native language*
2. 強勢的、主導的：*dominant* (adj.)　複雜的：*complicated* (adj.)　文字：*character* (n.)
　初學者：*beginner* (n.)

 Sample •──•

1. 中文已經取代英文成為世界上最多人說的母語。

   Chinese has **replaced** English as the native language spoken by the most people in the world.

2. 中文和英文是世界上兩個強勢的語言。前者有複雜且困難的文字，後者對初學者來說較為簡單。

   Chinese and English are two dominant languages in the world. **The former** has complicated and difficult characters and **the latter** is easier for beginners.

Ⓑ

Keywords

1. 肢體語言：*body language*　　口語：*spoken language*　　場合：*occasion*（n.）
2. 生動地：*lively*（adv.）　　表達：*convey*（v.）　　誤解：*misunderstanding*（n.）

Practice

1. 肢體語言在一些場合上可以取代口語。

_____

2. 前者可以生動地表達更多訊息，而後者會產生較少誤解。

_____

_____

Ⓒ

Keywords

1. 簡訊：*text message*　　傳統的：*traditional*（adj.）　　電話通話：*phone call*
2. 表情符號：*emoticon*（n.）　　結合：*combine with*

Practice

1. 為了節省更多時間，簡訊在某些場合常被用來取代傳統的電話通話。

_____

_____

2. 前者可以結合表情符號，而後者可以直接地傳達使用者的感覺。

_____

_____

Part I : Cloze Test

Ⓐ   A vacation to the moon sounds crazy. People, however, have already landed there, and such a trip will probably come true. In the future, when traveling to the moon, you will have to bring along all your own oxygen and water, since __1__ is available there. You will not have to bring earplugs, though, because the lack of air means that sound does not __2__. Furthermore, it never rains on the moon, so your umbrella can be __3__. Take a walk and enjoy the moon's scenery. With your body weight only one-sixth of its weight on Earth, you may feel as if you are walking on air. Dangers __4__ exist on the moon. For example, small earthquakes, called "moonquakes," are quite common. However, for those __5__ want a vacation that is truly out of this world, a trip to the moon may be the perfect choice.

_____ 1. (A) the other   (B) neither   (C) both   (D) none

_____ 2. (A) transfer   (B) carry   (C) convey   (D) communicate

_____ 3. (A) called on   (B) crossed out   (C) left behind   (D) broken into

_____ 4. (A) do   (B) have   (C) need   (D) seldom

_____ 5. (A) ×   (B) that   (C) which   (D) who

---

land v. 登陸　　*bring along* 把…帶來　　*oxygen* n. 氧氣　　*earplug* n. 耳塞
scenery n. 景色　　*one-sixth* 六分之一

---

moonquakes 月震

在月球上所發生的地震，由阿波羅號太空人於 1969 年至 1972 年間所發現，遠比地球的地震來的微弱，目前觀測到的 28 次月震所得知的最大震度可達芮氏地震規模 (Richter magnitude scale) 5.5 級。

Ⓑ   The word "planet" means wanderer, because it travels across the sky. Mercury approaches closer to the sun, about thirty million miles, than ___1___ planet. A few times each year, Mercury appears, after dark, low in the western sky. Other times, before the sun rises, we can ___2___ it low in the eastern sky. With a telescope, we can easily notice changes in its shape and even in its size. What we are seeing is similar ___3___ the changes of our moon. The reason for both the moon's and Mercury's changes is ___4___ light and shadow affect the way they are seen from our planet. As Mercury travels along its orbit, there are times that it is clearly visible. However, as Mercury approaches Earth, fewer sunlit areas remain visible. This ___5___, of increasing and decreasing in size, begins all over again as Mercury begins to move away again.

_____ 1. (A) all other   (B) the other   (C) some other   (D) any other

_____ 2. (A) skip   (B) attract   (C) spot   (D) predict

_____ 3. (A) as   (B) for   (C) to   (D) with

_____ 4. (A) that   (B) which   (C) because   (D) what

_____ 5. (A) glimpse   (B) cycle   (C) description   (D) procedure

---

wanderer n. 漫遊者   *Mercury* n. 水星   *telescope* n. 望遠鏡   *orbit* n. 軌道

Mercury 水星

太陽系 (Solar System) 中最靠近太陽及最小的行星，繞行 (orbit) 太陽公轉一周約為 87.969 天，每自轉 3 周同時也繞行太陽 2 周。關於水星的觀測資料中發現，水星與月球在外觀上很相似，同樣都沒有大氣層 (atmosphere) 及衛星 (satellites)。只有在日食 (solar eclipse)，否則在陽光的照耀下，是看不到水星。在北半球低緯度國家，比較容易在春分 (Spring Equinox) 後凌晨或黃昏時的暮光 (twilight) 中看見，而南半球則是在秋分 (Autumn Equinox)。人類觀測最早的紀錄出現在西元前 4 世紀，希臘天文學家認為水星是兩個不同的天體，在日出時稱為阿波羅 (Apollo)，日落則稱之赫米斯 (Hermes)。而英文中水星的名字就是來自羅馬神話中的墨丘利 (Mercury)，其實也就是希臘神話中赫米斯。

Ⓒ   Though our solar system contains a large ___1___ of asteroids, meteors, and other cosmic debris, it was long believed to have only nine planets. ___2___ Earth, the other planets include Mercury, Venus, Mars, Jupiter, Saturn, Uranus, Neptune, and Pluto. However, a surprise announcement has challenged this ___3___ belief. Astronomers in the United States claim that they have discovered a new planet in our solar system. This tenth planet was first detected on January 8, 2005, ___4___ the help of a powerful telescope at an observatory in California.

So far, the new planet has remained unnamed officially and is called 2003UB313 ___5___. It is larger than Pluto and also three times ___6___ away from the sun than the solar system's ninth planet. But the discovery has also caused some debate among astronomers. Some say that this new planet is in fact not a planet at all and that it may ___7___ be a large asteroid or even just an icy rock. Other astronomers think that it is ___8___ soon to tell if the new planet really orbits around the sun ___9___ is one of the requirements for being considered a planet. Will this new planet really become the tenth in our solar system? Will it be accepted as a planet by other astronomers? The answers to these questions are eagerly awaited in the future ___10___.

_____ 1. (A) number　　　(B) amount　　　(C) sum　　　　　(D) deal

_____ 2. (A) In addition　(B) Except　　　(C) Besides　　　(D) Like

_____ 3. (A) much-expected　(B) short-lived　(C) self-centered　(D) long-held

_____ 4. (A) by　　　　　(B) with　　　　　(C) because　　　(D) so

_____ 5. (A) at times　　　　　　　　　　　(B) in no time

　　　　　　(C) for the time being　　　　　　(D) from time to time

_____ 6. (A) as far as　　(B) farther　　　(C) farthest　　　(D) so far

_____ 7. (A) thus　　　　(B) nevertheless　(C) yet　　　　　(D) instead

_____ 8. (A) too　　　　　(B) so　　　　　(C) not　　　　　(D) enough

_____ 9. (A) it　　　　　　(B) , which　　　(C) that　　　　　(D) which

_____ 10. (A) beforehand　(B) on time　　　(C) to come　　　(D) by all means

---

asteroid n. 小行星　　*meteor* n. 流星　　*cosmic debris* 宇宙碎片　　*Venus* n. 金星
Mars n. 火星　　*Jupiter* n. 木星　　*Saturn* n. 土星　　*Uranus* n. 天王星
Neptune n. 海王星　　*Pluto* n. 冥王星　　*astronomer* n. 天文學家

Part II : Translation Practice

Sentence Patterns

1. S + be + 倍數詞 +
$$\begin{cases} \text{as Adj. + as....} \\ \text{the N + of....} \\ \text{Adj-er + than....} \end{cases}$$

用來表示「是…的幾倍」的句型。兩倍用 twice/two times，三倍 three times，四倍 four times 以此類推。注意 half（一半）和 twice（兩倍）只能放在 as...as 或 the N of 的前面。

2. a large amount of + 不可數名詞
   a large number of + 可數名詞

英文的量詞要注意修飾的是可數或不可數名詞。

a large/small amount of
a good/great deal of } + 不可數名詞 + 單數動詞

a large/small number of + 可數名詞 + 複數動詞

a large quantity of
a lot of/plenty of } + 可數或不可數名詞

Keywords

1. （光或聲音）傳播，運行：*travel* (v.)
2. 歷史上：*throughout history*　研究：*research* (n.)　（實驗、研究）進行：*conduct* (v.)
   測量：*measure* (v.)

Sample

1. 光線運行的速度比聲音快好多倍。

   Light travels **several times faster than/as fast as/at the speed of** sound.

2. 歷史上一直有許多測量光速的科學研究在進行。

   Throughout history, **a large amount of** scientific research has been conducted to measure the speed of light.

Ⓑ

Keywords

1. 火星：*Mars*（n.）　將近、幾乎：*approximately*（adv.）　體積大：*massive*（adj.）

2. 證據：*evidence*（n.）

Practice

1. 地球將近為火星的十倍大。

2. 火星上有微量的水，很多人將其視為生命的證據。

Ⓒ

Keywords

1. 據估計：*it is estimated that...*　星座：*astrology*（n.）

2. 雇主、老闆：*employer*（n.）　訴諸於、依靠：*resort to*　相處：*get along with*

Practice

1. 據估計對星座有興趣的女生比男生多一倍。

2. 現在也有很多女性老闆靠著星座來選擇好相處的員工。

Part I : Cloze Test

Ⓐ   As our world becomes more and more computerized, even the age-old practice of volunteering is finding life online. Virtual volunteering, as this emerging practice __1__, provides an opportunity for people who wish to work on charitable causes but might not have the time to do more traditional volunteering. This method also works well for those who are handy with computers or have a disability that prevents them __2__ home easily. Some examples of work that can be done online include conducting Internet research, translating documents, or designing web pages. Cyber service even allows for one-on-one contact between volunteers and people __3__ assistance. For those who are interested, numerous websites post listings describing the types of help needed and the amount of time __4__ to complete each task. By offering the choice of virtual volunteering, charities are able to use technology to increase the amount of good they can __5__.

_____ 1. (A) commonly known   (B) is commonly known

      (C) commonly knows   (D) commonly knowing

_____ 2. (A) to leave   (B) from leaving   (C) as leaving   (D) left

_____ 3. (A) in terms of   (B) in control of   (C) in need of   (D) in times of

_____ 4. (A) which estimated (B) estimate   (C) estimating   (D) estimated

_____ 5. (A) work   (B) discover   (C) make   (D) do

---

computerized adj. 電腦化   *age-old* adj. 行之有年的   *virtual* adj. 虛擬的
volunteer n. 義工   *emerging* adj. 新興的   *charitable* adj. 慈善的
be handy with 擅長…   *disability* n. 殘障   *conduct* v. 進行 (活動)
cyber adj. 網路的   *one-on-one* adj. 一對一的   *assistance* n. 協助

Ⓑ　Oxfam International was founded in England in 1995. Today, this organization has offices in 12 countries and provides assistance around the world. Oxfam, short for "The Oxford Committee to Fight Famine," takes a unique ___1___ to reaching its charitable goals. Rather than dealing directly with people in need of help, Oxfam deals with over 3,000 local organizations so that people ___2___ from poverty and grief can take control of their own lives. To achieve their goals, Oxfam focuses on specific causes. Oxfam fights for civilized working conditions and also works to provide basic services such as schooling and medical care ___3___ training local citizens to be teachers and health workers. After disasters, people are at greater ___4___ of violence, disease and abuse, so Oxfam works to provide shelter and clean water. Finally, this organization fights for human rights, so it helps women, religious and racial minorities, and people with disabilities gain social equality. In short, Oxfam strives to bring ___5___ to the mistreated and help the unheard have a voice.

_____ 1. (A) attitude　　(B) tendency　　(C) approach　　(D) measurement

_____ 2. (A) suffering　　(B) suffer　　(C) suffered　　(D) to suffer

_____ 3. (A) to　　(B) with　　(C) though　　(D) by

_____ 4. (A) cost　　(B) length　　(C) risk　　(D) sight

_____ 5. (A) justice　　(B) advantage　　(C) exhibition　　(D) conclusion

---

Oxfam (The Oxford Committee to Fight Famine) 國際樂施會　*in need of* 需要
poverty n. 貧窮　*take control of* 控制　*schooling* n. 學校教育　*disaster* n. 災難
abuse n. 虐待　*human rights* 人權　*racial minorities* 少數種族族群
social equality 社會公義　*mistreat* v. 虐待　*unheard* adj. 被忽視的

Ⓒ   In 1966, the Buddhist nun, Master Cheng Yen, founded the Tzu Chi Foundation in Taiwan. Back then, the organization consisted of 30 housewives saving two cents a day to help __1__ . Today, this organization has around 10 million volunteers and supporters providing humanitarian __2__ in 47 countries.

The organization's charitable works include feeding the poor and hungry, providing __3__ to victims of disasters such as floods and earthquakes, and visiting senior citizens in their homes to help them with their daily lives. They even have their own radio and television stations to help __4__ their ideas. __5__ , they try to help and educate people.

The Tzu Chi Foundation has opened a number of schools and hospitals. The Tzu Chi Academy, with locations around the world, __6__ people about Chinese culture, Buddhist principles, and even flower arrangement. The Tzu Chi Parent Child Program does the same __7__ bringing families closer together. This organization has also opened clinics that offer free and low-cost medical care in areas __8__ people need it most. The Tzu Chi International Medical Association has over 5,000 medical professionals volunteering their time in Asia and North and South America. On top of this, Tzu Chi dental vans __9__ bring dental care to remote places without access to basic service.

From __10__ a small beginning, the Tzu Chi Foundation is an excellent example of how much good can come from just a little giving.

_____ 1. (A) less fortunate   (B) the less fortunate
          (C) the less fortune   (D) less fortune

_____ 2. (A) aid   (B) forecast   (C) companion   (D) threat

_____ 3. (A) distribution   (B) relief   (C) portrait   (D) retreat

_____ 4. (A) donate   (B) inspect   (C) spread   (D) infect

_____ 5. (A) Instead   (B) On the contrary (C) Overall   (D) To be honest

_____ 6. (A) teaches   (B) teaching   (C) which teaches (D) teach

_____ 7. (A) rather than   (B) without   (C) so that   (D) while

_____ 8. (A) where   (B) which   (C) how   (D) why

_____ 9. (A) are capable of (B) are able to   (C) have access to (D) know the key to

_____ 10. (A) so   (B) such   (C) how   (D) that

Buddhist nun (佛教) 比丘尼   *humanitarian* adj. 人道主義的   *senior citizen* 年長者
clinic n. 診所

Part II : Translation Practice

Sentence Patterns

1. ...by + V-ing = by means of + N/V-ing

by + V-ing 表示「藉由…」，可代換成 by means of + N/V-ing。

例：Oxfam works to provide basic services such as schooling and medical care **by** training local citizens to be teachers and health workers.

by + N 通常指「搭乘…交通工具」。

例：I go to school by bus.

2. be able to + V/capable of V-ing = have the ability/capability to V

be able to + V = be capable of + N/V-ing 都表示「能夠…」，需注意後面字的詞性。

例：Charities **are able to** use technology to increase the amount of good they can do.

 **Keywords**

1. 提倡：*promote* (v.)　人道主義：*humanitarianism* (n.)

　救援：*assistance* (n.)　緊急、急難：*emergency* (n.)

2. 分配：*distribute* (v.)　災難：*disaster* (n.)　賑災物品：*relief* (n.)　援助：*support* (v.)

Sample

1. 國際紅十字會 (The International Committee of the Red Cross) 藉由在緊急情況時提供救援，來提倡人道主義。

The International Committee of the Red Cross promotes humanitarianism **by providing** assistance in emergency situations.

2. 這個組織能夠分配災難救援物品，以及援助當地的健康計畫。

The organization **is able to distribute** disaster relief as well as support local health projects.

Ⓑ

✈ Keywords ●

1. 致力於…：*dedicate...to + N/V-ing*　　福利：*welfare* (n.)　　貧窮：*poverty* (n.)

　社會不公：*social injustice*

2. 提供…給…：*provide sb with sth*　　機會：*opportunity* (n.)

✈ Practice ●

1. 台灣世界展望會 (World Vision Taiwan) 藉由幫助孩童克服貧窮和社會不公，致力於他們的福利。

_____

_____

2. 它能夠提供孩童們醫療照顧及教育的機會。

_____

_____

Ⓒ

✈ Keywords ●

1. 災民：*victim* (n.)　　洪水，水災：*flood* (n.)　　定期的：*regular* (adj.)　　贊助：*sponsorship* (n.)

2. 藉由，靠著：*with...*　　只／僅：*no more than*　　做出…貢獻：*make a contribution*

✈ Practice ●

1. 那些水災災民的生活可以藉由這個定期贊助計畫而得到改善。

_____

_____

2. 藉由一個月不超過一千元，我們每個人就都能做出貢獻。

_____

_____

Unit 19 Environmental Protection (I)

Part I : Cloze Test

Ⓐ　Tourism is a double-edged blade for the impoverished cities and countries whose livelihood depends on it. Jamaica and Cancun (Mexico) cannot compete with developed countries in terms of technology, or precious resources. Such countries ___1___ these rely on tourists for as much as 30 percent of their yearly income, but within this profit comes at a price. This is ___2___ side of that sword—their ecosystems are paying dearly for these yearly visits. For example, Cancun is one of the most visited vacation spots in Mexico and while much of its business depends on tourism, its rain forests are now dying ___3___ the overpopulation of vacationers. Moreover, Jamaica's wildlife has over 25 species that do not exist in other places, but these animals are currently ___4___ extinction. The challenge these places face is how to save their environment, while continuing to ___5___ economic growth.

_____ 1. (A) as 　　　　(B) like 　　　　(C) for 　　　　(D) than

_____ 2. (A) one 　　　　(B) the other 　　(C) another 　　(D) other

_____ 3. (A) regardless of 　(B) despite 　　(C) according to 　(D) owing to

_____ 4. (A) in need of 　　(B) in danger of 　(C) in terms of 　(D) in favor of

_____ 5. (A) remain 　　　(B) preserve 　　(C) sustain 　　(D) recover

---

tourism n. 觀光業　　*double-edged blade* 雙面刃　　*impoverished* adj. 貧困
livelihood n. 生計　　*Jamaica* 牙買加　　*Cancun* 坎恩　　*Mexico* 墨西哥
developed country 已開發國家　　*at a price* 付出代價　　*ecosystem* n. 生態環境
dearly adv. 代價極大地　　*overpopulation* n. 人口過剩　　*vacationer* n. 觀光客
economic growth 經濟發展

Ⓑ   Protecting natural areas is a challenge. One way to protect nature is to set up national parks and other protected areas __1__ visitors require permission before entering. This helps control the number of visitors who can go in at any given time, so that the amount of damage caused could be reduced. Another way to protect natural areas is to put __2__ on what activities people can do there. For example, many parks don't allow people to build fires—a human activity that causes damage to huge amounts of forest every year. Such laws are fine, but they don't work __3__ people follow them. Education is desperately needed. People who head for the wilderness need __4__ aware of how easily the natural environment can be damaged. This education must start early, and responsibility for it lies with parents, teachers, and governments. Only when people appreciate what they have __5__ protect it.

_____ 1. (A) when   (B) which   (C) what   (D) where

_____ 2. (A) stress   (B) limits   (C) doubts   (D) emphasis

_____ 3. (A) unless   (B) when   (C) if   (D) even though

_____ 4. (A) being made   (B) be made   (C) make   (D) to be made

_____ 5. (A) they do   (B) they will   (C) will they   (D) had they

---

national park 國家公園　*protected area* 保護區　*permission* n. 許可　*build fire* 升火
desperately v. 極、非常地　*wilderness* n. 荒野　*only when* 只有在…時才…
appreciate v. 重視

Ⓒ　Al Gore, formerly known as Vice-President of the U.S. under President Clinton, is also a film producer who created the award-winning documentary *An Inconvenient Truth*. This movie clearly defined the growing problem of global warming and ___1___ it is directly caused by humans. The reason why he named it *An Inconvenient Truth* is ___2___ for many years global warming has been an issue which has been hotly ___3___. There are those who don't want to believe it's true, and others who believe that it is but don't wish to change their lifestyles. Governments in particular have ___4___ the problem under the rug because of the great cost and trouble of changing energy, fuel, water and many other resources to be more ecologically ___5___.

　　The film was produced by showing clips of Gore's speeches ___6___ climate change with stories from his own experience that helped shape his opinions, such as his sister's early death from lung cancer. He was alarmed at the dramatic changes in our environment over the past decade ___7___ he decided to educate the public about global warming. This film is one way he can make people understand that we must change our lifestyles to save the earth. Once this film came out, it became clear that we cannot ignore the problem because the climate is changing more rapidly than previously ___8___. This film became an important start to the current "green" and "LOHAS" movements. It has also opened the eyes of governments worldwide ___9___ the necessity for core changes in policy towards non-renewable resources. Now it's no longer "convenient" for people just to look the other way; ___10___ we see that the time to fix the problem is now.

_____ 1. (A) where　　　(B) how　　　　(C) what　　　　(D) who

_____ 2. (A) why　　　　(B) that　　　　(C) because of　　(D) for

_____ 3. (A) embraced　　(B) inspired　　(C) debated　　　(D) challenged

_____ 4. (A) accepted　　(B) tackled　　　(C) transformed　(D) swept

_____ 5. (A) efficient　　(B) protective　(C) useful　　　　(D) effective

_____ 6. (A) for　　　　　(B) at　　　　　(C) on　　　　　　(D) in

_____ 7. (A) therefore　　(B) so　　　　　(C) though　　　　(D) until

_____ 8. (A) to think　　(B) thinking　　(C) thought　　　(D) think

_____ 9. (A) for　　　　　(B) to　　　　　(C) at　　　　　　(D) beyond

_____ 10. (A) however　　(B) otherwise　(C) moreover　　　(D) instead

---

documentary n. 紀錄片　　*sweep... under the rug* 對於…迴避不談　　*LOHAS* n. 樂活
movement n. 運動

 **Part II : Translation Practice**

Sentence Patterns

1. such...as...

表示「像…這樣的…」。

例：**such** beautiful girls **as** Mary and Susan　像 Mary 和 Susan 這樣漂亮的女孩

as 有時可作為關係代名詞用

例：**such** students **as** go to school late　像這樣上學遲到的學生

2. The reason why + S + V + is that...

表示「…的原因是…」，需注意此句型用 that 而不是 because。

例：**The reason why** Gore named it *An Inconvenient Truth* **is that** for many years global warming has been hotly debated.

Ⓐ

 Keywords ••

1.怪罪：*blame...on...*　氣候變化：*climate change*　工業的：*industrial* (adj.)

2.減少：*cut down on*　二氧化碳：*carbon dioxide*　排放量：*emission* (n.)

Sample •••

1.有些人把氣候變化的原因怪罪在像是美國這樣的工業國家。

Some people blame climate change on **such** industrial countries **as** the United States.

2.地球變得越來越暖的原因是，這些國家不願意減少二氧化碳的排放量。

The reason why the earth is getting warmer **is that** these countries are not willing to cut down on the emission of carbon dioxide.

Ⓑ

Keywords

1. 開拓發展：*exploit* (v.)　可再生的：*renewable* (adj.)　風力：*wind power*
2. 產生動力：*generate* (v.)　可持續，可支撐下去的：*sustainable* (adj.)
   天然資源：*natural resources*

Practice

1. 許多國家正在發展像風力這樣可再生的能源。

   _____

2. 可再生能源珍貴的原因是，它們都是由可持續的天然資源所產生的。

   _____

   _____

Ⓒ

Keywords

1. 無節制的：*unregulated* (adj.)　禁止：*prohibit* (v.)　伐木：*logging* (n.)
2. 嚴格的：*strict* (adj.)　對⋯造成傷害：*do damage to*　生態：*ecology* (n.)
   無法彌補的：*irreparable* (adj.)

Practice

1. 像無節制的捕魚和伐木這樣非法的人類活動應該被禁止。

   _____

2. 為何應有嚴格法律禁止這些活動的原因是，它們會對生態造成無法彌補的傷害。

   _____

   _____

Part I : Cloze Test

(A)   Many consumers like the idea of buying earth-friendly or "green" products because they think such __1__ help the environment. This type of buying choice also seems very fashionable to consumers __2__ they see famous people supporting environmental concerns in popular magazines or television programs. A variety of products __3__ bath and beauty products to cars claim that they are friendly to the environment. However, consumers must give some serious thought to __4__ buying a product labeled as "green" in fact helps the environment. The harsh truth is that it is not possible to prevent global warming simply by buying "green" things. It is not enough to own earth-friendly cars. The better way to reduce carbon dioxide emissions is to own only one earth-friendly car, use it to carpool with your co-workers or friends, ride your bicycle or walk over shorter distances and take public transportation __5__ it is possible.

_____ 1. (A) promotions   (B) purchases   (C) investigations   (D) excuses

_____ 2. (A) as   (B) although   (C) unless   (D) before

_____ 3. (A) range from   (B) to range from   (C) ranged from   (D) ranging from

_____ 4. (A) which   (B) whether   (C) that   (D) what

_____ 5. (A) whether   (B) no matter   (C) whenever   (D) if not

---

earth-friendly adj. 環保的   *give thought to sth = give sth thought* 仔細認真考慮
label v. 標示   *carbon dioxide emissions* 二氧化碳排放   *carpool* v. 共乘
co-worker n. 同事

Ⓑ　Ecological art, as the name suggests, is art that is practiced in an ecological, or natural way. The ecological art movement started in 1960s, when people started realizing the importance of ___1___ nature. Some artists saw ___2___ fragile and delicate nature was and they began to create artwork that would raise concerns about the environment. To create art that reflects harmony between man and nature, ecological artists use materials that are natural and eco-friendly. For example, artist Alan Sonfist is actively ___3___ with creating ecological artwork. One of his most famous works is the *Time Landscape* in New York. He took a small area and planted it with native trees and forests that once ___4___ the entire city of New York. The artwork is ___5___ of the plants that were lost over time because of human interference. Ecological art is an innovative way to awaken people's ecological consciousness.

_____ 1. (A) preserving　　(B) exploring　　(C) retaining　　(D) reserving

_____ 2. (A) whether　　(B) that　　(C) so　　(D) how

_____ 3. (A) acquainted　　(B) involved　　(C) combined　　(D) puzzled

_____ 4. (A) are used to cover　　　　(B) used to cover
　　　　(C) are used to covering　　　　(D) used to covering

_____ 5. (A) deprived　　(B) typical　　(C) symbolic　　(D) convinced

---

practice v. 實踐、實行　　*movement* n. 運動（活動）　　*fragile* adj. 脆弱的
delicate adj. 纖細的　　*raise concern about* 對…表示擔憂　　*harmony* n. 和諧
human interference 人為干預　　*innovative* adj. 創新的
ecological consciousness 生態意識

Ⓒ The fashion industry is often associated with selfishness. We tend to think of its customers as foolish rich people with more money than sense. Recently, __1__ , some in the fashion industry have been taking steps to change that image by promoting environmental or moral concerns along with their clothing products. Many designers have become concerned about the __2__ of the materials they use. Some have declared that their products are based on the principles of "fair trade"—meaning that the workers who make the materials, often in poor countries, will earn a fair __3__ and be treated well.

Though many of the new environmentally-aware fashion designers proudly announce their use of natural materials, some scientists believe __4__ materials might actually be better for the environment. This is because some of them can be washed effectively __5__ lower temperatures, therefore __6__ less energy. The scientists have also suggested that we rent clothes rather than buy them, but almost no one thinks this will ever __7__ .

It remains to be seen how long these new environmental concerns in the fashion industry will last. In the 1990s, several famous models spoke out against fur clothes. The project seemed __8__ successful during the past ten years. Nowadays, though, fur has become popular again. Some of the models who once spoke out against it have even __9__ it! So it remains to be seen whether environmental concern in the clothing industry is __10__ , or whether it's just a passing fad.

_____ 1. (A) hence   (B) undoubtedly
　　　　(C) nevertheless   (D) on the other hand

_____ 2. (A) amount   (B) quality   (C) source   (D) comfort

_____ 3. (A) accommodation (B) wage   (C) dignity   (D) agency

_____ 4. (A) organic   (B) delicate   (C) raw   (D) artificial

_____ 5. (A) at   (B) on   (C) for   (D) in

_____ 6. (A) which require   (B) require   (C) requiring   (D) to require

_____ 7. (A) get over   (B) take over   (C) dig in   (D) catch on

_____ 8. (A) to be   (B) to have been   (C) having been   (D) being

_____ 9. (A) been spotted wearing   (B) spotted wearing
　　　　(C) been spotted worn   (B) spotted to wear

_____ 10. (A) hard to find   (B) here to stay   (C) yet to come   (D) second to none

selfishness n. 自私　　*moral concern* 道德考量　　*catch on* 變得流行

here to stay 持續下去　　*a passing fad* 一時的流行

Part II : Translation Practice

Sentence Patterns

1. used to V

表示「過去的習慣」，注意和以下句型的比較：

be used to + V-ing 表示「習慣於…」，be used to + V 表示「被用來…」。

例：Alan Sonfist took a small area and planted it with native trees and forests that once **used to** cover the entire city of New York.

2. ..., which + V
→ ..., V-ing

非限定的關係代名詞 ", which" 用來代替前面一整個句子，可省略 which 將動詞改為

", V-ing"，後面動詞為單數，注意此用法關係代名詞不能用 that。

例：This is because some of them can be washed effectively at lower temperatures, **which** requires/**requiring** less energy.

 **Keywords** •

1.名人：*celebrity*（n.）　認為：*regard...as...*　毛皮和皮革（皮草）：*fur and leather*　元素：
element（n.）

2.殘忍：*cruelty*（n.）　批評：*criticize*（v.）　反應：*reflect*（v.）　關心：*concern*（n.）

Sample •

1.很多名人過去認為皮草是時尚的元素。

Lots of celebrities **used to regard** fur and leather as elements of fashion.

2.然而，殘忍殺害動物被廣泛地批評，這反映出對環境越來越關心。

However, the cruelty of killing animals has been widely criticized, **which reflects**/
reflecting the increasing concern for the environment.

Ⓑ

✈ Keywords

1. 壯觀的：*spectacular* (adj.)　海岸：*coast* (n.)　珊瑚礁：*coral reef*
2. 生態系統：*ecosystem* (n.)　造成威脅：*pose a threat to*　生存：*survival* (n.)

✈ Practice

1. 過去在台灣海岸附近有很多壯觀的珊瑚礁。

_____

_____

2. 嚴重的污染改變了海底的生態系統，這對珊瑚礁的生存造成很大的威脅。

_____

_____

Ⓒ

✈ Keywords

1. 素食：*vegan diet*　被認為：*be considered + N/Adj*　支持：*embrace/support* (v.)
2. 消耗：*consume* (v.)　飼養：*raise* (v.)　牛群：*cattle* (n.)

✈ Practice

1. 素食過去被認為只是一種健康的生活方式，只有少數人支持。

_____

_____

2. 然而，種植蔬菜所消耗的能源比飼養牛群少，這使它成為一個保護地球的好方法。

_____

_____

Unit 21 Geography

🌍 Part I : Cloze Test

Ⓐ　Our planet has many interesting features such as canyons, lakes, rivers, and plains. Interesting __1__ they are, these sites are not the most distinctive features on the planet. What is most likely to catch your eye from far above is Earth's mountains. They are arranged in long chains called "ranges." The most __2__ mountain ranges are located in the Americas, Asia, and Africa. The mountain ranges there are the highest and most visible features on our planet's surface; __3__ none of these counts as the world's longest mountain range. It is the mountains beneath the surface of the oceans that should retain this title. If you __4__ the oceans, you would see a chain of ridges that are more than 64,000 kilometers long! __5__ visible on the surface of Earth or not, the world's mountain ranges are an amazing part of our planet's landscape.

_____ 1. (A) so　　　　　(B) as　　　　　　(C) for　　　　　(D) since

_____ 2. (A) prominent　 (B) genuine　　　　(C) dynamic　　　(D) occasional

_____ 3. (A) instead　　　(B) what's more　　 (C) therefore　　(D) yet

_____ 4. (A) had drained　(B) drain　　　　　(C) have drained　(D) were to drain

_____ 5. (A) No matter how (B) If　　　　　　(C) Whether　　　(D) However

> *feature* n. 特色、特徵　　*canyon* n. 峽谷　　*plain* n. 平原　　*range* n. 山脈
> *distinctive* adj. 出色的　　*catch one's eye* 引起…注目　　*chains* n. 一連串山脈
> *count* v. 認可、算數　　*retain* v. 保有　　*ridge* n. 山脈、山脊

B Few people know how to define *El Nino*. The name, *El Nino*, means "little boy" in Spanish, and was given that name because *El Nino* usually happens around Christmas time, the same time of Jesus Christ's birth. *El Nino* typically occurs off the west coast of Africa. *La Nina*, however, is mostly the __1__ effects of *El Nino*. *La Nina* means "little girl" in Spanish, and typically affects the southern hemisphere. Both of these effects were first recognized by a scientist Sir Gilbert Thomas Walker. Walker was the first __2__ southern oscillation, which is the monthly change in air pressure between the island of Tahiti and Darwin, Australia. __3__ the effects in these specific regions, *El Nino* and *La Nina* have affected the worldwide weather by causing weather patterns to change. This has a profound impact __4__ the earth and the global economy, __5__ many of these economies are largely dependent on agriculture and fishing.

_____ 1. (A) side   (B) tremendous   (C) opposite   (D) immediate

_____ 2. (A) to notice   (B) that he noticed   (C) noticing   (D) noticed

_____ 3. (A) With   (B) Thanks to   (C) In addition to   (D) Despite

_____ 4. (A) for   (B) on   (C) in   (D) about

_____ 5. (A) to consider   (B) considered   (C) considering   (D) consider

---

El Nino 聖嬰現象   *Jesus Christ* 耶穌基督   *occur* v. 發生   *La Nina* 反聖嬰現象
hemisphere n. 半球   *oscillation* n. 擺動   *Tahiti* 大溪地   *Darwin* 達爾文（澳洲地名）
weather pattern 天氣型態   *profound* adj. 深刻的   *global economy* 全球經濟
agriculture n. 農業

Ⓒ   Sitting between Lake Pontchartrain and the Mississippi River near the Gulf of Mexico, New Orleans was a thriving U.S. city, famous for its Mardi Gras celebrations and talented jazz artists,   1   Hurricane Katrina flooded the city in 2005. In fact, the city's nickname   2   be "The Big Easy" because of the people's carefree nature. New Orleans   3   about two meters below sea level, and it is protected from the water around it by a system of levees that surround the city. These levees, or water barriers, circle the entire city and   4   water from Lake Pontchartrain and the Mississippi River from rushing into the city.

In 2005, Hurricane Katrina hit New Orleans   5   . The damage from Katrina's high winds and storm surge, which destroyed some levees, was terrible. More than 80 percent of the city was left completely underwater, leaving hundreds of thousands of people homeless without food, fresh water or electricity.   6   , the major roads going in and out of the city were   7   destroyed   7   underwater, making it very difficult for survivors to leave the city or for aid workers to get into the city.

To help these people and their city, the federal and local governments have spent billions of dollars   8   the mess, building better levees and rebuilding damaged homes and businesses. The damage, however, was   9   some experts estimated that it would take more than ten years for the city to   10   .

_____ 1. (A) unless   (B) after   (C) while   (D) until
_____ 2. (A) is used to   (B) was used to   (C) has used to   (D) used to
_____ 3. (A) places   (B) lays   (C) rests   (D) seats
_____ 4. (A) prevent   (B) prohibit   (C) warn   (D) escape
_____ 5. (A) in no time   (B) at full force (C) without delay (D) by all means
_____ 6. (A) On one hand   (B) To make matters worse
           (C) What's better   (D) To put it in another way
_____ 7. (A) either...or   (B) neither...nor (C) such...that   (D) so...that
_____ 8. (A) to clean up   (B) clean up   (C) cleaning up   (D) cleaned up
_____ 9. (A) so that   (B) such that   (C) so great as to (D) too great that
_____ 10. (A) retrieve   (B) renovate   (C) recall   (D) recover

| *thriving* adj. 繁榮的   *Mardi Gras* 狂歡節   *hurricane* n. 颶風 |
| *carefree* adj. 無憂無慮的   *levee* n. 防洪堤 |

Part II : Translation Practice

Sentence Patterns

1. NP + be such that...

此句型意為「如此…以至於」。用來強調前面的名詞，也可和 such...that/so...that 互換。

例：**Her beauty is such that** all the boys are mad about her.

→ She is **such a beautiful girl that** all the boys are mad about her.

→ She is **so beautiful a girl that** all the boys are mad about her.

2. N/Adj/Adv + as/though + S$_1$ +V$_1$, S$_2$+V$_2$

此句型和 Although「雖然」意義一樣，但更強調移到句首的形容詞，副詞和名詞。需注意使用此句型時，句首如為名詞，不加任何的冠詞。

例：Although Jim is a child, he is very brave.

→ Child **as**/**though** Jim is, he is very brave.

Although Tina is young, she is mature and considerate.

→ Young **as**/**though** Tina is, she is mature and considerate.

Although Tony worked hard, he was fired.

→ Hard **as**/**though** Tony worked, he was fired.

(A)

 Keywords •————————————————————————————————•

1. 廣大：*vastness* (n.)　穿越：*cross* (v.)　極度地：*extremely* (adv.)

2. 探險：*expedition* (n.)　一輩子：*lifetime* (n.)

 Sample •————————————————————————————————•

1. 撒哈拉沙漠 (Sahara Desert) 是如此的廣大，以至於要徒步穿越它是極為困難的。

The vastness of Sahara Desert is **such that** it is extremely difficult to cross through it on foot.

2. 雖然可能會很危險，對大多數人而言去撒哈拉沙漠探險是一輩子才有一次的機會。

Dangerous **as** it may be, an expedition to Sahara Desert is a chance of a lifetime for most people.

Ⓑ

Keywords ••

1.奪走 (生命)：*claim* (v.)　生態環境：*ecology* (n.)

2.恢復：*restore*　重建：*rebuild* (v.)　受地震摧殘的：*quake-stricken* (adj.)

Practice ••

1. 921 地震的威力是如此大，以至於它不僅奪走很多生命也破壞了生態環境。

_____

2.雖然要恢復原有的美景很困難，我們還是應該盡全力重建這個受地震摧殘的地區。

_____

_____

Ⓒ

Keywords ••

1.神秘：*mystery* (n.)　數不清：*countless* (adj.)　傳說：*legend* (n.)　謠言：*rumor* (n.)

2.冒險家：*adventurer* (n.)　怪物：*monster* (n.)

Practice ••

1.尼斯湖 (Loch Ness) 是如此神秘，以至於一直以來有數不清關於它的傳說和謠言。

_____

2.雖然很多冒險家和科學家努力嘗試，我們還是無法得知湖裏是否住有怪物

_____

_____

Part I : Cloze Test

Ⓐ The new science of nanotechnology may soon change our world. Before we __1__ these changes, we must be aware of any hidden dangers. Nanotechnology is about building things from atoms that can help us in our daily lives. We can use it to create protective coverings, better medicines and maybe even more powerful weapons. For example, the chemical silver, if __2__ into tiny particles, can be used to cover children's clothing and kill germs in food preparation. One of the biggest worries about nanotechnology is __3__ the particles are so small that they could pass through the skin. There is a danger of poisoning the body because the chemicals could __4__ in our lungs and maybe even in our brains. Modern science and nanotechnology are offering us the chance to create a better world. Perhaps we had better __5__ this brand-new world more closely.

_____ 1. (A) confess　　　(B) permit　　　(C) embrace　　　(D) pursue

_____ 2. (A) is breaking　　(B) to break　　(C) breaks　　　(D) broken

_____ 3. (A) which　　　(B) that　　　(C) why　　　(D) what

_____ 4. (A) build up　　　(B) carry on　　(C) put off　　　(D) hold up

_____ 5. (A) examine　　　(B) to examine　(C) examining　　(D) examined

---

nanotechnology n. 奈米科技　*be aware of* 察覺、發現　*atom* n. 原子
covering n. 遮蓋物　*particle* n. 粒子　*germ* n. 細菌
food preparation 食物製作　*poison* v. 毒害　*lung* n. 肺
brand-new adj. 全新的

Ⓑ　The latest hi-tech toys might have too many people jumping for joy. However, computer hackers also can't wait to steal customers'　1　information! It is a concern that has many people　2　about plugging into the future. From MP3 players, navigation tools, to smartphones anything that plugs into a computer may contain a virus. These viruses may either change settings or　3　important information. Some viruses can even steal passwords and other important information, including credit card numbers! Some viruses are　4　uploaded in the early stages of product production by malicious hackers who intend to cause harm. Other viruses come from factories where the lack of supervision may allow hackers to easily upload more dangerous viruses. Experts advise that each individual user　5　the latest anti-virus software and update it regularly. It is the best way to keep a step ahead in the future.

_____ 1. (A) intellectual　　(B) private　　(C) academic　　(D) technological

_____ 2. (A) let on　　(B) lose track　　(C) take after　　(D) think twice

_____ 3. (A) reflect　　(B) delete　　(C) insult　　(D) oppose

_____ 4. (A) occasionally　　(B) purposefully　　(C) inevitably　　(D) doubtfully

_____ 5. (A) to have　　(B) has　　(C) have　　(D) had

---

hi-tech adj. 高科技的　　*jump for joy* 雀躍、興奮　　*hacker* n. 駭客
can't wait to v. 等不及要去…　　*concern* n. 顧慮　　*navigation* n. 導航
smartphones n. 智慧型手機　　*virus* n. 病毒　　*setting* n. 設定　　*password* n. 密碼
upload v. 上傳　　*malicious* adj. 惡意的　　*supervision* n. 監督　　*a step ahead* 領先

Ⓒ   Nanotechnology will soon be closely involved in our daily lives. It is not something remote that only exists in ___1___, but something we will wear, see, and touch every day. One of the most remarkable nanotechnology-___2___ products is the NanoDetecto watch. This amazing device will not only tell the time, but also warn you ___3___ any hidden dangers in the environment such as dangerous chemicals or bacteria. For example, if someone close to you sneezes, the NanoDetecto watch can detect its ___4___ in the air and sound a warning.

Another great invention is superstick nanotape. It's just like ordinary sticky tape ___5___ much more powerful. It can stick to any surface, even under water. Some researchers believe that with a special suit or gloves made from superstick nanotape, humans would be able to climb walls, just like lizards or spiders!

Moreover, certain people have to wear very special sets of clothes to do their jobs such as firefighters and soldiers. Their clothing is usually uncomfortable. However, ___6___ nanotechnology, their lives may be about to get much easier. Scientists are working on clothing that can adapt itself ___7___ different tasks. For example, if a firefighter has to go through a fire, the clothes could change themselves to become more ___8___ to high temperatures. Skiers, ___9___, usually operate in cold environments, so their clothes could become tighter to help keep body temperature up. To sum up, nanotechnology has many fascinating ___10___ and shows that technology can be interesting.

_____ 1. (A) laboratories   (B) chambers   (C) submarines   (D) conventions

_____ 2. (A) base   (B) based   (C) basing   (D) to base

_____ 3. (A) in   (B) with   (C) on   (D) of

_____ 4. (A) alarm   (B) content   (C) strategy   (D) presence

_____ 5. (A) otherwise   (B) except   (C) including   (D) even

_____ 6. (A) in addition to   (B) regardless of   (C) thanks to   (D) considering

_____ 7. (A) to   (B) for   (C) in   (D) of

_____ 8. (A) vulnerable   (B) threatening   (C) allergic   (D) resistant

_____ 9. (A) in turn   (B) by contrast   (C) as a consequence (D) so far

_____ 10. (A) themes   (B) motives   (C) applications   (D) possessions

---

remote adj. 遙遠的   *remarkable* adj. 令人驚嘆的   *detect* v. 偵測   *bacteria* n. 細菌
lizard n. 蜥蜴

 **Part II : Translation Practice**

Sentence Patterns

1. Thanks to + N, S + V
表示「幸虧有…、因為有…、由於…」，用法和 due to/owing to/as a result of 一樣。 例：**Thanks to** Ray Kroc, McDonald can enjoy such a phenomenal growth.
2. either...or...
表示「不是…就是…」。用於對等連接詞，注意句子的動詞需和最靠近的主詞一致。 例：Either you or **John has** to be responsible for the mistake. 例：The major roads of the city were **either** destroyed **or** under water.

Keywords

1. 發明：*invention*（n.）　更好：*for the better*
2. 處理：*process*（v.）　資料：*data*（n.）　有效率地：*efficiently*（adv.）

Sample

1. 由於電腦的發明，我們的生活變的更好。

   Thanks to the invention of computers, our lives have been changed for the better.

2. 電腦不是能幫我們處理資料，就是可以更有效率地找到資訊。

   Computers can **either** help us process data **or** find information more efficiently.

B

Keywords

1. 人工智慧：*artificial intelligence*　　在…協助下：*with the help of...*　　機器人：*robot* (n.)
2. 家事：*household chores*　　協助：*assistance* (n.)　　在工作：*at work*

Practice

1. 幸虧有人工智慧的發展，人們能在機器人的協助下，過著更方便的生活。

　　　　　　　　　　　　　　　　　　　　　　　　　　　

　　　　　　　　　　　　　　　　　　　　　　　　　　　

2. 在未來，機器人不是能幫忙做家事，就是能提供工作上的協助。

　　　　　　　　　　　　　　　　　　　　　　　　　　　

　　　　　　　　　　　　　　　　　　　　　　　　　　　

C

Keywords

1. 像…這樣的：*such...as...*　　平板電腦：*tablet computer*　　科技產品：*gadget* (n.)
   上網：*surf the Net*
2. 得知：*keep abreast of*　　最新的：*latest* (adj.)

Practice

1. 因為有像智慧手機和平板筆電這樣的科技產品，我們可以輕鬆地上網。

　　　　　　　　　　　　　　　　　　　　　　　　　　　

　　　　　　　　　　　　　　　　　　　　　　　　　　　

2. 在家或上班，我們都可以得知最新的資訊。

Part I : Cloze Test

A With stores selling food from every country, the Japanese __1__ enjoy leisurely meals of their own culture. Food there is both fast and foreign. However, critics of this fast food culture have started a "Slow Food" movement to __2__ this trend. They are getting support from the public. Some Japanese agree that the quick pace and the low quality of fast foods affect the quality of life in Japan, and that deserves attention.

The Slow Food movement began in Italy in the 1980s, __3__ some people felt that the Italian public had to be re-educated about the benefits of healthful food. They also recommended that food __4__ more slowly. These ideas are difficult to promote in Japan. Cost and time are the key factors determining the way the Japanese eat. __5__ is offered must remain fast and cheap, or it will never be accepted, at least not in today's Japan.

_____ 1. (A) mostly   (B) rarely   (C) conventionally   (D) initially

_____ 2. (A) reverse   (B) balance   (C) mend   (D) contrast

_____ 3. (A) which   (B) during that   (C) what   (D) when

_____ 4. (A) to be eaten   (B) is eaten   (C) eaten   (D) be eaten

_____ 5. (A) Anything   (B) Whatever   (C) It   (D) Which

---

leisurely adj./adv. 悠閒地　　*Slow Food* 慢食　　*trend* n. 風潮　　*pace* n. 步調
quality of life 生活品質　　*deserve attention* 值得重視　　*key factor* 關鍵的因素

Ⓑ   Modern medicine has accomplished remarkable things. For example, many infectious diseases, __1__ , diseases that are spread from one person to another, have been eliminated or are under control. However, there is a whole other class of diseases that are __2__ . They are called "lifestyle diseases" which are illnesses caused by our own bad habits.

   The major lifestyle diseases are heart disease, stroke, some types of cancer, Type 2 diabetes, and lung disease. These diseases are caused by such things __3__ a poor diet, being overweight, not exercising, and cigarette smoking. Most of the other diseases are tied to the combination of poor diet and lack of exercise. Eating more calories than your body uses __4__ being very overweight, which leads to heart disease and stroke. There are other lifestyle factors that contribute to disease __5__ including alcohol, drug abuse, and stress.

_____ 1. (A) yet   (B) in addition   (C) on the contrary   (D) that is

_____ 2. (A) on the rise   (B) in private   (C) at odds   (D) off the record

_____ 3. (A) for   (B) like   (C) as   (D) included

_____ 4. (A) stems from   (B) results in   (C) is given rise to   (D) thanks to

_____ 5. (A) for instance   (B) either   (C) as well   (D) so

---

accomplish v. 完成   *infectious* adj. 傳染性   *lifestyle diseases* 文明病
eliminate v. 消除   *under control* 受到控制   *diabetes* n. 糖尿病   *stroke* n. 中風
cigarette n. 香煙   *combination* n. 綜合   *contribute* v. 導致   *alcohol* n. 酒、酒精
drug abuse 藥物濫用

---

lifestyle diseases 文明病

又作 diseases of longevity 或 diseases of civilization，多發生在已開發的先進國家，物質生活條件良好，使得人們變得更長壽，伴隨而來的疾病，如阿茲海默症 (Alzheimer's disease)、腫瘤 (tumor)、哮喘 (asthma)、動脈硬化 (atherosclerosis)、中風 (stroke)、骨質疏鬆症 (osteoporosis)、心臟病 (heart disease)、糖尿病 (diabetes)、肥胖症 (obesity) 等。

Ⓒ   Toshi Uechi is 92 and she still practices traditional Okinawan dance. She avoids snacks and eats "goya" every day. "Goya" is a vegetable __1__ zucchini with warts and it tastes bitter. This kind of diet and active lifestyle have made Okinawa home to many centenarians. It has one of the highest __2__ of centenarians in the world. Among every 100,000 residents, 39.5 people are over 100. However, Okinawa was ruled by Americans from the end of World War II __3__ 1972. Today, the Americans still keep their military bases there. Years of contact with the Americans have made many Okinawians lose their traditional eating habits, __4__ at the same time it has raised their standard of living.

The Americans brought in food such as the hamburgers and canned meat, and the local lifestyle began to change. Young people are dying earlier __5__ the older people live longer. Older people such as Uechi grew up eating lots of local vegetables, tofu, and seaweed. The diet of young people in Okinawa is completely different. They'd rather eat hamburgers, fries and other fast-food items __6__ be on a goya diet; __7__, they reject the idea of exercise. Part of the reason is __8__ the island lacks public transportation and, as in America, young Okinawians have developed a love for cars. The result of this trend is shown in the following data: longevity for Okinawan men had fallen to the 26th place among Japan's 47 areas in 2000, down __9__ from the 4th in 1995 and the 1st in 1985. The local health department is trying to alert people __10__ the importance of a balanced diet and the right way to prepare food.

_____ 1. (A) which resemble (B) resembled   (C) resembling   (D) to resemble

_____ 2. (A) data   (B) percentage   (C) membership   (D) manners

_____ 3. (A) for   (B) in   (C) until   (D) by

_____ 4. (A) and   (B) nevertheless   (C) otherwise   (D) but

_____ 5. (A) though   (B) while   (C) because   (D) unless

_____ 6. (A) than   (B) for   (C) as   (D) to

_____ 7. (A) in fact   (B) consequently   (C) what's more   (D) however

_____ 8. (A) which   (B) that   (C) ×   (D) because

_____ 9. (A) largely   (B) undoubtedly   (C) specifically   (D) considerably

_____ 10. (A) of   (B) on   (C) to   (D) with

---

goya n. 沖繩苦瓜   *zucchini* n. 櫛瓜   *wart* n. 突出物   *centenarian* n. 百歲人瑞
seaweed n. 海菜   *longevity* n. 長壽

Part II : Translation Practice

Sentence Patterns

1. would rather V₁... than V₂...

此句型為「寧願做…而不願做…」之意。注意句中的兩個動詞均為原形動詞。

此句型也可代換為 $\begin{cases} \text{prefer} + \text{to V}_1 + \text{rather than} + \text{V}_2 \\ \text{prefer} + \text{V}_1\text{ing} + \text{to} + \text{V}_2\text{ing} \end{cases}$

例：Young people **would rather** eat hamburgers and other fast foods **than** go on a diet.

2. (原因) + contribute to/give rise to/lead to/result in + N/V-ing (結果)

用法為表示句中的「因果關係」。以上均為「造成，導致」之意，這些片語均無被動語態。

例：There are other lifestyle factors that **contribute to** disease as well, including alcohol and stress.

Ⓐ

 Keywords •─────────────────────────────•

1. 節食：*go on a diet*　　減肥：*lose weight*
2. 限制：*restrict...to N/V-ing*　　傷害：*do harm to*　　厭食症：*anorexia*

 Sample •─────────────────────────────•

1. 有些少女寧願節食也不願做運動來減肥。

   Some teenage girls **would rather go** on a diet **than do** exercise to lose weight.

   → Some teenage girls **prefer to go** on a diet **rather than do** exercise to lose weight.

   → Some teenage girls **prefer going** on a diet **to doing** exercise to lose weight.

2. 限制自己一天只能吃一餐，會傷害身體，甚至會導致厭食症。

   Restricting oneself to one meal a day will do harm to the body and can even **lead to** anorexia.

Ⓑ

Keywords

1. 上班族：*white-collar/nine-to-five workers*　　電梯：*elevator*（n.）　　走樓梯：*take stairs*
2. 懶惰：*laziness*（n.）　　肥胖：*obesity*（n.）　　心臟病：*heart disease*　　糖尿病：*diabetes*（n.）

Practice

1. 很多上班族寧願花時間等電梯也不願走樓梯到辦公室。

_____

_____

2. 他們的懶惰導致像是肥胖、心臟病、糖尿病等種種問題。

_____

_____

Ⓒ

Keywords

1. 富含：*rich in*　　維他命：*vitamin*（n.）
2. 成年人：*adult*（n.）　　不均衡的：*unbalanced*（adj.）　　過度攝取：*overtake*（n.）
   高血壓：*high blood pressure*

Practice

1. 越來越多孩童寧願選擇速食，也不願去吃富含維他命 C 的蔬菜水果。

_____

_____

2. 當他們成年後，不均衡的飲食和過度攝取脂肪會導致高血壓。

_____

_____

Part I : Cloze Test

(A)   Nowadays, many mothers face a dilemma, not knowing whether they should continue with their jobs or stay home to look after their babies. According to recent studies, there are pros and cons of ___1___ sides. Some scientists have found that mothers who go back to their careers feel independent and proud. However, office jobs may ___2___ very long working hours, so working women may worry they are sacrificing family life. ___3___, stay-at-home mothers enjoy seeing their child grow day by day. But with numerous household chores to be done, they might feel lonely, bored, or jealous of their husbands' careers. Many women have ___4___ take on a "middle way." They may work part-time or in companies that have a kindergarten ___5___ they can see their kids at break time throughout the day. In this way, many women have found that they can be truly happy working mothers!

_____ 1. (A) both   (B) all   (C) either   (D) neither

_____ 2. (A) reserve   (B) replace   (C) require   (D) reduce

_____ 3. (A) Instead   (B) In contrast   (C) As a result   (D) On the one hand

_____ 4. (A) yet   (B) so   (C) nevertheless   (D) therefore

_____ 5. (A) so that   (B) lest   (C) until   (D) never

---

dilemma n. 兩難的情況   *pros and cons* 利與弊   *career* n. 事業、工作
independent adj. 獨立的   *office job* 上班工作   *working hour* 上班時間
working woman 職業婦女   *sacrifice* 犧牲   *stay-at-home* adj. 待在家裡的
household chores n. 家務工作，家事   *middle way* 折衷的方法
kindergarten n. 幼稚園   *break* n. 休息時間

Ⓑ　Today's working environment is full of pressure, often ___1___ long weekends and nights at the office. Although many men love this working culture, others are tired of ___2___ seeing their children, and feeling like a stranger to their own family. Traditionally, the husband has gone out to work and the wife has stayed at home. But now this is changing: More and more stay-at-home dads have decided to leave the business world to ___3___ their children.

　　For example, Joe is a father of two small children, who worked as a manager in a big international company. Two years ago, he decided to quit his job, ___4___ his wife went out to work instead. The positive side of his new life, Joe explains, includes being able to spend time ___5___ fun activities with his kids. It can be assumed that this trend is here to stay.

_____ 1. (A) involves　(B) to involve　(C) it involves　(D) involving
_____ 2. (A) frequently　(B) economically　(C) rarely　(D) partially
_____ 3. (A) take to　(B) look after　(C) leave behind　(D) see off
_____ 4. (A) unless　(B) while　(C) for fear that　(D) however
_____ 5. (A) to do　(B) do　(C) doing　(D) done

pressure n. 壓力　working culture 工作職場文化　feel like 想要…　manager n. 經理
positive adj. 正面的　assume v. 假設　be here to stay 將持續很久

Ⓒ   Every parent wants his or her child to do well. However, in an effort to guide their children, some parents go too far. They become __1__ and wish to be involved in every part of their children's lives. These parents, often called "helicopter parents," have trouble __2__.

In 1990, Foster Cline and Jim Fay first __3__ the term "helicopter parents" in their book *Parenting with Love and Logic*. Officers at colleges noticed that some parents wanted their children to get into certain schools very badly. This led parents __4__ their children about their choices of colleges. They try to force their children to get better grades and take certain jobs. Some parents even wrote essays and filled out the college __5__ for their children, hoping to increase their chances of getting in.

Helicopter parents soon spread to areas __6__ college admissions. Cell phones allow parents to call their children at any time, __7__ them and trying to protect them. One of the problems is __8__ helicopter parents can keep children from learning to do things for themselves. This can actually hurt them later in life.

Children must become adults sometime. They need to learn to be responsible __9__ their own future. Unfortunately, helicopter parents can delay this, __10__ more harm than help in their children's lives.

_____ 1. (A) informative   (B) optimistic   (C) overprotective   (D) moral
_____ 2. (A) to let go   (B) let go   (C) be let go   (D) letting go
_____ 3. (A) introduced   (B) grieved   (C) raised   (D) translated
_____ 4. (A) nagging   (B) nag   (C) to nag   (D) nagged
_____ 5. (A) plots   (B) applications   (C) regulations   (D) investigations
_____ 6. (A) except   (B) instead of   (C) besides   (D) in addition
_____ 7. (A) looking down upon   (B) keeping track of
          (C) losing sight of   (D) catching up with
_____ 8. (A) ✕   (B) why   (C) what   (D) that
_____ 9. (A) for   (B) on   (C) with   (D) despite
_____ 10. (A) which causes   (B) and causing   (C) to cause   (D) caused

---

in an effort to V 為了   *go too far* 太過頭   *be involved in* 參與
helicopter parents 直升機父母   *nag* v. 嘮叨抱怨   *admission* n. 入學 (許可)

Part II : Translation Practice

Sentence Patterns

1. S + have + trouble/problems/difficulty/a hard time + (in) + V-ing....

此句型表示「在⋯有困難」，in 通常可省略。類似用法還有 have + fun/a good time + (in) V-ing 則表示「做⋯很開心」。

例：These parents, often called helicopter parents, **have trouble** letting go.

2. ...so that...

so that 用於連接兩個句子，用以表示「目的」，意思為「如此一來」。類似用法有 S + V + in order that.../so as to +V。

例：Some kites had whistles attached to them **so that** they would make musical sounds while they flew.

 Keywords •--•

1. 取得平衡：*strike a balance between*　　事業：*career* (n.)

2. 減少：*reduce* (v.)　　工作量：*workload* (n.)　　教養，撫育：*nurture* (v.)

Sample •--•

1. 有些母親難以在事業及家庭兩者之間，取得平衡點。

　Some mothers **have problems striking** a balance between career and family.

2. 她們試著減少工作份量，如此一來就可以花較多的時間在教養子女上。

　They try to reduce their workload **so that**/**in order that** they can spend more time nurturing their children.

Ⓑ

Keywords •••

1. 很多：*a great number of*　青少年：*teenager* (n.)　溝通：*communicate* (v.)
2. 吐露心聲：*confide in*

Practice ••

1. 很多青少年和他們父母溝通有困難。

_____

_____

2. 父母應成為好的傾聽者，如此一來他們的小孩會對他們吐露心聲。

_____

_____

Ⓒ

Keywords •••

1. 親密的：*intimate* (adj.)
2. 分享，分擔：*share* (v.)　家事：*household chores*　和…親近：*feel close to...*

Practice ••

1. 有些父親在和家人保持親密關係方面有困難。

_____

_____

2. 他們應多分擔家事，如此來家人會覺得和他們較親近。

_____

_____

Part I : Cloze Test

Ⓐ   Victor Hugo is well known for his novel *Les Miserables* and   1   of his famous works is *Notre-Dame de Paris*, which is often called *The Hunchback of Notre-Dame*. Hugo's novel is not really about the hunchback, Quasimodo, but about events that happen in and around the church, the Notre Dame. The church's leader, Claude Frollo, has fallen in love with a beautiful woman named Esmeralda. Trying to murder Esmeralda's lover, Frollo put the blame on her. She is   2   hanged as a punishment. *Notre-Dame de Paris* has several important meanings. Esmeralda was convicted   3   a crime she did not commit, which   4   the uselessness of France's government. Quasimodo is treated with hatred just because he is ugly,   5   the reader of the importance of pity and compassion. *Notre-Dame de Paris* tells a story about what happens to people when justice and power are not used correctly.

_____ 1. (A) the other   (B) another   (C) other   (D) one

_____ 2. (A) consequently   (B) definitely   (C) obviously   (D) initially

_____ 3. (A) with   (B) to   (C) against   (D) of

_____ 4. (A) symbolized   (B) graced   (C) manipulated   (D) strengthened

_____ 5. (A) that reminds   (B) reminds   (C) reminding   (D) which reminding

---

Victor Hugo 雨果   *Les Miserables*《悲慘世界》   *Notre-Dame de Paris*《巴黎聖母院》
The Hunchback of Notre-Dame《鐘樓怪人》   *hunchback* adj. 駝背的；n. 駝背的人
murder v. 謀殺   *put the blame on sb* 怪罪於某人…   *hang* v. 絞刑
punishment n. 懲罰   *commit* v. 犯（罪）   *hatred* n. 仇恨

B First published in 1943, *The Little Prince* is a children's book written by Antoine de Saint-Exupéry. *The Little Prince* is a fantasy story about a pilot stranded in the desert, who meets a boy from another planet—the Little Prince. The boy is searching for knowledge, and asks the pilot many questions. Its __1__ is based on its charming way of addressing simple but important truths, especially those that adults often forget __2__ they age. A famous quote from the story is, "It is only with the heart that one can see rightly; what is essential is __3__ to the eye." Its simple, imaginative fantasy setting makes this story entertaining for children, and its universal concepts attract adults as well. This __4__ makes the novel very popular. __5__, the story has been translated into more than 250 languages and is one of the top 50 best-selling books in the world.

_____ 1. (A) peculiarity   (B) appeal   (C) criticism   (D) contribution

_____ 2. (A) unless   (B) until   (C) as   (D) if

_____ 3. (A) fundamental   (B) precious   (C) invisible   (D) impractical

_____ 4. (A) combination   (B) contradiction   (C) distribution   (D) recognition

_____ 5. (A) Nevertheless   (B) Otherwise   (C) Likewise   (D) In fact

---

children's book 童書   *fantasy* n. 幻想   *strand* v. 滯留擱淺   *desert* n. 沙漠
age v. 年紀增長   *quote* n. 引言   *setting* n. 情節背景   *concept* n. 概念
best-selling adj. 暢銷的

Antoine de Saint-Exupery 安托尼‧德‧聖修伯里 (1900－1944)

20 世紀初法國作家、飛行員，著有代表作《小王子》(*Le Petit Prince*) (1943)、《夜間飛行》(*Night Flight*)(1931)、《風沙星辰》(*Wind, Sand and Stars*)(1939)。在二次大戰前是位擔任運送郵件的飛行員，大戰開始後加入法國空軍，於 1944 年執行一次任務中不幸罹難。法國政府曾將其肖像放置 50 法朗紙鈔上，另外家鄉里昂的機場，也以其名改為里昂聖修伯里機場。

Ⓒ　If there is one word to describe the Irish dramatist Samuel Beckett's play, *Waiting for Godot*, it's absurd. This absurd play ___1___ two themes: the meaninglessness of human life and the uselessness of language. Structurally, *Waiting for Godot* is centered on two homeless characters, Estragon and Vladimir. Throughout the play, they have nothing to do ___2___ sit by a tree and wait for another character named Godot, who never arrives. At the end of the play, Godot is still a mystery. One theme that runs deep in *Waiting for Godot* is the idea ___3___ man's life is meaningless. Originally written in French in 1948, *Waiting for Godot* was partially influenced by World War II ___4___ people built weapons powerful enough to destroy the human race. Beckett believed that the war proved man's insignificance. ___5___, in *Waiting for Godot,* much of the dialogue between the characters is full of nonsense, which demonstrates that language is a useless tool.

　　Waiting for Godot stands out among other dramas because it challenges the conventions of traditional theater. ___6___, main characters in traditional dramas after some life-changing events will discover a truth about themselves, which serves as a moral for the human race. However, in *Waiting for Godot*, it seems that just the ___7___ occurs. Estragon and Vladamir begin the same way as they end, with nothing important ___8___ in between. The characters don't understand each other, the plot is illogical, and the audience can't help ___9___ if mankind really is absurd. After all, Beckett implies that the next day, ___10___ there was one, would be very much the same.

_____ 1. (A) gets away with　(B) deals with　(C) means by　(D) agrees to

_____ 2. (A) besides　(B) but　(C) without　(D) than

_____ 3. (A) in which　(B) whose　(C) that　(D) how

_____ 4. (A) , where　(B) , which　(C) when　(D) , during which

_____ 5. (A) As a result　　　　　　(B) On the other hand
　　　　　(C) On the contrary　　　　(D) To be more specific

_____ 6. (A) Typically　(B) Originally　(C) Ideally　(D) Fortunately

_____ 7. (A) composition　(B) motivation　(C) opposite　(D) disagreement

_____ 8. (A) to happen　(B) happen　(C) happening　(D) happened

_____ 9. (A) wondering　(B) but to wonder　(C) wonder　(D) but wondering

_____ 10. (A) because　(B) but　(C) although　(D) if

---

absurd adj. 荒謬　*meaninglessness* n. 無意義　*uselessness* n. 無用
character n. 角色　*insignificance* n. 微不足道　*convention* n. 慣例

 **Part II : Translation Practice**

Sentence Patterns

1. N that S+V

that 子句用來說明解釋前面名詞或名詞片語的內容，作為同位語用，所以不可以省略。

例：One theme in *Waiting for Godot* is the idea **that** man's life is meaningless.

2. V_1-ing/V_1-en, S + V_2

此句型為分詞構句用法。當兩句子前後主詞一樣時，可省略連接詞，將附屬子句的主詞省去，動詞為主動時改成 V-ing，如為 being + Adj，則可省略 being，被動則改為 V-en。

例：**Trying** to murder Esmeralda's lover, Frollo put the blame on her.

→ **After** Frollo tried to murder Esmeralda's lover, **he** put the blame on her.

Ⓐ

 Keywords ────────────────────────────────

1. 主題：*theme*（n.）　人人生而平等：*all men are created equal*　平等的：*equal*（adj.）

   觀念：*concept/idea*（n.）

2. 爭議：*controversy*（n.）　突出：*stand out*（v.）

 Sample ──────────────────────────────────

1. 這本小說的一個重要主題就是「人人生而平等」的這個觀念。

   One important theme of this novel is **the concept that** all men are created equal.

2. 因為充滿爭議，這本小說與其他小說顯得突出不同。

   Because the novel is full of controversy, it stands out among other novels.

   → **Full of** controversy, this novel stands out among other novels.

Ⓑ

Keywords

1. 浪漫小說：*romance novel*　挑戰：*challenge*（v.）　一見鍾情：*fall in love at first sight*
2. 受⋯的歡迎：*be popular with/among*　各個年齡層的人：*people of all ages*

Practice

1. 這本浪漫愛情小說挑戰「一見鍾情」這種想法。

_____

_____

2. 在 50 年前寫成，這本小說受到各年齡層的歡迎。

_____

_____

Ⓒ

Keywords

1. 議題：*issue*（n.）　一再地：*repeatedly*（adv.）　強調：*highlight/emphasize*（v.）
2. 提倡：*advocate*（v.）　女性主義：*feminism*（n.）　造成轟動：*cause a sensation*
　批評：*criticism*（n.）

Practice

1. 女性應享有更多自由的這個議題，一再地在這個劇本中被強調。

_____

_____

2. 由於提倡女性主義，這個劇本造成轟動但也引發批評。

_____

_____

Part I : Cloze Test

Ⓐ   The Grimm Brothers have given us some of the most loved stories like "Little Red Riding Hood" and "Snow White." Since childhood, Jacob and Wilhelm Grimm ___1___ around the countryside to listen to and collect folktales. They combined different ___2___ of a story into one, trying to stay as close to the original as possible. Yet, the brothers intentionally added violence ___3___ the stories to teach values of justice, obedience, and morality. One example is the story "Cinderella," originally called "Aschenputtel." In "Cinderella," neither of the step-sisters was the girl the prince wanted, ___4___ the glass shoe did not fit them. However, in "Aschenputtel," the brothers deliberately put in a horrible twist—the step-sisters wanted to marry the prince so much that they cut off parts of their heels! This story shows that it is wrong to tell lies, ___5___ if you do, you have to suffer.

_____ 1. (A) have traveled   (B) traveled
          (C) had traveled   (D) have been traveled

_____ 2. (A) scales   (B) versions   (C) conventions   (D) facilities

_____ 3. (A) by   (B) to   (C) in   (D) for

_____ 4. (A) as   (B) hence   (C) while   (D) yet

_____ 5. (A) but   (B) therefore   (C) and that   (D) so

Grimm Brothers 格林兄弟   *Little Red Riding Hood* 小紅帽   *Show White* 白雪公主
intentionally adv. 刻意地   *obedience* n. 服從   *morality* n. 道德
Cinderella/Aschenputtel 灰姑娘   *deliberately* adv. 刻意地   *twist* n. 故事轉折
step-sister n. 繼姐（妹）

Ⓑ　Nathaniel Hawthorne has been recognized as one of America's most important writers. Though ___1___ by critics of his day, he still experienced a lot of frustrations throughout his literary career. Before he became famous, Hawthorne was unable to earn a living as a writer, so he worked at the custom house of the Port of Salem. One day he came home ___2___ after being fired. Sophia, his bright and cheerful wife, did something that American literature will thank her forever. She did not yell at him for losing his job; ___3___ she said, smiling, "Think of it as a great opportunity. Now you can have all the time to complete your book ___4___ you never had time." It was her positive attitude ___5___ convinced him to start working on his new book, *The Scarlet Letter* now considered to be his best novel and one of American's literary treasures.

_____ 1. (A) praised　　　(B) criticized　　　(C) appreciating　　　(D) recognizing

_____ 2. (A) distress　　　(B) distressing　　　(C) distressed　　　(D) to be distressed

_____ 3. (A) thus　　　　(B) moreover　　　　(C) namely　　　　(D) instead

_____ 4. (A) that　　　　(B) where　　　　(C) what　　　　(D) for which

_____ 5. (A) and　　　　(B) that　　　　(C) where　　　　(D) why

---

recognize v. 認定　　*frustration* n. 挫折　　*career* n. 事業生涯　　*custom house* 海關
opportunity n. 機會　　*positive* adj. 正面的　　*convince* v. 說服
The Scarlet Letter《紅字》

Nathaniel Hawthrone 納森尼爾・霍桑 (1804–1864)

19 世紀美國著名作家，著有長篇小說《紅字》(*The Scarlet Letter*) (1850)、短篇故事〈年輕的布朗大爺〉("Young Goodman Brown") (1835) 等代表作。1828 年以不署名方式出版首部小說《范肖》(Fanshawe)，之後在許多雜誌上陸續發表短篇小說。曾經兩度在海關工作，同時繼續寫作。後來也因為辭去海關工作，才有機會將《紅字》此小說完成。

Ⓒ The Trojan War, one of the most important stories in Greek legend, is thought to have been __1__ by a beauty. The war started when Eris, the goddess of discord, was angered because she had not been invited to the wedding of Peleus and Thetis. Eris hurried to their wedding feast upon __2__ the news and threw a golden apple onto the table. She said that it belonged to __3__ looked the best. Hera, Athena, and Aphrodite all wanted the apple. Then, Zeus announced Paris, the Prince of Troy, to be the judge.

__4__ Paris choose them, the three goddesses tried to bribe him with something he desired. He was offered power by Hera, wisdom by Athena, and the best-looking woman in the world by Aphrodite. __5__, Paris chose Aphrodite. Therefore, he was promised Helen, wife of Menelaus. Despite the advice of his mother, Paris left for Sparta to find Helen. There, Menelaus treated Paris wonderfully __6__ find his wife, Helen, and much of his riches __7__ away by Paris one day when Menelaus left Sparta to attend a funeral.

As a result, a war between Troy and Greece began. After fighting for nine years, the army of Greece __8__ an idea. They made a wooden horse and hid in it secretly. The Trojans then took the wooden horse back to the city, thinking it would bring them good luck. However, __9__ their great shock, the Greeks got out of the horse and beat the Trojans at midnight. This ended the war—a war that was caused by and famous __10__ a beauty.

_____ 1. (A) brought up	(B) brought out	(C) brought down	(D) brought about
_____ 2. (A) hear	(B) she heard	(C) hearing	(D) to hear
_____ 3. (A) anyone	(B) whoever	(C) who	(D) what
_____ 4. (A) For making	(B) To make	(C) Making	(D) Make
_____ 5. (A) In consequence	(B) Nonetheless	(C) In fact	(D) Rather
_____ 6. (A) but to	(B) rather than	(C) only to	(D) as well as
_____ 7. (A) taking	(B) to be taken	(C) take	(D) taken
_____ 8. (A) came up with	(B) occurred to	(C) struck	(D) dawned on
_____ 9. (A) for	(B) to	(C) by	(D) with
_____ 10. (A) as	(B) in	(C) by	(D) for

---

legend n. 傳說　*discord* n. 糾紛　*feast* n. 盛宴　*bribe* v. 賄賂　*wisdom* n. 智慧

Part II : Translation Practice

Sentence Patterns

1. S + be thought + to V → It is thought that S + V

S + be thought + to V = It is thought that S + V　表示「被認為…」。
S + be thought + to have + V-en = It is thought that S + V-ed　表示「被認為過去…」
另外相類似的用法還有 S + be + said/reported/believed + to V
→ It is said/reported/believed + that S + V 表示「據說／據報導」。
例：The Trojan War **is thought to** have been brought about by a beauty.

2. only to + V

此句型用來表示「卻只是、卻…」，後面接和預期相反的事實或是令人驚訝的事。
例：I desperately ran up to the MRT station **only to** find (that) the train just departed.

Keywords

1.等待以久的：*long-awaited*（adj.）　系列：*series*（n.）　銷售最好的：*best-selling*（adj.）

排行榜：*chart*（n.）

2.…迷：*fan*（n.）　賣完：*be sold out*

Sample

1.大家等待已久《哈利波特》系列的完結篇，被認為會成為銷售排行榜的冠軍。

The long-awaited final novel of the *Harry Potter* series **is thought to become** the top one on the best-selling chart.

2.許多書迷在書店外面等了一整夜，卻發現書已經賣完了。

Many fans waited outside the bookstores for the whole night **only to find** that all the books were sold out.

Ⓑ

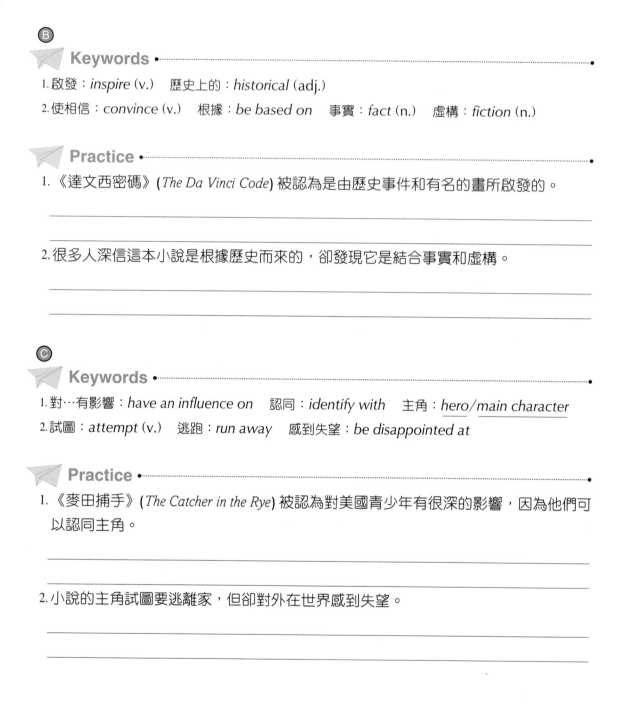

Keywords •————————————————————————————————————•

1. 啟發：*inspire* (v.)　歷史上的：*historical* (adj.)

2. 使相信：*convince* (v.)　根據：*be based on*　事實：*fact* (n.)　虛構：*fiction* (n.)

Practice •————————————————————————————————————•

1. 《達文西密碼》(*The Da Vinci Code*) 被認為是由歷史事件和有名的畫所啟發的。

_____

_____

2. 很多人深信這本小說是根據歷史而來的，卻發現它是結合事實和虛構。

_____

_____

Ⓒ

Keywords •————————————————————————————————————•

1. 對…有影響：*have an influence on*　認同：*identify with*　主角：*hero/main character*

2. 試圖：*attempt* (v.)　逃跑：*run away*　感到失望：*be disappointed at*

Practice •————————————————————————————————————•

1. 《麥田捕手》(*The Catcher in the Rye*) 被認為對美國青少年有很深的影響，因為他們可以認同主角。

_____

_____

2. 小說的主角試圖要逃離家，但卻對外在世界感到失望。

_____

_____

Unit 27 Idioms and Phrases (I)

Part I : Cloze Test

Ⓐ   In English, sometimes there are interesting stories behind the origin of a phrase. One example is "face the music" __1__ today means "suffering the results of something you have done." In 1850, however, it meant "being strong in difficult times." There are different opinions about how the phrase first __2__ . One is that it referred to a soldier who __3__ the army. The soldier would be placed on a horse, facing its tail. Then a military band would be playing music to watch him leave. Another story is related to theater. New performers might be worried before their __4__ . Besides the crowd, they would have to face the musicians who were often unkind to rookies. "Facing the music" thus describes someone __5__ a little afraid. When coming across a strange phrase, you may be provided with a chance to know an interesting story.

_____ 1. (A) that   (B) which   (C) , which   (D) it

_____ 2. (A) resulted from   (B) ran out   (C) went by   (D) came into being

_____ 3. (A) was made to leave   (B) was made leave

        (C) was made left   (D) was made leaving

_____ 4. (A) debut   (B) prominence   (C) operation   (D) recognition

_____ 5. (A) become   (B) becoming   (C) to become   (D) that become

---

opinion n. 看法   *refer* v. 指的是…   *rookies* n. 菜鳥、新手   *come across* 遇到、碰見

B   Many expressions in the English language are related to animals. These expressions come from different ___1___, such as mythology, folk tales, literature, religion, and old customs. Many expressions in use today have come from Aesop's Fables. For example, Aesop wrote a story about a clumsy donkey in a pottery shop. Later, Europeans changed the pottery shop into a china shop and replaced the donkey ___2___ the bull because the bull was bigger. Thus, the phrase "Bull in a China Shop" describes somebody who cannot help ___3___, and often breaks things. There are also many phrases whose origin is not so certain. The phrase "It is raining cats and dogs" means it is raining heavily. According to one ___4___, this phrase originated in England in the 17th century ___5___ streets were considerably filthy and heavy rains would wash away dead animals. All these animal-related idioms help make English more interesting.

_____ 1. (A) elements   (B) sources   (C) outcomes   (D) compositions
_____ 2. (A) in   (B) for   (C) with   (D) to
_____ 3. (A) but being clumsy (B) being clumsy   (C) to be clumsy   (D) be clumsy
_____ 4. (A) explanation   (B) significance   (C) impression   (D) prediction
_____ 5. (A) during which   (B) that   (C) , where   (D) , when

---

expression n. 用語   *mythology* n. 神話   *folk tale* 民間故事   *custom* n. 習俗
Aesop's Fables 伊索寓言   *clumsy* adj. 笨拙的   *pottery* n. 陶器   *china* n. 瓷器
originate v. 源起於…   *filthy* adj. 骯髒的

Ⓒ The term "butterflies in the stomach" is thought ___1___ in England in 1908 by a now-forgotten writer. The phrase was originally used to describe the funny feeling we get in our stomachs when we are nervous or feeling ___2___. Of course the feeling is not caused by butterflies and has a very simple ___3___ explanation.

When we experience a rush of emotion such as fear, nervousness or even excitement, the body produces chemicals which take blood away from the stomach and send it to the muscles. This causes the stomach muscles ___4___, which feels like fluttering or movement in the stomach to us. The word "fluttering" is often used to describe the way ___5___ a butterfly moves. This extra strength in the muscles is also the reason why we seem to be stronger in dangerous situations.

When we are in ___6___, a number of different things will happen in the body. However, not everyone's reaction is exactly the same. Other ___7___ of nervousness can include sweating, cold hands, a ___8___ of appetite (which might be because the stomach muscles are tighter), a racing heartbeat or a dry mouth. The symptoms can be worse, including upset stomach and being sick, ___9___ the nervous feeling is very strong and persistent. Knowing what causes these physical reactions and understanding them will be ___10___ great help in controlling them and it's also good to remember that everybody has these feelings from time to time.

_____ 1. (A) to have been first used (B) to be first used

(C) that had been first used (D) that it was first used

_____ 2. (A) to stress (B) stressing (C) stressed (D) be stressed

_____ 3. (A) biological (B) emotional (C) oral (D) historical

_____ 4. (A) tightening up (B) tighten up (C) tightened up (D) to tighten up

_____ 5. (A) why (B) in which (C) where (D) by how

_____ 6. (A) delight (B) panic (C) confusion (D) grief

_____ 7. (A) signs (B) causes (C) ingredients (D) features

_____ 8. (A) lose (B) lost (C) loss (D) losing

_____ 9. (A) while (B) unless (C) if (D) whether

_____ 10. (A) of (B) with (C) to (D) for

---

rush n. 一陣強烈的感受 *fluttering* n. 撲動；激動、緊張 *racing* adj. 快速的
persistent adj. 持續的

Part II : Translation Practice

Sentence Patterns

1. mean + V-ing/N   mean to + V

mean+ V-ing/N 為「意義為⋯」之意。

例：Love **means** never **having to say** you are sorry.

例：The word "planet" **means** wanderer.

而 mean to +V 則為「有意去⋯」之意。

例：Henry didn't **mean to harm** you. He just wanted to tell you the truth.

2. cause + O + N   cause + O + to + V

cause + O + N 為「造成⋯得到什麼結果」之意。

例：The death of his wife **caused** him much **pain**.

cause + O + to + V 則為「造成⋯去⋯」之意。

例：The heavy fog **caused** many airlines **to cancel** their flights.

例：A rush of emotion many **cause** the stomach muscles **to tighten** up.

A

Keywords

1. 片語：*phrase* (n.)　無理的：*irrational* (adj.)　極度地：*extremely* (adv.)

　熱切的：*enthusiastic* (adj.)　反應：*reaction/response* (n.)

2. 餵食：*feed* (v.)　來源：*origin* (n.)

Sample

1. "to go bananas" 這個片語意思為做出無理或極度熱切的反應。

   The phrase "to go bananas" **means making** irrational or extremely enthusiastic reaction/response.

2. 被餵食太多香蕉，會使猴子變得有野性，這可能是這個片語的來源。

   Being fed too many bananas will **cause** monkeys **to go** wild, which may be the origin of the phrase.

Ⓑ

Keywords

1. 系列：*series*（n.）　擁有：*possess*（v.）　魔法：*magical power*
2. 廣告商：*advertising agency*　傳達訊息：*get the message across*

Practice

1. 在《哈利波特》系列中，"muggle" 這個字意為「沒有擁有任何魔法的人」。

_____

_____

2. 這本小說的成功，已經造成很多廣告商使用小說內的語言，來傳達訊息。

_____

_____

Ⓒ

Keywords

1. 造字：*coin*（v.）　十年：*decade*（n.）　信：*mail/letter*（n.）
2. 取笑：*mock*（v.）　郵件遞送：*mail delivery*　緩慢：*slowness*（n.）
   不方便：*inconvenience*（n.）

Practice

1. "snail mail" 這個名詞是十年前被造出來的，意思是為由郵局所寄出的信。

_____

_____

2. 這個用語取笑傳統郵件遞送的緩慢，因為這可能造成人們很多的不方便。

_____

_____

Unit 28 Idioms and Phrases (II)

Part I : Cloze Test

Ⓐ Through the centuries colors have been used to describe many things. The phrase, "white elephant," which came from Southeast Asia, means something that is not worth __1__ because of the problems it creates. A white elephant was considered sacred, so the owner could neither force the animal to work __2__ get rid of it. Also, an elephant can be very expensive to feed. Therefore, the gift of a white elephant was not __3__ even if it might come from the king. The phrase, "blue blood," is an expression that means someone __4__ noble birth. The oldest families of Castile would claim to have never mixed with the Moors and they were pure. Their veins appeared bluer than __5__ of the Moors. This was because their skin was lighter and their blue-colored veins could be seen through the fair skin. Now when you hear a color expression, you will know that it may have an interesting history.

_____ 1. (A) to have   (B) having   (C) had   (D) being had

_____ 2. (A) nor   (B) can't   (C) and   (D) or

_____ 3. (A) refused   (B) enforced   (C) recommended   (D) appreciated

_____ 4. (A) to   (B) at   (C) of   (D) within

_____ 5. (A) ones   (B) all   (C) that   (D) those

---

worth adj. 值得的   *get rid of* 丟棄、拆掉   *noble birth* 貴族出身   *Castile* 卡斯提爾
Moors 摩爾人   *claim* v. 宣稱   *vein* n. 靜脈   *sacred* adj. 神聖的   *fair* adj. 淺色的

B We can know the culture of a country through its language. For many people, expressions like "Get to the point," "Speak your mind," or "Just do it" are so American. The direct, stand-up-for-what-is-right American style can be good, __1__ it might surprise people from other parts of the world. For example, American children are not afraid of __2__ the ideas of their parents or teachers. Office workers are encouraged to speak up in front of the manager. However, respect for the __3__ and those in power is very important in some cultures. They prefer using hints __4__ hurting the feelings of anyone. Another feature of American style is competition. It drives people to "think big," "make it happen," and be the "A player." Sometimes Americans may be considered pushy or not easy __5__ because they like the no-nonsense type of guys who waste no time.

_____ 1. (A) so　　　　　(B) however　　　(C) for　　　　　(D) yet

_____ 2. (A) admitting　　(B) pondering　　(C) questioning　(D) embracing

_____ 3. (A) elderly　　　(B) miserable　　(C) fortunate　　(D) educated

_____ 4. (A) in　　　　　(B) than　　　　(C) to　　　　　(D) with

_____ 5. (A) that works along　　　　(B) to be worked along with
　　　　　(C) to work along with　　　　(D) to work along

---

get to the point 講重點　　speak your mind 實話實說
stand-up-for-what-is-right 對的事情就挺身去做　　speak up 有話直說
in power 掌權　　competition n. 競爭　　think big 夢想要大
make it happen 主動積極　　pushy adj. 咄咄逼人　　nonsense n. 廢話

Ⓒ Imagine someone telling you that you are "worth your salt." If you hadn't heard that phrase before, you might be confused, especially if it seemed out of context with the conversation. The modern meaning is __1__ "you have earned your reward, be it your salary or just __2__ for a job well done." But how that idiom __3__ is a different story.

The popular belief is that it __4__ to Roman soldiers, who were paid with salt instead of currency, salt __5__ quite valuable at the time. Some linguists believe that the word "salary" also came from the same Latin source. Many idioms and cliches have a long history, which can be traced back to familiar __6__ such as the Bible, Shakespeare, and even more distant sources like Confucius, the Chinese philosopher. There are countless examples to be found in literature, politics, film, sports and music as well. Even the phrase "rock 'n' roll" started out __7__ a slang term to describe that style of music.

The English language is always changing, so new terms are __8__ to match new trends and new realities. But where does it end? There are __9__ unique cliches to suit every moment, and it isn't possible to learn them all, even for a native English speaker. The best thing to do is keep your chin up and take it one step __10__.

_____ 1. (A) that (B) what (C) when (D) because
_____ 2. (A) punishment (B) technique (C) application (D) praise
_____ 3. (A) resulted from (B) came from (C) came about (D) brought about
_____ 4. (A) turns back (B) dates back (C) traced back (D) holds back
_____ 5. (A) had been (B) being (C) was (D) been
_____ 6. (A) roots (B) glances (C) resources (D) acquaintances
_____ 7. (A) with (B) in (C) as (D) for
_____ 8. (A) abolished (B) discovered (C) translated (D) coined
_____ 9. (A) more than one (B) thousands of (C) many a (D) a good deal of
_____ 10. (A) at times (B) for the time being
            (C) at a time (D) just in time

---

context n. 上下文　*salary* n. 薪水　*currency* n. 貨幣　*linguist* n. 語言學家
politics n. 政治　*slang* n. 俚語　*cliche* n. 陳腔濫調；俗語
keep one's chin up 別氣餒

 **Part II : Translation Practice**

Sentence Patterns

1. S₁ + V₁-ing/V₁-en, S₂ + V₂

此句型為獨立分詞構句，當兩個句子中間省略連接詞時，若主詞不同需保留，其中一句的動詞改為分詞形式，主動用 V-ing，被動則用 V-en。

例：There **was** no bus, **so** we had to walk home.

　　→ There **being** no bus, we had to walk home.

例：**As** he saw the dream girl, his heart **started** to beat faster.

　　→ He saw the dream girl, his heart **starting** to beat faster.

2. be worth + N/V-ing

be worth + N/Ving 表示「價值／值得…」之意。

例：This book **is worth** five hundred dollars.

　　His latest novel **is worth** reading because the plot is intriguing.

另外也可用 it pays to + V 句型來表示相同的意思。

Ⓐ

 Keywords ●━━━━━━━━━━━━━━━━━━━━━━━━━━━━━━━━━━━

1. 情境喜劇：*sitcom* (n.)

2. 集：*episode* (n.)　　字彙：*vocabulary* (n.)　　片語：*idiom/phrase* (n.)　　背誦：*memorize* (v.)

 Sample ●━━━━━━━━━━━━━━━━━━━━━━━━━━━━━━━━━━━━

1. 美國情境喜劇很好笑又有趣，很多學生喜歡看它們學英文。

American sitcoms **being** funny and interesting, many students like to watch them to learn English.

2. 每集所使用的字彙及片語很值得背起來。

The vocabulary and phrases used in each episode **are worth memorizing**.

B

Keywords •————————————————————————————————•

1.指涉：*allusion to N*　劇作家：*playwright* (n.)　對…有貢獻：*contribute to*

2.引言：*quotation* (n.)　每天使用：*in daily use*

Practice •————————————————————————————————•

1.在英文中對莎士比亞 (Shakespeare) 的指涉到處可發現，這名偉大的英國劇作家對英語很有貢獻。

_____

_____

2.很多他的引言還是每天被使用，而且很值得學習。

_____

_____

C

Keywords •————————————————————————————————•

1.俚語：*slang* (n.)　廣泛地：*widely* (adv.)　對話：*conversation* (n.)　校園中：*on campus*

2.常見的：*common* (adj.)　表達：*expression* (n.)　文化的：*cultural* (adj.)

　重要性：*significance* (n.)　注意：*pay attention to*

Practice •————————————————————————————————•

1.由於俚語在學校被廣泛地使用，外國學生可能覺得要去了解校園中的對話很困難。

_____

_____

2.有些常見的美國俚語表達是有文化上的重要性，值得好好注意。

_____

_____

Part I : Cloze Test

Ⓐ Michael Jackson, known around the world as the King of Pop, died at the age of 50. Jackson earned millions of fans around the world with his catchy songs and incredible dance moves. Michael Jackson __1__ to fame at the age of 11 as the lead singer of the Jackson 5, a singing group __2__ him and four of his brothers. By the late 1970s, Michael __3__ a successful solo artist, and his fame reached a new level with the release of the album *Thriller* in 1982, which won eight Grammy Awards and became the best-selling album __4__. Because of his achievement in music, more than 17,000 people attended a __5__ service for Jackson. Jackson's 11-year-old daughter, Paris, made a touching tribute to her father at the end of the ceremony, holding back tears to declare that Michael Jackson was "the best father you could ever imagine."

_____ 1. (A) aroused   (B) rose   (C) raised   (D) arose

_____ 2. (A) consisted of   (B) consisting of   (C) consists of   (D) consist of

_____ 3. (A) had become   (B) has become

        (C) will have become   (D) becomes

_____ 4. (A) at times   (B) time after time   (C) of all time   (D) all the time

_____ 5. (A) memorial   (B) sacrifice   (C) military   (D) psychological

---

Michael Jackson 麥克・傑克森　　*earn* v. 獲得　　*catchy* adj. 動聽的、易記的
incredible adj. 難以置信的　　*fame* n. 名聲　　*lead singer* 主唱
solo artist 單飛歌手　　*release* n. 發行　　*Grammy Awards* 葛萊美獎
best-selling adj. 最暢銷　　*touching* adj. 感人的　　*tribute* n. 獻詞

Ⓑ   In a surprising upset, Scottish singing sensation Susan Boyle finished second in the television competition *Britain's Got Talent*. The unlikely star shocked judges and charmed people around the world after her ___1___ for the show. Originally, the judges seemed to dismiss her before she even started singing because of her ___2___ appearance and simple background. Her performance, however, stunned and touched every one. More than 100 million people around the world watched Boyle's performance on YouTube, and she became an overnight celebrity. The media quickly embraced Boyle ___3___ modest background made her story even more appealing. Before the show, she had no job ___4___ had cared for her sick mother for many years. Boyle worried that her unassuming looks would lead people to prejudge her, but her mother's death ___5___ her to pursue her dream. And the result proved her to be a diamond in the rough.

_____ 1. (A) contribution   (B) review   (C) audition   (D) registration

_____ 2. (A) stunning   (B) plain   (C) cunning   (D) attractive

_____ 3. (A) , who   (B) of whom   (C) with   (D) , whose

_____ 4. (A) along with   (B) but   (C) in addition to (D) nor

_____ 5. (A) prompted   (B) convinced   (C) discouraged   (D) devoted

---

upset n. 意外擊敗、冷門   *unlikely* adj. 不太可能的   *dismiss* v. 不接受
stun v. 使震驚、令人印象深刻   *touch* v. 感動   *overnight* adj. 一夜之間
embrace v. 接納   *unassuming* adj. 保守的、不起眼的   *prejudge* v. 對…有成見
diamond in the rough 未琢磨的鑽石

Britain's Got Talent (BGT) 英國星光大道選秀節目

為英國獨立電視台 (ITV) 製作的電視選秀節目，目的在發掘業餘的影藝人才。自 2007 年 6 月 9 日開播，至今已產生許多英國的歌壇新秀，如第一屆的冠軍是手機銷售員出身的保羅‧帕茲 (Paul Potts)，以及當時六歲的亞軍得主康妮‧塔波特 (Connie Talbot)，第三屆亞軍的蘇珊‧波爾 (Susan Boyle) 等。

Ⓒ Although the Beatles broke up in 1970, their music remains as popular as __1__. Now, thanks to a new video game, people can relive the magic. In *The Beatles: Rock Band*, players take on the roles of John, Paul, George, and Ringo, playing and singing along __2__ 45 of the band's best-known songs.

Because the Beatles carefully control their image, some people were __3__ that they should lend their likenesses to a video game. It started when Dhani Harrison (son of the late George Harrison) met Harmonix, the company that produced the graphics for the video game, and discussed the idea of creating something that would honor the Beatles' __4__. Paul McCartney and Ringo Starr, the two remaining Beatles, __5__ the plan.

The result is a musical trip through time. All eras of the band's works are __6__. Players earn points for their skill in following the on-screen prompts for their instruments, and poor performers can get booed off the stage.

Some reviewers have called *The Beatles: Rock Band* the most important video game ever invented __7__ it demonstrates the band's universal appeal. For people who grew up listening to the Beatles, the game is a chance to travel back in time; for those __8__ familiar with the band, it is a chance to experience the most influential rock music ever made. In __9__ case, the game lets people feel __10__ it was like to be one of the Fab Four.

_____ 1. (A) it   (B) was   (C) never   (D) ever
_____ 2. (A) in   (B) to   (C) for   (D) against
_____ 3. (A) surprised   (B) relieved   (C) content   (D) confident
_____ 4. (A) legacy   (B) tragedy   (C) determination (D) instruction
_____ 5. (A) frowned upon (B) agreed to   (C) objected to   (D) cut down on
_____ 6. (A) omitted   (B) stated   (C) featured   (D) inspected
_____ 7. (A) therefore   (B) due to   (C) but   (D) because
_____ 8. (A) less   (B) more   (C) only   (D) who
_____ 9. (A) both   (B) either   (C) neither   (D) all
_____ 10. (A) that   (B) how   (C) what   (D) whether

---

break up 拆散、解散   *relive* v. 重溫   *take on* 擔任   *likeness* n. 肖像
legacy n. 遺留之物   *feature* v. 以…為特色   *on-screen* adj. 在螢幕上的
prompt n. 提示   *boo* v. 給…噓聲、喝倒采   *reviewer* n. 評論家
demonstrate v. 證明   *The Fab Four* 披頭四人組

 **Part II : Translation Practice**

Sentence Patterns

1. whose

whose 為關係代名詞，表示先行詞的「所有格」用法，有時可代換為 of which。

例：Ha Jin is a relatively newcomer **whose** grasp of English is so masterly that he has won Pen/Faulkner awards twice.

例：This is the boy **whose** mother is our principal.

I like the house **whose** roof is red.

= I like the house the roof **of which** is red.

2. S_1 + V_1 + because S_2 + V_2 = S + V + because of + N

because 為連接詞，須連接兩句子，為「因為、由於…」之意。

because of = due to = owing to = as a result of = thanks to 後面需接名詞。

例：The judges seemed to dismiss Susan Boyle before she even started singing **because of** her plain appearance and simple background.

例：We finished the project **because** he came to help us in time.

= We finished the project **because of** his timely help.

 A

 Keywords •••

1. 風靡：*take...by storm*   流行指標：*fashion icon*

2. 崇拜：*worship* (v.)   多才多藝的：*multi-talented* (adj.)   獨特的：*unique* (adj.)

舞台表演：*stage performance* (n.)

 Sample ••

1. **Lady Gaga**，她的音樂風靡全世界，現在是流行指標。

Lady Gaga, **whose** music takes the world by storm, now becomes a fashion icon.

2. 青少年崇拜這個多才多藝的歌手，因為她獨樹一格的舞台表演。

Teenagers worship this multi-talented singer **because of** her unique stage performance.

Ⓑ

✈ Keywords

1. 由…所組成：*consist of*　手足：*sibling*（n.）　經得起時間考驗：*stand the test of time*
2. 熱門的事物：*hit*（n.）　與眾不同的：*distinct*（adj.）　風格：*style*（n.）

✈ Practice

1. 木匠兄妹 (The Carpenters) 是由兩個兄妹組成的，他們美麗的歌曲經得起時間的考驗。

_____

2. 他們的歌成為熱門曲子，因為他們在當時創立一種與眾不同的音樂風格。

_____

_____

Ⓒ

✈ Keywords

1. 義大利文：*Italian*（n.）　流行音樂界：*pop music*　傳奇的人物：*legend*（n.）
2. 得到…認可：*achieve/gain/get/receive/win...recognition*　全球的：*global*（adj.）
　勇於挑戰：*dare to challenge*　傳統觀念：*convention*（n.）

✈ Practice

1. Madonna，她的名字在義大利文是 My Lady 之意，在流行音樂界是個傳奇人物。

_____

_____

2. 她得到全球的認可肯定，因為她勇於挑戰社會傳統觀念。

_____

_____

Part I : Cloze Test

(A)   In the past, men in Asia were not very concerned about their looks. Most were __1__ worried about making money and getting ahead at work. However, during the past few years, more and more men in Asia have begun to pay closer attention to their __2__. These men have been called "metrosexuals." Working out for hours in the gym every day, metrosexuals would spare no efforts to keep fit; __3__, they are buying moisturizers and skin lotions to look good. These men are also using a large amount of their salary to buy the latest fashions, including brand-name and designer clothes. There are many reasons for the __4__ growth of metrosexual population. Some Asian metrosexuals say that looking good gives them more confidence. Others hope it will bring them success in the business world. One thing is clear, __5__ the reason. The metrosexual trend is big in Asia.

_____ 1. (A) very   (B) more   (C) less   (D) never

_____ 2. (A) degree   (B) performance   (C) appearance   (D) relationship

_____ 3. (A) in addition   (B) in contrast   (C) on the whole   (D) instead

_____ 4. (A) shrinking   (B) convincing   (C) exploding   (D) inspiring

_____ 5. (A) whether   (B) despite   (C) whatever   (D) except

---

be concerned about 關注⋯   *metrosexual* n. 都會美型男   *gym* n. 健身房
spare no effort to V 不遺餘力去⋯   *keep fit* 保持身材   *moisturizer* n. 保濕霜
skin lotion n. 潤膚乳液   *fashion* n. 流行服飾   *brand-name* adj. 名牌的
big adj. 狂熱的；受歡迎的

Ⓑ Playing video games can be a beneficial family activity. Many of today's parents __1__ 30 or 40 grew up playing *Pac-Man*, and even as adults, they still enjoy video games. That's hardly surprising. What is surprising is __2__ video games, long criticized for taking people away from friends and family, are turning out to be a way for parents and children to communicate. Parents say that playing Wii or video games such as *Mario Party* offers them a rare chance to relate to their children as __3__, because being stronger or older has nothing to do with winning. In fact, children often have the technical edge __4__ their parents. Playing video games also gives parents something in common to talk about with their children, even though it is mostly "geek talk" about computers; __5__, gaming time offers parents and children an informal opportunity to discuss family issues.

_____ 1. (A) to be aged   (B) aging   (C) age   (D) aged
_____ 2. (A) that   (B) how   (C) which   (D) ✕
_____ 3. (A) rivals   (B) inferiors   (C) equals   (D) seniors
_____ 4. (A) for   (B) over   (C) with   (D) in
_____ 5. (A) otherwise   (B) instead
　　　　 (C) what's worse   (D) more importantly

---

beneficial adj. 有益的　*Pac-Man* 小精靈　*turn out to* 變成　*Mario Party* 瑪利歐派對
relate v. 瞭解、體恤　*edge* n. 優勢　*in common* 共同、相同　*issue* n. 議題

Ⓒ   In the age of political correctness (PC), companies are removing traditional stereotypes and images from advertising. Perhaps the best example of this change is Darkie toothpaste, now called Darlie, with a more race-__1__ image on the box. But __2__ different races have been treated with more respect in recent years, women seem to have been left behind in the PC movement. Nowhere __3__ more obvious than in beer commercials.

Around the world, beer companies continue to exploit female sexuality. Bars and stores in nearly every country have posters of women in swimsuits __4__ their beer of choice. The German beer, Saint Pauli Girl, __5__ the image of a servant girl on the bottle. A video from a beer festival in Kenting, popular on the Internet, shows thinly dressed young ladies dancing on stage. Unfortunately, it is not just women's sexuality __6__ is still being exploited in beer commercials. An Italian ad pokes fun at the stereotypical idea that "women are bad drivers." A group of female lawyers, __7__, did not see the humor. They decided to sue the beer company __8__ being sexist and discriminatory.

It is unclear why women have been largely ignored by beer companies in the PC movement. Perhaps it is because of the undeniable biological differences between men and women and the ways __9__ men and women interact, especially when drinking. Whatever the cause, it is important that we __10__ this issue.

_____ 1. (A) neutral   (B) sensitive   (C) related   (D) based

_____ 2. (A) because   (B) while   (C) until   (D) despite

_____ 3. (A) it is   (B) is this   (C) it would   (D) does it

_____ 4. (A) hold   (B) to hold   (C) held   (D) holding

_____ 5. (A) stars   (B) stresses   (C) features   (D) acknowledges

_____ 6. (A) which   (B) that   (C) what   (D) who

_____ 7. (A) therefore   (B) instead   (C) however   (D) additionally

_____ 8. (A) as   (B) in   (C) with   (D) for

_____ 9. (A) ×   (B) why   (C) where   (D) which

_____ 10. (A) lose sight of   (B) get rid of   (C) give thought to   (D) take for granted

---

political correctness (PC) 政治正確   *stereotype* n. 刻板形象   *Darkie* 黑人牙膏
commercial n. 廣告   *exploit* v. 剝削、濫用   *sexuality* n. 性感   *poke fun at* 取笑
discriminatory adj. 歧視的   *biological difference* 生理差異

 **Part II : Translation Practice**

Sentence Patterns

1. S + have + a lot/little/much/nothing/something + to do with
have...to do with 表示「和…有關」，中間可放入 nothing, little, something, much 來修飾。 例：Being stronger or older **has nothing to do with** winning.
2. Nowhere/Never/Little + Be-V + S 　　Nowhere/Never/Little + Aux + S + V
否定詞或帶有否定意義的詞置於句首時，句子必須以「倒裝」句型來呈現。be 動詞和主詞掉換位置，如為一般動詞，則須改為助動詞 + 主詞 + 原型動詞。另外相關的否定副詞有：neither/no sooner...than/no longer/rarely/seldom 等。 例：**Nowhere** is this more obvious than in beer commercials.

Ⓐ

 Keywords •───────────────────────────•

1. 生態旅遊：*ecotourism*（n.）　越來越多的，增加的：*increasing*（adj.）　關注：*concern*（n.）
　環境：*environment*（n.）

2. 過去：*in the past*　想到：*occur to...*　古蹟：*historic site*　破壞：*destruction*（n.）

 Sample •───────────────────────────•

1. 生態旅遊和我們對環境越來越多的關注很有關係。

　Ecotourism **has a lot to do with** our increasing concern for the environment.

2. 過去人們都沒想過，拜訪古蹟可能會帶來破壞。

　In the past, **never did it occur to people** that visiting a historic site could bring destruction.

Ⓑ

Keywords

1. 線上書店：*online bookstore*　　受歡迎；流行；普及：*popularity* (n.)

　取得，使用（電腦、資訊）：*...access to*

2. 沒有地方：*nowhere* (adv.)　　瀏覽：*browse* (v.)　　在網路上：*on the Internet*

Practice

1. 線上書店的日益普及，和現在容易上網有些關係。

2. 沒有比在網路上，能讓人們瀏覽更多書的地方。

Ⓒ

Keywords

1. 偏好：*preference* (n.)　　單身的：*single* (adj.)　　影響：*influence* (n.)

2. 扶養：*raise* (v.)

Practice

1. 寧願選擇單身，和西方文化的影響沒有任何關係。

2. 一個單身的人很少需要扶養太多家人。

英文素養寫作攻略

郭慧敏　編著

108 課綱英文素養寫作必備寶典

將寫作理論具象化，打造一套好理解的寫作方法！

掌握關鍵，瞄準致勝！

學測指考英文致勝句型

王隆典　編著

致勝關鍵

★關鍵１　名師嚴選80個句型重點！
完整收錄大考常見句型，並比較易混淆的句型，清楚掌握重點，舉一反三。

★關鍵２　解說清楚明瞭一看就懂！
重點一目瞭然，說明淺顯易懂好吸收，考前衝刺神隊友，迅速提升考場即戰力。

★關鍵３　隨堂評量實戰練習現學現用！
隨書附贈20回隨堂評量，及時檢視學習成果、熟悉句型，以收事半功倍之效。

From Cloze Test to Translation Practice

從克漏字到
翻譯練習　解析本

王郁惠、鄭翔嬬　編著

獨家首創
反覆練習
模式

三民書局

Keys & Analysis

Unit 1

Part I: Cloze Test

Ⓐ

　　大多數的蝙蝠只在夜晚覓食時才出來活動。為了能在黑暗裡到處行動，牠們仰賴一種叫回聲定位的特殊方法來適應黑暗。蝙蝠會發出高頻聲波，並且以脈衝方式發射出去。那些聲脈衝會反射回來形成回音，這樣可讓蝙蝠知道牠與物體之間的距離。由於這種方法靠的是聲音，所以大多數蝙蝠都有一雙超級敏銳的大耳朵。

　　此外，許多種類的蝙蝠在口鼻附近有形狀奇怪的皮膚突起物。這些突起就像皮瓣一樣，可以用來控制聲脈衝。

　　為了要在一片漆黑裡獵取蟲子，蝙蝠還需要優越的飛行技術。牠們的翅膀是由皮革般的皮膚所構成，在兩手的指間延展開來。沒錯，蝙蝠的翅膀就是牠們的手。

　　這些真的是令人驚奇的適應環境的特徵，讓蝙蝠可以飛行、獵食，以及在黑暗中暢行無阻。

1.	C	此處 how 所引導的名詞子句，作 know 的受詞，為間接問句，主詞與動詞的位置須對調，故選(C)。
2.	B	(A)明理、明智的(B)敏感的(C)轟動的、聳人聽聞的(D)多愁善感的。蝙蝠回聲定位的系統需仰賴聲音，因此大多數蝙蝠的耳朵都很大而且很敏感，故選(B)。
3.	A	長在蝙蝠口鼻附近的皮膚生長物，可以用來控制聲音的脈動。be used to + V 被用於…，是 S + use + O + to V 的被動語態，故選(A)；be used to + V-ing 表示「習慣於做…」。
4.	B	(A)部分 + make up + 整體，為「組成」(B)物品 be made of 原料，仍可辨認出原料，「製造、構成」之意(C)理解、認出(D)物品 be made from 原料，無法辨認出原料，為「製造、做」之意。蝙蝠的翅膀 (事實上是手) 是像皮革一樣的皮膚所構成的，故選(B)。
5.	D	(A)態度(B)突破(C)示範、示威；(D)特色、特徵。這些特徵 (包括敏銳的耳朵可以聽聲辨位、口鼻附近可以控制聲音脈動的皮膚生長物、像翅膀的手) 是蝙蝠適應環境在黑暗中飛行、捕捉獵物的方法，故選(D)。

Ⓑ

　　在嬰兒學會說話之前，有很重要的一點是，他們能學習將父母的表情與說話聲音連結配對。有趣的是，一項動物研究顯示，獼猴具有跟人類相似的配對能力。

　　在那項研究實驗中，數隻猴子被安排待在兩台電視機前，兩台電視各自播放一段無聲影片。其中一個螢幕上顯示一隻恆河猴發出友善的「咕」聲時臉上慣有的表情。另一個螢幕上則是那隻猴子在發出生氣的「威脅」聲時所做出的不同表情。接下來，科學家用擴音器播放「咕」聲或「威脅」聲。聽到聲音信號之後，那些猴子移動到正確的螢幕，看著和聲音相符的正確表情。研究人員還注意到，當配對的臉孔發出友善的「咕」聲時，那些猴子觀看的時間會比較長。

　　不管是人類還是猴子都一樣，他們將聲音與意思互相連結的能力，使他們能夠與自己的同類溝通。

1.	B	文章第一句提到，在嬰兒掌控說話能力之前，先學會將語音和父母的臉部表情做配對是很重要的，接著提到恆河猴和人類很像，也有這種配對的能力，故選(B)。
2.	C	此處為分詞構句，原句為：… monkeys were placed in front of two TVs, and each (TV) played a silent film. 省略連接詞 and，兩個子句主詞不同 (monkeys, each TV)，予以保留，動詞主動改為 V-ing，故選(C)。
3.	D	前面提到兩台電視機，一台是… (on one monitor) 另一是… (on the other monitor)，故選(D)。
4.	A	從語意判斷可知，是在聽到提示的聲音之後，猴子會到相對應的螢幕前，看發出該聲音的臉孔，故選(A)。
5.	C	(A)結合(B)命令(C)溝通(D)競爭。本文認為猴子和人類一樣有連結語音和意義的能力，這樣的能力使他們可以和自己的同類溝通，故選(C)。

Ⓒ

　　許多動物都具有一種稱為「保護偽裝」的能力，可以避免被發現而遭受攻擊。「保護偽裝」是指動物的顏色或外型看起來與周圍環境融合一起。

　　例如，鹿、松鼠和老鼠等動物有樹木和森林地面土壤的顏色。許多像是鯊魚和海豚等海洋生物都有灰藍色的外觀，使牠們較容易融入光線微弱的水中環境。有很多種動物發展出特殊的適應性能力，讓牠們能隨著環境變化來改變身上的顏色。動物的周遭環境產生最大變化

的情形之一，是發生在季節轉換的時候。森林在夏季也許都是綠色與褐色，但到了冬季會覆蓋上一層白雪，使顏色鮮豔的動物容易成為受攻擊的目標。為了應付這種變化，許多鳥類以及像狐狸與兔子等動物，會依不同時節生長出不同顏色的毛皮或羽毛。有些藏匿技術高超的動物，例如像變色龍與章魚，已學會如何立刻依環境變化改變身體的顏色。而有些動物會像某種蝴蝶一樣完全不躲藏，把自己偽裝成危險的東西來迷惑掠食者。

在世界上各個地方，你會發現動物的各種保護偽裝。這種適應能力，比起牙齒或腳爪等威脅性防衛武器通常是較有效的求生方式。畢竟，避免注意比非得展開戰鬥要好許多。

1.	C	(A)帶來、導致(B)以…維生(C)混合(D)求助某人。第一句提到許多動物發展出偽裝的能力，讓牠們不被攻擊者 (掠食者) 發現，因此可知，所謂偽裝就是動物的形狀或顏色和周圍的環境看起來十分相近，而形成保護，故選(C)。
2.	D	許多像鯊魚和海豚等的海洋生物有種灰藍色，這使得牠們較容易融入水底輕柔微亮的顏色，此處為 make it + adj. + (for sb.) + to V 的句型，it 為虛受詞，真正的受詞是 to V，此句中，形容詞 easier 為受詞補語，用來修飾 to blend in with the soft light underwater，故選(D)。
3.	A	許多動物發展出適應環境的方法，讓牠們隨著環境的變化而改變顏色，此處為 let + O + V 的句型，使役動詞 let 之後，若受詞與其後動詞為主動關係則用原形動詞，故選(A)。
4.	D	(A)渴望、欲望(B)工具(C)允諾、承諾(D)靶子、目標。夏天森林是綠色和褐色，但冬天被白雪覆蓋，這使得色彩鮮豔的動物很容易成為掠食者的目標，故選(D)。
5.	A	(A)處理應付(B)前往(C)安排、注意(D)調查。當周圍環境改變時，許多鳥類和狐狸、兔子這類的動物就會視季節的更迭，藉由長出不同的皮毛或羽毛的顏色，來應付這樣的變化，故選(A)。
6.	D	此處為關係子句 which depends on the time of year 所省略而來的分詞片語，用來修飾前面的句子，此處為主動，故選(D)。
7.	D	(A)代表(B)更別說…(C)與…有關(D)與…一致。例如變色龍和章魚這些有技巧的躲藏者，會瞬間改變自己的顏色和四周的環境一致，故選(D)。

8.	B	(A)設計(B)偽裝(C)分開(D)主宰、支配。有些種類的蝴蝶根本不躲藏，而是把自己偽裝成危險的生物來混淆掠食者，故選(B)。
9.	A	(A)有侵略性的(B)有建設性的(C)實驗的(D)有影響力的。文中提到的這些適應環境的偽裝，比起像牙齒、爪子這類具有侵略性的防衛武器，反而是更有效的生存工具，故選(A)。
10.	C	(A)更糟的是(B)相反地(C)畢竟(D)此外。此處再進一步說明，畢竟，被攻擊者完全地忽略是比要和對方打一場架來得好多了，故選(C)。

Part II: **Translation Practice**

B	1.	Hummingbirds' long and slender beaks **allow** them **to** probe into flowers for food.
	2.	Moreover, their stiff feathers **let** their wings **beat** fast for many hours at a time.
C	1.	Polar bears' white fur **allows** them **to** easily blend in with the snow and ice in the Arctic.
	2.	Furthermore, their thick fur and fat **let** them **stay** warm in a freezing cold climate.

Unit 2

Part I: **Cloze Test**

Ⓐ

有些種類的鯨魚屬於世上最稀有的生物。牠們生存的最大威脅是人類的獵捕——也就是捕鯨產業。

1868 年，第一艘配有魚叉槍——設計用來對鯨魚發射魚叉的槍枝——的捕鯨船從挪威駛出。這些新型的捕鯨船行駛快速，能追捕最巨大的鯨魚。超過一百年的時間，商業捕鯨一直都是大規模的產業。數以百計的捕鯨船捕捉了成千上萬的鯨魚，不久之後，藍鯨、抹香鯨、座頭鯨以及其他許多種類都瀕臨絕種。1980 年代，國際捕鯨委員會決定要全面禁止捕鯨。只有挪威和日本不顧其他許多國家的抗議，仍繼續獵捕鯨魚。

即使今天，也就是多數捕鯨活動終止 20 年之後，北露脊鯨大約只剩下 600 隻。數量之所以沒有增加，是因為鯨魚的繁衍速度不足以取代死亡的鯨魚。

1.	D	(A)企圖(B)努力(C)支持(D)威脅。從語意可判斷，人類的獵殺 (捕鯨業) 是對鯨魚存活最大的威脅，故選(D)。

2.	B	(A)提醒(B)維持、保持(C)保有(D)撤退。從語意可知，新的捕鯨船既快速又可追捕最大的鯨魚，因此 100 年來，商業捕鯨一直是很興盛的產業，故選(B)。
3.	D	(A)爆發(B)熄滅(C)突出、與眾不同(D)去除、消滅。前半句提到數百艘的捕鯨船捕撈了數千頭的鯨魚，因此很快地藍鯨、抹香鯨、座頭鯨和其他鯨魚都快要被捕捉殆盡，故選(D)。
4.	A	儘管許多其他國家抗議，日本和挪威仍舊獵捕鯨魚。despite 和 in spite of 一樣，之後接名詞，故選(A)。though 為連接詞，之後接子句；regardless 需接 of 再接名詞；even 為副詞。
5.	C	此處為句型 there is/are + N + V-ing/V-en，若 N 可以主動做某個動作，則用 V-ing；若 N 為某個動作的接受者，則用 V-en。此句說明即使大部分捕鯨業已停止約 20 年了，也只剩大約 6 百頭的北露脊鯨存留下來。leave 此處做「剩餘、遺留」解，故選(C)。此處若選(D) leaving，則做「離開」解，在此語意不合。

Ⓑ

約在 1598 年首度發現的度度鳥，是種不會飛的大型鳥類，只曾出現在印度洋上的模里西斯島。許多人相信，早期的水手將度度鳥視為新鮮肉品的來源，捕殺到牠們絕種。然而，這看法已遭到反駁，因為度度鳥的肉據說非常難吃。

度度鳥之所以滅絕，是因為人類闖入牠們獨特的生存環境。早期的移民人口擾亂了度度鳥的棲息地，他們引進外來品種的動物，那些動物不是獵食牠們，就是破壞鳥巢。最後一次確認有見到度度鳥的蹤跡是在 1681 年。絕跡的度度鳥是歷史紀錄上首次列為絕種的物種。正因如此，度度鳥已成為滅絕的象徵。像是「如同度度鳥一樣消逝」或「走上與度度鳥相同的道路」等用語，如今都用來形容已經永遠消失或即將永遠消失的事物。

1.	B	(A)此外(B)然而(C)此外(D)因此。前一句提到許多人相信早年水手們視度度鳥為新鮮肉類的來源，因此將牠們捕殺至絕種。但接著說到這種說法被駁斥，因為度度鳥的肉並不美味。因此前後語意轉折，故選(B)。
2.	B	(A)保護、保育(B)打擾、干擾(C)提供(D)維持。第一句提到度度鳥絕種的原因是因為人類侵入了牠們獨特的生存環境。接著說明早期的定居者干擾了度度鳥的棲息地，故選(B)。

3.	C	(A)繼續(B)依賴(C)掠食(D)打開。此句說明早期的定居者引進了新的動物，而這些新動物不是會掠食度度鳥就是會破壞牠們的巢穴，故選(C)。
4.	D	(A)結果(B)代表團(C)特權(D)象徵。前句提到度度鳥的消失是歷史上第一個有官方紀錄的絕種物種，因此渡渡鳥成為了絕種的象徵，故選(D)。
5.	C	lose 的動詞三態為 lose-lost-lost；「像度度鳥一樣消逝」和「踏上度度鳥的後塵」這樣的說法，在今日被用來描述已經或將要永遠消失的東西，此處須用被動，故選(C)。

Ⓒ

有愈來愈多的動物正處於瀕臨絕種的危機。就連美國深愛的國鳥禿鷹都面臨過這種可怕的命運。曾經，禿鷹在除了夏威夷州以外的其他 50 州都找得到，但到了 1967 年時，只剩下幾百隻而已。

有兩項原因導致了禿鷹的數量減少。從 1940 年代開始，為了趕上人口成長的速度，美國的城市不斷迅速發展。隨著城市進一步擴展到鄉村，許多樹木遭到砍伐，破壞了禿鷹所棲息的森林。

也大約是在這段時期，農民為了控制蟲害，開始在農作物上噴灑一種叫 DDT 的有毒藥劑。老鼠吃了作物，同時把毒劑一起吃下肚。DDT 也隨水流入湖泊與河川，毒害魚類。當禿鷹吃下中毒的老鼠與魚類時，DDT 便進入食物鏈之中。毒劑導致雌性禿鷹產下異常薄殼的蛋，使很多蛋都無法孵化。科學家警告，除非立刻採取辦法拯救禿鷹，否則牠們很快就會永遠消失。

1972 年，美國政府下令禁止使用 DDT。隨著毒劑從食物鏈中消失，禿鷹的數量開始回升。1974 年，美國大約只有 791 對築巢的禿鷹。到了 1998 年，這個數字已上升到約 5,948 對。這表示如果人類肯認真而堅定地做出努力，就算是最危急的情況也都能扭轉過來。

1.	A	「面臨」的用法有 face + O = confront + O = encounter + O = meet with + O = be faced with + O = be confronted with + O。此句說明即使深受美國人喜愛的國家象徵——禿鷹，也面臨這樣恐怖的命運。(B)應改為 confronted；(C)應改為 met with；(D)應改為 encountered。
2.	A	(A)趕上(B)和解(C)忍受(D)和某人商量某事。此處說明從 1940 年代開始，美國的城市持續地快速成長，是為了趕上日益增加的人口，故選(A)。

3.	B	隨著城市拓展至鄉村，許多樹木都被砍掉，破壞了曾是禿鷹棲息地的森林，that were the bald eagle's habitat 為形容詞子句，用來修飾先行詞 the forests。
4.	B	此為分裂句 It is...that... 的句型，it is 和 that 之間放入要強調的部份，句子剩餘的部份置於 that 之後。此句原本為 Around this time farmers began spraying a poison called DDT on their crops to control pests.；此處要強調的部分為時間，that 亦可替換成 when。
5.	C	poison 作「毒殺」解，此句為分詞構句，原句為 DDT was also making its way into lakes and rivers, and poisoned the fish.，DDT 也流入了湖泊和河流中，因此毒害了魚，省略連接詞 and 後，主動用 V-ing，故選(C)。
6.	D	「臥躺、位於」的動詞三態為 lie, lay lain；「說謊」的動詞三態為 lie, lied, lied；「產卵」的動詞三態為 lay, laid, laid，此處說明 DDT 這種毒使得母鷹產下的蛋，蛋殼異常的薄，cause + O + to V，故選(D)。
7.	D	(A)既然(B)一旦、曾經(C)當、然而(D)除非。科學家警告除非立即採取行動拯救禿鷹，否則牠們很快將永遠消失，故選(D)。
8.	B	(A)允許、准許(B)禁止(C)注意(D)促進、推廣。1972年，美國政府禁止 DDT 的使用，下一句也提及 DDT 從食物鏈中被移除，故選(B)。
9.	D	此處為句型，「By + 過去時間, S + had + V-en」，到 1998 年時，這數字已上升至 5,948 對，主要子句用過去完成式，故選(D)。
10.	C	(A)分析(B)使複雜(C)使相反、顛倒(D)容忍、忍耐。這篇文章主要說明禿鷹的復育與成效，這個事件顯示，如果人們下定決心努力以赴，即使最危急的狀況也可以被扭轉，故選(C)。

Part II: Translation Practice

B	1.	**There are** around twenty thousand polar bears **living** in the wild at present.
	2.	**By the time** scientists realized that global warming damaged their habitat, the ecology in the Arctic **had been** greatly **altered**.

C	1.	**There is** not enough natural habitat **left** to sustain giant pandas in the world.
	2.	**By the time** enough bamboo forests are restored, giant pandas **will have starved** to death.

Unit 3

Part I: Cloze Test

Ⓐ
　　當你進行運動競賽時，盡全力去贏得比賽很重要。但頂尖運動員還知道，真正重要的不是輸贏，而是比賽中的表現如何。

　　缺乏運動精神在許多方面都會破壞一場比賽。運動員侮辱對手或抱怨比賽過程中發生的事，會令所有人感到反感，為觀看的群眾立下壞榜樣。大多數最出色的運動員不管賽場上發生什麼事都會保持風度。

　　做個有風度的運動員還有其他好處。把情緒控制好也會使你表現得更出色。最優秀的教練與父母會教導孩子要努力比賽，並尊重他們參與的賽事。這些訣竅不僅在比賽中很受用，而且在學校和職場上也很有幫助。畢竟，沒有人喜歡跟沒風度的運動員比賽。

1.	B	not A but B 不是 A 而是 B。此處說明比賽時，重要的不是輸或贏 (whether you win or lose) 而是比賽的態度和過程 (how you play the game)，此外還需注意本句是一分裂句，it is...that...。
2.	C	(A)競爭、爭奪(B)打敗(C)侮辱、冒犯(D)發射、開辦。前一句提到缺乏運動家精神會使得比賽在許多方面受到破壞，此句接著舉例說明侮辱對手和抱怨比賽中發生的事，都是沒有運動家精神的表現。
3.	C	(A)期待(B)使終止、結束(C)立下壞榜樣(D)利用、佔便宜。此句接著說明這些沒有運動家精神的情況，會帶給每個人負面的觀感，同時也給觀眾立下壞榜樣。
4.	A	(A)好處(B)缺點(C)設施(D)榮譽、榮耀。本段後面提到若運動員能控制情緒，則能有較好的表現，此外運動家精神不只適用於比賽中，對學業或工作也很有幫助，可知此段在說明擁有運動家精神的好處。

| 5. | D | ㈎首先、一則㈏相反地㈐不久㈑畢竟。此句為結論句，說明畢竟沒有人喜歡和沒有運動家精神的人比賽。 |

Ⓑ

　　運動是有趣又健康的活動，受到許多人喜愛，但體育活動有受傷的風險。

　　運動傷害可分為急性或慢性兩種類型。急性傷害是突然發生的，例如：瘀傷、肌肉拉傷或骨折。然而，慢性傷害是經過時間累積產生的。舉例來說，疲勞性骨折是由於反覆過度使用而造成骨頭有輕微的裂傷。

　　當然，不管大家多麼小心，有時候還是會受傷。如果你受傷了，別試圖想忍痛繼續運動。你可以按照「RICE」的步驟處理傷害。這個頭字語裡的字母是提醒你要休息 (Rest)、冰敷 (Ice)、壓迫 (Compression) 和抬高 (Elevation)。這些做法有助於避免傷處腫脹，接著就能開始治療。

　　受傷的風險不該讓你懼怕起體育活動。反過來說，具有正確的危險意識可以讓運動既好玩又安全。

1.	B	㈎兩者皆是㈏兩者任一㈐兩者皆非㈑不僅…還…。此段說明運動傷害可分為急性和慢性兩種，故選㈏。
2.	B	㈎因此㈏然而㈐此外㈑同樣地。前句在說明急性運動傷害像是瘀青、肌肉拉傷和骨折等，是屬於突然發生的，與此句說明慢性運動傷害是經過一段時間逐漸形成的，語意出現轉折，故選㈏。
3.	C	㈎用藥過量㈏推翻㈐過度使用㈑體重過重。此句接上一句，舉例說明何謂慢性運動傷害，像是重力骨折 (stress fracture) 就是由於反覆的過度使用導致骨頭出現細微裂縫，故選㈐。
4.	C	㈎定義㈏暗示㈐字首縮略詞㈑智慧。從下一句可知 RICE 這縮略詞中每個字母各代表一項運動傷害時需要做的事情，故選㈐。
5.	D	㈎此外㈏因此㈐否則㈑而是、取而代之的是。前一句提到運動傷害的風險不應該讓我們因此而害怕運動，接著說明反倒是因為適當地注意這些危險，才能使運動更有趣也更安全，語意上出現轉折，故選㈑。

Ⓒ

　　每四年舉行一次的殘障奧運與奧運相似。不過，殘障奧運只有身體殘疾者才能參加。第一屆的殘障奧運是在 1948 年舉行。一開始的比賽是由二次世界大戰的傷殘軍人坐在輪椅上進行一些競賽，其中有許多人是遭受脊髓損傷。直到 1960 年才舉辦了正式的第一屆殘障奧運。從 2001 年以後，夏季與冬季的殘障奧運都與一般奧運一同舉行。從 2012 年開始，所有獲選主辦奧運的城市，必須也要主辦殘障奧運。

　　有些人或許會問，為什麼殘障人士的運動應該受到提倡？事實上，運動對他們在許多方面都能有所幫助。運動不但能增強他們的體力，也能增強他們的心理素質。運動也能幫助殘障人士建立自信。這點非常重要，因為只有當他們對自己有信心時，才能試圖開創成功的人生。參與運動給他們一個機會證明自己也能像其他人一樣靈活，同時還幫忙鼓勵其他數百萬的殘障人士。例如，德國的滑雪金牌得主安妮梅・施耐德儘管有一隻腿截肢到膝蓋以上，卻仍不斷贏得比賽。當她沒有進行訓練時，她會給予年輕殘障運動員和他們的父母一些指導與鼓舞，還會造訪復健中心，鼓勵那裡的年輕病患。她就像其他的殘障奧運選手，為所有人樹立了榜樣。

1.	B	㈎此外㈏然而㈐的確㈑或許。第一句雖然提到殘障奧運和奧運很相似，都是四年舉辦一次，但接著說明殘奧是為身心障礙人士所舉辦的，語意出現轉折，故選㈏。
2.	C	關係代名詞前可加上數量詞，如 all/many/some of + whom/which，此處 whom 代替前述的先行詞 the disabled soldiers of World War II。此空格若選㈎則必須在 many of them 前加上連接詞 and，或和前句分開寫成兩個句子，因為關係代名詞同時兼具有代名詞和連接詞的功能，但 them 只是代名詞。
3.	C	此句 it is...that 為強調句，是由 The first official Paralympic Games were not held until 1960. 改變而來，將要強調的部分 not until 1960 置於 it is 和 that 中間，剩餘的部分則放到 that 之後。
4.	D	㈎有鑑於㈏儘管㈐萬一、倘若㈑和…一起。從 2001 年起，夏季和冬季殘奧開始和奧運一起舉辦，故選㈑。
5.	C	此處為關係子句省略而來的分詞，原句為 ...any city that is chosen to host the Olympics must also host the Paralympics.，表被動，省略關係代名詞 that 後改為過去分詞 chosen，故選㈐。

6.	D	(A)區別(B)消滅(C)中斷、打斷(D)提倡。本文第一段在說明殘障奧運的由來和發展過程，接著第二段則在說明運動對身障人士的好處，此句承接上段，先點出有些人質疑為何要<u>提倡</u>這類運動，再開啟下文說明理由，故選(D)。
7.	A	A as well as B「不僅 B 而且 A」，此片語中 A 和 B 在文法結構上必須平行對稱，前半為 increase their physical strength 故後半為 make them mentally stronger，故選(A)。
8.	B	only when 放句首時要改為<u>倒裝</u>，原句為 They can try and make their life a success only when they have belief in themselves.。
9.	B	此處的用法為 have + O + OC，腿是被截肢的，表示被動，受詞補語用過去分詞 removed 當作形容詞，修飾 leg (受詞)。
10.	D	(A)吸引(B)導致、帶來(C)撞見 (某人) (D)當作。施耐德和許多其他殘奧選手一樣，都可<u>當作</u>所有人的模範。

Part II: Translation Practice

	1.	The coach **as well as** the players/**Not only** the players **but also** the coach understands that sports injuries are hard to avoid.
B	2.	Thus/Therefore, they do stretching exercises **not** to relax their muscles **but** to protect themselves.
C	1.	Through Paralympic Games **as well as** Olympic Games/**not only** Olympic Games **but also** Paralympic Games, outstanding athletes are honored for their excellent performance.
	2.	Their names will be remembered **not** because of their records **but** because of their perseverance.

Unit 4

Part I: Cloze Test

Ⓐ

棒球史上最糟糕的時刻之一是發生在 1919 年的世界大賽。那一年，辛辛那提紅人隊贏得了比賽，但所有人記得的都是他們的對手：芝加哥白襪隊。

有一群賭客想從這場系列賽裡賺取財富。白襪隊被看好能贏得比賽，所以以下注在白襪隊輸而且成真的話就能有很高的賠率。為了確保白襪隊輸掉比賽，那些賭客花錢收買其中八位球員，要他們故意失誤。這項計畫成功了，那些賭客因這些比賽發了大財。

系列賽結束之後，許多人對白襪隊的表現感到懷疑，因此組了大陪審團來調查比賽。最後，涉案的八位球員全都被逐出大聯盟。

芝加哥白襪隊因此蒙羞，甚至還陷入魔咒。他們一直到 2005 年才終於再次贏得世界大賽，與醜聞事件相隔了 86 年之久。

1.	C	what = the thing that，此句的主詞為 what 所引導的名詞子句 what everyone remembers，人們所記得的卻是他們 (Cincinnati Reds) 的敵隊——Chicago White Sox，故選(C)。
2.	D	此處敘述過去發生的事，故用 would lose。
3.	B	(A)至少(B)故意地 (intentionally) (C)接觸、聯繫(D)伸手所及的範圍。賭徒賄賂八位球員，要他們<u>故意</u>失誤，故選(B)。
4.	B	be involved in 涉及…；此處為關係子句 who were involved in the case 所省略而來的分詞片語，用來修飾 all eight players；涉入這案子的八位球員都被禁止出賽大聯盟，故選(B)。
5.	A	(A)醜聞(B)利益(C)活動(D)預算；直到 2005 年，也就是這醜聞案發生的 86 年後，芝加哥白襪隊才再次贏得世界大賽，故選(A)。

Ⓑ

所有運動都是「觀賞性運動」——意思是觀眾或球迷在安全的距離外觀看運動員比賽。但這條「看不見的」界線有漏洞。有球迷曾跨越界線，通常都導致悲慘的結果。例如在 1993 年，世界第一的網球選手莫妮卡·莎莉絲遭到一名德國球迷刺傷。2002 年，棒球的一壘指導教練湯姆·甘博瓦遭到一對父子攻擊。

造成球迷行使暴力的原因是什麼？有些人認為，在大多運動場都有販售的酒精飲料會助長球迷的熱情，使熱情轉變成暴力。歷史與文化也占了部分原因。如果是兩個國家互相競賽，而且在政治上彼此為敵，很容易就會有暴力發生。

運動賽事的管理當局已經考慮要在比賽活動當中禁止飲酒，有些還加強了維安措施。他們也已毫不猶豫

對違法的球迷與選手提出控訴。畢竟他們是應該阻止球迷煽動暴力的。

1.	A	(A)屏障、阻礙物(B)距離(C)地理(D)測量。前句提到觀眾或球迷是在一個安全距離之外觀賞運動員比賽，但這無形的<u>屏障</u>有漏洞，故選(A)。
2.	B	(A)具體的(B)不幸的、悲慘的(C)鼓舞人心的(D)正面的、積極的。從後面兩個例子 (網球選手被德國球迷刺傷、棒球教練被一對父子攻擊) 可知，一但球迷跨越了這個界線，通常都會帶來<u>不幸</u>的結果，故選(B)。
3.	B	此處為關係子句 which is sold in most sporting arena 所省略而來的分詞片語，用來修飾 the alcohol；多數運動場所販售的酒精飲料會讓球迷更興奮，而濫用熱情，故選(B)。
4.	D	(A)不惜任何代價(B)失控(C)無疑地(D)遙遠。此處提到歷史和文化也在球迷暴力中扮演重要的因素，如果是兩國比賽，再加上這兩國又是世仇，那麼暴力可說是<u>一觸即發</u>，故選(D)。
5.	C	charge sb. with... 控告某人 (罪名)。相似的用法還有 accuse sb. of...; sue sb. for...，故選(C)。

Ⓒ

　　班・強森通過百米終點線的那刻，觀眾都雀躍而起，場中充滿尖叫聲，他在首爾奧運創下 9.79 秒的紀錄，成為史上跑得最快的人。

　　僅僅三天之後，強森就被發現違規使用類固醇。他被摘下金牌，遭到禁賽。然而，他不是唯一一位因用藥而受罰的人。由於在現今這個殘酷的運動界裡，只有贏得比賽才重要，所以沒有人會費心考慮倫理道德和行為規範。世人一再為此類不堪事件受到震驚。

　　這種體能增進藥物的研發與使用，是科技發展所不希望發生的結果之一。醫生會收錢去取得並提供這些藥物，通常還會要求一大筆封口費。科學家則收錢研發會讓運動員的競爭力勝過其他人的新藥。

　　為了掃除這類惡劣的事件，已經有成立「世界反禁藥組織」在任何重要的國際體育競賽開始前，檢查選手是否使用類固醇。不過，該組織的成效難以認定。

　　奧運金牌是許多運動員的終極目標。他們陷入贏得獎牌的渴望之中，忘記了奧運的宗旨——頌揚人道精神。運動員採取作弊手段會讓他們的國家、球迷，甚至是全人類蒙羞。

1.	C	此處為關係子句 which made him the fastest human ever 所省略而來的分詞片語，用來修飾前面的句子；班・強森在首爾奧運以破記錄的 9.79 秒跨越了百米終點線，這使他成為有史以來最快的人，為主動之意故選(C)。
2.	B	(A)意識到的(B)有罪的(C)懷疑的(D)典型的。三天後，班・強森被揭發使用禁藥，故選(B)。
3.	B	此處為關係子句 that is punished for the use of drugs 所省略而來的分詞片語，用來修飾 the only person；班・強森並不是唯一因為使用禁藥而被罰的選手，為被動意涵故選(B)。
4.	A	(A)倫理道德(B)人類(C)目標(D)所有物、財產。在今日殘酷的運動世界中，唯一重要的是贏得比賽，因此沒有人會在乎倫理道德，此句後半還提到 code of conduct，其同義字為(A)。
5.	D	(A)有益的、有幫助的(B)顯著的、傑出的(C)暫時的(D)不受歡迎的。這類增進表現藥品的發展與使用是科技發展中<u>不願見到</u>的影響，故選(D)。
6.	B	seal 封緘、密封；此處為 keep + O + OC 的句型，使他們封口，用過去分詞 (sealed) 修飾 their lips。醫生會要求一大筆錢為這類非法使用禁藥的事保守秘密，故選(B)。
7.	A	(A)優勢(B)對手(C)勝利(D)天職、號召。有人付錢給科學家，要他們研發新的藥品，讓球員更有競爭<u>優勢</u>，故選(A)。
8.	C	(A)遇見(B)解雇(C)設立、裝設(D)轉變成。為了避免此類惡意違規事件，因此<u>設立</u>了世界反禁藥組織，在重要國際運動比賽之前，檢測運動員是否使用禁藥，故選(C)。
9.	A	(A)然而(B)此外(C)否則(D)因此。為防止禁藥違規而設立世界反禁藥組織，<u>但是</u>這組織是否成功很難下定論，前後有語意轉折，故選(A)。
10.	D	(A)迷戀、被騙(B)照顧(C)延遲、拖延(D)訴諸於 (不良手段)。運動員<u>採取</u>犯規的方法贏得勝利，讓他們的國家、球迷、甚至人類蒙羞，故選(D)。

Part II: Translation Practice

B	1.	**What** the athlete did to enhance his performance in the game **was** disgraceful.

	2.	He **was stripped** of his gold medal and **banned** from competing for life.
C	1.	**What** made the football fans lose their mind **was** that they drank too much alcohol.
	2.	They **were arrested** on the spot and later **charged** by the local police.

Unit 5

Part I: Cloze Test

Ⓐ

如果你感到疲勞，有背痛的毛病，或只是身材走樣，那麼瑜珈可以幫你解決問題。瑜珈具有五千年歷史，是風行全世界的一種運動與冥想方式。

瑜珈的美妙之處在於，它是以安全、有效又方便的方式幫你處理壓力。伸展動作會減輕身體疼痛，並幫助強健肌肉。冥想使心靈脫離憂慮。深呼吸能將身體內部的能量釋放出來。瑜珈藉由將身體與心靈合而為一，能同時處理壓力，比其他運動帶來更良好的效果。

許多人加入健身俱樂部，購買運動器材，或是從事團體運動。這麼做可能花費昂貴又耗費時間。相對來說，瑜珈可以在任何地方練習，不需要特殊的器材，而且可以單獨或一群人一起從事。最重要的是，做瑜珈帶來永久的體能，有助於日後紓解壓力！

1.	C	關係子句 that is practiced all over the world 是用來修飾 a 5,000-year-old form of exercise and meditation；瑜珈是一種有五千年歷史在世界各地都有人做的運動與冥想方式，此處須用被動，故選(C)。
2.	D	(A)意外(B)失敗(C)饑餓(D)壓力。從本段的最後一句 yoga treats stress... 可知，此處要填入(D)，瑜珈非常的好，因為它以一種安全、有效、方便的方式處理各種壓力的來源。
3.	B	release...from... 將…從…釋放出來，故選(B)。
4.	B	此處為關係子句 which provides better results than other exercises 所省略而來的分詞片語，用來修飾前面的句子；藉由結合身體與心靈，瑜珈同時處理壓力，這和其它運動相比，更能提供較好的效果，故選(B)。
5.	A	(A)獨自地(B)事先(C)每天的(D)免費的。此句與本段的第一句正好呈現對比，瑜珈可以在任何地

方做 (不需上健身房)，不用特殊的裝備 (不需買昂貴裝備)，也可以單獨或和團體一起做 (不需組隊)。

Ⓑ

有時候我們或許會羨慕魚兒在色彩繽紛的水中花園裡自由自在地游泳。為了進入水中世界裡遨遊，我們需要學習水肺潛水。水肺潛水 (SCUBA diving) 這個名稱的由來，是來自它字面上所代表的意義——自給式水中呼吸裝置 (Self Contained Underwater Breathing Apparatus)。意思是潛水者帶著在水中生存所需的所有東西，而不用靠呼吸管吸取水面上的空氣。

水肺潛水者背著一具高壓氣瓶。他們也穿著潛水衣保暖，穿著蛙鞋協助打水，還要繫一條配重帶來避免他們浮上水面。他們還穿著一件特殊的背心。氣瓶裡的空氣會打入背心或從背心裡抽出，有助於潛水者待在適當的深度。太多空氣會讓他們浮上去，而太少則會讓他們沉到海底。一旦你具備了潛水技術，就能隨心所欲去探索令人興奮的海底世界。

1.	D	(A)爆發(B)復原 、 走出損失和悲傷(C)熄滅(D)代表。SCUBA diving (水肺潛水) 這名稱來自於它所代表的詞 Self Contained Underwater Breathing Apparatus (自給式水中呼吸裝置)，故選(D)。
2.	A	(A)沒有…而…(B)不顧(C)儘管、即使(D)因此。水肺潛水是潛水者攜帶在海底存活所需的東西，而不需要依賴管子供給他們氧氣，故選(A)。
3.	C	(A)剝奪(B)告知(C)阻止、避免(D)勸阻。水肺潛水者會穿戴配重帶，避免浮出水面，故選(C)。
4.	D	(A)雖然(B)自從、既然(C)當…時(D)然而。while 作「然而」解，用於前後語意相對時。背心中空氣太多時，會讓潛水者往上浮，然而空氣太少時，會讓潛水者往下沉到海底，故選(C)。
5.	B	(A)取得(B)使配備(C)評論(D)牽涉、涉及。一旦你具備了這些技巧，你就能自由自在地探索令人興奮的海底世界了，故選(B)。

Ⓒ

極限運動也稱作冒險運動 ，比起傳統運動風險較高，更能刺激腎上腺素分泌，並帶給個人更大的成就感。這種運動的出現也帶來全新的一群運動員！

從事極限運動具有風險。對那些運動員來說，這通常是在嘗試一種現有運動的危險版本。例如，將跳板跳

水發揮到極限，就會得出像懸崖跳水這樣的危險運動。如果你在懸崖跳水時沒控制好身體跳落的位置，可能會使背部撞擊岩床而碎裂，而非只是在入水時濺起一個大水花！

科學家認為，極限運動員天生就有承受這些風險的能力。腎上腺素能導致極度的興奮程度，驅使這些人們做出我們大多數人幾乎連看都不敢看的驚險動作。他們做完那些危險特技之後，腦中會釋放出一些化學物質，因而使他們對那些運動上癮。那也是他們不管摔得多重都樂此不疲的原因。

極限運動吸引執著於個人成就的運動員。這種運動都幾乎沒有規則或裁判，運動員要靠創造力、技術和勇氣來達到個人的最佳表現。

雖然我們不是每個人都敢嘗試這種運動，但好奇心仍使我們忍不住想觀看這些無懼驚險的表演。如果你看膩了傳統運動，可以選擇改看極限運動。雖然舒服坐在沙發上的你不會贏得任何獎牌，但卻能在不需承受風險的情況下，得到腎上腺素激增的快感！

1.	B	⒜攻擊⒝運動員⒞觀眾⒟獎賞。從接下來的幾段可知極限運動不僅和傳統運動不同，更孕育出不同類型的運動員，故選⒝。
2.	B	attempt 嘗試；mean + V-ing 作「意思是」解；此處在解釋何謂極限運動；極限運動指的是嘗試將現有的運動變得更危險，故選⒝；mean + to V 作「打算」解，相當於 plan to + V。
3.	D	⒜出其不意⒝視為理所當然⒞列入考慮⒟變成極端。將跳板跳水極端化，就成了一種危險的運動像是懸崖跳水，故選⒟。
4.	A	⒜而非⒝比…更多⒞及時、趕上做⒟關於。在懸崖跳水時，若你弄錯了著地點，你可能摔在岩石上而摔斷了你的背脊，而不是水花四處飛濺，故選⒜。
5.	C	⒜害怕⒝保持⒞忍受⒟等待。barely 幾乎不；我們大多數人可能連看都不敢看的特技，這些人在腎上腺素的驅使下卻會去嘗試，故選⒞。
6.	C	release 釋出；此處為關係子句 which are released in the brain 所省略而來的分詞片語，用來修飾 chemicals；他們迷上這些運動，因為他們表演了這些危險的特技後，腦中會釋放出某些化學物質，故選⒞。

7.	B	前一句解釋了為何這些人不管摔得多重，仍舊會一再地嘗試這些極限運動的原因，故選⒝，此處省略了 the reason。
8.	D	⒜適用、申請⒝沉溺於⒞補考、虛構、組成⒟依賴。運動員要依賴他們的創意、技巧、和無畏的精神才能達到個人最佳的表現，故選⒟。
9.	C	⒜脫掉、(飛機) 起飛⒝頂嘴⒞轉到 (某個頻道)⒟結果變成。從下一句的 from your comfortable couch 可知是坐在沙發上看電視；如果你厭倦了觀賞傳統的運動，不妨轉到另類運動，故選⒞。
10.	D	雖然你坐在舒服的沙發上不能得到任何獎牌，但你無需冒險就能感受到腎上腺素狂飆的快感，故選⒟。

Part II: Translation Practice

B	1.	The potential danger of extreme sports doesn't **keep/prevent/stop** thrill seekers **from** playing these crazy sports.
	2.	**Instead of** giving up, they are willing to take the risk and attempt difficult tricks. = They do not give up. **Instead**, they are willing to take the risk and attempt difficult tricks.
C	1.	The intensive training course and additional expenses don't **keep/prevent/stop** sea lovers **from** taking to scuba diving.
	2.	**Instead of** trying some easier activities, they are eager to enjoy a whole new experience. = They won't try some easier activities. **Instead**, they are eager to enjoy a whole new experience.

Unit 6

Part I: Cloze Test

Ⓐ

尼爾森・曼德拉 (1918−) 在消除南非種族歧視這件事，扮演著重要的角色。在他出生的時候，南非是個相當不公平的國家。因為「種族隔離」制度把非白人與白人隔開，使非白人族群不得擁有投票權，並受到不公

的對待。為了對抗不公的體制，曼德拉成為一位律師，並且在 1944 年參加非洲民族議會。1962 年，他到衣索比亞推動非洲自由化，但回國後以非法出境的罪名遭到逮捕，被判處終身監禁。他在囚禁獄中期間繼續為自己的理念奮鬥。1990 年，總統戴克拉克 (1936-) 廢止種族歧視的法令，釋放了許多政治犯，其中就包括曼德拉。3 年後，戴克拉克與曼德拉一同獲得諾貝爾和平獎，此獎表彰「他們為種族隔離制度和平結束所做的貢獻」。1994 年，曼德拉成為首位非白人的南非總統。雖然他在 1999 年已退休，但他依舊為世界各地的自由鬥士帶來鼓舞。

1.	D	先行詞為 time 用表時間的關係副詞 when 修飾，此句說明曼德拉出生於南非仍舊是個十分不公平國家的<u>時代</u>。
2.	B	此為 Because the non-whites <u>were separated from</u> the white population through the apartheid system, they were refused the right to.... 省略的分詞構句，被動用 V-en。
3.	D	(A)控告 (+ of) (B)負擔得起、有足夠的 (金錢、時間) 去 (做某事) (C)使煩惱 (D)逮捕。從<u>非法出境和被判終身監禁</u>可知，曼德拉回國時<u>被逮捕</u>，故選(D)。
4.	A	(A)廢除 (B)執行、強迫 (C)觀察、遵守 (D)違反、冒犯。從後半句，戴克拉克總統<u>釋放了包括曼德拉在內的政治犯</u>可知，戴克拉克<u>廢除</u>了種族歧視的法律，故選(A)。
5.	C	(A)成就 (B)解釋 (C)鼓舞的人 (物) (D)行業、佔據。此句由 though 連接，呈現一<u>轉折語氣</u>，雖然曼德拉在 1999 年<u>卸下公職</u>，但是他<u>依舊鼓舞</u>了世界各地自由鬥士，故選(C)。

Ⓑ

　　出生在富有家庭的聖雄甘地 (1869-1948)，年輕時到英國研讀法律。回到印度之後，他努力為自己的理念奮鬥。其中包括公平稅賦、提升女性地位、救助貧困、鼓勵印度不同社會階級之間建立手足情誼並平等對待。就像他的許多同胞一樣，甘地認為印度應該脫離英國統治，成為一個自由國家。他開始盡已所能促成這種改變。

　　甘地因為自己的信念而被視為叛亂份子，但他與一般叛亂份子之間有個重要的區別。他認為應採取和平抗爭手段。他鼓勵追隨者起來反抗，但絕不要出手回擊。他教導他們，打鬥只會導致更多的打鬥，採取非暴力方

式是帶來改變的最佳辦法。甘地就是以這樣的方式，最終成功帶領印度在 1947 年獲得獨立。

1.	C	included 後接一連串的<u>名詞</u>：公平賦稅、改善婦女現狀、幫助窮人、鼓勵同胞愛和印度不同階層間的平等對待。選動名詞 encouraging，和 improving, assisting 對稱。
2.	A	(A)改變 (B)事實 (C)任務 (D)練習、實行。甘地開始做任何事讓這個改變成為可能。此句中的 this change 指的是印度應該是個自由國家，而非被英國統治。
3.	B	A be considered (to be) B；A be regarded as B。因為他的信念，Gandhi <u>被認為是謀反者</u>，選(B)。(A)應改為 was considered (to be); (C)(D)應改為 was regarded as
4.	C	(A)軍事的 (B)有組織的 (C)和平的 (D)宗教的。從下面幾句可知甘地鼓勵他的追隨者<u>反抗</u>，<u>但不要反擊</u>。同時帶來改變最佳的方式是用<u>非暴力</u>。故(C)為最佳答案。
5.	D	(A)想出 (B)補償 (C)接管 (D)帶來、導致。前半句提到甘地教導人民打鬥只會<u>帶來</u> (lead to) 更多的打鬥，接著用 and 連接後半句，而非暴力才是<u>帶來改變最佳的方式</u>，lead to 和 bring about 為同義詞。

Ⓒ

　　非裔美籍牧師馬丁・路德・金恩二世 (1929-1968) 在他所處的當時，是最重要的黑人領袖之一。他將非暴力策略植入激進的民權運動之中，因而聞名於世。

　　金恩最初是在大學裡學習到非暴力理論，後來他對梭羅與甘地教導的非暴力抗爭留下深刻印象。金恩預見到反對種族歧視制度的組織性非暴力抗爭行動，會引發支持民權運動的浪潮。對金恩來說，非暴力是比暴力更徹底、激進的作法，暴力只會使一個族群對另一族群的迫害持續下去而已。他體認到暴力絕對無法帶來真正的公平正義。暴力並不會削弱惡行，反而會使之愈演愈烈。

　　金恩帶領的「蒙哥馬利市拒乘公車運動」使他獲得首次勝利，在這項運動中，阿拉巴馬州蒙哥馬利市的黑人市民拒絕搭乘市公車長達 11 個月，強烈要求廢止公車座位黑白隔離的規定。市政府最後讓步，從此以後，黑人市民高興坐哪個座位都行。這項運動成功之後，產生了「南方基督教領袖會議」，是黑人教會與牧師所組成的一個團體。在金恩的領導之下，該團體將非暴力抗

爭的原則應用得十分成功。

　　金恩成為了史上最年輕的諾貝爾和平獎得主，得獎原因是他所領導的非暴力抗爭，消除了美國的種族偏見。現在他是舉世公認的自由、和平與非暴力公民不合作運動的象徵。

1.	C	(A)挑戰(B)結果(C)策略(D)傾向。從下文可知，金恩在激進的民權運動中以採用非暴力的策略著名。
2.	B	(A)追隨(B)使印象深刻、使感動(C)擁有(D)拒絕。金恩最早是在大學時得知非暴力的概念，之後他又被梭羅和甘地的理念所感動。
3.	D	that 所接的子句缺少動詞，故選(D)，金恩預見有組織且非暴力反抗種族歧視的抗爭，將會帶來一股支持民權運動的浪潮。
4.	C	(A)節省的(B)政治的(C)徹底的、激進的(D)技術的。從句末的關係子句中可知，暴力只是延續了一個團體對另一團體的暴虐，(亦即暴力無法解決問題)，因此非暴力是比暴力更徹底、更激進的作法。
5.	B	(A)分割、除(B)增加、乘(C)減少(D)禁止。從 instead of 可知，本空格應填入 diminish 的反義詞，暴力只會帶來更多的邪惡，而不能讓邪惡減少，故選(B)。
6.	D	in which 在此所代替的是在這事件中 (in the Montgomery Bus Boycott)，在蒙哥馬利市拒乘公車運動中，該地區的黑人長達 11 個月拒絕搭乘公車。
7.	C	此句為 ...the black citizens of Montgomery, Alabama refused to use the city buses for eleven months, and they demanded an end to the policy.... 省略而來的分詞構句，主動用 V-ing。
8.	A	wherever 為複合關係副詞，作「無論在任何地方」解，從那時起，黑人公民搭公車時可以坐在任何他想坐的地方。
9.	A	with success 此為 with + N 轉化成副詞的用法，等同於 successfully。
10.	D	(A)突破、重要的新發現(B)里程碑(C)訊號(D)象徵、代表。金恩現在被全世界認為是自由、和平、非暴力不服從的象徵。

Part II: Translation Practice

B	1.	In the Gettysburg Address, **which** is regarded as one of the greatest speeches, Abraham Lincoln restated the principle of human equality.
B	2.	The Address was delivered during the American Civil War, **when** the U.S. was torn apart by the slavery issue.
C	1.	Barack Obama's acceptance speech, **which** was addressed to more than two hundred thousand supporters, restored people's faith.
C	2.	They believed that the time **when** all things are possible has come to America.

Unit 7

Part I: Cloze Test

Ⓐ

　　埃及擁有超過 4 千年持續不斷的文明，是個尚未把所有秘密揭開的古老國度。其中有個令歷史學家著迷的奧秘是關於一座消失的埃及城市——希拉克里昂。大約在 1300 年前，它憑空消失了。沒有人確知是什麼使這座城市滅亡。

　　最近，潛水員在離埃及海岸數哩的地中海中，發現了希拉克里昂這個消失的城市。這處保存良好的廢墟位在阿布奇爾海灣的 30 呎水深處。潛水員從海沙底下取回了隱藏數個世紀的藝品。初步的研究顯示，希拉克里昂可能與現代的威尼斯相似，有運河、美麗莊園與神殿。歷史學家指出，這座城市頗為富裕，以當地多種娛樂聞名。希望這些藝品有助於人們更加了解埃及後期的偉大文明。

1.	D	(A)出現(B)繁榮(C)除去、脫掉(D)消失。下一句提到沒有人知道導致希拉克里昂城毀滅的原因，所以選(D)。大約 1 千 3 百年前，這城市不知為何就消失了。
2.	B	recently 通常與過去式或現在完成式連用。
3.	A	(A)收回、尋回(B)撤退(C)減輕、緩和(D)收到。潛水人員從海底下尋回埋藏了好幾世紀的物品，故選(A)。

4.	D	(A)沿岸的(B)原始的(C)原產的 、 本國的(D)富有的。上句提到最初的研究顯示希拉克里昂城很像當代的維尼斯，有<u>運河</u>、<u>別墅</u>、和<u>寺廟</u>，可推知希拉克里昂城應該很<u>有錢</u>。
5.	C	(A)跟上、趕上(B)盼望、期待(C)使明白、闡明，亦可用 cast/throw light on (D)以⋯為榮。文章一開始提到希拉克里昂城的消失是謎團，因此<u>歷史家想透過這些挖掘出來的工藝品進一步了解埃及這古文明的最後階段</u>。

B

　　大約建立在西元前 6 百年的龐貝城 ，在西元前 80 年成為羅馬帝國的殖民地 。 龐貝城非常靠近維蘇威火山，但人們既不害怕，也不擔心。儘管在火山爆發前有出現明顯的警訊，但居民們還是措手不及。西元 79 年，維蘇威火山爆發，噴出濕灰與毒氣。火山爆發持續了一天，改變了當地河流的流向，也使得海灘上升。這場悲劇發生之後，龐貝城不再是個迷人又平靜的城市，而是成千上萬人的墳場。

　　龐貝城直到 1748 年才再度被發現。許多遭火山灰包覆而維持原狀的建築、神殿與壁畫被挖掘出來，給我們一個難得的機會去了解古羅馬地方城鎮的日常生活。龐貝城不僅是個讓歷史學家了解古羅馬社會與文化的珍貴機會，也是個吸引數百萬名遊客前來的特殊景點，他們都對這個特別的城市感到著迷。

1.	C	(A)不僅 A 而且 B (B)不是 A 就是 B (C) AB 兩者皆非(D)既 A 且 B。本句前半提到龐貝古城很靠近維蘇威火山，接著出現 but，語意上呈現<u>轉折</u>，故選(C)，但是人們<u>卻不害怕也不擔心</u>。
2.	B	(A)記住(B)出奇不意(C)聯絡(D)白費、徒勞無功。和上一句一樣，此句也是在語意上呈現<u>轉折</u>，儘管之前有明顯的<u>警告訊號</u>，居民對於火山爆發依舊<u>大感意外</u>。
3.	C	此處為關係代名詞的省略 ，原本應是 The eruption lasted one day, <u>which changed</u> the course of the local rivers and <u>raised</u> the sea beach.；which 代替前一句：火山爆發持續了一整天，省略後主動改為 changing 和 raising。
4.	B	此處也是關係代名詞的省略，原本應是 Many buildings, temples and wall paintings, <u>which have been preserved</u> by the ashes, have been found...，省略後被動改為 preserved。

5.	A	(A)使著迷(B)支配(C)傳達(D)拋棄。上百萬的遊客因這個不尋常的<u>龐貝</u>古城市而<u>著迷</u>。

C

　　19 世紀時，在墨西哥與瓜地馬拉的茂密叢林裡，發現數量龐大的古城位於樹林與藤蔓之中。筆直的道路連接這些城市，城市裡遍布著美麗的石造神殿與宮殿。這些是馬雅城市，但馬雅人是什麼人？

　　馬雅人是由許多不同的美洲印地安民族所組成，他們是住在中美洲，大約從西元前 1 千年到西元 1572 年，前後長達了 2 千 5 百多年的時間。他們的文化以農業為基礎，主要是種植玉米。由於他們十分仰賴季節的循環，因而成為能力高超的天文學家，發展出極為精準的曆法——甚至比現今廣泛使用的羅馬曆法還要準確。他們建造出用來觀測天象的巨大圓頂建築，建築裡的窗戶位置在宗教慶典的日子裡可以對準特定的行星與恆星。

　　女人在馬雅社會裡備受尊重，與男人有同等地位。在許多情況中，她們擔任要職，而且有些女人還被視為是女神。馬雅人是個篤信宗教的民族，他們敬拜雨水、沃土與大地。

　　大約從 3 世紀到 16 世紀是馬雅文化的黃金時期。儘管在那段期間創造出各種成就，但馬雅文化幾乎都消失了。是因為玉米歉收、族群內鬥，還是被另一個文化取代了？沒有人知道。如今只有語言、少數傳統以及一些古老的偉大成就留存下來。

1.	C	(A)溝通(B)競爭(C)連接(D)建造。筆直的道路<u>連接</u>這些城市，選(C)。
2.	B	consist of/be made up of/contain/be composed of/comprise 表示「組成」，前面主詞為代表「整體」，後接「部份」內容。而 constitute 則為「部分 + constitute + 整體」。
3.	A	(A)農業(B)商業(C)手工藝品(D)工業。此句後半段提到主要是<u>玉米的種植</u>，因此馬雅文化是建立在<u>農業</u>上的。
4.	B	depend on/upon 仰賴、取決於
5.	A	(A)天文學家(B)顧問(C)技工(D)哲學家。此句後半提到馬雅人發展出十分精確的<u>曆法</u>，故可推論他們為傑出的<u>天文學家</u>。
6.	D	with 為附帶法，表示「有」的意思。指的是這些大型圓頂的建築物<u>有</u>可以在宗教慶典時觀測到天象的窗戶。

7.	C	(A)較高的(B)較低的(C)相等的(D)社會的。前半句提到在馬雅文化中，女性是極為被尊重的 (well-respected)，因此女性和男性的地位是<u>相等的</u>；若選(A)之後應改為 Women had higher standing <u>than</u> men.
8.	D	(A)勤勞的(B)暴力的(C)專業的(D)虔誠的。此句提到馬雅人<u>崇拜雨水、富饒和大地</u>，故選(D)。
9.	B	(A) because (+ S + V) 因為(B) because of (+ N) 因為(C) in spite of (+ N) 儘管(D) in regard to (+ N) 關於。此句在探討馬雅文化滅亡的原因，且所接的是<u>名詞片語</u>，故選(B)。
10.	C	(A)維持、保持(B)消失(C)留存(D)保存、維護。沒有人知道馬雅文明滅亡的原因，現今<u>只有語</u>言、一些傳統和偉大的成就有<u>留存</u>下來，選(C)。

Part II: Translation Practice

B	1.	Stonehenge **is** mainly **composed of**/**is** mainly **comprised of**/**is** mainly **made up of**/mainly **consists of**/**comprises** many tall and large stones.
	2.	Archeologists are trying to explain **how** these huge stones were transported here.
C	1.	Angkor Wat **is composed of**/**is comprised of**/**is made up of**/**consists of**/**comprises** dozens of stone temples.
	2.	Visitors/Tourists all wonder **who** created it and **how** it was constructed.

Unit 8

Part I: Cloze Test

Ⓐ
　　勞力士錶在全世界各地都是財富、品味與高品質的象徵。這個品牌的名氣與不朽傳奇是建立在他們創造的商品，以及他們堅守機械手錶技術的決心，那是一種已臻於完美的技術。

　　這家公司的創立人漢斯‧威爾斯道夫夢想以完美運轉的手錶取代一般的懷錶。雖然手錶在當時是時尚產品，不過尚未有人製造出的手錶，可以像體積大但不方便的懷錶那樣精確又可靠。然而在 1910 年，威爾斯道夫創造出的一只手錶，受到瑞士的鐘錶學院高度讚譽，這所學院是世界第一的鐘錶製造學校。1926 年，威爾

斯道夫以全球首創的防水手錶，再度引起轟動，而接著又一次在 1931 年推出了世界第一只自動手錶。

　　現今的勞力士就如同 1920 年代一樣，還是鐘錶業的龍頭品牌。它成功度過了從機械轉變為電子技術的變遷過程。

1.	A	(A)名聲(B)偶像(C)標語、口號(D)衝動、渴望。前一句提及勞力士 (Rolex) 代表的是<u>財富、品味和高品質</u>，而這正是勞力士的<u>名聲</u>，故選(A)。
2.	C	replace A with B 用 B 取代 A
3.	B	(A)因此(B)然而(C)相似地(D)否則。前一句提到沒有人能夠製造和懷錶一樣準確可靠的手錶，<u>可</u>是在 1910 年威爾斯道夫做出了連世界頂級的鐘錶製造學校都稱讚的手錶，前後語意出現<u>轉折</u>，故選(B)。
4.	D	此處提到<u>另一個</u> Wilsdorf 的發明，故選(D)。
5.	B	(A)翻譯(B)轉變(C)運輸(D)傳達、傳送。勞力士成功地從機械技術<u>轉換</u>到數位技術中存活下來。

Ⓑ
　　麥當勞公司的成功是出自於三位男人之手。一開始的兩位是麥當勞兄弟，他們在 1940 年代創造出一家新型態的餐廳。他們使用簡單的菜單，並設計出像工廠一樣的廚房，受過訓練的員工如同生產線上的工人一般，在那裡製作出菜單上的餐點。高效率的服務吸引了顧客上門，不久之後，這對兄弟開設了更多家餐廳。他們也開始開放加盟，也就是允許其他商人使用麥當勞的名字與標準作業流程開設餐廳。這對兄弟會收取營業額的一小部分來作為授權的代價。

　　第三位男人是雷‧克洛克。他驚訝於顧客隊伍雖長卻移動快速，說服了這對兄弟讓他負責加盟事業，將餐廳擴展到全國。到了他去世的 1984 年，麥當勞每隔 17 個小時就會在世界的某處新開一家店！多虧有他們 3 人，麥當勞才能享有這樣卓越的成長。

1.	C	關係副詞 where 代替的是 in a factory-like kitchen，意即<u>在這像工廠似的廚房中</u>，訓練有素的職員能夠做出菜單上的各項食物。
2.	B	(A)時薪(B)裝配線(C)例行公事(D)衣著規定。這些訓練有素的員工做菜就像在工廠<u>裝配線</u>上組裝的工人一樣。
3.	C	mean + V-ing 作「意味著…」解，mean + to V 作「打算做…」解。which 所引導的關係子句說明 franchising：經銷權意味著允許其他商

		人以麥當勞的商標和標準作業流程開餐廳。
4.	B	persuade sb. to V 勸某人做某事
5.	D	(A)深度(B)寬度(C)溫暖(D)成長。前一句提到在克洛克於 1984 年過世時，每 17 個小時就有一家麥當勞在世界的某個角落出現，因為這 3 個人，麥當勞才能有如此驚人的成長。

Ⓒ

供應世上最受歡迎汽水的可口可樂公司所擁有的特點是推銷商品的本領，再加上持續擴展市場的衝勁。

1886 年約翰‧潘伯頓博士發明了最初配方的幾個月之後，可口可樂在美國一份地方報紙刊登廣告。他推銷可口可樂是種可以治療頭痛的提神飲料，但宣傳標語卻是簡潔有力的「喝可口可樂」。

可口可樂公司在 1892 年成立之後，緊接著就將事業拓展到全國。在阿沙‧錢德勒的領導之下，這家公司在亞特蘭大郊區建造裝瓶廠，使得可口可樂的銷售擴展到美國各州。伴隨這項擴展的還有貼在全美國倉庫門上和建築物側面的廣告，以及聘用知名歌手、演員與運動明星來推銷可口可樂。

在 20 世紀時，可口可樂向國際拓展，在歐洲、南美洲、非洲和亞洲建造裝瓶廠。從 1920 年代開始，在全世界各城市的電子看板上，隨處可見可口可樂的商標圖案。可口可樂利用新興大眾媒體，在廣播以及之後的電視上打廣告，創出好聽易記的口號，例如：「就是可口可樂！」

可口可樂公司 1923 年的董事長羅伯特‧伍德拉夫說過，他希望可口可樂成為每個人「垂手可得的渴望」。該公司一直秉持著他的抱負與遠見，繼續不停追求開發新市場，為的是要確保達到如 1927 年的廣告所說的，可口可樂「不管在哪都垂手可得」。

1.	D	couple 在此作動詞用，A be coupled with B 作「A 和 B 同時發生或存在」解。此處過去分詞 coupled，為關係子句 which is coupled with 省略而來。可口可樂公司的特色是它行銷的能力<u>加上</u>不停地擴張市場的動力。
2.	A	早在 1886 年可口可樂最初的秘方被潘伯頓發明之後的幾個月，就已經在美國當地的報紙上有廣告在宣傳促銷。秘方是被發明的，故用「被動語態」，且此動作和前半句 promote 的動詞時間點相比，是發生在更早的時候，因此用「過去完成式」表示，故選(A)。

3.	B	(A)身分(B)標語、口號(C)冒犯(D)許可證。從句末的 "Drink Coca-Cola" 可知空格要填的是(B)，它的<u>標語</u>是有效且簡單的。
4.	C	under the leadership of... 「在…的領導下」。
5.	B	enable sb. to V 「使某人能夠做某事」。
6.	A	(A)伴隨、隨…而來(B)延遲(C)發布(D)限制。伴隨著可口可樂擴展的是在全美倉庫門上和建築物側邊所張貼的廣告及聘請知名的歌手、演員和運動明星來宣傳他們的產品，故選(A)。
7.	B	(A)國內地(B)國際地(C)秘密地(D)可看見地。從後半句可看出可口可樂<u>在歐洲、南美、非洲和亞洲設立工廠</u>，就是要朝國際拓展，故選(B)。
8.	C	(A)太陽能(B)蒸汽機(C)大眾傳播媒體(D)大眾運輸工具。從後半句提到可口可樂<u>先透過廣播接著利用電視來廣告</u>，得知可口可樂是利用新的<u>大眾傳媒</u>來進行密集宣傳。
9.	D	(A)到達(B)長度(C)觸碰(D) (伸手所及的) 範圍。1923 年可口可樂的主席伍德拉夫希望可口可樂成為每一個人渴望<u>垂手可得的</u>飲料。
10.	C	(A)技術(B)發明(C)市場(D)產品。全文的重心放在可口可樂如何<u>行銷宣傳與擴展</u>，此句再一次呼應第一句，可知可口可樂不斷地在追求新的<u>市場</u>，同時本句後半可提到他們的目標是要讓可口可樂<u>出現在世界的每個角落</u>，故選(C)。

Part II: Translation Practice

B	1.	People did **not** put **as/so** many toppings on the pizza **as** they do today.
	2.	**However/Nevertheless**, after the food spreads across the world, various ingredients are added.
C	1.	When blue jeans were made, they were **not as/so** stylish **as** they are today.
	2.	**However/Nevertheless**, later they become a fashion and attract people of all ages.

Unit 9

Part I: Cloze Test

Ⓐ

　　到羅馬旅行的遊客一定會造訪當地其中一個最古老且著名的地方：圓形競技場。

　　西元 72 年，羅馬皇帝維斯帕先要求人民建造競技場來舉辦各種體育活動。成千上萬的工匠花了 8 年時間建造完成。競技場外圍圍牆的高度約有 157 呎，長度大約是 1,788 呎，裡頭可容納 5 萬名觀眾。

　　過去在那裡舉行的活動主要分成兩類。一種是為了展現人類體能，而另一種則是為了娛樂。在前者的活動中，受過訓練的戰士與另一名戰士或危險動物進行搏鬥。在後者，由受過訓練的猴子與獅子表演一些把戲，讓觀眾開懷大笑。

　　到了 6 世紀，羅馬人停止舉行這些活動。在那之後，經過多年荒廢，再加上兩次地震，競技場受到了嚴重的毀壞。直到現在，它的外觀仍未完全修復。

1.	D	此處 to hold 是 in order to hold 的省略，表示建造古羅馬圓形大競技場是為了舉辦各種的體育活動。
2.	B	(A)能力(B)容量(C)可能性(D)可能性。圓形大競技場可容納五萬人，故選(B)。
3.	B	(A)訓練(B)娛樂(C)告知、通知(D)說服。本段提到競技場所舉辦的活動可分為兩類，一是能展現人的力量 (受過訓練的戰士對打或與危險的動物較勁)，另一類則是受過訓練的猴子和獅子會表演一些把戲逗群眾笑，故選(B)。
4.	C	(A)遲的、晚的(B)以後(C) (兩者中的) 後者(D)最後地。與前一句的 in the former kind (前者) 相對，此處為 in the latter kind。
5.	A	(A)破壞、衰敗(B)經常出沒於、縈繞於心(C)拋棄(D)使孤立、隔絕。前半句提到經過多年疏於管理照顧，再加上兩次的地震，因此大競技場嚴重毀壞了。

Ⓑ

　　轟立在台北的台北 101 大樓絕對是棟引人注目的建築物。但除了驚人的高度之外，台北 101 還有其他許多特別之處。

　　台北 101 是一項建築成就。頻繁的地震與強烈颱風帶來的風雨，是它需要面對的主要挑戰。因此，這棟大樓必須夠堅固，才能承受台灣的極端氣候。它擁有的極大彈性可防止大規模傾斜，確保結構完整。此外，帷幕牆會增強像支撐這樣的關鍵結構要素。

　　台北 101 以八層樓為一個單位做分隔。中文的「八」聽起來像「發」，具有繁榮與興盛之意。台北 101 的外型看起來像一棵向上長的竹子，象徵台灣的積極精神。

　　簡單來說，台北 101 確切展現出人類改變景觀的能力。它是我們應引以為榮的建築物。

1.	C	(A)長度(B)寬度(C)高度(D)重量。第一句提到台北 101 高聳於台北之上，是棟引人注目的建築物，但是除了這一點 (亦即它令人側目的高度)，台北 101 還有許多特別的地方。
2.	A	(A)因此(B)然而(C)此外(D)相反地。前一句提到原因：經常性的地震和颱風帶來的強風豪雨是建造台北 101 最主要的挑戰，因此，建築物必須強度夠強才能抵擋台灣氣候的考驗，此處呈現上下文的因果關係，故選(A)。
3.	B	(A)特色(B)彈性(C)進步(D)技術。要避免強烈的左右搖晃並且確保建築的完整性，因此建築十分需要有彈性，故選(B)。
4.	D	(A)保守的(B)聰明的(C)樂觀的(D)繁榮的、興盛的。數字「八」的中文發音和「發」相近，意思相當於繁榮、興盛。此處要選 blooming 的同義字 prosperous。
5.	A	(A)簡單地說(B)說來奇怪(C)首先(D)比較而言。從全文可知，台北 101 可說是建築上的壯舉，因此最後一段總結說明台北 101 是人們改變地貌的具體實例，故選(A)。(C)通常用於說明理由或原因的第一點；若比較兩樣事物時用(D)。

Ⓒ

　　從遠處看雄偉的泰姬瑪哈陵，就像是看到一顆閃閃發光的寶石漂浮在一大片藍色之上。但你知道在這座宏偉宮殿的白色石牆背後，有段悲傷的愛情故事嗎？

　　蒙兀兒帝國的皇帝沙‧賈汗在 1628 到 1658 年統治印度。1612 年，這位皇帝娶了艾珠曼德‧巴奴，就是後來的泰姬瑪哈。從他們結婚之後，這對愛侶不管做什麼都在一起。這位君王甚至連出兵打仗都帶著妻子同行。泰姬瑪哈一直支持著沙‧賈汗，陪他度過勝仗與敗仗──她是皇帝的妻子、情人，也是他的朋友。

　　不幸的是，他們共度的時光不久就結束了。1631 年泰姬瑪哈在生下他們第 14 個孩子的過程中去世了。深愛的妻子逝去令沙‧賈汗深受打擊，據說打擊大到他的

頭髮僅在數個月間就全部變得雪白。沙·賈汗陷入悲傷,並渴望紀念愛妻,他下令建造泰姬瑪哈陵作為亡妻最後的長眠之地。因此,在 1632 年,開始了泰姬瑪哈陵的建造工程在阿格拉。

1.	**B**	本句為一倒裝句,句子的主詞是 a sad tale of love,主要為陳述現狀,故選(B)。在這華麗宮殿的白色石牆背後有著一段悲傷的愛情故事。
2.	**C**	from...to...「從…到…」。
3.	**C**	(A)脫掉(B)接管(C)帶著…一起(D)帶走。前一句提到兩人結婚後,不論做什麼事情都在一起。因此國王上戰場時也帶著妻子一起去,故選(C)。
4.	**A**	(A)失敗(B)命運(C)發現(D)爭論。不論勝利或失敗,瑪哈始終支持著賈汗,此處要選 victory 的相反詞 defeat。
5.	**B**	(A)幫助(B)結束(C)成立、產生(D)生效。前一段提到兩人甜蜜相處的時光,但此段一開始就出現 unfortunately (不幸地) 語意呈現轉折,兩人在一起的時間很快就結束了。
6.	**D**	(A)閃光(B) (臉頰) 發紅、沖 (馬桶) (C)墜毀、轟然作響(D)壓碎、摧毀。後半句提到賈汗的頭髮據說在幾個月內就變白了,可知愛妻的死訊深深地打擊了賈汗,故選(D)。
7.	**D**	order 所接的 that 子句中,should 可以省略,直接用原形動詞。泰姬瑪哈陵是被建造的,要用被動語態,原句為 Shah Jahan ordered that the Taj Mahal (should) be built...。
8.	**C**	(A)家鄉(B)建築學,建築物(C)建造(D)裝飾。由前一句下令建造泰姬瑪哈陵可以推測 1632 年應該為泰姬瑪哈陵開始建造的時間。
9.	**A**	談論花多少「時間」做某事用:it takes + 人 + 時間 + to V;若談論花多少「金錢」做某事用:it costs + 人 + 金錢 + to V。若以人為主詞還可用:人 + spend + 時間／金錢 + V-ing。
10.	**B**	instill...into...「灌輸…到…」。

Part II: Translation Practice

B	1.	Around 220 B.C., Chinese emperor Qin Shi Huang **ordered that** the Great Wall **be built** to defend the empire.
	2.	Rumor has it that **inside the Great Wall** are countless dead bodies of the slaves.
C	1.	In 1163, Bishop of Paris Maurice de Sully **ordered that** Notre Dame de Paris **be built** in honor of the Virgin Mary.
	2.	**Inside the cathedral** are the world-renowned stained glass and sculptures.

Unit 10

Part I: Cloze Test

Ⓐ

穿戴黑色帽子與長袍的亨利感到非常光榮:他終於畢業了。畢業典禮的演說與祝禱結束了。當院長叫到他的名字時,他緊張上台接下畢業證書。在最後一位學生拿到畢業證書之後,所有學生大聲歡呼,並把學士帽拋向天空。

大學畢業典禮已經有近千年的時間都沒有太大的改變。在 12 世紀的歐洲,羅馬天主教會首先創立一些大學來培養神職人員。到了畢業的時候,那些學生便成了神職人員,有資格穿上黑袍。這些大學本來只教授神學,但隨著文明進步而擴充了課程。

雖然今日多數的大學都是世俗教育,但現代畢業典禮的傳統是來自中世紀教會大學的儀式。祝禱儀式與穿戴方帽與長袍都是悠久傳統的例子。

1.	**B**	(A)接受(B)畢業典禮(C)競選(D)就職。前句提到亨利終於要畢業了,故選(B)。
2.	**D**	to accept 為 in order to accept 的省略,表示亨利走上台是為了要領畢業證書。
3.	**A**	(A)使有資格(B) be devoted to + V-ing 奉獻、專心致力(C)拒絕(D) be opposed to + V-ing 反對。畢業之後學生就成為神職人員,因此有資格穿上黑袍。
4.	**B**	(A)設計(B)擴大(C)跟隨(D)介紹。前半句提到這些早期的大學原來只教授神學,接著出現 but,語意上呈現轉折,但是隨著文明的進展,學校開始擴充課程,故選(B)。
5.	**C**	derive from... 起源於、源自於。

B

　　古代文明之中有許多著名的高等教育中心。例如，柏拉圖學院或許是世上最古老的大學，而印度的第一所「大學」，那難陀大學，以研究佛學聞名。但如果「最古老」指的是「持續經營最久的」，那麼，無論是柏拉圖學院或那難陀大學都無法擁有這樣的稱號，因為這兩所學校早在好幾世紀前就關門了。

　　根據金氏世界紀錄的記載，世上最古老的大學是摩洛哥菲茲的卡魯因大學。這所在西元 859 年創立的學校，至今仍在運作。

　　這所大學起初是一座清真寺的一部分，雖然現在教授的學科包括政治、科學與語言，但仍舊是個很重要的宗教學校。在中世紀時，這所大學是分享知識，使穆斯林和歐洲人之間彼此了解的中心。如今，這所學校的使命大致上還是一樣：展現伊斯蘭社會在世界上所能扮演的積極角色。

1.	B	(A)取而代之的是(B)舉例而言(C)相反地(D)因此。第一句提到古文明有許多深造學習的中心，接著舉柏拉圖學院和那難陀大學為例，故選(B)。
2.	A	(A)兩者皆是(B)兩者任一(C)兩者皆非(D)三者以上皆非。歷史最悠久的大學既不是柏拉圖學院也不是那難陀大學，因為這兩所學校很久以前就已經關閉了，故選(A)。
3.	C	(A)在建造中(B)無法描述、難以形容(C)在運作中(D)未獲得許可。上一段有提到 oldest 指的是 longest continuously operating，而根據金氏世界紀錄卡魯因大學是最老的大學，創立於西元 859 年，現在仍舊有開課，故選(C)。
4.	A	(A)保持、依然是(B)提醒(C)保留(D)辭職。此句用 although 連接兩子句，語意前後出現轉折，前半句提到這所學校現在雖然有政治、科學、語言等課程，但在宗教研究上依然很重要。
5.	D	play a...role in... 在…中扮演～的角色

C

　　教育在中世紀期間跟現在大不相同。孩童並沒有受教育的義務。孩童接受教育的方式取決於所屬家庭的社會階級與他們的性別。

　　最初的學校是由教會辦理，提供給富家公子就讀。本身只受過基本教育的神父，擔任這些學校的教職。學校的上課時間是從日出持續到日落，因此可能長達 12 個小時之久。由於印刷費用太貴，學生並沒有課本。他們藉由讀聖經來學習閱讀與書寫。他們也學習邏輯、拉丁文、天文學、哲學與數學。他們還學習行為規範。在中世紀的歐洲，最初的大學是在 12 世紀由教會創立的。男性可以在 14 或 15 歲時進入就讀。

　　住在城鎮或鄉間的孩童有時候是到由當地神父授課的小學校上課。農家小孩通常從父母或兄姊那裡學習耕種技術與處理家務。然而，他們沒有學習識字或寫字。男性有時候是成為學徒，以習得工藝技能。跟著師傅學習與工作幾年之後，他們就可以自己開業，例如像是開麵包店。

　　現今的我們有較普及的教育。我們知道，不論社會階級或性別，每個人都有受教育的權利。此外，在大多數國家裡，教會與學校是各自獨立。

1.	A	(A)取決於(B)沉溺於(C)暴露於(D)從…中恢復。前一句提到並非所有的小孩都必須受教育，同時他們所受的教育是取決於家庭的社會地位和性別，故選(A)。
2.	C	(A)出席、參加(B)注意(C)經營(D)認為。最早的學校是教會所創辦的，故選(C)。
3.	B	(A)遠至…(B)長達…(C)一…就…(D)也。學校從太陽升起開始上課，直到太陽西下，所以上課時間可能長達 12 小時，故選(B)。
4.	A	學生沒有書本是因為印刷太昂貴了，此句呈現因果關係，故選(A)。
5.	C	allow sb. to V → sb. be allowed to V 允許某人做某事，故選(C)。
6.	D	從下一句可知，農夫的小孩沒有學習如何閱讀和寫作，可推出他們所學的是農場上所需的技能和家務，故選(D)。
7.	B	(A)會計(B)學徒(C)大使(D)申請者。為了要學會某種技藝，男孩子有時要先成為學徒。下一句也提到，要先在師傅的指導下學習數年，故選(B)。
8.	D	(A)根據(B)在…之旁(C)因為(D)像是。此處舉例說明學徒可以做的生意，像是麵包店，故選(D)。
9.	D	(A)傳統的(B)間接的(C)科學的(D)普遍的、廣泛的。此處呈現對比，以前受教權依社會地位和性別而定 (是侷限的)，然而現在教育是更為普遍的。
10.	C	(A)代表(B)因此(C)不顧、不管(D)取而代之的是。不管一個人的社會地位和性別為何，每個人都有接受教育的權利。

Part II: Translation Practice

B	1.	**On/Upon** receiving her master degree, Mary went abroad for further studies. → **As soon as** Mary received her master degree, she went abroad for further studies.
	2.	Because she was aggressive and intelligent, a committee gave her scholarship **regardless of** her background.
C	1.	**On/Upon** acquiring/obtaining his teaching certificate, Rick applied for a job in a remote area. → **As soon as** Rick acquired/obtained his teaching certificate, he applied for a job in a remote area.
	2.	Because he was enthusiastic and passionate, a principal offered him the position **regardless of** his age.

Unit 11

Part I: Cloze Test

Ⓐ

根據考古學家的說法，史前人類也會嚼口香糖，但他們實際上只是純粹喜歡嚼樹脂塊。

在美國，最早的口香糖要追溯到西元 1848 年，當時是用樹脂來製作「雲杉口香糖」。19 世紀中期，一位名叫湯瑪斯・亞當斯的攝影師把橡膠和糖膠樹膠 (一種具有黏性的無味物質) 混合在一起，想要製造出較好的輪胎。雖然亞當斯沒有成功製出輪胎，但他創造出完全用糖膠樹膠製成的口香糖，並且開始販售。在成功製出口香糖之後，亞當斯嘗試添加味道。新產品雖然大受歡迎，但卻有個缺點：味道無法持久。味道的問題直到 1880 年才解決。威廉・懷特用了幾種味道做實驗，結果是把糖和玉米糖漿加進去混合便解決了問題。他使用的第一種味道是薄荷，那味道在咀嚼過程中一直都留在口香糖上。

1.	A	date back to = go back to = be traced back to 追溯至…
2.	C	mix A with B「將 A 和 B 混合在一起」。

3.	C	(A)優點(B)好處(C)缺點(D)失敗。本句前半提到這樣新產品很受歡迎，接著出現 but，語意上呈現**轉折**，故選(C)，但是**卻有一個缺點**。
4.	B	not...until 直到…才。味道的問題**直到** 1880 年**才**解決。
5.	D	add A to B「將 A 加入 B」。

Ⓑ

大多數人都認為「呼拉圈」是 1950 年代在美國發明的，但其實不是。早在西元前 1 千年，埃及兒童就把乾燥葡萄藤圍成的大圈圈當玩具玩。他們把這些圈圈套在腰間搖晃，或是沿著地面滾動。後來，在中世紀後期，英格蘭有種叫做「搖圈圈」的活動開始流行。大約 5 百年之後，來到夏威夷群島的英國水手看到當地的「呼拉」舞與「搖圈圈」非常相似。就在這個時候，第一次出現了「呼拉圈」這個名稱。

1957 年，兩位美國商人得知木製圈圈在澳洲被當成玩具販售。他們的玩具公司 Wham-O 在 1958 年開始製造並販售「呼拉圈」。經過大力宣傳之後，他們新產的亮色塑膠圈深受小孩歡迎，使 Wham-O 玩具公司在僅僅四個月內就賣出 2 千 5 百萬個。

1.	D	(A) driven 為 drive (開車、逼迫) 的過去分詞(B) drawn 為 draw (畫、拉、吸引) 的過去分詞(C) shot 為 shoot (射擊、拍照) 的過去分詞(D) swung 為 swing (擺盪、旋轉) 的過去分詞。呼拉圈是用搖的，故選(D)。
2.	A	此句為分裂句 it is...that，用於加強語氣；原句為：The name "Hula Hoop" first appeared at this time. 將要強調的部分置於 it is 和 that 之間，其餘的部分置於 that 之後，**就是在那時**，Hula Hoop 這名字首次出現，選(A)。
3.	A	be/become aware of + N「意識到、察覺到…」之意。
4.	C	(A)批評(B)遭遇、邂逅(C)促銷(D)抵抗。Wham-O 這家公司製造了自己的呼拉圈後，就開始販賣與**促銷**，故選(C)。
5.	B	so...that... 如此…以至於…。這些色彩鮮豔的塑膠呼拉圈變得**如此**受小孩歡迎，**以至於** Wham-O 這家公司在四個月內就賣了兩千五百萬個。

C

雖然現在世界各地都找得到風箏，但很多人可能不知道，風箏最早來自中國。中國最早的風箏出現在西元前 5 世紀。最初的風箏並不是玩具，而是使用在戰場上，通常是飛越敵軍陣營以傳遞情報。有些風箏甚至大到可以把人帶上天空，讓他們觀察敵軍的動靜。風箏在中國還有其他用處。有些配備鉤子和魚餌，可以用來釣魚。有些是附有哨子和特殊弦線，所以在飛舞的同時會發出音樂聲。

放風箏的活動很快就遍及亞洲各地，但直到 16 世紀晚期，風箏才在歐洲出現。18 世紀時，風箏開始使用在科學研究上。為了更瞭解風與天氣，科學家在風箏上加裝特殊儀器與攝影機，然後讓風箏飛到高空中。飛機等早期飛行器的發明家，也將風箏當作參考範本。

今日，飛機已經取代風箏，使用在大多的科學與軍事用途上，而風箏主要則是用來玩樂。雖然很多人都認為風箏是玩具，但美國國家航太博物館卻授予它一份殊榮。在館內用來放飛機和太空船的展區裡，有個牌子簡單標示著：「最早的航空工具是中國的風箏。」

1.	C	(A)然而(B)因此(C)反而是(D)否則。前一句提到最早的風箏並不是玩具，而是使用於戰爭中，語意上呈現轉折，應選(C)。
2.	B	(A)生產、製造(B)觀察(C)懷疑(D)運輸、運送。前半句提到有些風箏可能大到可以載人，而他們就可以藉此從空中觀察敵人的動靜，選(B)。
3.	A	be equipped with...「裝備有…」。
4.	B	此為 have + O + OC 的句型，受詞為 whistles and special strings，而這些哨子和特殊的繩子是被繫在風箏上的，用 V-en 表被動。
5.	A	此句為分裂句 it is...that，用於加強語氣；原句為：The kite did not appear in Europe until the late 1500s. 將要強調的部分 (劃線部分) 置於 it is 和 that 之間，其餘的部分置於 that 之後，直到 16 世紀晚期，風箏才出現在歐洲，選(A)，此強調用法需注意不用倒裝。
6.	D	此處的 to + V 為 in order to + V 的省略，表示「為了」；科學家之所以要將特殊的工具和照相機綁在風箏上，並將風箏放到天上，是為了得到更多有關風和天氣的資訊，故選(D)。
7.	B	(A)方法、方式(B)模型(C)鑄模、模子(D)心情。早期創造像飛機這類飛行器的人，也將風箏當作參考模型。
8.	C	(A)教育的(B)醫療的(C)軍事的(D)社會的。此句呼應第一段提及風箏可用於戰爭中，及第二段風箏可用於科學研究中；現在飛機已取代了風箏在科學與軍事目的。
9.	A	(A)尊敬、給予榮耀(B)巧合、同時發生(C)使印象深刻(D)陳設、佈置。前半句提到雖然大多數人將風箏視為玩具，但是在美國國家航太博物館中卻被給予了特殊的榮譽。
10.	D	(A)受歡迎的娛樂(B)有用的武器(C)音樂樂器(D)空中交通工具。前半段特別提到在飛機和太空船這一展示區，而風箏也被歸為同一類，這些都屬於(D)。

Part II: Translation Practice

	1.	B	Bar codes **were not** widely used in grocery stores **until** the early 1970s. → **Not until** the early 1970s **were** bar codes widely **used** in grocery stores. → **It was not until** the early 1970s **that** bar codes were widely used in grocery stores.
	2.		They can be **so** easily read by a scanner **that** customers can check out more quickly.
	1.	C	Microwave ovens **were not** invented by an American scientist **until** the late 1940s. → **Not until** the late 1940s **were** microwave ovens **invented** by an American scientist. → **It was not until** the late 1940s **that** microwave ovens were invented by an American scientist.
	2.		They are **so** easy to operate nowadays **that** everyone can fix a meal without much effort.

Unit 12

Part I: Cloze Test

A

雖然大多數人都聽過尼斯湖水怪，但很少人知道這隻神秘生物的歷史。

最早是在 1 千 5 百年前開始有這隻怪物的記載。記載裡描述了一名神父在尼斯湖畔散步時，目睹一隻巨大生物正準備要攻擊一名男子。因為有上帝的幫助，神父才能命令怪物離開，拯救了可憐男子。

然而，尼斯湖水怪的現代傳說則是開始於 1933 年。有對夫婦曾駕車經過尼斯湖附近的新闢道路，他們表示看見了一隻巨大動物在湖水裡游泳。有關這隻奇怪生物的消息，迅速散播開來。

在 1957 年，與這隻怪物相關的記述與圖畫集結成冊出版了。因為有了這本書，使人們開始較認真看待尋找怪物這件事。雖然什麼怪物都沒找到，但研究人員的確有找到證據顯示，湖水中有龐大的物體。

1.	C	order sb. to + V 命令某人做某事
2.	B	(A)否則(B)然而(C)因此(D)因此。上一段在說明尼斯湖水怪最早在 1500 年前有被記錄，但此段則說明現代尼斯湖水怪的傳奇開始於 1933 年，前後呈現一時間上的轉折，故選(B)。
3.	B	此句的主要動詞為 said，此格為關係子句 who drove on a new road near the Loch 省略而來的分詞片語，driving on a new road near the Loch 用來形容主詞 a couple。
4.	A	(A)記述報導(B)硬幣(C)獎章、勳章(D)郵票。空格後提到圖畫，可推測還有文字敘述。在 1957 年，發行了關於尼斯湖水怪的記述和圖畫。
5.	D	(A)謎(B)影子(C)生物(D)證據。用 though 連接，呈現轉折語氣，前半句提到雖然沒有找到任何生物 (也就是沒有實證)，但是研究者真的有發現深海下有巨大物體存在的證據，故選(D)。

Ⓑ

亦有「福爾摩沙三角」之稱的「魔鬼海」，位於日本、台灣與雅蒲島之間的三角海域。就像美國東部外海的百慕達三角一樣，魔鬼海之所以變得著名，是因為有大量的大型船隻與漁船在那裡消失。

有各種不同的看法解釋這個現象。有些人說是不明飛行物讓那些船消失的。有些人則相信，就像在百慕達三角一樣，在其他海域能正確顯示方位的羅盤，到了這裡會失靈，但這點已經被證實是不實的說法。還有一些人認為，這塊三角海域底下的劇烈火山活動，是造成這些船隻消失的原因。

無論這些異常事件發生的原因是什麼，在 1940 和 1950 年代期間，因為有太多船艦消失，使日本政府派出一艘研究船去調查，結果同樣失蹤，船上一百名人員也跟著消失。日本當時便宣告那裡是危險海域。

| 1. | B | be known for + 原因。就像美國東岸的百慕達三角，福爾摩沙三角也因為許多船隻和漁船在 |

那消失而聞名。另外，be known as + 身份。

2.	D	(A)實際的(B)有罪的(C)無罪的、清白的(D)不正確的。前半句提到有人認為此處就像百慕達三角一樣，羅盤的指針讀數和其他地方不同，後半句先出現連接詞 but 語意呈現轉折，「但是這點被證實是不正確的」，推翻前半句的說法，故選(D)。
3.	A	(A)消失(B)離開(C)拋棄(D)抵達。此段在討論船隻在此消失的原因，除了幽浮、羅盤讀數之外，還有說法是海底火山劇烈活動所造成的。
4.	C	so...that... 如此…以至於…，表示「因果關係」。因為在 1940 和 1950 年代有如此多的船隻消失以至於日本政府派遣研究船調查此事。
5.	B	(A)舒適區(B)危險區域(C)戰區(D)地震帶。前句提到就連日本政府派遣去的研究船連同船上 100 名人員都消失在此處，所以日本政府宣布此區為危險區域，故選(B)。

Ⓒ

2007 年 11 月，有人在尼泊爾聖母峰一帶發現了一連串腳印。那些腳印的長度約有 12 吋，看起來像一種出現在圖畫裡的神秘生物的腳印，那種生物被稱作「喜馬拉雅山雪人」，或是「雪怪」。雪怪是喜馬拉雅原住民所說的一種古代生物，這說法已流傳了數百年之久。他們描述這種生物有猿人的特徵，例如像大拇指、無毛的耳朵以及能用後腳站立。「雪怪」這個名稱來自於西藏語的 yeh-teh，意思是「像人的小動物」。

有許多關於雪怪的調查是由動物科學家來完成，他們專門研究絕種、傳說中或神話中的動物。收集起來的調查結果顯示，大部分的目擊情況，都只不過是誤認像熊這類的森林動物，但有一些採集到的毛髮樣本無法辨認。有些專家宣稱，大多的目擊情況，很可能都是看見瀕臨絕種的棕熊，這種熊能單靠後腳走路。然而，新的目擊事件層出不窮，也為雪怪的存在帶來新希望與更多關注。

從 1950 年代開始，雪怪就一直是許多電視節目與電影的題材，吸引了大量的觀眾，其中不管是相信還是不相信雪怪存在的人都有。曾經以雪怪為題材的包括華納兄弟的卡通、電視影集《超時空博士》以及 1987 年的電影《大腳哈利》。無論雪怪到底存不存在，直到發現進一步的證據之前，都會是個未解之謎，這只會使牠成為更令人興奮想看的題材！

1.	B	measure (測量) 一詞用主動代替被動，此外腳印是在 2007 年被發現的，用<u>過去式</u>。腳印約 12 英吋長。
2.	B	傳說中喜馬拉雅山雪人<u>又稱</u> Yeti，故選(B)。
3.	A	(A)特色(B)演化、進化(C)聰明才智(D)代表。such as 之後所描述的包括<u>有拇指、耳朵上無毛髮和可能用後腳站立</u>，這些都是猩猩或猴子的<u>特色</u>，故選(A)。
4.	C	(A)站起來(B)突出、與眾不同(C)代表(D)支持、準備待命。Yeti 一字源自於西藏語 yeh-teh，<u>意思指的是</u> (此西藏字代表的是)「小的、像人的動物」，故選(C)。
5.	A	(A)絕種的(B)室內的、國內的(C)海洋的(D)走失的、流浪的。此空格後出現的形容詞有 legendary (傳奇的) 和 mythological (神話的)，可推知最可能的答案是(A)。
6.	D	(A)絕不(B)相似的(C)和…無關(D)不過是、僅是。從文意可推論出<u>沒有人</u>真的親眼看過雪怪，大多數得知的目擊報告<u>不過是</u>像熊這類的森林動物被誤認為是雪人罷了，故選(D)。
7.	D	(A)維持、維修(B)保有(C)支持(D)依然是。此句語意有出現轉折，雖然沒人看過雪怪，<u>但是</u>卻有<u>依舊</u>無法辨認的毛髮樣本。
8.	C	關係代名詞 which，代替的是前面的句子 new sightings are constantly surfacing (新的目擊事件不斷地出現)，這件事讓人對雪怪的存在抱持著希望與注意。
9.	B	Whether S + V or not, …「無論…與否」。不論雪怪存在與否，這將成為一個無解之謎。
10.	C	(A)雖然(B)自從、既然(C)直到(D)當、然而。<u>直到</u>找到近一步的證據前，這謎團仍是無解。

Part II: Translation Practice

| B | 1. | Easter Island **is famous for** its huge/enormous stone statues which resemble human heads. |
| | 2. | **Whether** they were carved for religious purposes **or not**, they remain an example of human creativity. |

| C | 1. | Machu Picchu **is renowned for** its architecture which is perfectly combined with its natural surroundings. |
| | 2. | **Whether** the site was a royal retreat **or not**, it is one of the most visited tourist attractions in Peru. |

Unit 13

Part I: Cloze Test

Ⓐ

　　一位勇敢的加拿大青年泰瑞·福克斯，證明了他的夢想可以帶來改變。他在 18 歲時被診斷出患有骨癌，而且右腿遭到截肢。親身經歷了癌症病人的痛苦令泰瑞瞭解到，需要有更多的資金投入癌症研究。因此，他籌畫了一項橫越加拿大的慈善路跑活動。

　　「希望馬拉松」在 1980 年 4 月開跑，泰瑞每天都跑超過 20 哩的路程。除了要忍受劇烈的痛苦之外，他還要面對許多人的冷漠對待。開車經過的人會按喇叭逼他離開道路。不過，泰瑞每天誠摯地在加拿大廣播電台上作進度報告，逐漸開始引起大眾的注意。不久之後，許多民眾開始捐錢支持他的目標。

　　不幸的是，泰瑞在 1981 年 6 月 28 日去世，無法完成他的路跑活動。然而，他的夢想繼續存在——他的努力鼓舞了其他人為癌症研究募款。

1.	D	be diagnosed with「被診斷出有…疾病」。
2.	C	此句為分詞構句，原句為 Because Terry experienced the suffering of a cancer patient firsthand, he realized that....，省略連接詞 Because 和主詞 Terry 後，主動用 V-ing 變為 Experiencing the suffering..., Terry realized that.... 故選(C)。
3.	B	(A)同情(B)漠不關心(C)悲觀(D)革命。下一句提及開車經過的人會對泰瑞按喇叭把他趕到路邊，表示大家對泰瑞的慈善路跑<u>漠不關心</u>，故選(B)。
4.	D	(A)因此、結果(B)相同地(C)此外(D)然而。前一句提到大家對泰瑞的慈善跑步漠不關心，而後面提到泰瑞的報告慢慢地開始引起大家的注意，語意上出現<u>轉折</u>，故選(D)。

| 5. | A | (A)鼓舞、激發(B)侮辱、羞辱(C)打算(D)干涉、介入。前一句提到泰瑞的夢想仍舊存在，他的努力**鼓舞**了其他人繼續為癌症募款，故選(A)。 |

Ⓑ

1995 年 5 月 27 日這天，克里斯多夫・李維的一切都變了。這位在電影裡飾演過超人的演員，在一場馬術比賽裡墜馬受傷。一瞬間，他從一個運動愛好者，變成一個受限在輪椅上的傷殘人士。他無法移動，甚至也無法正常自行呼吸。不過，李維就和他在銀幕上所扮演的角色一樣。即使在養傷期間，他就開始利用自己的巨星身分來幫助他人。他成立了「克里斯多夫・李維基金會」，為脊髓損傷研究募取資金，也協助改善殘障人士的生活品質。

他曾說過：「所謂的英雄是個找到力量堅持下去的凡人…儘管面對巨大的障礙也會堅持下去。」李維符合了自己對英雄的定義，拒絕放棄自己。他是真正的英雄。

1.	B	(A)使適應…(B)限制(C)專心致力於…(D)反對。下一句提到李維無法移動也不能自行呼吸，所以他只能坐輪椅，故選(B)。
2.	A	(A)達成(B)敬重、尊敬(C)廢除(D)逃過…的懲罰。接下來的句子提到李維的成就，因此雖然他不能動，但還是**做到**了跟他在螢幕上所扮演的(超人)角色一樣的事，故選(A)。
3.	B	關係代名詞 which 代替前句 He established the Christopher Reeve Foundation，說明基金會的成立有助於研究經費的募集與殘障人士生活的改善。
4.	D	(A)要求、需要(B)情緒(C)回答、反應(D)阻礙、障礙。英雄是儘管在重重**障礙**中，仍然能找出力量堅持下去的平凡人。
5.	C	(A)接受、贊同(B)創造力(C)定義(D)例外。前一句引號中的話就是李維對英雄的**定義**，而他不放棄的精神正符合他自己對英雄的定義。

Ⓒ

想像你自己既盲又聾。你認為自己還能夠有一份職業，對社會有所貢獻嗎？在你回答之前，先想想海倫・凱勒的故事。

海倫・凱勒在 1880 年出生時是個健康的寶寶。然而，在 18 個月大的時候，一種不明的腦膜炎造成她失去視覺與聽覺，使她的生活變得困難。海倫不停打破東西、尖叫，因沮喪而大發脾氣。她的家人無法處理這樣

的情況，所以為她找來一位老師，也就是安・蘇利文。

安一開始先藉由在海倫手上寫字來教導她。她也教她餐桌禮儀，還有像是梳頭這樣的日常工作。海倫經常行為粗暴，但安會處罰她。漸漸地，海倫學會了一些簡單的日常工作。這是她人生中最困難的時期之一，但海倫並沒有放棄。

儘管海倫患有殘疾，她仍然堅持想過充實的生活。她想上大學，因此在蘇利文老師的協助之下──她用手語幫她翻譯課本與上課內容──海倫成為第一位取得學士學位的聾盲人士。還在就讀大學時，海倫就撰寫了一本自傳，名為《我的生活故事》。在瞭解到自己能用寫作來鼓舞許多人之後，她又寫了一些關於殘障、社會問題與婦女權利的作品。由於她深具影響力又極富成就，世界各地有許多大學頒給她多項榮譽博士學位。

海倫・凱勒的故事證明了永不放棄的重要。是海倫的積極態度幫助了她克服難關，而現在也為數百萬人帶來幫助。

1.	A	contribute to + N/V-ing「對…有所貢獻」。
2.	B	leave + O + OC，在此受詞為 her (Helen Keller)，受詞補語為 blind and deaf；不明的腦膜炎使得海倫失明又失聰。
3.	C	(A) 樂趣、娛樂(B)好奇心(C)挫折、沮喪(D)減輕、放心。前句提及海倫失明、失聰後，日子變得很難過、痛苦，因此經常因為**挫折**而亂摔東西、大叫和發脾氣，故選(C)。
4.	B	by + V-ing，藉由某種方式做…，在此安藉由將字拼在海倫的手上，開始教海倫，故選(B)。
5.	D	(A)優雅地(B)完美地(C)有責任感地、盡責地(D)激烈地、粗暴地。後半句提到安會處罰海倫，是因為海倫經常表現得很**粗暴**，故選(D)。
6.	A	**儘管海倫殘障**，她仍堅持要過充實有用的一生，despite 之後接名詞，故選(A)。(B)應改為 In spite of；(C) Although 為連接詞，其後要接子句；(D)為副詞，表「然而」。
7.	C	要用不定詞 to earn 修飾 the first person，應選擇(C)。
8.	D	原句為 which is entitled *The Story of My Life*，修飾先行詞 her autobiography，省略後改為分詞 entitled，故選(D)。

| 9. | B | so...that...，如此…以至於…。Helen Keller 是<u>如此</u>的有影響力與成就，<u>以至於</u>她獲頒了來自世界各地大學的榮譽博士學位。 |
| 10. | C | 此為分裂句 It is...that... 的句型，it is 和 that 之間放入要強調的部份，句子剩餘的部份置於 that 之後。此句原本為 <u>Helen's positive attitude</u> helped her overcome her difficulties and has now brought help to millions. |

Part II: Translation Practice

B	1.	**In spite of/Despite** his physical disability, he never gives up his dream of becoming an athlete. → **Although** he suffers from physical disability, he never gives up his dream of becoming an athlete.
	2.	**It is** his strong determination **that** inspires others to live life to the full.
C	1.	**In spite of/Despite** the fact that he died young, he will always be remembered as a real fighter for freedom/liberty. → **Although** he died young, he will always be remembered as a real fighter for freedom/liberty.
	2.	**It is** his tremendous courage **that** teaches us never to accept any limitation.

Unit 14

Part I: Cloze Test

Ⓐ

很多研究顯示，一般人都喜歡充滿自信的人。相對來說，缺乏自信則令人感到不愉快。但不用擔心，有些簡單的訣竅可以讓你變得有自信！

其中一個訣竅是學習正面思考。當你有缺乏自信的想法時，試著努力將那些想法轉變成正面思考。然後，設法找出是否有其他解決問題的方法，而不要只是感到悲傷難過，什麼事都不做。另一個訣竅是，試著不要根據發生在你身上的事來對自己做評斷，一定要知道遇上挫折並不代表你就是失敗。有自信的人對人生之禍福均甘之如飴。

要始終保持自信並不容易。如果你學著遵照這些方法，你不僅會變得更有自信，而且會開始真正享受人生！

1.	A	(A)缺少(B)一瞥(C)一些(D)一筆 (金額)。前一句提到大家喜歡有 (with) 自信的人，接者由<u>相反地</u> (In contrast) 引出下一句，語意上呈現<u>轉折</u>，故選(A)，<u>缺乏自信</u>會讓人感到不愉快。
2.	B	make an effort to + V「<u>盡力、努力做…</u>」。
3.	C	(A)為了(B)就…而言(C)取而代之(D)萬一。此處提到當你缺乏自信時，<u>不要傷心</u>或什麼都不做，<u>反而</u>應該試著找出處理問題的方法，故選(C)。
4.	C	此處提到<u>另一個</u>增強自信的方法，故選(C)。
5.	D	否定詞放句首主詞與 (助) 動詞要<u>倒裝</u>，原句為 You will not only become more confident....

Ⓑ

我們的人生在很多方面都像一條河流。

一條河是由來自各種不同源頭的水所構成。雨水在山坡上聚積而成的細流，以及從一些小溪緩緩流入的水，都促成一條河流形成，還有污水下水道和工廠廢水也是。河流最後會是乾淨的，還是受污染的，就取決於流入的水。這情況同樣也適用在我們身上。我們會變成什麼樣的人，主要是由我們選擇接受什麼來決定。

河流裡的水不停流動，潺潺流過石頭，流向它最終的目的地──海洋。這或許是我們能從觀察河流所得到的最正面教育意義──只有當我們積極向目標邁進，才能到達目的地。如果我們因為過於害怕而不敢追求目標，我們的人生就會變得停滯不前。

1.	C	(A)背景(B)指示、說明(C)來源(D)味道、品味。下一句說明河川的水可能來自雨水、小溪、下水道或工廠的廢水，說明河水的<u>來源</u>，故選(C)。
2.	B	在此 whether...or... 所引導的子句為名詞子句，當主詞用，表示「是否…」。
3.	B	(A)遞送、傳送(B)決定(C)描述(D)設計。此句承接上面的敘述：河水是乾淨還是受污染的，<u>取決</u>於水的來源，而人也是一樣，我們將成為怎樣的人也是由我們選擇要接受的事物來<u>決定</u>。
4.	A	(A)最終的(B)特定的(C)有決定性的(D)野心勃勃的。海洋是河水<u>最終</u>的目的地，故選(A)。
5.	D	only when 放句首時後面的主詞與動詞要<u>倒裝</u>，原句為 We can reach our goals only when we are actively moving towards them.

Ⓒ

《長路》是戈馬克‧麥卡錫所撰寫出的一則駭人故事，內容描述一場災難摧毀了世界之後，一個男孩和他慈愛的父親一同緩步走過一片毀壞的景象。文明滅亡，而留存下來的只有一顆星球冰冷、黯淡的外殼，以及少數幾名倖存者。森林與城市遭到焚毀，造成河水污黑，也使所有一切覆上一層灰燼。在這樣的核子冬天裡，男孩和父親走在焦屍遍佈的「長路」上，拚命對抗險惡的氣候、暴力，以及其他因嚴重毀壞而造成的無數困境。他們偶爾也會經過一個令他們想起過去世界的景物。

這本小說呈現出死亡本身的概念，不過讀者始終都不知道是什麼造成了這樣大規模的破壞。麥卡錫描述一個孤獨的人物找不到食物、住所，也得不到安全、同伴或希望。這則故事充滿絕望，但也含有溫情，麥卡錫以精采的描繪獲得了讚揚，不僅寫出故事人物的外在處境，也寫出他們的內在生命與想法。

這則故事的主要內容是關於生存、父親為了保護孩子所做的努力。那父親有強烈的生存意志，儘管情況絕望且未來渺茫，他仍決心要成功活下去。

這不是個輕鬆的故事，而是在探討面對困境要保有希望與信念的課題。故事用極大的對比提醒我們，不管這世界遭到破壞後變得多麼糟糕，都要熱愛生命。

1.	B	⒜申請、應用⒝文明⒞分送⒟膨脹、擴大。第一句提到可怕的事情摧毀了世界、到處是一片破壞的景象，因此文明已經死亡，故選⒝。
2.	D	此處為關係代名詞的省略，原本應是 which leaves，主動改為分詞 leaving。
3.	C	⒜原因⒝缺點⒞例子⒟系統。前面所提到屍體、恐怖的天氣和暴力等等都是世界被嚴重破壞後的例子，故選⒞。
4.	C	remind sb. of sth. 「讓人想起…」。
5.	D	have difficulty + V-ing 「做…有困難」。
6.	D	⒜沮喪⒝嚴苛、殘酷⒞印象⒟溫柔。前半句提到這故事充滿了絕望，後半句由連接詞但是引出，語意上要呈現轉折，故選⒟，與 despair 意思相反。
7.	A	⒜內在的⒝社交的、社會的⒞家庭的⒟學術的。此句提到 McCarthy 同時描述了故事人物的內心世界和外在處境，inner 正好與 exterior 相對照。
8.	B	dedication to + V-ing/N「獻身、致力於…」。

		to 為介系詞，devotion 的用法亦同。
9.	A	⒜處理⒝發生⒞回應⒟修復、恢復。此句提到《長路》不是個輕鬆的故事，而是處理在面臨可怕的情況時，希望和信念的問題。⒝ arises 為不及物動詞，用法為 questions arise，若改為 raises (questions) 用法才正確，⒞要改為 responds to。
10.	B	⒜難怪⒞ however = no matter how 無論如何⒟不論是否…。此處缺少一連接詞，語意上要用無論…，選⒝ No matter + wh-clause。

Part II: Translation Practice

1. B	**No matter how** disastrous the defeat/failure is, you should learn to take it well. → **However** disastrous the defeat/failure is, you should learn to take it well.
	Only when you are aware of your shortcomings / drawbacks / weaknesses can you succeed in the future.
1. C	**No matter what** is/stands in your way, you should stay calm and stick to your principles. → **Whatever** is / stands in your way, you should stay calm and stick to your principles.
2.	**Only when** you have confidence / faith in yourself can you manage to defeat/overcome your fear.

Unit 15

Part I: Cloze Test

Ⓐ

1854 年，倫敦蘇活區爆發了霍亂疫情。博德街方圓 250 碼內，有 5 百人在一週之內喪生。有些人怪罪空氣不好，有些人則認為是上帝帶來的懲罰。但醫生約翰‧斯諾發現，幾乎所有的死者都住在博德街的抽水幫浦附近。不過，其中有 10 個人即使沒住在幫浦附近也死亡了。在民眾愈來愈恐慌的情況之下，他前往這些死者的家中拜訪。他發現在這 10 名死者當中，有 5 名因為好喝的關係，經常從博德街的幫浦帶水回來，而其他有 3 名是在那附近上學的孩童。確定了原因之後，他現身在政府官員面前，要求把抽水幫浦的把手拆掉。疫情

隨即就停止擴散了。雖然斯諾沒有發現霍亂弧菌——引起霍亂的細菌——他那像偵探的調查方法卻有助於現代流行病學的創立。

1.	B	用法 some.... others/some 有些…有些…。例：Some like classical music and others love rock music.；one...the other 一是…另一是…。例：I have two brothers. One lives in Taipei and the other lives in Taichung.
2.	B	(A)因此(B)然而(C)此外(D)事實上。前一句提到幾乎所有的受害者都住在幫浦附近，而接下來的句子提到有 10 個人沒住在幫浦附近也死了，語意上出現轉折，應選(B)。
3.	C	(A)幾乎(B)幾乎不(C)規律地(D)很少。此句說明調查結果，其中有五人因為這裡的水味道好，常常將這的水帶回家，這解釋了為何他們沒住在幫浦附近也成為受害者，故選(C)。
4.	D	此句為「斯諾要求把幫浦的把手移除」。ask...to + V 要求…去做…。因為 water pump handle 是被移除，要用被動語態。
5.	A	(A)雖然(B)甚至、即使 (為副詞) (C)自從、既然(D)除非。此處要選連接詞，連接兩個子句，前半句是「斯諾沒有發現導致霍亂的細菌」，後半句是「他像偵探般的調查方法有助於現代流行病學的創立」，用「雖然…」連接兩句，選(A)。

Ⓑ

在過去 100 年被當作是特效藥的阿斯匹靈，似乎每年都在增加對健康的益處。除了可以舒緩疼痛或治療頭痛之外。有些研究發現阿斯匹靈可能有降低罹患心臟病與中風的機率。由於阿斯匹靈不是處方藥，因此可以廣泛取得。對大多數人來說，服用了阿斯匹靈後，會使他們的血液稀釋，阻斷一種叫做血栓素的化學物質形成。這種化學物質負責凝結血液，有時可能會導致中風。當血栓素形成受阻，就不會產生血塊。這可能降低罹患心臟病及中風的危險。但有些人無法享有這些好處，有凝血功能失調或胃潰瘍等健康問題的人就不能常常服用這萬靈藥。使用阿斯匹靈可能會讓有抗藥性的病人產生嚴重的副作用。每種藥有其功效及風險。記住，沒有一種藥是絕對地安全，即使萬靈藥也是如此。

1.	C	(A)增加(B)測量(C)減少、降低(D)冒…的風險此句在說明阿斯匹靈的好處，根據句意判斷，應選(C)降低心臟病或中風的風險。
2.	A	(A)可取得的(B)傳統的(C)處方箋的(D)規律的。此句前半提及阿斯匹靈是非處方箋藥，(over-the-counter drug)，因此這種藥是(A)很容易取得的。
3.	B	關係代名詞 which 代替前面的句子 (This chemical is responsible for creating blood clots.)，說明這種現象會導致中風。
4.	A	those who + 複數動詞，指凡是…之人此句說明凡是有凝血功能失調或胃潰瘍等健康問題的人不能常常服用這萬靈藥。 若選(B)要改為 having。
5.	B	(A)預防(B)抵抗(C)症狀(D)治療。此句提到服用阿斯匹靈對有些病人會有嚴重的副作用，特別是對阿斯匹靈是有(B)抗藥性的病人。

Ⓒ

你有沒有想過你聞到的味道可能影響你的心情？有一種稱作「芳香療法」的新治療方式宣稱，氣味可以影響我們的心情，甚至我們的健康。「芳香療法」這個字是由一位法國科學家在 1920 年代首先開始使用。這個字是將意為「香氣」的 aroma 與意為「治療」的 therapy 兩個字結合起來。

基本上，芳香療法是一種使用植物萃取精油與化合物的另類療法。進行芳香療法時，會讓人吸入精油與植物的香味。換句話說，就是一個人拿著一瓶精油靠近鼻子深深呼吸。也可以使用按摩方式讓精油直接滲入肌膚，或是將精油加入熱水泡澡。

芳香療法已成為一些人喜愛的紓壓方式。此外，有些醫生現在也在醫院使用芳香療法來為病人減輕疼痛，尤其是那些需要經歷劇烈產痛的母親。但有些人對芳香療法提出了批評。他們說沒有科學證據顯示這種方法真的有療效。而且，有些市售的「芳香療法」產品聞起來很香，但實際上卻是假貨。

儘管有這些批評存在，芳香療法受歡迎的程度仍然持續增加。但是關於療效的爭議也持續不斷。許多人不確定芳香療法是一種有效療法，或只是一種斂財方式。這一切只有靠時間來證明了。

1.	B	claim 宣稱，為此句的動詞，主詞為 a new therapy "called aromatherapy" 為關係子句 which is called aromatherapy 省略而來的分詞，用來修飾先行詞 a new therapy，故選(B)。

2.	**A**	(A) combine A with B 結合 A 和 B (B) communicate with... 和…溝通 (C) confine...to... 將…限制於…之內 (D) connect...to/with... 將…連接
3.	**D**	extract 提煉、榨取；此處為關係代名詞的省略用法，原句為 which are extracted from plants，用來修飾先行詞 essential oils and compounds，省略後改為過去分詞 extracted，故選(D)。
4.	**B**	(A)因此(B)換句話說(C)就某種程度而言(D)另一方面 (常與 on the one hand 成對出現)。此句進一步解釋前一句 (如何吸入精油)，故選(B)。
5.	**A**	be popular with... 「受…歡迎」。
6.	**C**	(A)忍受、忍耐(B)增加(C)減輕、緩和(D)受苦、遭受。前句提及芳香療法有助於紓壓，此外醫生也用芳療來減輕病人的疼痛。
7.	**C**	(A)爭辯、主張(B)確認(C)批評(D)讚美。此句一開始以 But 點出語意上轉折，前半段說明芳香療法的好處，而後半段則提出質疑，故選(C)。
8.	**D**	(A)相反地(B)大體而言(C)簡單地說、總之(D)此外。此處說明為何有人批評芳香療法，一方面是沒有科學依據，此外，有些產品是假的。
9.	**D**	這些字意思皆為「雖然、儘管」，但用法上需注意：although 和 even if 為連接詞，之後需接子句，Although/Even if there are some criticisms；in spite of 和 despite 為介系詞 (片語) 之後接名詞，故選(D)。
10.	**A**	許多人想知道芳香療法是有效的療法或只是種賺錢的方法，whether 在此引導間接問句，做「是否」解。

Part II: Translation Practice

B	1.	**With** the rapid development in medicine/**As** medicine develops rapidly, modern people are able to live longer.
	2.	**To welcome** an aging society, the government should pay attention to the welfare of senior citizens.

C	1.	**With** a longer lifespan/life expectancy/**As** the life expectancy extends, people become more health-conscious than before.
	2.	**To improve** the quality of life, more and more people are willing to spend more time on leisure activities.

Unit 16

Part I: Cloze Test

Ⓐ

「黑人英語」常被認為是「黑人的英語」，或指非裔美國人的說話風格。「黑人英語」這個字是由「黑」和「語音學」組合而成。非裔美國人往往會在非正式場合使用黑人英語。會在非正式場合使用這種語言的人，可能會在比較正式的場合使用標準英語，比如工作場合。黑人英語通常可以透過幾種方式分辨出來。舉例來說，「ain't」會被用來代替「don't」和「isn't」等字。因此像「Why you ain't tell me?」這句話，就是「Why didn't you tell me? (你為什麼沒告訴我)」的意思。除此之外，我們也常會聽到「Ima tell you...」這種說法，意思是「I am going to tell you... (我要跟你說…)」。有些人認為黑人英語是一種次級語言，因為常常是一些教育程度較低的人在使用它。然而，其實它自有一套系統。它不是因為懶得使用標準英語而形成的語言類型，相反地呈現出一種不同的文化。

1.	**A**	(A)混合(B)食譜(C)發音(D)起源。由拼字可知，ebonics 是 "ebony" 和 " phonics" 的混合字。
2.	**D**	on some occasions 表示「在某些場合」。
3.	**C**	本句是指 "ain't" 被用來取代 "don't"。「A 取代 B」可用 A replace B/A substitute for B/A is in place of B，故選(C)。
4.	**C**	(A)一般的，平均的(B)想像的(C)較次等的(D)冒犯人的。從上下文可知，有些人覺得黑人英語是較次等的語言，因為它常被教育程度低的人們 (low levels of education) 所使用。
5.	**B**	本句為 do/does/did + V 的加強語氣句型，說明黑人英語真的是有遵循一套系統。(D) be + to + V 則表示「將要…」。

Ⓑ　　華裔美籍小說家已在文學會議、頒獎典禮和讚許有加的書評中嶄露頭角。 你一定讀過其中一些作家的作品，比如譚恩美、任璧蓮和哈金。這些第二代和第三代的華裔美國人，是在對自己的能力和表達自我的權利有著充分自信的環境中成長。支持她們創作的重要情感有兩個，其一是歸屬感，其二是對歷史的興趣。譚恩美的小說 (《喜福會》和《接骨師的女兒》) 常常將華人童年記憶和當代美國生活相互結合。任璧蓮探討認同問題，並得到來自主流美國和華人社群雙方的讚揚。哈金是比較新進的作家，他對英語的掌握能力爐火純青，甚至兩度獲得筆會／福克納獎的殊榮。這些作家證明，以英語表達東方經驗確實不只是曇花一現而已。

1.	B	must have + V-en 表示「過去必定…。」本句表示「你一定曾經讀過這些作家的作品」。(A) should have + V-en 表示「過去應該做而未做」(C) do + V 表示「真的…」(D) can't have + V-en 表示「以前不可能…」。
2.	D	grow up + Adj 表示「…的長大」，此處 Adj 為主詞補語。
3.	A	(A)以及(B)而不是(C)取代(D)除了。此句表示她受到美國主流市場以及華人圈的推崇。
4.	C	so Adj/Adv that... 表示「如此…以至於」。本句表示他的英文掌握這麼好，以至於他兩次贏得福克納獎。(A)表示「太…以至於不能…」(B)表示「為了…」(D) such 後面需接名詞。
5.	A	(A)東方的(B)本土的(C)不正式的(D)創新的。從上下文得知，這些成功的華裔作家，證明了用英文所表達的東方內容，不會只是曇花一現。

Ⓒ　　今日，科技和廣告正以全新但不尋常的方式改變英語。科技在新式英語的發展中也許扮演最重要的角色。在過去十年間，電子郵件、網際網路聊天室、即時訊息和簡訊成為受歡迎的溝通方式，以這些方式溝通的人創造出一種新風格的語言。例如，縮寫就經常被使用。意指「大笑」的縮寫「LOL」，是以文字的形式說某件事非常好笑。數字也被用來取代字母，比如「Gr8」是表示「真棒」，而「L8r」則表示「待會兒」。對人們來說，使用這種新型態的英語很方便。在使用更快速溝通而有字數限制的簡訊時，這是很重要的。除此之外，有些人認為電子郵件和即時訊息是比較不正式的溝通方式，因此也不需遵守在較正式場合應遵守的標點符號和文法

規則。廣告也對新式英語有所貢獻。為了凸顯自己 (以及引起注意)，有些廣告會使用新式英語，特別是新的拼字。今日，我們常常可以看到標榜「X-treme」(極限) 或「x-tra valu」(超值) 的產品廣告。

　　當然，在寫報告或考試的時候使用過多這些新式縮寫是不太恰當的。除此之外，雖然這種新式英語在簡訊和電子郵件中很受歡迎，在口語英文中還是不太流行。在跟其他人對話時，很少人會說「BTW」或「IMHO」，而是會說「順帶一提」或「依我的淺見」。不過就目前而言，新式英語仍是正在蓬勃發展的一個語言區塊。

1.	C	此句上文指出科技和廣告正在改變英文。由下文討論 e-mail, chatroom, text messaging 可得知此處是說前者 (technology) 或許是改變的最大主因。
2.	A	(A)取代(B)以…的論點(C)以…之名(D)紀念推崇…。此句表示數字常用來取代字母。
3.	A	原句應為 ...in text messages, in which the space for messages is limited. ，這裡的 "in which" 可用 "where" 取代。
4.	D	此句承接上文，指出這樣的語言受到歡迎，是因為它很快速方便，此外，使用者覺得在電子郵件或簡訊中所用的語言，不需過於正式，這兩項都是造成這種非正式語言流行的原因。
5.	A	本句表示因為使用者在非正式的場合 (text messaging, chatrooms)，不需太正式，反之他們會在正式場合使用合乎文法的文字。
6.	C	make contributions/contribute to + N 表示「對…有貢獻」。
7.	D	(A)發音(B)文法(C)字彙(D)拼字。由下句的 x-treme, x-tra valu 可知廣告對英文的拼字方面造成影響。
8.	B	由下文可得知很少人在說話的時候，使用這些新英文，亦即這種英文尚未在口語上流行起來。has yet to + V 表示「尚未…」。
9.	A	(A)而是(B)因此(C)然而 conj. (D)再者。此處應為副詞，表示他們不說 BTW 而是說 by the way。
10.	C	(A)遲早(B)一再地(C)目前(D)有時候。本句和上文語氣有所轉折，表示雖然這種英文在口語上不流行，但目前它仍屬英語正發展中的一部份。

Part II: Translation Practice

B	1.	Body language can **take the place of** spoken language on some occasions.
	2.	**The former** can lively convey more messages while **the latter** can cause less misunderstanding.
C	1.	To save more time, text messages are often used **in place of/to replace/to substitute for** traditional phone calls.
	2.	**The former** can be combined with emoticons while **the latter** can express the user's feelings directly.

Unit 17

Part I: Cloze Test

Ⓐ

到月球度假聽來瘋狂。不過既然已經有人登陸月球了，這樣的旅程也許可能成真。在未來，當你到月球旅遊時，必須攜帶自己所需的一切氧氣和水，因為這兩樣東西月球上都沒有。但你不需要帶耳塞，因為沒有空氣意味著聲音也無法傳送。此外，月球上從不下雨，因此你可以不用帶雨傘。散個步，享受月球的景緻吧。你的身體重量只有在地球上的六分之一，走起來會感覺宛如在空中漫步。月球上也會有危險。舉例來說，被稱作「月震」的小地震時常發生。然而，對於想體驗真正「遠離塵世」假期的人來說，到月球旅遊可能是個完美的選擇。

1.	**B**	根據上下文可得知，到月球旅行需要自己帶氧氣及水，因為在月球上兩者皆無法獲得，故選(B)表示「兩者皆不…」。(D) none 多用在表示「三者以上皆不…」的情況。
2.	**B**	(A)調職(B)傳遞(C)傳達訊息(D)溝通。本句是說明月球上沒有空氣因此聲音無法傳遞，故選(B)。
3.	**C**	(A)拜訪(B)刪除(C)留下(D)入侵。月球上不下雨，因此可以把雨傘留下不帶去，故選(C)。
4.	**A**	do/does/did + V 用來加強語氣，本句是說明月球上真的有危險存在，故選(A)。
5.	**D**	those who S + V 表示「那…類型的人」，故選(D)。

Ⓑ

「行星」這個字意指漫遊者，因為它會在天空中旅行。水星距離太陽大約 3 千萬英哩，是離它最近的一顆行星。水星每年有幾次會在天黑之後出現在西邊天空的低處。其他時候，日出前我們都可以在東方天空的低處看到它。透過望遠鏡，我們很容易看出它的形狀甚至大小產生變化。我們所看到的跟月球變化相似。月球和水星產生變化的原因，都是因為光線和陰影影響了我們從地球上看到它們的樣子。當水星循著軌道運行時，有時候非常清晰可見。但水星接近地球時，被太陽照亮的地方也較不容易被我們看到。當水星再次遠離我們時，這種大小變化的循環也會重新開始。

1.	**D**	比較級 ...than any other + 單數名詞，表示「最…」，此句表示水星比任何其他的行星更接近太陽，故選(D)。
2.	**C**	(A)略過(B)吸引(C)看到(D)預測。此句表示在日出前，我們能在東方天空的低處看到水星。
3.	**C**	be similar to 表示「和…相似」，故選(C)。
4.	**A**	The reason...is that... 表示「原因為…」，that 子句用來說明解釋前面 reason 的內容，故選(A)。
5.	**B**	(A)瞥一眼(B)循環(C)描述(D)步驟。此句是表示水星大小改變的這個循環，會再度開始，故選(B)。

Ⓒ

儘管我們的太陽系裡有數量龐大的小行星、流星和其他宇宙碎片，長久以來人們都相信只有九大行星存在。除了地球之外，其他行星包括水星、金星、火星、木星、土星、天王星、海王星和冥王星。然而，一項驚人的宣言挑戰了這份長久以來的信念。美國的天文學家聲稱他們在太陽系發現一顆新行星。拜位於加州一座天文台的強力望遠鏡之賜，這第十顆行星在 2005 年 1 月 8 日首次被人發現。

到目前為止，這顆新行星還沒有正式名稱，暫時被稱為「2003UB313」。它比冥王星還大，跟太陽的距離也比第九行星 (即冥王星) 到太陽的距離遠三倍。但這項發現也在天文學家之間引發一些爭論。有些人認為這顆新行星事實上根本還算不上行星，只是一顆大型的小行星，或甚至只是一顆冰凍的岩石。有些天文學家則認為，要認定這顆新行星確實繞著太陽轉，現在還言之過早，而這是被判定為行星的必要條件之一。這顆新行星真的會成為太陽系第十顆行星嗎？其他天文學家會承認它是一顆行星嗎？這些問題尚待未來能有人解答。

1.	A	表示「大量的…」。a large number of + 可數名詞。asteroids, meteors 為可數名詞，故選(A)。a large amount of + 不可數名詞。a large sum of + 不可數名詞。a good deal of + 不可數名詞。
2.	C	從 "the other plants include…." 得知此句應是說明「除了地球以外，其他的行星還包括…」，故選(C)。(A)需改為 In addition to。
3.	D	(A)高度期待的(B)壽命短的(C)自我中心的(D)長久保持的。由 However 得知語氣有轉折，此句說明這個發現挑戰了「太陽系只有九個行星」這項長久以來的想法，故選(D)。
4.	B	with the help of N 表示「有了…的幫助」，故選(B)。(A) by 表示「藉由…」，多半以 by + V-ing 型式出現。
5.	C	(A)有時候(B)很快地(C)目前暫時(D)偶而。由 remain unnamed 可得知，此星球尚未被命名，目前暫時被叫做 2003UB313，故選(C)。
6.	B	倍數 (three times, four times, etc) + 比較級 + than 表示「是…的幾倍」。故選(B) farther 為 far 的比較級，此句表示此星球離太陽的距離比太陽系第九個行星跟太陽的距離還要遠三倍。
7.	D	(A)因此(B)然而(C)然而(D)反而。此句說明有些人認為這個星球不是個行星，反而應該可能只是小行星或冰岩，故選(D)。
8.	A	too…to 表示「太…以至於不能…」。此句表示有些天文學家認為現在要說這顆星球繞著太陽轉還太早了，故選(A)。
9.	B	此處應選(B) ", which" 代替前面一整句。表示「繞著太陽轉」是成為行星的條件之一。
10.	C	in the future to come 表示「未來」。也就是在未來大家期待知道這些問題的答案。

Part II: Translation Practice

B	1.	Earth is approximately **ten times as massive as** Mars.
	2.	There is **a small amount of** water on Mars, which many people regard as evidence of life.

C	1.	It is estimated that there are **twice as many girls as** boys who are interested in astrology.
	2.	Nowadays, **a large number of** female employers resort to astrology to choose workers easy to get along with.

Unit 18

Part I: Cloze Test

Ⓐ

　　隨著我們的世界變得越來越電腦化，進行之有年的義工活動也在線上獲得新生。這項新興活動一般稱為虛擬義工，它提供機會給一些沒有時間進行較傳統義工活動，但仍希望從事慈善工作的人。對一些擅長使用電腦的人，或行動不便以致於無法輕易離開家的人來說，這也是一種好用的方法。可以在線上完成的工作包括進行網路研究、翻譯文件，或設計網頁等。網路服務甚至能讓義工和需要幫助的人進行一對一接觸。若對這樣的活動有興趣，在許多網站上都有清單，描述所需要的幫助和完成這些事情預計要花的時間。透過提供虛擬義工這項選擇，慈善團體能運用科技做的好事也更多了。

1.	B	此句意思為「就如同大家所知道的，這種上網做善事的舉動，就是 virtual volunteering」。as 為關係代名詞，需用被動式表示「為…所知道」。
2.	B	prevent + O + from + N/V-ing 表示「使…不能…」。
3.	C	(A)就…而言(B)控制(C)需要(D)在…的時候。此句表示網路可提供義工和需要幫助的人，一對一接觸的機會，故選(C)。
4.	D	原句應為 …the amount of time (which is) estimated to complete each task. 省略關係代名詞和 be 動詞，故選(D)。
5.	D	do good (to + N) 表示「對…誰有好處」。

Ⓑ

　　國際樂施會在 1995 年成立於英國。今日，這個組織在 12 個國家設有辦公室，在世界各地提供援助。「樂施」這個名字是「牛津對抗飢荒委員會」的簡稱，它採取一種獨特的方式來達到慈善目標。樂施會不直接和需要幫助的人接觸，而是跟超過 3 千個在地組織合作，讓飽受貧窮和悲慘之苦的人對自己的生活有掌控權。為了

達到目標，樂施會把焦點集中在特定議題上。他們爭取文明的工作環境，並致力於提供一些基本服務，如教育和醫療，方法是訓練當地居民成為教師和醫療人員。在巨大災難發生之後，人們會很容易受到暴力和疾病的侵襲，甚至可能遭到虐待，因此樂施會致力於提供庇護所和乾淨飲水。最後，這個組織也爭取人權，因此它協助婦女、宗教和種族上的少數者，以及殘障人士獲得社會公義。簡而言之，樂施會努力幫遭到不當對待者爭取正義，並幫助受人忽略者發聲。

1.	C	(A)態度(B)傾向(C)方法(D)測量。本句表示這個機構採取一種特殊的<u>方法</u>，去達到它助人的目標，故選(C)。
2.	A	本句原為 ...so that people who suffer from poverty and grief can take control of their own lives. 省略關係代名詞，動詞改為分詞 suffering from 來修飾 people。
3.	D	by + V-ing 為「藉由…」。本句表示 Oxfam 希望<u>藉</u>由訓練當地人民為老師及醫護人員來提供教育及醫療資源。
4.	C	at the risk of 表示「有…的風險」。
5.	A	(A)公平(B)優點(C)展示(D)結論。bring justice to + N 表示「為…找回公平正義」。

Ⓒ

1966 年證嚴法師在台灣創立慈濟功德會。在當時，該組織由 30 名家庭主婦組成，每個人每天存兩毛錢來協助弱勢者。今日，這個組織有一千萬名義工及支持者，在世界 47 個國家提供人道協助。

這個組織的慈善工作包括提供食物給貧窮和飢餓的人，為大災難如水災和地震的受災者提供賑災物資，還有到年長者家中探訪，協助他們的生活起居。他們甚至有自己的廣播電台和電視台，以便傳播他們的理念。總結來說，他們努力幫助和教育民眾。

慈濟基金會開設許多學校和醫院。慈濟學院在世界各地都設有學校，主要教導中華文化、佛教規章，甚至還有插花課程。慈濟親子計畫除了進行這些活動之外，還同時促進家庭感情。這個組織也在最需要醫療的地方開設診所，提供免費或收費低廉的醫療服務。慈濟國際醫療協會有超過 5 千名醫療專業人員志願到亞洲、北美洲及南美洲服務。最值得注目的是，慈濟牙醫專車還能把牙醫服務帶到沒有這項基本服務的偏遠地區。

從如此小的起步點開始，慈濟基金會是一個精彩的

例子，讓我們看到一點點付出就可以產生如此多的善。

1.	B	the + Adj 表示「那一類型的人」為複數。the less fortunate 表示「較不幸的人」。
2.	A	(A)協助(B)預測(C)同伴(D)威脅。此句表示這個組織在全世界有義工提供人道<u>協助</u>，故選(A)。
3.	B	(A)分配(B)賑災物資(C)畫像(D)撤退。本句表示慈濟會提供<u>賑災物資</u>給水災或地震的災民。
4.	C	(A)捐獻(B)檢視(C)散布(D)傳染。本句表示慈濟有自己的電視和廣播，去幫忙散布他們的理念。
5.	C	(A)反而(B)相反地(C)整體而言(D)老實說。本句承接上文，慈濟會賑災、散布理念，<u>整體而言</u>，他們想做的就是幫助及教育人們。故選(C)。
6.	A	本句主詞 The Tzu Chi Academy 為單數名詞，空格應為本句的動詞，故選(A)。
7.	D	本句表示慈濟親子計畫也做同樣的事，一邊還同時讓家庭關係更緊密，while 此處表示「在…的同時」。
8.	A	原句應為 areas in which people need it most，用 where 代替 in which。
9.	B	be able to + V 表示「能夠…」，故選(B)。若選(A)句子應改為 be capable of bringing... (C) have access to + N 表示「能夠使用…」(D) know the key to N 表示「知道…的訣竅」。
10.	B	such + N 表示「如此…」。若選(A)，應改為 from so small a beginning。

Part II: Translation Practice

B	1.	World Vision Taiwan dedicates itself to the welfare of children **by helping** them overcome poverty and social injustice.
	2.	It **is capable of providing** children with opportunities of education and medical care.
C	1.	Life of those victims in the flood can be improved **by means of** this regular sponsorship program.
	2.	With no more than NT$ 1000 a month, each of us **is able to make** a contribution.

Unit 19

Part I: Cloze Test

Ⓐ

　　觀光業對於陷入貧困而必須倚靠觀光來生存的城市和國家而言，是一把雙面刃。牙買加和坎恩 (墨西哥) 沒辦法在科技或珍貴資源上跟已開發國家競爭，這樣的國家年收入 30% 都要靠觀光，但這樣的收益卻伴隨著相對的代價。這就是刃的另一面——它們的生態系統要為這些年復一年出現的觀光客付出昂貴的代價。舉例而言，坎恩是墨西哥觀光客最常造訪的度假地點之一，雖然當地商業大幅倚賴觀光，它的雨林卻因為來度假的人太多而瀕臨死亡。此外，牙買加有超過 25 種當地才有的野生物種，但這些動物如今正瀕臨絕種。這些地區面臨的挑戰是如何在持續保有經濟成長的同時，拯救它們的環境。

1.	A	such...as... 表示「像…這樣的…」。此句表示<u>像是墨西哥、牙買加這樣的國家</u>，每年人民的收入，有 30% 是依賴觀光旅遊，故選(A)。
2.	B	從第一句 Tourism is a <u>double-edged</u> blade 可得知旅遊業是一把<u>雙面</u>刃。前一句提到旅遊業帶來的<u>獲益</u>，此句則說明旅遊業的另外一面，故選(B)。
3.	D	(A)不管、不論(B)僅管(C)根據(D)因為。<u>因為</u>過多的遊客，雨林正面臨毀滅，故選(D)。
4.	B	(A)需要(B)處在…的危險中(C)以…而論(D)支持。此句表示「這些動物<u>正面臨絕種的危險</u>」，故選(B)。
5.	C	(A)維持(B)保存(C)持續(D)恢復。此句表示這些地方面臨的挑戰是，一邊要拯救環境，同時也要持續經濟方面的成長，故選(C)。(A) remain 是指「維持在…的狀況」，如接名詞，為主詞補語，例：He remains a bachelor all his life.

Ⓑ

　　保護自然區域是一項挑戰。保護自然的其中一種方式是設立國家公園及其他保護區，遊客要進入之前必須先申請許可。這有助於控制在特定時間內進入該處的遊客數量，降低遊客所造成的損害。另一種保護自然區域的方式是限制能在該區域進行的活動項目。舉例來說，許多公園禁止遊客在境內生火，這是每年造成大量森林損害的一項人類活動。類似這樣的法律很好，但除非人們真的遵守，否則無法發生作用。教育是非常急迫要做

的事。想前往野外的人必須知道自然環境多麼容易受到傷害。這項教育必須及早開始，父母、老師和政府都有責任採取行動。只有在人們珍惜自己所擁有的事物時，他們才會去保護它。

1.	D	原句應為 "...other protected areas in which visitors require permission before entering."。其中 in which 可代換為 where，故選(D)。
2.	B	(A)壓力(B)限制(C)懷疑(D)強調。根據下一句可知，很多公園現在不准遊客生火，可知此句是表示另一個保護保育區的方式就是去<u>限制</u>遊客能夠做的活動，故選(B)。
3.	A	此句表示，<u>除非</u>人們遵守，否則規定是沒有用的，故選(A)。
4.	D	此句表示去野外的人，必須要知道環境是很容易被破壞的。need to be V-en = need V-ing，故選(D)。
5.	C	only 放句首時，主詞與動詞需倒裝。但如果句中有助動詞時，則只需要 (助動詞) 部份倒裝即可。此原句為 They will protect what they have only when they appreciate it. 故選(C)。

Ⓒ

　　厄爾・高爾曾在美國總統柯林頓執政時代擔任副總統，他也是一名製片家，製作過得獎紀錄片《不願面對的真相》。這部電影清楚定義越來越嚴重的全球暖化問題，以及它是怎麼直接由人類所造成。他之所以將這部片命名為《不願面對的真相》，是因為多年來全球暖化一直是一個引發熱烈爭論的議題。有些人不願意相信這是事實，也有些人相信這是事實，但卻不願改變自己的生活方式。尤其政府更對這項問題避而不談，因為將能源、燃料、水和其他許多資源改得更具環保效益，這將帶來龐大的花費和麻煩。

　　這部電影的產生，是透過剪輯一些他對氣候變遷的談話片段，再加上形成這種看法的自身經驗，例如他的姊姊因肺癌而英年早逝。他對過去十年來環境的劇烈變遷感到憂心，因此決定針對全球暖化問題開始教育大眾。這部電影是表達此項理念的方式之一，他讓人們瞭解到：我們必須改變自己的生活方式才能拯救地球。這部電影上映之後，人們清楚瞭解到這個問題不能再被忽視了，因為氣候變遷比先前預估的更快。這部電影成為讓現在的「綠色」和「樂活」運動得以展開一個重要的開始。它同時也使世界各地的政府不得不正視這個問

題，明白它們必須對無法再生的資源做出政策上的根本改變。如今，無視於問題的存在，對人們而言已經不再是「方便」的，反而，此時此刻正是解決問題的契機。

1.	B	這部電影說明了溫室效應的問題，及它是<u>如何</u>由人類直接造成的，故選(B)。
2.	B	The reason why S + V is **that** S + V 是表示「…的理由為…」，故選(B)。
3.	C	(A)擁抱、支持(B)啟發(C)辯論(D)挑戰。此句是說明電影取名的原由，好幾年來，溫室效應一直是個被<u>熱烈討論</u>的議題，故選(C)。
4.	D	sweep something under the rug 表示「對…置之不理」，故選(D)。
5.	A	(A)有效益的(B)保護的(C)有用的(D)有效的。此句表示「政府一直對全球暖化的問題置之不理，是因為害怕，要把能源變得更具<u>環保效益</u>，會帶來很多金錢花費及麻煩」。
6.	C	speeches/lectures/books/topics + <u>on</u>/about + N 表示「關於…的演講／授課／書／議題」，故選(C)。
7.	B	本句是表示高爾很擔憂近年來氣候的劇烈改變，<u>因此</u>他決定教導人們關於溫室效應的議題，故選 (B)。(A) therefore 為副詞，無法連接兩個句子。
8.	C	本句表示「氣候比原先所想的變化更快速」，原本句子應為 ...because the climate is changing more rapidly than (it is) previously thought，故選(C)。
9.	B	open sb's eyes **to** N.... 表示「讓…看到／正視到…」，故選(B)。
10.	D	現在對於人們而言，對於問題視而不見已經不再是不便之事，<u>反而</u>，已經知道現在就是要解決問題的時候，故選(D)。

Part II: Translation Practice

	1.	Many countries are exploiting **such** renewable energy **as** wind power.
B	2.	**The reason why** renewable energy is valuable **is that** they are generated by sustainable natural resources.

	1.	**Such** illegal human activities **as** unregulated fishing and logging should be prohibited.
C	2.	**The reason why** there should be strict laws against these activities **is that** they will do irreparable damage to the ecology.

Unit 20

Part I: Cloze Test

Ⓐ

許多消費者對購買環保或「綠色」商品很有興趣，因為他們認為這樣的消費能對環境有所幫助。這種消費選擇似乎也很合乎流行，因為他們看到名人在暢銷雜誌或電視節目上支持環保訴求。從沐浴、美容保養品到車子，有各種各樣的商品聲稱自己是環保的。然而，消費者必須認真考慮一下，購買標榜「綠色」的商品是否真的是對環境有利。殘酷的真相是，我們不可能光靠購買「綠色」商品來防止全球暖化。擁有環保的車子也還不夠。減少二氧化碳排放較好的方式是擁有一台環保的車子，並且和同事或朋友共乘，若路程較短就騎腳踏車或走路，並盡可能搭乘大眾運輸工具。

1.	B	(A)促銷(B)購買(C)調查(D)藉口。從 buying green products 可得知，本句是表示很多消費者覺得這樣的<u>購買</u>可以幫助地球，故選(B)。
2.	A	本句是表示因為消費者在電視或雜誌上看到名人支持環保時，會覺得做這樣的購買活動來說是很時尚的，故選(A)。
3.	D	原句應為 A variety of products which range from bath and beauty products to cars claim that...，省略關係代名詞，故選(D)。
4.	B	本句表示消費者應仔細思考，購買這些綠產品<u>是否</u>真的能夠幫助環境，故選(B)。
5.	C	此處表示<u>當可能的時候</u>，應搭乘大眾交通工具，故選(C)。whenever = anytime when

Ⓑ

生態藝術正如其名，是以生態或自然的方式創作藝術。生態藝術運動始於 1960 年代，那時人們開始瞭解到保護生態的重要性。有些藝術家發現自然原來是這麼脆弱和細緻，於是開始創作能引起環境關懷的藝術作品。為了要創作出能反映人與自然和諧共存的作品，生態藝術家使用天然而環保的素材。舉例而言，藝術家 Alan Sonfist 積極參與生態藝術作品創作，他最知名的

作品之一就是位於紐約的《時間風景》。他在一小塊區域上種滿原本曾長滿整個紐約市的原生樹木和森林。這個作品象徵因為人類干預而隨時間消逝的許多植物。生態藝術是喚醒大眾生態意識的一種創新方式。

1.	A	(A)保護、保存(B)探險(C)維持(D)保留。本句表示「1960 年代，人們開始了解保護自然的重要性」，故選(A)。
2.	D	本句表示「很多藝術家發現大自然是多麼脆弱」，故選(D)。
3.	B	(A)熟悉(C)結合(D)困惑。be involved with/in 表示「參與…，加入…」，故選(B)。本句表示 Alan Sonfist 積極地參與創作生態藝術作品。
4.	B	used to + V 表示「過去曾經…」。他在一塊區域，種植了過去曾經覆蓋整個紐約市的植物，故選(B)。
5.	C	(A)剝奪(B)典型(D)相信。這個藝術作品是象徵因為人類干擾而消失的植物。be symbolic of 表示「象徵，代表…」，故選(C)。

Ⓒ 時尚產業常常跟自私自利聯想在一起。我們傾向把會去消費這些東西的消費者想成是錢太多的蠢蛋。然而，近來有些時尚產業中的人開始採取行動，改變這種既定形象，方式是在促銷服飾商品的同時推動環保或道德議題。許多設計師開始關切自己使用的衣料是從何而來。有些人聲明他們的產品是在「公平交易」原則下的產物，意思是製造這些布料的工人 (往往是貧窮國家居民) 會得到合理薪資和良好待遇。

儘管許多新的、有環保意識的流行設計師驕傲地宣稱他們使用天然素材，但有些科學家相信，使用人工材質可能實際上更環保。這是因為有些人工材質可以在更低的溫度下有效洗滌，因此需要用到的能量也更少。這些科學家也建議人們租衣服而不是買衣服，但幾乎沒有人認為真的會流行起來。

這些新興的環境關懷會在時尚產業裡持續多久，這點還有待觀察。在 1990 年代，有好幾位名模公開反對皮草服飾。這項計畫在過去十年間似乎頗為成功，但如今皮草又再度開始受歡迎。有些曾宣稱反對皮草的模特兒，竟然被人看到身上也穿了一件！所以，環境關懷到底會在時裝業持續下去還是一時流行，仍有待觀察。

1.	C	(A)因此(B)無疑地(C)然而(D)在另一方面。前文說明過去對時尚界的印象是負面的 (selfishness, foolish rich people)。然而，有些時尚界人士已經開始採取行動去改變這種形象。
2.	C	(A)數量(B)品質(C)來源(D)舒適。從下一句 Some have claimed... **the principle of fair trade.** 可得知現在很多設計師關心的是他們原料的來源，故選(C)。
3.	B	(A)住宿(B)薪資(C)尊嚴(D)代理。公平交易是指保護勞工，確保他們得到合理的薪資，故選(B)。
4.	D	由 though 可得知此處有所轉折，本句表示雖然設計家自豪使用天然的素材，但有些科學家相信人工材料事實上對環境較好，故選(D)。(A)有機的(B)精緻的(C)未加工的(D)人工的。
5.	A	at...temperatures「在…的溫度下」，故選(A)。
6.	C	原句為 This is because...temperatures, and therefore requires less energy.。省略 and 並將動詞 require 改成為分詞而形成分詞構句，故選(C)。
7.	D	(A)恢復(B)接管(C)開始吃(D)流行。本句表示幾乎沒有人認為租衣服這件事會流行，故選(D)。
8.	B	seem to V 表示「似乎…」，seem to have + V-en 表示「似乎…過去…」，本句表示過去 10 年這項活動似乎很成功，故選(B)。
9.	A	當時反對穿皮草的模特兒，被看到穿著它們。be spotted V-ing 表示「被看到…做…」，本句為完成式，故選(A)。
10.	B	(A)很難找到(B)持續下去(C)尚未來到(D)最棒的。時尚界的環保意識是否會持續下去，或只是一時的流行，仍有待觀察，故選(B)。

Part II: Translation Practice

B	1.	There **used to be** a great number of spectacular coral reefs around the coast of Taiwan.
	2.	Serious pollution has changed the ecosystem under the sea, **which poses/posing** a great threat to the survival of coral reefs.
C	1.	Vegan diet **used to be** considered just a healthy way of living embraced/supported by few people.

2.	However, growing vegetables consumes less energy than raising cattle, **which makes** / **making** it a good way to protect the Earth.

Unit 21

Part I: Cloze Test

Ⓐ

　　我們的星球有許多引人入勝的特色景致 ，例如峽谷、湖泊、河流，以及平原。雖然它們都很有意思，但還不是地球上最出色的。最能從遠處就吸引你目光的是地球的山。它們峰峰相連，形成所謂的「山脈」。最雄偉的山脈位於美洲、亞洲和非洲。那裡的山脈是地球表面上最高也最顯眼的特色景致，不過它們都不是地球上最長的山脈。這項殊榮該屬於海面下的山。如果把海水抽乾，我們就會看到一條超過 64,000 公里長的山脈！無論能否從地球表面上看到，這條世界最長的山脈仍然是這個星球上令人驚嘆的景致之一。

1.	B	此句為 Adj/Adv/N as S + V, S + V 的句型，表示「雖然，儘管…」。這裡是說明雖然他們很有趣，卻不是地球上最明顯的地貌，故選(B)。
2.	A	(A)顯著的(B)真正的(C)有活力的(D)偶爾的。由下句 the highest and most visible features，可得知此句說明最顯著突出的山脈在美洲、亞洲和非洲。
3.	D	此句是說明最顯著突出的山脈在美洲、亞洲和歐洲，然而沒有一個是世界上最長的山脈。此為語氣轉折之處，故選(D)。
4.	D	此句為假設語氣的用法 If S + were to + V, S + would/could/should/might + V，表示「未來不可能發生」的事實。此句說明如果你將來有一天將海水排乾 ，你會發現有超過 64,000 公里長的山脈，故選(D)。
5.	C	Whether...or not 是表示 「不論 / 是否…與否」，故選(C)。If 做「是否」時，不可放句首，也不和 or not 合用。

Ⓑ

　　很少人知道怎麼定義「聖嬰現象」。這個字在西班牙文裡意指「小男孩」。之所以用「聖嬰現象」為名，是因為這個現象往往發生在聖誕節，也就是耶穌誕生的時間。典型的聖嬰現象發生在非洲西部海岸外，而「反聖嬰現象」則是聖嬰現象的相反。反聖嬰現象這個字在

西班牙义中意指「小女孩」，主要影響範圍是南半球。這兩個現象都是首先被吉伯特‧湯馬斯‧渥克爵士這位科學家所發現。渥克是第一個注意到南方震盪現象的人，那是每個月發生在大溪地群島和澳洲達爾文地區之間的氣壓變化現象 。 除了這些特定區域造成影響之外，聖嬰現象和反聖嬰現象導致天氣型態改變，對全球氣候都產生影響。 這對地球和全球經濟都造成深遠衝擊，因為這些地區的經濟體之中有許多都大幅倚靠農業和漁業。

1.	C	(A)次要的(B)巨大的(C)相反的(D)立即的 。 由 El Nino 表示 little boy ，而下文 La Nina 表示 little girl，可推論出 La Nina 是 El Nino 的相反事物。(A) side effect 為副作用。
2.	A	此為 the first + to V 的用法，故選(A)。
3.	C	此句表示除了影響這幾個特定地區 ，El Nino 和 La Nina 也影響了全球的天氣，故選(C)。
4.	B	have an impact on 表示「對…有影響」。
5.	C	以連接詞 considering (that) S + V 的用法，來連接兩個句子，表示「考慮到…」，故選(C)。

Ⓒ

　　紐奧良位於龐恰特雷恩湖和密西西比河之間，鄰近墨西哥灣，曾是個蓬勃發展的美國城市，向來以狂歡節嘉年華會和才華洋溢的爵士樂手聞名。直到 2005 年，卡崔娜颶風肆虐這城市而淹沒在洪水中。事實上，由於居民的樂天個性，這個城市素有「樂天之都」的暱稱。

　　紐奧良的地勢低於海平面約兩公尺，由一個環繞全市的防洪系統保護它不受洪水侵襲。這些防洪堤或是水屏障，環繞整個城市，防止龐恰特雷恩湖和密西西比河的水湧入市區內。

　　2005 年，卡崔娜颶風全力直撲紐奧良。颶風挾帶的強風和暴潮摧毀了部分防洪堤，造成可怕的損害。整個城市有超過八成地區完全被水淹沒，數以萬計的人無家可歸，沒有食物、清水，甚至沒有電力可用。更雪上加霜的是，進出這個城市的主要道路不是被摧毀就是被淹沒，使生還者很難逃離這個城市，而救援人員也很難進去。

　　為了協助這些居民和這座城市，聯邦和地方政府花費數十億美元進行災後清理，建造更好的防洪堤，並重建被摧毀的房子跟商業活動。然而由於遭受的損害如此巨大，有些專家預估要花上超過十年，這個城市才能恢復原貌。

1.	D	此句是表示在 2005 年的卡崔娜颶風淹沒這個城市前，紐奧良是個非常繁榮的城市，until 表示「到…為止，在…之前」，故選(D)。
2.	D	此句是表示紐奧良過去的名字是 the Big Easy，故選(D)。be use to + N/V-ing 表示「習慣於…」，used to + V 表示「過去習慣…」，be used to + V 表示「被用來…」。
3.	C	(A)放置(B)放置、下蛋(C)座落在(D)坐下 seat oneself。此句表示紐奧良座落於海平面下兩公尺處，故選(C)，類似用法的動詞還有 sit, lie, stand 等。
4.	A	prevent A from B 表示「阻止…不要」。此句表示這些防水屏障阻止密西西比河的水灌入這個城市，故選(A)。
5.	B	(A)很快(B)全力、全面(C)沒有延誤(D)一定、絕對。此句表示卡崔娜颶風全面地摧毀了紐奧良，故選(B)。
6.	B	承接上文，此句表示「有數萬人無家可歸，百分之八十的城市泡在水中，更糟的是，主要連外道路都被摧毀」，故選(B)。
7.	A	主要對外道路不是被摧毀就是泡在水中，使得救難工作很困難，故選(A)。
8.	C	spend time/money V-ing/on + N，故選(C)。
9.	B	N be such that 用來強調名詞，此句表示這傷害是多麼大，以至於專家估計要花十年以上這城市才能恢復原貌，故選(B)。選項(A)，應改為 The damage is so great that…。
10.	D	(A)重新拿回(B)整修(C)回想(D)恢復。此句表示「這傷害是多麼大，以致於專家估計要花十年這城市才能恢復」，故選(D)。

Part II: Translation Practice

| B | 1. | The power of the 921 earthquake is **such that** it not only claimed many lives but also damaged the ecology. |
| | 2. | Difficult **as/though** it is to restore the original beauty, we still should try our best to rebuild this quake-stricken area. |

| C | 1. | The mystery of Loch Ness is **such that** there have been countless legends and rumors about it. |
| | 2. | Hard **as/though** many adventurers and scientists have tried, we are still unable to know whether there is a monster living in the lake. |

Unit 22

Part I: Cloze Test

Ⓐ
　　奈米科技這項新科學也許很快就會改變我們的世界。在接受這些改變之前，我們必須先對可能隱藏的危險有所認識。奈米科技是從原子組成能對日常生活有所幫助的東西。我們可以利用它來製作保護套、更好的藥品，甚至更強的武器。舉例來說，化學銀如果被打散成很小的粒子，就能用來覆蓋在兒童的衣服上，以及在製作食物的過程中殺菌。對於奈米科技最大的疑慮之一，就是這些粒子如此微小，以至於它們可能會穿透皮膚。由於這些化學物質可能會堆積在我們的肺部甚至腦部，因此會有毒害身體的風險。現代科學和奈米技術提供我們機會，讓我們能創造一個更好的世界。也許我們最好能更仔細檢視眼前這個新世界。

1.	C	(A)坦承(B)允許(C)擁抱、接受(D)追求。此句表示「在我們接受這些改變之前，要先知道一些隱藏的危險」，故選(C)。
2.	D	原句為 the chemical silver, if it is broken into tiny particles, can be used to cover children's clothing…，省略字句中的主詞，改為分詞構句只留下 if broken，故選(D)。
3.	B	此處句型為 …is that S + V。that S + V 為主詞補語，補充說明前面的 worries。
4.	A	(A)累積(B)繼續(C)延後、拖延(D)持槍強劫。此句表示「這些化學物質會在我們肺部甚至腦部累積而有危害身體的危險」，故選(A)。
5.	A	had better (not) + V 表示「最好(不要)…」之意，故選(A)。

Ⓑ
　　最新的高科技玩具也許會讓許多人雀躍不已。然而，電腦駭客也等不及要偷取消費者的個人資料了！這項隱憂使許多人猶豫要不要急著連結未來。從 MP3 播

放器、導航工具到智慧型手機，任何能插取至電腦的東西都有可能包含病毒。這些病毒會改變設定或消除重要資訊。有些病毒甚至能偷取密碼或其他重要資料，包括信用卡號碼！有些惡意的駭客甚至在產品製作的早期就把病毒植入，刻意造成損害。有些來自工廠的病毒則是因為缺乏監督，讓駭客很容易上傳更危險的病毒。專家勸告每個使用者都該擁有最新版本的防毒軟體，並定期更新。這是能早先一步防範的最好方法。

1.	B	(A)智力的(B)私人的(C)學業的(D)科技的。此句表示「電腦駭客已經等不及要偷取顧客的<u>私人</u>資料了」，故選(B)。
2.	D	(A)洩露(B)失去…的行蹤(C)像…、模仿(D)三思。這種擔憂會讓人對於上網有所顧慮要<u>三思而後行</u>。
3.	B	(A)反映(B)刪除(C)污辱(D)反對。此句表示「這些電腦病毒不是改變設定，就是會<u>刪除</u>重要的資訊」，故選(B)。
4.	B	(A)有時候(B)故意地(C)不可避免地(D)可疑地。由 malicious hackers who intend to cause harm「那些心懷惡意，有意造成破壞的電腦駭客」可得知這些病毒是<u>故意</u>被上傳的，故選(B)。
5.	C	advise + O + that S + (should) + V，表示「建議…該做…」，後面 that 子句中 should 可省略，只留下原型動詞，故選(C)。

C

奈米科技很快就會跟我們的日常生活密切結合。它並不是只遙遠地存在於實驗室，而是我們每天都會穿到、看到以及碰到的東西。以奈米科技為基礎的最神奇產品就是奈米偵測錶。這個令人驚嘆的裝置不止能顯示時間，還能針對四周環境裡的危險對你提出警告，例如危險的化學物或細菌等。比如，如果你附近有人打噴嚏，奈米偵測錶就會偵測到空中出現的噴嚏，並發出聲音警告你。

另外一項偉大發明是超級奈米膠帶。它就像普通膠帶，但黏力強很多。它能黏在各種表面上，甚至在水中也可以用。有些研究人員相信，只要有一套由超級奈米膠帶製作的特製衣或手套，人類就能飛簷走壁，就跟蜥蜴和蜘蛛一樣！

除此之外，像消防員和士兵這些需要穿著特殊服裝來執行工作的人，他們的服裝往往很不舒適。然而，拜奈米科技之賜，他們的生活將會變得舒服許多。科學家正在努力研究能因應不同任務而自行變化的衣服。例

如，若一名消防員必須穿過火場，他的衣服就能自行變得較能抵抗高溫。相反地，滑雪者往往必須在低溫環境中行動，因此他們的衣服則會變得更貼身，能保持身體溫暖。總之，奈米科技有許多驚人的應用產品，證明科技也可以很有趣。

1.	A	(A)實驗室(B)房間(C)潛水艇(D)傳統習俗。奈米科技不是只是在實驗室會出現的東西，而是我們每天會看到接觸到的東西，故選(A)。
2.	B	N-based 為複合形容詞的用法。此處表示「以奈米科技為基礎所做的產品。」
3.	D	warn + O (sb) + of N 表示「警告…什麼事…」，故選(D)。
4.	D	(A)警告(B)內容(C)策略(D)出現、存在。當你附近有人打噴嚏時，奈米偵測錶可以得知噴嚏的<u>存在</u>，並發出警告。
5.	B	由下文可知這種膠水可以黏著在任何表面上，所以可得知此處表示它可能看起來像普通膠水，<u>除了</u>功能更強大之外，故選(B)。
6.	C	(A)除了(B)不管(C)幸虧有、因為(D)考慮到。此句表示「<u>因為</u>奈米科技的緣故，他們的生活可能會變得更方便」，故選(C)。
7.	A	adapt oneself + to N 表示「使…適應」。
8.	D	(A)脆弱的(B)威脅的(C)過敏的(D)可抵抗的。此句表示「消防員身上的衣服在通過火場時，可以調整為抵抗高溫」。be resistant to 表示「可以抵抗…的」，故選(D)。
9.	B	(A)依次地(B)相對地(C)結果是(D)到目前為止。與前文介紹消防員抗高溫的衣服做比較，此處表示「<u>相對地</u>，滑雪者的衣服需要能保持溫度」，故選(B)。
10.	C	(A)主題(B)動機(C)應用(D)擁有物。此句承接上文，表示奈米科技有很多有趣的<u>應用</u>，故選(C)。

Part II: Translation Practice

1.	B	**Thanks to** the development of artificial intelligence, people may live a more convenient life with the help of robots.
2.		In the future, robots can **either** help do the household chores **or** offer assistance at work.

| C | 1. | **Thanks to** such gadgets as smartphones and tablet computers, we can surf the Net easily. |
| | 2. | We can keep abreast of the latest information **either** at home **or** at work. |

Unit 23

Part I: Cloze Test

Ⓐ

因為商店裡販賣著來自各國的食物，日本人很少悠閒地享受屬於自己文化的餐飲。那些店裡的食物既快速又具異國風味。然而，對這種速食文化有所批評的人開始進行一種「慢食」運動，以扭轉這種潮流。他們得到來自大眾的支持。有些日本人同意，速食的快步調和低品質正對日本的生活品質造成影響，值得大家重視。

「慢食運動」源起於 1980 年代的義大利，當時有些人覺得應該重新教育義大利人民有關健康食物的益處。他們也建議大家食物應該慢慢品嚐。這些理念難以在日本推展。因為費用和時間是決定日本人飲食方式的關鍵因素。無論是什麼食物，必須既快速又便宜，否則永遠不會被日本人接受，至少在今日的日本是如此。

1.	B	⒜大部份地⒝很少地⒞習慣上地⒟起初地。由下句可得知，日本人喜歡吃速食及外來的食物，因此最好的選項為⒝，表示日本人<u>很少</u>慢慢地享受自己國家的食物。
2.	A	⒜扭轉⒝平衡⒞修補⒟對比。從 However 可得知與上一句的句意有轉折，故選⒜。指現在有慢食活動來<u>扭轉</u>之前的飲食趨勢。
3.	D	此處應選⒟ when，來指出西元 1980 年代所發生的事，⒝應改為 during which。
4.	D	recommend that S + (should) + V，故選原形動詞⒟。
5.	B	此句意義為<u>任何提供的飲食</u>應該還是要快速和便宜，故選⒝。⒜應該改為 anything that。

Ⓑ

現代醫學完成許多驚人的成就。舉例而言，許多具有傳染性，也就是會由一個人傳給另一個人的疾病已經被完全消除或得到控制。然而，還有另一種完全不同的疾病正在興起。它們被稱為「文明病」，也就是由我們自己的壞習慣所引發的疾病。

主要的文明病有心臟病、中風、幾種癌症、第二型糖尿病，以及肺病。這些疾病是由不良飲食習慣、體重過重、缺乏運動和抽煙等原因所造成。大多數的疾病是由不良飲食習慣再加上缺乏運動而引起。吃下比身體所需還更多的熱量，會導致體重過重，引起心臟病和中風。還有其他生活方式的因素會導致人生病，包括喝酒、濫用藥物，以及壓力。

1.	D	⒜然而⒝除此之外⒞相反地⒟也就是說。在此 that is，用來更進一步說明 infectious disease 的定義為何。
2.	A	⒜增加⒝私底下⒞不同意⒟未列入記錄。根據上下文，此處應是介紹有一類型的疾病正在迅速<u>增加</u>，故選⒜。
3.	C	such...as 表示「像…這樣的…」，故選⒞。
4.	B	此處表示攝取過多的卡洛里 (eating more calories than your body uses) 會導致過胖及相關疾病。故選⒝。⒜起因於⒟幸虧…⒞應改為 gives rise to。
5.	C	由 other 可得知，此句說明<u>還有</u>其他和生活型態相關的疾病，故選⒞。

Ⓒ

上地敏 (Toshi Uechi) 已經高齡九十二歲，她還是能表演傳統沖繩舞蹈。她不吃零食，並且每天吃「沖繩苦瓜」(Goya)。沖繩苦瓜是一種跟櫛瓜相似的蔬菜，長有許多凸出物，吃起來苦苦的。這種飲食習慣加上積極的生活方式使沖繩有許多百歲人瑞，是世界上人瑞比例最高的地方之一，每十萬名居民之中就有 39.5 人超過百歲。然而從二次世界大戰結束到 1972 年，沖繩一直是由美軍統治，直到今天還有美軍基地在那裡。幾十年來跟美國人的接觸使他們的生活水平有所提高，但同時許多沖繩人失去傳統的飲食習慣。

美國人把漢堡和罐頭肉品等食物帶進沖繩，讓當地生活方式開始改變。年輕人的壽命變短，而老人則活得更長。像上地敏這樣的老年人從小就吃許多當地蔬果、豆腐和海藻，但沖繩年輕人的飲食習慣則完全不同，他們寧願吃漢堡、薯條和其他速食而不吃沖繩苦瓜；更糟的是，他們拒絕運動。之所以如此，一部份原因在於島上缺乏大眾運輸系統，再加上就跟在美國的情況一樣，沖繩年輕人發展出對車子的愛好。這股潮流的結果呈現在以下資料中：2000 年時，在全日本 47 個地區中，沖繩長壽男性的排名下滑到第 26 名，遠比 1995 年的第 4 名和 1985 年的第 1 名下降許多。當地衛生健康當局正試圖喚醒人們的警覺，讓他們明白均衡飲食習慣以及正確烹煮食物的重要。

1.	C	此處為關係代名詞的省略用法，原本應是 which resembles，改為分詞 resembling。
2.	B	(A)資料(B)百分比(C)會員(D)禮貌。此句說明沖繩全世界人瑞百分比最高，故選(B)。
3.	C	本句說明沖繩人從第二次世界大戰結束直到1972 年，都被美國人所統治，故選(C)。
4.	D	本句表示「美國人讓沖繩人喪失原有的飲食習慣，但同時也提高了他們的生活水準」，故應選表示語氣有所轉折的連接詞(D)。(B) nevertheless 語氣雖表示「轉折」，但並不是連接詞，在此文法不合。
5.	B	本句表示「年輕人早死，而老年人活的比較長」，此處應選擇表示兩句差異的連接詞(B) while「然而」。
6.	A	本句為 would rather V₁ than V₂「寧願做…而不願…」的句型，故選(A)。
7.	C	此處承接上句，表示「年輕人寧願吃速食也不願吃傳統食物，再者，他們還不喜歡運動」。故選(C)。
8.	B	此處 that S + V 做為同位語，用來解釋說明 part of the reason 的內容，故選(B)。
9.	D	(A)大部份地(B)無疑地(C)特別地(D)可觀地。沖繩人的壽命排行在日本的 47 區中，從 1985 年的第 1 名，下降至 2000 年的第 26 名，降幅十分可觀，故選(D)。
10.	C	alert sb to sth「讓…警覺到…」，故選(C)。

Part II: Translation Practice

B	1.	Many white-collar workers **would rather spend** time waiting for the elevator **than take** stairs to the office.
	2.	Their laziness **results in** problems such as obesity, heart disease, diabetes and so on.
C	1.	More and more children **would rather choose** fast food **than eat** vegetables and fruit which are rich in vitamin C.
	2.	When they become adults, an unbalanced diet and overtake of fat will **lead to** high blood pressure.

Unit 24

Part I: Cloze Test

Ⓐ
　　現今許多母親面臨到一種兩難局面，不曉得到底要繼續工作，還是留在家裡照顧孩子。根據最近的研究顯示，兩方面都各有利弊。有些科學家發現，重返工作職場的母親會感覺到獨立與自我肯定。然而，上班的時間可能會非常長，因此職業婦女們會擔心自己犧牲了家庭生活。相反地，留在家裡的母親能享受每天看著孩子成長的喜悅。但有無數的家事必須要處理，她們可能會感到孤獨、無聊，或對丈夫的事業感到嫉妒。許多女性因此採取折衷的辦法。她們可能會從事兼職工作，或在設有幼稚園的公司上班，這樣她們一天中都能在休息時間看到自己的孩子。透過這樣的方式，許多女性發現自己真的可以成為快樂的工作媽媽！

1.	A	根據上文，很多婦女不知該繼續待在職場或是回家照顧小孩當全職媽媽，而研究指出兩者都有優缺點，故選(A)。若選(C)後面名詞應改為單數。
2.	C	(A)保留(B)取代(C)需要(D)減少。此句表示「辦公室的工作會需要很長的工作時數」，故選(C)。
3.	B	此處上文指出職業婦女會擔心犧牲家庭，相反地全職媽媽可以感到喜悅，看到他們的子女一天天成長。因前後兩者之間有比較的關係，有強調後者比前者的差異時，由此推斷應選(B)。
4.	D	上文指出職業婦女和全職媽媽各有優缺點，因此很多婦女選擇一條折衷的路線，故選(D)。
5.	A	(A)因此(B)以免(C)直到…(D)決不。此處表示「他們會選擇有幼稚園的公司，如此一來就可以在休息時間去看小孩」，故選(A)。

Ⓑ
　　今日的工作環境充滿壓力，時常使人週末和夜晚都得長時間加班。雖然許多男性喜愛這種工作文化，其他人則已經不想老是看不到自己的孩子，或感到自己彷彿家中的陌生人。傳統上，丈夫必須出外工作，而妻子則留在家裡。但如今這種情況正在改變。越來越多家庭主夫選擇離開職場，以便能照顧自己的孩子。

　　舉例來說，Joe 有兩個很年幼的小孩，他原本在一家大型跨國公司擔任經理。兩年前他決定辭職，轉而讓太太出去工作。Joe 表示，這種新生活的好處包括能花時間和小孩一起從事有趣的活動。想必這將會是一個持

續的潮流。

1.	**D**	此處原句為 ..., which often involves long weekends and nights at the office. 省略 which 將動詞改為 ..., involving...。involve 在此指「需要、包含」。
2.	**C**	(A)經常地(B)經濟地(C)很少地(D)部份地。由下文可知，有些父親覺得自己像陌生人，對<u>很少</u>看到家人的情況感到厭煩，故選(C)。
3.	**B**	(A)開始從事(B)照顧(C)丟下(D)送行。越來越多父親決定離開事業，<u>照顧</u>小孩去。
4.	**B**	此處應為連接詞，表示「他決定辭職，<u>然而</u>他的太太則去工作」。while 用來比較兩個相反的事物及情況，故選(B)。
5.	**C**	spend time/money + V-ing，故選(C)。

Ⓒ

　　每個父母都希望自己的孩子表現優秀。然而，有些父母為了引導孩子卻做得太過頭了。他們變得過度保護小孩，希望能參與孩子生活的每一個部分。這些父母常常被稱為「直昇機父母」，他們的問題就是無法放手。

　　「直昇機父母」這個名詞是在 1990 年由 Foster Cline 及 Jim Fay 在《用愛與邏輯的教養》一書中開始提到的。大學的職員注意到，有些父母非常想讓孩子進入某些學校，以至於他們會對孩子的入學選擇不斷叨念。他們試圖逼孩子獲得更好成績並去從事某些特定工作。有些父母甚至替孩子寫作業，替他們填寫大學申請表，希望能增加孩子錄取的可能性。

　　直昇機父母很快就把干涉範圍擴展到大學入學以外的領域。手機讓父母能隨時打電話給孩子，掌握孩子行蹤和試圖保護他們。這當中的問題之一，是直昇機父母會使孩子無法學會靠自己完成事情。這實際上會在未來對孩子造成傷害。

　　孩子們總有一天要學習當個大人。他們必須學會為自己的未來負責。不幸的是，直昇機父母只會延遲這樣的過程，對孩子生命造成的傷害大於幫助。

1.	**C**	(A)有知識性的(B)樂觀的(C)過度保護的(D)道德的。有些父母變得<u>過度保護</u>子女，子女生活的每一部份，他們都想要參與，故選(C)。
2.	**D**	have trouble + (in) + V-ing 表示「在…有困難」。have trouble letting go 表示「很難放手」。

3.	**A**	(A)開始(B)使悲傷(C)撫養、舉起(D)翻譯。此句表示首先<u>開始</u> "helicopter parents." 這個名詞
4.	**C**	lead + sb + to V 表示「導致…去…」。這讓父母們會去嘮叨子女關於選擇大學的問題。
5.	**B**	(A)情節(B)申請表(C)規定(D)調查。「有些父母甚至會替子女填好<u>申請表</u>」，故選(B)。
6.	**C**	這樣的父母除了<u>在大學入學申請方面</u>，在其它事情上也會如法泡製，應選(C)。如選(D)，需改為 in addition to。
7.	**B**	(A)瞧不起(B)得知…的行蹤(C)忽視(D)趕得上。手機讓父母可以隨時打電話給子女，<u>得知他們的行蹤</u>並試著保護他們，故選(B)。
8.	**D**	that S + V 用來解釋說明前面名詞的內容，為補語用法，且不可省略。
9.	**A**	be responsible for 表示「為…負起責任」。
10.	**A**	, which 用來代替前面一整件事，this 也就是指 They (Children) need to learn to be responsible for their own future，故選(A)，此處 , which causes …也可改為 , causing。

Part II: Translation Practice

B	1.	A great number of teenagers **have difficulty communicating** with their parents.
	2.	Parents should become good listeners **so that** their children can confide in them.
C	1.	Some fathers **have trouble keeping** an intimate relationship with their families.
	2.	They should share the household chores more **so that** their families will feel closer to them.

Unit 25

Part I: Cloze Test

Ⓐ

　　雨果以他的小說《悲慘世界》聞名，他的另一部知名作品是《巴黎聖母院》，也常常被叫做《鐘樓怪人》。這部小說並不是真的關於那名駝背人科西莫多，而是關於發生在聖母院的事件。這座教堂的執事克勞德·浮羅諾愛上一位名叫艾美拉達的美麗女子。他試圖謀害艾美

拉達的愛人,並把這項罪過推給她,結果她因此被處以吊刑。這本小說有幾項重要涵義。艾美拉達因為一樁她其實沒有犯的罪行而被判罪,這象徵法國政府的無能。科西莫多只因為長相醜陋就被人憎恨,這提醒了讀者保有憐憫和同情心的重要。《鐘樓怪人》的故事告訴我們,如果正義和權力沒有被正確行使時,人類會變成怎樣。

1.	B	從上下文並未說雨果只寫了兩本小說,故(A)不正確。因前句有提及他所寫的一本小說,承接上句介紹另一本,故選(B)。
2.	A	(A)結果是(B)肯定;明確地(C)明顯地(D)一開始。由上下文可得知,此句應為說明艾美拉達最後的結果,故選(A)。
3.	D	be convicted of 是指「被判了…罪」,故選(D)。
4.	A	(A)象徵(B)使優美(C)操弄(D)加強。此句應是說明「雨果利用艾美拉達無辜被冤枉的情節,來象徵法國政府的無能」,故選(A)。
5.	C	本句使用的文法為「, which」,或「, V-ing」來代替前面所提到的一整個句子,故正確選項為(C)。

B

《小王子》在 1943 年首度出版,是一本由安東尼‧聖修伯里所撰寫的童書。它是一個幻想故事,描寫一名迫降在沙漠的飛行員遇到一名來自外星的小男孩,也就是小王子。這名男孩渴求知識,問了這名飛行員許多問題。這本書吸引人的地方在於它以迷人的方式處理一些簡單但重要的真相,特別是一些人們會隨著年齡增長而遺忘的事。出自這個故事的名言之一,就是「只有用心去看,才能看見對的東西;眼睛往往看不到最關鍵的東西。」這本書簡單而有想像力的幻想場景,使這個故事不止對兒童來說很有娛樂性,其中一些普世皆然的觀念也吸引了大人。這種結合使這本書非常暢銷。事實上,它已經被翻譯成超過 250 種語言,是全世界賣得最好的 50 本書之一。

1.	B	(A)奇異(B)吸引力(C)批評(D)貢獻。此句說明「這本書吸引人的地方在於用有趣的方式說明簡單的道理」,故最適合的答案為(B)。
2.	C	隨著人們年紀漸長,會逐漸忘記這些道理。故最適合的連接詞為(C) as。
3.	C	(A)基礎的(B)珍貴的(C)看不見的(D)不實際的。此句前一句說明只有用心靈才能看得清楚,因此

		可推論出事物的基本道理時常是肉眼所看不見的,故選(C)。
4.	A	(A)結合(B)矛盾(C)分配(D)認可。從上文可知本書的幻想情節吸引孩童,而講述的想法吸引成人,這兩點的結合使它很受全世界讀者的歡迎。
5.	D	此句更進一步說明本書受歡迎的程度,故最適合的選項為(D)。

C

如果要用一個詞來形容愛爾蘭劇作家山繆‧貝克特的作品《等待果陀》,那就是「荒謬」。這齣荒謬劇論及兩個主題:人生的沒有意義以及語言的無用。就結構而言,《等待果陀》圍繞著兩名無家可歸的人——Estragon 和 Vladimir。在整齣劇裡,他們就是無所事事地坐在一棵樹旁邊,等待另一個名叫果陀的人來,但那個人始終沒有出現。到這齣戲結束的時候,果陀還是一團謎。一個貫穿《等待果陀》的主題就是:人生是沒有意義的。這齣戲最初是在 1948 年以法語寫成,有部份受到二次世界大戰的影響;在這場戰爭裡,人們製造出足以摧毀全人類的強力武器。貝克特相信,這場戰爭證明了人類的渺小。另一方面,在《等待果陀》裡,人物之間大部分的對話都是胡言亂語,顯示語言是一種無用的工具。

《等待果陀》之所以比其他戲劇突出的原因在於,它挑戰了傳統劇場的慣例。在典型的傳統戲劇裡,主要角色經歷過一些人生巨變之後,總會對自己有更真實的認識,這也是給人類的道德教訓。然而《等待果陀》卻似乎正好相反。Estragon 和 Vladimir 從頭到尾都沒有什麼改變,整齣戲裡沒有發生任何重要事件。角色們既無法彼此瞭解,劇情發展也沒有邏輯可言,而觀眾不由得懷疑人類是否真的很荒謬。畢竟貝克特告訴我們,明天 (如果我們還有明天的話) 大概跟今天也差不了多少。

1.	B	(A)逃過…處罰(B)論及(C)意義(D)同意。此句說明這部劇作處理的主題,故選(B)。
2.	B	此句說明他們除了整天坐在樹下等 Godot 以外,沒有其它事可做,為「have nothing to do but + V」的句型,故選(B)。
3.	C	that S + V 用來說明前方名詞的內容做為同位語,故選(C)。
4.	D	World War II 為一特定時間,其後的關係代名詞或關係副詞前必須打上逗號,此句應是說明

		在二次大戰期間發生的事，故選(D)
5.	B	由本段主題句得知這段在說明《等待果陀》所論及的兩個主題：一個是人的生命是無意義的，另一個則是語言是無用的。此格前文說明了第一個主題，此格應選(B)，說明第二個主題。
6.	A	(A)典型地(B)原先地(C)理想地(D)幸運地。本句應是說明「典型地傳統戲劇中，主角會有的變化」，故選(A)。
7.	C	(A)組成(B)動機(C)相反的事物(D)不同意。由此句開頭 However 轉承詞可得知，與上一句語氣相反，故選(C)。
8.	C	此句為 with + O + V-ing/V-en 附帶說明的句型，happen 當「發生」之意應用主動語態，故選(C)。
9.	A	「不得不…忍不住」的句型為「can't help + V-ing」或「can't help but + V」故正確答案為(A)。
10.	D	此句承接上下文的插入句。說明如果還有明天，事情也不會有變化。以語意推測應選(D)。

Part II: Translation Practice

B	1.	This romance novel challenges **the idea that** lovers can fall in love at first sight.
	2.	**Written** fifty years ago, this novel is very popular with people of all ages.
C	1.	**The issue that** women should have more freedom is repeatedly highlighted in this play.
	2.	**Because this play advocated** feminism, it caused a sensation but aroused criticism as well. → **Advocating** feminism, this play caused a sensation but aroused criticism as well.

Unit 26

Part I: Cloze Test

Ⓐ
　　格林兄弟帶給我們一些最受人喜愛的故事，像是〈小紅帽〉和〈白雪公主〉。打從孩提時代起，Jacob 和 Wilhelm 兩兄弟就會到鄉間四處旅行，傾聽和收集民間故事。他們將不同版本的故事結合成一個，盡可能貼近

最初的故事。不過這對兄弟刻意在故事中加入暴力成分，教導人們正義、服從和道德的價值。〈灰姑娘〉就是一個例子，這個故事的原名是 *Aschenputtel*。在〈灰姑娘〉的故事裡，她的兩個繼姐都不是王子要的女孩，因為她們都穿不下那雙玻璃鞋。不過在 *Aschenputtel* 這個故事裡，這對兄弟刻意加進一個可怕的故事轉折：由於這兩名繼姐太想嫁給王子，她們竟然把自己的腳後跟切掉一部份！這個故事讓我們看到：說謊是不對的，而萬一你說了，就得付出慘痛代價。

1.	C	since + 時間點，後面的子句常接完成式，故選(C)。(A)時態不合，應用過去完成式。此句表示「自從孩童時期，這對兄弟就走遍德國鄉村收集故事」。
2.	B	(A)秤(B)版本(C)習俗(D)設備。此句表示「格林兄弟將同一個故事的不同版本合併成一個」，故應選(B)。
3.	B	add...to 表示「將…加入…」，故選(B)。
4.	A	此句表示「兩個姐妹都不是王子要找的人，因為他們穿不進玻璃鞋」，故選(A)。
5.	C	此句為 show (that) S + V and that S + V 的句型，if you do, you have to suffer 也是 show 後面的受詞，前面要有 and that。

Ⓑ
　　霍桑向來被公認是美國最重要的作家之一。雖然當時的評論家對他讚許有加，但他在文學生涯中仍歷經許多挫折。在成名之前，霍桑無法靠當作家維生，因此他在塞勒姆港的海關工作。有一天他被開除了，很沮喪地回到家中，這時他那位聰明又開朗的妻子蘇菲亞作了一件事，而美國文學會永遠為此感謝她。她沒有大聲斥責他丟了工作，而是微笑著對他說：「把它想成一個很棒的機會吧。現在你有充分的時間完成你一直找不到時間完成的作品了。」正是她這份正面的態度，說服他開始寫作新書，那就是如今被認為是他的代表作，也是美國文學瑰寶之一的《紅字》。

1.	A	(A)讚美(B)批評(C)欣賞(D)認出。此句表示「雖然被他當代的批評家所讚美，他寫作生涯一路上體驗到很多挫折」。故選(A)，而(C)則須改為 appreciated。
2.	C	此句表示他回家感到沮喪，come 後面常接主詞補語，修飾主詞。故選(C)而(B)則表示「令人沮喪的」。

3.	D	(A)因此(B)此外(C)換句話說(D)反而。此句表示他太太沒有斥責他，<u>反而</u>微笑鼓勵他，故選(D)。
4.	D	此句原來應該是 you have all the time to complete your book which you never had time for，將 for 放到關係代名詞前，故選(D)。
5.	B	此句表示「<u>就是</u>她正面的態度讓他深信自己，去寫自己的書」。為 It is...that... 的強調句型，故選(B)。

C

特洛伊戰爭是希臘傳說中最重要的故事之一，這是場因一名美女而起的戰爭。當糾紛女神厄莉絲因為沒被邀請參加培勒斯和賽提絲的婚禮而大發雷霆時，這場戰爭就開始了。厄莉絲一得知這個消息就衝到婚禮會場，把一顆金蘋果扔到婚宴桌上，說這顆蘋果屬於最美麗的女神。赫拉、雅典娜和艾芙戴蒂都想要這顆蘋果，於是宙斯宣布由特洛伊王子巴里斯來擔任裁判。

為了讓巴里斯能選擇自己，這三名女神企圖用他想要的東西來賄賂他。赫拉表示要給他權力，雅典娜要給他智慧，而艾芙戴蒂則要給他世界上最美的女人。結果巴里斯選了艾芙戴蒂，因此艾芙戴蒂允諾他能擁有曼尼勒斯的妻子海倫。巴里斯不顧母親勸告，前往斯巴達找海倫。曼尼勒斯待他很好，結果卻發現巴里斯趁他離開斯巴達去參加一場葬禮的時候，竟然把海倫和許多金銀財寶一起帶走了。

於是，特洛伊和希臘展開一場大戰。戰爭打了九年之後，希臘軍隊想到一個點子。他們打造一座木馬，然後偷偷藏身在裡頭。特洛伊人把木馬拖回城內，以為它會帶來好運。然而讓他們大吃一驚的是，希臘人在夜裡從木馬中跑出來，把特洛伊人打得落花流水。這場戰爭就此結束——這是場因一名美女而起，也因此聞名的戰爭。

1.	D	(A)撫養(B)說明(C)使落下(D)導致。特洛伊戰爭被認為是由一名美女所<u>導致</u>引發的，故選(D)。
2.	C	Upon + N/V-ing, S + V 表示「一…就…」，故選(C)。
3.	B	whoever = anyone who。此句表示「這顆蘋果屬於<u>任何</u>一個最美的人」，故選(B)。
4.	B	此句表示「<u>為了</u>使巴里斯選擇她們，這三位女神試圖去賄賂他」，故選(B)，此處的 to 為 in order to 的省略。

5.	A	(A)結果(B)然而(C)事實上(D)反而。此句表示「<u>最後結果</u>，巴里斯選擇了艾芙戴蒂」，故選(A)。
6.	C	only to + V 表示「卻…」，後面接和預期相反的結果，故選(C)。
7.	D	此處為 find + O + Ving/V-en 的句型，表示「斯巴達國王發現他的妻子和財富<u>被</u>巴里斯帶走了」。語意呈現被動，故選(D)。
8.	A	come up with 表示「想出…主意」。(B)(C)(D)均需用「事情」當主詞。
9.	B	to one's N 表示「讓…很…的是」。此處表示「讓他們很驚訝的是」，故選(B)。
10.	D	be famous for 表示「因…而聞名」，故選(D)。

Part II: Translation Practice

B	1.	*The Da Vinci Code* **is thought to have** been inspired by historical events and famous paintings.
	2.	Many people are convinced that the novel is based on history **only to find** that it combines facts with fiction.
C	1.	*The Catcher in the Rye* **is thought to have** a deep influence on American teenagers, because they can identify with the main character.
	2.	The hero in this novel attempted to run away from home **only to be** disappointed at the outside world.

Unit 27

Part I: Cloze Test

A

在英語裡，有時候一個片語的起源背後是個有趣的故事。face the music 就是個例子，今日它的意思是「承受自己行為的後果」。不過在 1850 年時，它的意思是「在艱困的時刻保持堅強」。關於這個片語最初是怎麼出現的，有不同的看法。一種是跟被軍隊遣返的士兵有關。這名士兵會被放在一匹馬上，面朝馬尾方向。接著一支軍樂隊會演奏音樂，目送他離開。另一種看法是跟劇場有關。新來的表演者可能會在第一次登台前感到很憂慮。除了觀眾之外，他們還得面對通常對菜鳥不太友善

的樂師。因此 facing the music 是描述人變得有點害怕的樣子。當你遇到一個陌生的片語，可能正是你瞭解一個有趣故事的好機會。

1.	C	face the music 為一固定片語，修飾限定的先行詞，關係代名詞前必須打上逗點，故選(C)。
2.	D	(A)起源於(B)用完(C)經過。N + come into being /existence 表示「某事開始出現。」
3.	A	make 使役動詞的被動式為 be made to + V，此處表示「一個被要求離開軍隊的士兵」。
4.	A	(A)初次登台(B)傑出(C)手術、操作(D)認可。此句表示新的表演者在初次登台前可能會很擔心。
5.	B	原句應為 describes someone who becomes a little afraid，省略關係代名詞 who，成為 describes someone becoming a little afraid。(D)應改為 that **becomes**。

B

　　英語中的許多用語都跟動物有關。這些用語出自不同來源，例如神話、民間故事、文學、宗教和舊習俗等。今日人們的用語有許多出自伊索寓言。舉例來說，伊索寫了有關一隻笨手笨腳的驢子在陶器店裡的故事。後來，歐洲人把陶器店變成瓷器店，把驢子換成公牛，因為公牛的身軀又更龐大。因此「在瓷器店裡的公牛」(Bull in a China Shop) 這句片語，就是在描述一個總是笨手笨腳又經常打破東西的人。除此之外還有許多來源不明的片語。「天在下貓下狗」(It is raining cats and dogs) 這句片語的意思是雨下得非常大。有一種說法是這個句子源自十七世紀的英國，當時的街道非常骯髒，所以大雨會沖走動物的屍體。這些跟動物有關的習慣用語有助於使英語更有趣。

1.	B	(A)元素(B)來源(C)結果(D)作文、作曲。此處表示「這些表達用語，可能來自不同的來源，像是神話、民間故事、宗教等」，故選(B)。
2.	C	replace A with B 表示「用 B 取代 A」。
3.	B	cannot help + V-ing = cannot help but + V 表示「忍不住…，不得不…」，故選(B)。如選(A)需改為 cannot help but **be** clumsy.。
4.	A	(A)解釋(B)重要性(C)印象(D)預測。根據一種解釋，這個說法是在 17 世紀起源於英國，由此句意故選(A)。

5.	D	此處修飾前面的先行詞 the 17th century, 表示「在這段期間街道都很髒亂，下大雨能沖走動物的死屍」。為非限定用法，原為 , during which, 改為 ,when。

C

　　「胃裡的蝴蝶」這個詞，據說是在 1908 年由一名如今被人所遺忘的作家開始使用。這個片語原本是在描述人感到緊張或有壓力時，胃部的奇妙感覺。當然，這種感覺不是真的由蝴蝶造成，而且有一個很簡單的生物學解釋。

　　當我們感到一股突如其來的感情，比如害怕、緊張或甚至興奮等，會使身體會產生一些化學物質，使血液離開胃部進入肌肉。這導致胃肌緊縮，使我們感覺就像胃在撲動。「撲動」這個字常常被用來形容蝴蝶飛舞的樣子。這股在肌肉中的額外力量，也是在危急情況下我們似乎會變得更有力氣的原因。

　　當我們感到驚慌時，身體裡會有一些不同的事發生。然而，不是每個人都會產生一樣的反應。顯示緊張的其他徵狀可能包括流汗、雙手發冷、食欲不振 (可能是由於胃肌繃得比較緊)，心跳很快，或嘴巴發乾。如果緊張的感受非常強烈而持續，症狀可能更糟，包括反胃和嘔吐。如果能知道是什麼原因引起這些生理反應，並進一步瞭解它們，會非常有助於控制它們。而且，想到每個人不時都會有這些感覺，這點也很好。

1.	A	be thought to have + V-en 表示「據說…過去…」，此處表示 butterflies in the stomach 據說是 1908 年一位作家最先使用的。
2.	C	feel + adj 表示「覺得…」，此處 stressed 為過去分詞做形容詞用，為「有壓力的」之意。
3.	A	(A)生理的(B)情感的(C)口頭的(D)歷史的。從 the body produces chemicals 可推論這種緊張的感覺是有生理上的解釋，故選(A)。
4.	D	cause + O (sb/sth) + to V 表示「造成…」。
5.	B	the way that S + V = the way in which S + V = how S + V 表示「…的方式」，故選(B)。
6.	B	(A)喜悅(B)驚慌失措(C)困惑(D)悲傷。上文表示「緊張的時候，肌肉會比之前更有力量，所以此處表示當我們驚慌失措的時候，身體會有很多種不同的反應」。

7.	A	(A)表徵(B)原因(C)成份(D)特色。此處表示「其它緊張的表徵有流汗、雙手冰冷，食慾不振等」，故選(A)。
8.	C	此處應擺 lose 的名詞(C) loss，a loss of appetite 表示「食慾消退」。
9.	C	此句表示「假如緊張的情緒很強烈，並持續一段時間，這些症狀可能會更糟」。
10.	A	of great help = helpful。of + 抽象名詞 = 形容詞，with + 抽象名詞 = 副詞。

Part II: Translation Practice

B	1.	In the series of *Harry Potter*, the word "muggle" **means a person** who possesses no magical power.
	2.	The success of the novel has **caused** many advertising agencies **to use** its language to get the message across.
C	1.	Snail mail, coined a decade ago, **means letters** sent by the post office.
	2.	This expression mocks the slowness of traditional mail delivery as/because it may **cause** people much **inconvenience**.

Unit 28

Part I: Cloze Test

Ⓐ
　　幾世紀以來，色彩一直被用來描述許多東西。「白大象」這個片語源自東南亞，意指某種麻煩到不值得擁有的東西。白色大象被認為是非常神聖的動物，所以牠的主人既不能強迫牠工作，也不能丟了牠。除此之外，要餵飽一隻大象也所費不貲。所以，送一隻白色大象當禮物是不會被人感謝的，即便送禮的人可能是國王。「藍血」這個片語是意指某人出身皇家。卡斯提爾的最古老家族聲稱他們從未跟摩爾族混血，宣稱他們的血統純正。他們的靜脈看起來比摩爾族的還要藍。這是因為他們的皮膚更白，透過白嫩的皮膚能看到他們的藍色靜脈。現在，當你聽到一個富有色彩的用語時，你會知道它可能有一段有趣的歷史。

1.	B	be worth + N/V-ing 表示「價值 / 值得…」。

2.	A	neither...nor... 表示「既不…也不…」，此處表示主人既不能叫牠工作，也不能遺棄牠。
3.	D	(A)拒絕(B)執行(C)建議(D)感激。根據上下文，白色的大象是大而無用的東西，因此即使是來自國王的禮物，也不會被感激。
4.	C	of noble/humble birth 表示「出身高貴 / 貧寒」之意。
5.	D	原句為 Their veins appear bluer than veins of the Moors.。在比較對照的句子中，會用 that 代替前面提過的單數名詞，those 代替複數名詞，故選(D)

Ⓑ
　　我們可以透過一個國家的語言來瞭解它的文化。對許多人而言，「講重點」、「實話實說」，或「盡情去做」都很有美國風味。這種「直接了當」、「對的事情就挺身去做」的美式風格也許很好，但可能會使來自世界其他地區的人感到錯愕。舉例來說，美國孩子並不害怕去質疑父母或師長的主張。職員也很被鼓勵要在經理面前有話直說。然而在一些文化裡，尊敬長輩和上級是非常重要的。他們寧願用暗示，而不是傷害別人的感情。美式風格的另一個特色是競爭。它會激勵人「夢想要大」、「主動積極」，並成為「佼佼者」。有時候，美國人會被認為很咄咄逼人，或不容易共事，因為他們喜歡不說廢話，不浪費時間的人。

1.	D	這句表示「這樣的美式風格很好，然而會讓其他國家的人嚇一跳」。此處應為連接詞 yet 連接兩個句子。若選(B)則為副詞用法，前面需改為分號後面再加逗點。
2.	C	(A)承認(B)深思(C)質疑(D)擁抱、接受。此處承接上文說明美國人直接的風格，美國小孩不害怕去質疑老師及父母的想法。
3.	A	(A)年長的(B)悲慘的(C)幸運的(D)受過教育的。前文提到美國人對父母、老師，及老闆都會勇於發言，然而，在一些文化中，對長輩和掌權者的尊重是很重要的，故選(A)。
4.	C	prefer N/V-ing to N/V-ing 表示「寧願…而不是…」之意。
5.	C	S + is easy to work along with 表示「和…一起工作很容易」，to 後面不需用被動語態。

C

　　想像一下，某天有人說你「值得你的鹽」。如果你不曾聽過這個片語，可能會覺得莫名其妙，特別是若它跟正在進行的對話似乎搭不上邊的時候。這個片語的現代含意是指你的表現跟你的獎賞相稱，可以指你的薪水，或就是稱讚你很稱職地完成一項工作。但這個片語當初是怎麼產生的，則是另外一回事。

　　大多數人接受的說法是，這句片語可追溯到羅馬時代的士兵，他們的薪水是以鹽而不是貨幣來支付，因為當時的鹽很有價值。有些語言學家則相信，「薪水」這個詞也出自同樣的拉丁語源。許多片語和俗語有很長的歷史，可以追溯自我們熟悉的來源，比如聖經、莎士比亞，也可以來自較遠的來源，如孔子這位中國哲學家。在文學、政治、電影、運動和音樂中也可以找到無數例子。甚至連「搖滾」這個片語也始於一個用來形容那種音樂風格的俚語。

　　英語總是在變化，所以新詞彙也因應新的潮流和現實被創造出來。但要變到什麼地步才會停呢？有數千個獨特的俗語來配合所有的情境，不可能完全把它們學會，就連以英語為母語的人都辦不到。最好的辦法就是別氣餒，一步一步慢慢來。

1.	A	that S + V 為主詞補語，that 不可省略，用來解釋前面的 meaning。本句表示「這個說法的意思就是你已經贏得你的獎勵」。
2.	D	(A)處罰(B)技術(C)申請、應用(D)讚美。此處承接上文，表示「獎勵可能是你的薪水，或是對好表現的<u>讚美</u>」。
3.	C	(A)起因於(B)源起(C)發生、出現(D)引起。此處表示「這個片語是怎麼<u>出現</u>的，是完全不同的一回事」。而選項(B) come from 通常與疑問詞 where 連用。
4.	B	(A)回轉(D)退縮。date back to = be traced back to (同一段敘述，重複使用的用法) 表示「追溯到…」，故選(B)。
5.	B	此處為獨立分詞構句，原句應為 The popular belief is that Roman soldiers, who were paid with salt instead of currency, <u>because</u> salt <u>was</u> quite valuable at that time. 兩句子省略連接詞 because，保留不同的主詞，將動詞 was 改為分詞 being。
6.	A	(A)源頭(B)一瞥(C)資源(D)熟人。此句表示「很多片語可以追溯到一些我們熟悉的<u>來源</u>，如聖

		經、莎士比亞等」。
7.	C	as + N 表示「以…身份，當作…」。此處表示「甚至 rock n' roll 這個說法，一開始被<u>當做</u>俚語來描述這種音樂」。
8.	D	(A)廢除(B)發現(C)翻譯(D)造字。此處表示「英文一直在改變，所以新的字被<u>造出來</u>，去配合新的趨勢」。
9.	B	(A) more than one + 單數名詞，表示「不只一個…」(C) many a + 單數名詞，表示「很多…」(D) a good deal of 不可數名詞，表示「很多…」。cliches 為複數名詞，此處應該使用 thousands of 修飾，表示「數以千計的…」。
10.	C	(A)有時候(B)暫時、目前(C)一次(D)及時。最好的方法是下定決心，<u>一次</u>一步去學習。

Part II: Translation Practice

	1.	Allusions to Shakespeare widely **found** in English, the great playwright contributed greatly to the English language.
B	2.	Many of his quotations **are** still in daily use and **worth learning**.
	1.	Slang widely **used** in school, a foreign student may find it difficult to understand conversation on campus.
C	2.	Some common American slang expressions have cultural significance and are **worth paying** attention to.

Unit 29

Part I: Cloze Test

A

　　麥克・傑克森以「流行音樂天王」之名聞名全球，於 50 歲那年去世。傑克森以動聽歌曲和不可思議的舞步獲得全球數百萬歌迷支持。麥克・傑克森 11 歲就成名，當時他擔任 Jackson 5 合唱團的主唱，團員包括他和另外四名兄弟。到了 1970 年代末期，麥克已經成為一名成功的單飛歌手。當他在 1982 年發行《戰慄》這張專輯時，名氣更上一層樓，這張專輯獲得 8 座葛萊美獎，並成為有史以來最暢銷的專輯。由於他在音樂上的成就，有超過 1 萬 7 千人參加他的追思會。在儀式最後，

他 11 歲大的女兒 Paris 為父親致上感人獻詞，含著眼淚說麥克·傑克森是「我心目中最好的爸爸」。

1.	B	rise to fame 表示「開始成名」。(A)喚起(C)舉起、募款、撫養(D)興起、產生。
2.	B	原句應為…, a singing group which consisted of him and four of his brothers. 省略 which 改為分詞 consisting of。
3.	A	「By + 時間」表示「到了…的時候」，後面接的句子常用完成式。此句表示「到了 1970 年代，麥克·傑克森已經成為一個成功的單飛歌手」。
4.	C	(A)有時候(B)一再(C)有史以來(D)一直。此句表示這張專輯成為有史以來最暢銷的唱片。
5.	A	(A)紀念的(B)犧牲(C)軍事的(D)心理的。此句表示「因為他在音樂上的傑出成就，有超過 17000 人參加他的紀念儀式 (追思會)」。

Ⓑ

在一場出乎意料的大逆轉裡，來自蘇格蘭轟動一時的歌手蘇珊·波爾最終得到電視選秀節目《英國星光大道》的第二名成績。這名原本不被看好的新星在試唱之後就令裁判震驚不已也迷倒全球各地觀眾。由於她平凡的外表和樸素的出身背景使然，原本裁判們似乎在她開始唱之前就想淘汰她。然而她的表演震驚與觸動了每個人。全球超過一億人次在 YouTube 上觀看過她的表演，使她一夜之間聲名大噪。媒體很快就開始大肆報導她，她平淡的出身背景使她的故事更吸引人。參加這個選秀節目之前，她多年來沒有工作，全心照顧生病的母親。她原本擔心平凡的外表會使人對她有成見，但母親的死促使她勇於追求自己的夢想。結果證明，她其實是一顆尚未琢磨的鑽石。

1.	C	(A)貢獻(B)複習(C)試鏡(D)註冊。此句「表示她在節目中試鏡演出後，她的表演讓評審驚訝，也吸引了全世界的注目」。
2.	B	(A)光彩動人的(B)平凡無奇的(C)狡猾的(D)有吸引力的。從 simple background 可猜測蘇珊的外表也應該平凡無奇，才會讓原本在她表演前，就想淘汰她的評審們驚奇不已。
3.	D	Susan Boyle 為人名，關係代名詞前面需加上逗點。此句表示「她平凡的背景使她的故事更吸引人」。若選(C)則此句會有兩個動詞。

4.	B	but = except 此句表示「在表演之前，她除了長年照顧母親外，沒有其他的工作」，故選(B)。
5.	A	(A)促使(B)使確信(C)使氣餒(D)致力於。她母親的死促使她去追求她的夢想。

Ⓒ

儘管披頭四合唱團在 1970 年就已經解散，他們的音樂卻一直歷久不衰。現在，拜一款新電玩遊戲之賜，人們能親身體驗這些音樂了。在《披頭四：搖滾樂團》這個遊戲裡，玩家可以扮演約翰、保羅、喬治、林哥，跟著這個樂團的 45 首暢銷歌曲一起彈奏和演唱。

由於披頭四很小心保護他們的形象，有些人很訝異他們會把肖像權借給一個電玩遊戲。一切的開始，始於達尼·哈里森 (已經過世的喬治·哈里森的兒子) 遇上 Harmonix 這個電玩遊戲圖像製作的公司，他跟他們討論一些想法，希望製作出能發揚披頭四精神的作品。保羅·麥卡尼和林哥·史塔這兩位還在世的披頭四成員也同意這個計畫。

最後的成果，就是一場穿越時間的音樂之旅，可以體驗該團的所有作品時期。玩家跟著螢幕上的指示彈奏樂器來得分，彈得太差就可能被噓下台。

有些評論家將《披頭四：搖滾樂團》這個遊戲稱之為史上最重要的電玩遊戲，因為它展現了這個樂團的普世吸引力。對於聽披頭四音樂長大的人而言，這個遊戲是一個回到過去的機會；對於沒那麼熟悉這個樂團的人來說，這是一個好機會，可以體驗史上最有影響力的搖滾樂。這個遊戲讓人們能感受一下，成為超級四人組之一的感覺是什麼。

1.	D	as + adj/adv + as ever = as + adj/adv + as before 表示「和以前一樣…」。
2.	B	sing/dance to 表示「隨著…唱歌 / 跳舞」。
3.	A	(A)驚訝的(B)放鬆的(C)滿足的(D)有信心的。此句表示「因為披頭四對自己的形象很小心，有些人很驚訝他們會願意借肖像權給一個電玩」。
4.	A	(A)遺產(B)悲劇(C)決心(D)教導。此句表示「他們想要創造一個東西來紀念推崇披頭四所遺留下的事蹟」，故選(A)。
5.	B	(A)感到不悅(B)同意(C)反對(D)刪減。根據上下文，此句表示「剩下的兩名披頭四成員同意了這計畫，而有這電玩的產生」。
6.	C	(A)省略(B)陳述(C)做為特色(D)檢視。此句表示

		「所有時期的作品都被電玩收錄進去」做為特色。
7.	D	此處應為連接詞，連接兩個句子，表示「有人認為這是有始以來最棒的電玩，因為它展示了這個樂團全球性的吸引力」。(B) due to 表示「因為…」，後面需接名詞。
8.	A	此處和上文做對照，前文表示「對那些聽他們音樂長大的人，這電玩像是一場時空之旅，而對那些較不熟悉他們的人，這是一個機會去體驗有史以來最有影響力的搖滾樂」，故選(A)。
9.	B	承接上文，兩種情況任一種，這電玩都可讓人感受到身為超級四人組之中一員的感覺，故選(B)，若選(A)，case 須改為 cases。
10.	C	what it is like to V 表示「…的感覺為何」。

Part II: Translation Practice

B	1.	The Carpenters consists of two siblings, **whose** beautiful songs stand the test of time.
	2.	Their songs became a hit **because** they produced a distinct musical style at that time.
C	1.	Madonna, **whose** name means "My Lady" in Italian, is a pop music legend.
	2.	She wins global recognition **because** she dares to challenge the social convention.

Unit 30

Part I: Cloze Test

Ⓐ

在過去，亞洲男性不太在意自己的外表。大多數人更關心賺錢和在工作上勝人一籌。然而在過去數年間，有越來越多亞洲男性開始更注意自己的外表。這些人被稱為「都會美型男」。都會美型男每天在健身房運動好幾小時，為了保持身材不遺餘力，還會購買保濕霜和潤膚乳液來使自己看起來好看。這些人也會把薪水的一大部分拿去購買最新流行服飾，包括名牌與設計師品牌服飾。有許多原因導致都市美型男人口急遽成長。有些亞洲美型男表示，外表好看會讓他們更有自信。有些人則希望這能讓他們在職場獲得成功。可以確定的一點是，不管原因如何，都會美型男風潮正在亞洲發燒。

1.	B	從前一句知從前亞洲男人不太關心外表，可得知此處指他們比較關心賺錢和工作。
2.	C	(A)程度(B)表現(C)外表(D)關係。此句和前一句語氣有轉折，表示「然而現在亞洲男性開始注意他們的外表了」。
3.	A	(A)此外(B)相反地(C)整體而言(D)反而。此處承接上句，表示「亞洲男性開始健身，此外，他們也購買美容用品來使外表看起來更好」。
4.	C	(A)衰退的(B)有說服力的(C)激增的(D)有啟發性的。此處表示「亞洲重視外表的男性，人口激增的原因有很多」，故選(C)。
5.	C	此處表示不論理由為何。whatever the reason = no matter what the reason (is)，故選(C)。

Ⓑ

打電動可能是一項有益的家庭活動。今日，有許多年紀在 30 到 40 歲之間的父母都是玩「小精靈」遊戲長大的。甚至在長大成人後，他們也還是會打電玩遊戲。這其實沒什麼好奇怪的。真正令人感到驚奇的是，一直以來被批評會使人遠離朋友和家庭的電玩遊戲，如今正變成父母和孩子溝通的一種方式。父母們表示，玩 Wii 或《瑪利歐派對》這類電玩其實提供他們一個少有的相處機會，讓他們能以對等的方式和孩子互動，因為能否贏得遊戲跟你是否比較強壯、高大或年長無關。事實上，孩子們的技巧往往都贏過父母。打電玩遊戲也讓父母和孩子有一些共通話題可談，即便大部分是有關電腦的「科技狂對話」，但更重要的是，遊戲時間讓父母和孩子有機會以一種沒那麼正式的方式討論家庭議題。

1.	D	此句本來應為 parents who are aged 30 or 40 grew up playing...，省略關係代名詞及動詞，改為 parents aged 30 or 40，故選(D)。
2.	A	此處為 What... is that S + V 的句型，that + S + V 為主詞補語，that 不可省。
3.	C	(A)對手(B)較差的人(C)地位相同的人(D)年長的人。此句表示「玩電玩讓家長有機會和子女相處，平起平坐，因為比較強壯或年長和輸贏並無關係」，故選(C)。
4.	B	have the edge on/over... 表示「比…佔優勢」，故選(B)。over 常有「勝過、超過」之意。

| 5. | D | (A)除非(B)反而(C)更糟的是 (D 更重要的是。此處承接上句表示「即使只是關於電腦的談話，打電玩也讓父母和子女有共同的話題，<u>更重要的是</u>，這提供一個較平常 (不那麼正式) 的場合，讓父母和子女談論家庭議題」，故選(D)。 |

Ⓒ

　　在講求「政治正確」的時代，許多公司都會去掉廣告裡的傳統刻板形象。「黑人牙膏」也許是這種轉變的最佳例證，如今它的英文名稱改為「Darlie」，包裝盒上的形象也換成比較不具種族特徵的樣子。但近年來不同種族都受到更多尊重，女人卻似乎沒有被包含在這場政治正確運動之中。啤酒廣告就是最明顯的例子。

　　在世界各地，啤酒公司仍持續濫用女人的性感特質。在幾乎每個國家的酒吧和商店裡，都貼著女人身穿泳裝手拿推薦啤酒的海報。德國啤酒 Saint Pauli Girl 的特色標誌就是瓶子上有一個女傭圖樣。一部在墾丁啤酒節中拍攝的影片在網路上很受歡迎，內容是穿得很少的年輕女子在台上跳舞。不幸的是，女人不只有性感特質被啤酒廣告濫用。一個義大利廣告還拿「女人不會開車」的刻板印象開玩笑。不過，一群女律師並不覺得這哪裡有好笑，所以她們決定控告啤酒公司的性別歧視行為。

　　女人為什麼在政治正確運動裡被啤酒公司大幅忽略，原因並不清楚。也許是因為男人和女人之間無法否認的生理差異，以及男人和女人的互動方式，特別是在喝酒的場合。無論什麼原因，我們都應該思考這個問題。

1.	A	(A)中立的(B)敏感的(C)相關的(D)根據。此句承接上文，現在很多公司都把以前充滿著刻板印象的圖案移除，黑人 (Darlie) 牙膏現在是放上一個<u>較無</u>特定種族形象的圖案，故選(A)。
2.	B	根據上下文，本句是表示「<u>雖然</u>近年來不同的種族都被尊重，女人卻在這場政治正確的運動中被忽視」，故選(B)。
3.	B	此句是否定詞置於句首的倒裝句，主詞和動詞需調換位置，原句應為 This is nowhere more obvious than in beer commercials. 故選(B)
4.	D	此句原本應是 have posters of women in swimsuits <u>who hold</u> their beer of choice，省略 who 並改為分詞 <u>holding</u> …，故選(D)。
5.	C	(A)主演(B)強調(C)以…做為特色(D)認可。此句表示「這款德國啤酒是在瓶子上以一個女僕的圖案做為<u>它的特色</u>」，故選(C)。

6.	B	此句為 It is...that... 強調句型，表示「不是只有女性的性感特質成為啤酒廣告拿來濫用的主題」，故選(B)。
7.	C	從前一句 An Italian ad <u>poked fun at</u>...，及 a group of female lawyers <u>did not see the humor</u>，可得知語氣有轉折，故選(C)。
8.	D	sue sb for sth 表示「<u>因為</u> (某事) <u>而控告</u> (某人)」，故選(D)。
9.	A	the way in which S + V = the way (that) S + V= how S + V，表示「…的方式」，故選(A)。
10.	C	(A)沒有看到(B)去除(C)仔細想想(D)視為理所當然。表示「整個社會應該要<u>仔細思考</u>這個問題」。

Part II: Translation Practice

	1.	The increasing popularity of on-line bookstores **has something to do with** the easy access to the Internet.
B	2.	**Nowhere can people browse** through more books than on the Internet.
	1.	The preference for staying single **has nothing to do with** the influence of the Western culture.
C	2.	**Seldom <u>does a single person need to</u>** raise a big family.

誰說克漏字與翻譯
不能一次解決？

- 收錄克漏字測驗最常見之主題，共30單元，每單元皆有兩則
  短篇及一則長篇測驗，讓你充分熟悉各式題材，並從中觀察
  文章內容、學習字句用法，奠定作答實力。
- 連貫式翻譯每單元提供2組練習題目，並附上重要句型講
  解、題組所需的關鍵字彙及參考範例，透過本書獨特的反覆
  練習模式，提昇你的翻譯寫作能力。
- 隨書附有解析本，提供完整文章翻譯，並逐題加以詳解，幫
  助你確實掌握文章脈絡，並學習相關解題技巧及應答策略。